UNFORGETTABLE

"Upon my word, Miss Travers," Julian murmured, "you look at me with inviting eyes."

Collie forced her gaze back to his. His eyes were wary and intense, but beyond that inscrutable.

"I do," she agreed, her voice just above a whisper. Her chest rose and fell with her shallow breathing. Every nerve within her tingled. If he would just touch her, she thought, he would remember. If she could kiss him, he would come away knowing what they'd had together, she was suddenly sure.

She slid one foot toward him, closing the gap between them by half. She did not touch him, but as she neared, his hands rose to grasp her arms—whether to draw her in or hold her off she was not sure. His touch provoked a surge of pleasure along her skin and she closed her eyes with the sensation.

"Miss Travers," he said. His voice was brisk, but she met his gaze. "What is it you want from me?" he asked.

With deliberate care, she moved closer, until her body touched his, her breasts against his coat. Her hands rose to his arms. Her fingers touched the damp wool of his sleeves. She moved one hand up to his shoulder, his neck, then allowed herself to touch a lock of hair that fell to his nape.

His lashes dropped so that he regarded her through slitted eyes. "Miss Travers, are you seducing me?"

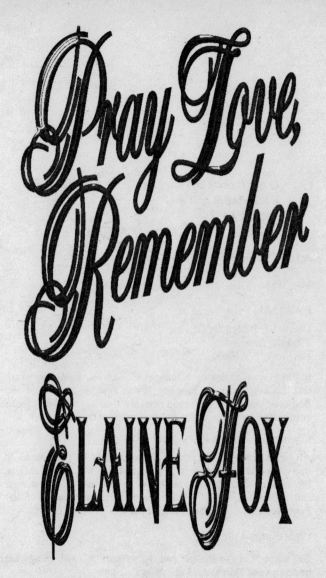

Pray Love, Remember

ELAINE FOX

LEISURE BOOKS   NEW YORK CITY

A LEISURE BOOK®

May 1998

Published by

Dorchester Publishing Co., Inc.
276 Fifth Avenue
New York, NY 10001

ISBN 0-8439-4384-X

To the pals who kept me sane while writing this book: Beth, Chris, Mary, Mary Kay, Nora and Pat. Tough times call for good friends, and you all have helped me so much more than you know.

Pray Love, Remember

Prologue

Carriage wheels crunched over the frosted grass and bramble of the ditch in front of the house. Cuff smoothed his mustache with one hand and gazed out the window of the coach at the tiny cottage.

Early morning sunlight struggled through a trickling fog to strike the mud walls and thatched roof with a dull warmth, illuminating the fact that the windows held no glass, nor even shutters to ward off the October chill. What appeared to be a blanket covered the right-hand window, but the left one ogled him with a black eye, empty and flat as an idiot's stare.

Why, it's nothing more than a shed, Cuff thought, and found himself issuing the unlikely prayer that his master, who if alive would now be the seventh Earl of Northcliffe, was not to be found in this hovel. Of course, if he were not to be found here, chances were he was well and truly dead, which would naturally be far worse than the notion that he'd spent the last five weeks in squalor. Still, Cuff contended to himself, for a man of the earl's impeccable sensibilities and personal superiority, staying even temporarily in a place like this was unthinkable.

The carriage stopped, the springs creaked as the body of the coach came to rest, and the horses blew restlessly through their noses while Cuff studied the problem. They'd gotten several false leads since the ship carrying Jonathan Coletun, the sixth Earl of Northcliffe, and his son Julian had gone down on its way to Italy, but this was the only one that held any degree of plausibility. Granted, it wasn't much, but based on the location of the wreck, a body could have washed up here, alive, if God was in His heaven and feeling merciful at the time.

And if what the commoners said was true, if the earl's son had injured his head seriously enough to cause a loss of all memory, all knowledge of who he was or from whence he'd come, then it was possible Lord Julian had survived the wreck and bided his time here. But he would have had to have been ignorant of his obligations, Cuff knew, to keep him from home. Ignorant, as well, of his past, his family, his blood.

But Cuff didn't believe it. The earl and his son were dead, all the authorities agreed. It had been too long and the wreck had been too severe for a survivor to turn up now. Indeed, sailors were still plucking pieces of the ruined ship from the sea, with cottagers along the coast finding crates and rigging washed up from Plymouth to Weymouth. For a body to have survived such destruction—well, as Cuff had said many a time, God would have had to have been in the mood for nothing short of a miracle.

He cleared his throat gruffly. Though he'd had weeks to get used to the idea that both his masters were gone, Cuff struggled to keep the hard lump from rising in his throat. If these folks here thought to toy with the memory of the earl and his son, Cuff would have a thing or two to tell them, he would.

Clearing his throat once again, he sat up and straightened his coat. Nothing to do now but follow through, he thought. He'd investigated the other shams; he'd investigate this one too. Buttoning his waistcoat over his ample belly, Cuff slid forward on the seat to open the door.

Jem, the coachman, had not descended from his perch to open the door, nor had Cuff expected him to. After all, Cuff was only steward to the Coletuns of Northcliffe, sent to investigate a claim, and one that did not hold enough promise to warrant the removal of the family to Lyme to investigate.

Cuff stepped down from the carriage just as the door to the hovel swung open and a lanky man came out, tugging his forelock in greeting and bowing.

Cuff nodded, flicking the carriage door shut with one hand and hearing it catch with a well-oiled click. He was quite conscious of the contrast between the lacquered grandeur of the coach behind him and the crumbling abode before him.

"You Harris?" he asked, stepping across the prickly weeds of the roadside ditch to the grass-tufted dirt front yard.

"Aye, sir," the man said, nodding his head and tugging again at his forelock. "We're right honored you've come, sir. We've naught to offer such gracious company, but—"

"I didn't come for you, Harris, so don't worry yourself about going to any lengths to be hospitable. Where is the man? If it's not his lordship, I got a lot of driving yet to do this day." He stepped over a pile of slop and eyed a pig that snuffled toward it. You'd think they'd at least build a pen, he thought. If they lived in Northcliffe they'd have a pen. His lordship would have made sure of it.

" 'E's in 'ere," Harris said, motioning to the hut behind him. " 'E's gettin' dressed."

Cuff harrumphed and stood awkwardly in the yard. "Let him come out here then. If he's the real thing, he'll come out here to me. I've known him since he was a boy."

He'd be damned if he was going inside the filthy place, he thought. He wasn't about to fall for a ruse like that, no sir. The last claim he'd investigated involved several unscrupulous characters looking for a reward, whether it was offered to them or not. But he'd managed to escape unscathed. Today Jem sat up on the driver's seat, and Jones and Cleary stood at the back, all ready to jump to his aid at a moment's notice if this escapade turned to treachery. No one was going to get anything out of a ploy like this if it wasn't the real thing.

He looked around himself while he waited. The fog thickened in spots, then lightened, swirling around two other huts that lay to the right. Each was sinking similarly into decrepitude; one had a passel of chickens milling about beneath a window. The other looked as barren as if empty, but a thin stream of smoke from the chimney gave the inhabitants away.

Nobody stirred. Cuff was certain the tenants of the two hovels were all inside, gathered around windows to peer out at him; after all, how often was it that an earl's conveyance even passed along this road, let alone stopped at one of its lodgings?

Sighing, he shifted his weight to stare at the house, focusing on the dumb left window, though he could see nothing inside. The minutes ticked by. No doubt it was all a hoax, he thought for the hundredth time, and the scoundrel perpetrating it didn't have the nerve to come out from the shack and try to pass himself off as Julian Coletun.

Cuff felt anger well up inside him at the gall of someone who'd try to impersonate the young lord. A man of class he'd been, a man of polish and integrity, a man of such imposing physical attributes as to make women swoon and men sit up and take notice. No, nobody who had known or ever seen him would attempt to pass for His Lordship. He was too rare, and too bloody dangerous.

If this turned out to be a sham, Cuff decided, he'd make damn sure nobody in these parts would ever think to pull such a trick again in their lifetimes. He pushed at the sleeve of his jacket, as if he might roll it up and challenge this Harris to fisticuffs.

Instead, he pulled a pipe from his pocket and gazed at the door, chewing the inside of his cheek in mild impatience. Cuff couldn't hope the imposter was Lord Julian. No, it had been too long and the chances were too remote that he could have survived. Besides, who had ever heard of someone forgetting his whole life? No, he'd wait to see what these people produced, but he had no intention of being disappointed again.

The fog comforted him. Like a blank sheet of paper, it asked nothing, offered nothing, and made no judgments.

Julian stared out the window of the house into the misty gray shroud and hoped it would never break, hoped he might stay here in blissful anonymity forever and let the murk in his mind swallow him as completely as the fog outside swallowed the trees.

He was to return to a home he did not know, people he could not remember, a life that was no longer his. He was terrified. And though he knew little else about himself, he knew that fear was foreign to him.

He had family, the Harrises had told him. A mother. A brother. A young sister.

A fiancée.

All devastated by the shipwreck that had claimed the life of his father and, supposedly, himself. How joyful they'd be to discover he'd been spared, they insisted. How anxious they all were to have him back, he'd been assured. Julian Coletun, the Earl of Northcliffe, in his father's stead.

But the storm had not spared him, he thought. Did they know that? He was alive, but he was without a life, without memory, without feeling. Did they know just how alien they all were going to be to him?

* * *

14

The moment the man appeared the sun broke through the fog. Cuff was busy filling his pipe and felt the warmth on his back as the man stepped into the doorway. Despite seeing him only peripherally, Cuff stopped, his actions arrested by the man's height and bearing. He jerked his head upward, forgetting the pipe and tobacco in his hands.

There, in the slanted shadow of the doorjamb, wearing a homespun shirt and mended breeches, stood the seventh Earl of Northcliffe. Hard morning sunlight struck one side of his face, leaving the other in shadow. But it was him.

"I'll be damned," Cuff murmured to himself.

With his eyes riveted to the man, Cuff wadded the tobacco bag in one hand and with his other shoved the half-filled pipe into a pocket, heedless of the way the leaves tumbled out of the bowl onto his jacket. He moved forward slowly, amazed, relishing the stubbled plane of the man's cheek and the glittering silver of his eyes. His dark hair was long and fell over his forehead, down to his collar in back, but he had never looked better to the steward.

Cuff started to break into a smile, but paused at the odd lack of expression on the man's face.

He was thinner, and studiously wary, but then he'd always appeared untrusting, Cuff knew. An angry red scar mottled the corner of his right brow at the temple, causing one eyelid to dip slightly in a lazy, piratical way.

"My lord," he said in wonder as he approached. With each step he grew more sure, his heart taking up a rapid tattoo the closer and more real the man became. Tears pricked at Cuff's eyes. "I will be damned," he repeated softly.

It *was* him, he thought with certainty. He was alive, by all the saints, *alive.*

"My lord," he repeated, expecting at any moment Julian's mouth to curl into that familiar, cynical smile at the joke he had played. "My lord, I can hardly believe my eyes. It's really you, sir!"

One lean, dark eyebrow arched at the exclamation, and the silver eyes pierced him with a familiar, shimmering intensity.

Then he spoke, the words low and unmistakably cultured. "Is it?"

Chapter One

The blunt, shaggy-whiskered man with the barrel chest stood several paces in front of the carriage. Even without the coat of arms on the side, the coach would have looked opulent and out of place next to the patch of weedy farmland strewn with pig slop and dust.

The man they'd decided was Julian Coletun, Earl of Northcliffe, looked dispassionately at the stranger.

He'd not been prepared for the look of shock that took over the man's face when he'd caught sight of him. The recognition had been immediate and unfeigned. So much for blissful anonymity, Julian thought.

"Y'see, he don't remember much about 'isself," Harris explained nervously, then turned to Julian. "My lord, this here's the man from Northcliffe."

"I see that," Julian said, and stared at the whiskered man.

He didn't know him. Didn't recognize the gold crest of lion and rose on the carriage. He felt nothing for this development except a vague feeling of hostility.

Harris backed up as the whiskered man approached Julian. His short stride was businesslike as he moved across the hard dirt. He might just as well have been striding down rows of barley, pointing out a weed or an infestation with an authoritative air. Julian stared at the barrel-chested man in the hope that he'd suddenly look familiar.

The other man opened his mouth to speak again, his eyes hard on Julian; then he closed it and opted for a smile instead.

Julian's nerves jumped at the smile, though he stayed perfectly still. It stirred something in him, he thought, the sight of this man. He could not tell if being under his scrutiny and the object of his crooked, delighted grin irked or gratified him.

Julian studied the man carefully, and determined, if he wasn't mistaken, that the man's eyes looked overbright, as if tears welled in them.

"By God, it *is* you. By Christ and all his disciples . . . we believed you dead, son." He stood there, shaking his grizzled head and grinning, oblivious to the complete lack of response he received.

Then, as suddenly as a dam breaking, the man took the last few steps toward him, one hand outstretched to shake, the other out as if to clap him on the shoulder, or embrace him, Julian wasn't sure which.

He made it as far as taking Julian's hand and pumping it, but something in Julian's expression and the stiffening of his body at the touch must have warned him off the rest, for he contented himself with squeezing hard on the one hand Julian had instinctively offered.

"Damnation, sir, it's good t' see you." The grin was genuine, Julian could tell. The brightness of his eyes was normal now.

Julian was not sure how to respond. "You know me," he said finally.

The man's shrewd eyes narrowed and the grin faded, though it didn't disappear. "It's true, then, what they said. You don't know who it is you are."

Julian didn't answer. The question was a stupid one—as if they'd all be standing there if he knew who he was. He glared insolently until the other man nearly squirmed with discomfort, his face turning a mottled red.

"The more immediate problem," Julian said mildly, "is not knowing who *you* are."

After one disconcerted moment, the man's laugh bounced dully off the thick mud walls of the house. "Cuff, my boy! I'm Cuff, your old retainer! Lord take me, if this isn't the oddest thing. Introducing myself to *you!* Why, I wiped your nose as a lad, picked you up when you fell down and brushed you off, told you to clean up your toys. Never once imagined the day I'd be telling you who I am." He shook his head, but the grin would not disappear. "Lord, but I can't help thinking what a blessing it is to be saying anything at all to you. Not after these last five weeks of hell, no sir."

Julian took a deep breath and glanced at Harris, watching the scene from near the door with something that looked like fear.

"It hasn't been hell," Julian murmured. No, he thought, hell was just beginning now.

* * *

They'd be told, the steward assured him. He'd send a courier ahead of them, once they got closer to the estate in Yorkshire, to tell the family of his condition. And once he was back among those who loved him, he'd recover, the steward asserted. He'd have his memory back in no time.

Julian did not share the man's optimism. For days after his family's emissary—this Cuff—had retrieved him and they'd started back to Yorkshire, he'd racked his brain, pushing, loathing himself for the infirmity of forgetting. But he could not produce even one dim memory of this place that was his home or these people who were his blood.

"Almost there, sir," his companion said, eyeing him as he had the entire trip, as if looking for the man who had disappeared five weeks ago.

Julian nodded once.

"Just around the next bend. Shame about the fog," the man added, shaking his graying head. "Seems it's been foggy the entire way, and there's such a lovely view of the house from the gate. Might have sparked a memory or two. Then again . . ." The man chuckled, eyes crinkling under bushy gray eyebrows. "This time of year the house is almost always in fog, so a clear day might throw you more than anything."

"I like the fog," Julian said, thinking his companion's opinion about the weather was at best irrelevant, at worst inappropriate. This man was a servant. Julian was the earl. He rubbed a hand over his eyes.

"Aye, and you always did, sir," Cuff said, smiling with what looked like relief.

Julian gazed at him. "Did I?"

He noted that the man called him "sir" instead of "my lord." Funny how he could remember the impropriety of that when he could not even remember his own mother's face. Perhaps he had been friends with this man, he thought, and then remembered. Cuff was a servant. He should not even be engaging the earl in conversation, especially not in such an informal way.

"Aye, you always loved the fog," his companion repeated. "Rain, thunder, weather that'd make ordinary folk tremble in their boots was always your cup of tea. Brooding sort, you were. Liked your books and your work. Some called you stern, but not those who knew you. No sir, you and the earl— the late earl, that is . . ." Cuff cleared his throat. "Well, you were both fine men to work for."

Julian listened, not wanting to question him, but thirsty for as much information as he could get. After mentioning Julian's father, however, the steward stopped talking, and sank back in his seat to look out the window, chewing the inside of his lip.

Julian studied the man's somber face a moment, then turned to look out his own window. Caution, he thought. He must proceed with caution. Watch and learn. There had to be a reason he was reluctant to arrive, a reason the thought of home filled him with dread.

Cuff was harmless enough. The servant did not inspire the fear that Northcliffe aroused in him. But with no knowledge or memory to guide him he had only his instincts. And his instincts told him to be careful of everyone.

Fog left rivulets of water on the windows. Through them Julian could make out the edge of a forest. Swathed in the thickened, moist air, the bare arms of the trees reached upward, their tips lost in the mist.

Julian frowned and looked down at his hands, turning them over, palm up. No calluses. At least, none permanent. He'd developed a few working with the Harrises; but the distinguishing lack of workworn hands had been a significant clue to his identity.

Noblemen didn't have to work for a living, the Harrises had pointed out; with Julian being such a young man in obviously robust health, rank could be the only explanation.

Looking at them now, Julian wondered if his hands had ever looked familiar to him. It didn't seem the kind of thing one would notice, if one were not in his unique situation. But his hands, while obviously his, had the look of anyone else's. They were square and straight. None of the fingers appeared ever to have been broken. There was a scar he wondered about, might have asked about had the hands been another's, that ran along the knuckles of his right hand.

He flexed the hand into a fist and watched the scar go flat and white.

The strangest part was that their unfamiliarity did not disturb him. Nor was it upsetting that his face was foreign to him. Why? he wondered. It seemed wrong to feel such detachment.

Cuff had produced a mirror after they'd left the cottage. The Harrises had not owned one, so Julian had looked at himself curiously for the first time since the shipwreck. If Cuff had expected any grand revelation, a swift burgeoning of memory, he'd hidden his disappointment well.

Julian had felt nothing but interest, seeing his face for, effectively, the first time. He looked severe, he had thought of himself, and unhappy. Dark, wavy hair crowned a lean face with heavy-lidded gray eyes and a wide mouth. His features were strong, maybe arrogant, and his jaw was shadowed with a week's worth of stubble. The scar above his right eye was obviously new, caused no doubt by the same blow that had inflicted his memory loss, but other than that he was without distinguishing marks. The country doctor the Harrises had summoned upon finding him had sewn the cut with skill, but he was still left with a red gash and a slight droop to his right eyelid.

Bodily, he was muscular, if on the thin side, though that was most likely due to his injuries. And he was tall—above six feet. He had, apparently, done something that required physical exertion in his previous life, for the labor he performed at the Harrises' had not taxed him overmuch.

His thoughts drifted to the people he was to meet. A fiancée, the steward had told him. Julian tried to examine the feelings such a relationship conjured in him, but could not tell if the inkling of relief was due to past feelings, or the hope that there might be one person with whom he could share his thoughts, one person who might help him through this dark, nameless fear.

Mothers could be distant and brothers competitive, he thought, dismissing the others. Then he wondered why he accepted those things as true. Did he know from experience? Or had he merely observed it in the families of others?

The coach made a hard left and the steady clopping of the horses' hooves sounded quicker, more lively. They sensed home, he thought, and he inhaled deeply to quell the anxious pounding of his heartbeat. He looked again out the window, saw nothing but the filmy gray fog, and let his eyes flick to the steward.

"Aye, we're close now, sir," the man said, compassion in his voice.

Julian frowned and unclenched his hands. The man had seen his unease.

"Fine," he said brusquely. "I'll need a bath."

The steward nodded. "I'll tell Helen. She'll have it drawn as soon as we arrive, sir."

Julian looked back at him. The tone of command, which had sprung so easily to his lips, had been accepted and acted upon as simply as if he'd asked the time of day. After weeks of hard labor with the Harrises, it amazed him that anything he wished for now could be had for the asking.

What had he done, he wondered, to deserve such a life? Or did he not deserve it? Could there even now be some sort of mistake? Up until the moment the steward had arrived, Julian had hoped the Harrises might be wrong, that he was not this Earl of Northcliffe. The idea of it had filled him with a shameful anxiety. But the steward had known him immediately—had nearly drawn him into an embrace, for God's sake—and the hope that he might savor the simple life of the Harrises was dashed.

The horses slowed as the coach neared the house, which appeared as nothing but a huge, dark shape in the fog. He could not see it, precisely; it was more as if he could feel its presence looming in the mist. Several windows glowed visibly, but it was the enormous front stoop that came most clearly into view. Sweeping up from two sides, the stone stairway curved up to impossibly tall, polished wood doors.

He waited for some spark of recognition, some inkling of familiarity, but none came. He was a visitor, nothing more.

He descended from the carriage and stood for a moment in the chill air, letting the mist coat his face and dampen his hair. What appeared to be the entire outdoor staff stood waiting, lined up from the drive to the stoop, trying not to stare. Julian did little more than glance at them, instead noting the pale green lichen that lined the lowermost stones of the stoop, and the gray surfaces of the steps, wet and glistening.

A housemaid hurried by with a quick smile that faded the moment their eyes met. His fear must be obvious, he thought. Indeed, he felt as if it shrouded him like the fog, warning all who saw him that danger hovered close by.

Julian lifted his eyes to the doors and the skin between his shoulder blades prickled with uncertainty. Liveried footmen flanked the portal. He did not want to enter, did not want to see what was beyond that door.

Cuff cleared his throat. Julian glanced back at him, then returned his gaze to the door. With what seemed an enormous effort, he moved himself forward.

His eyes hard, his mouth set, his heart hammering danger with every beat, he ascended the stairs. A couple of servants murmured "Welcome home, Lord Northcliffe" as he passed, and he nodded to them with what he hoped looked like the detachment of the privileged. With a deep breath he took the last stair, nodded to one of the footmen, and the door was opened to him.

"Move *forward*, Collie," Pam hissed. "Get in the front where he can see you."

Collette Travers shrugged off her friend's hand and glanced back at her. "They said he doesn't remember anything," she whispered back. "It won't matter if he sees me or not."

Pam rolled her eyes. "He ought to remember *you*, you silly fool. How could he forget his own—"

"*Shhh!*" Collie turned and drilled her friend with hard eyes. After a second she glanced around. No one seemed to pay any attention to them. She exhaled. "Don't make me sorry I told you."

The maid dropped her eyes with a sour look. "I'm just worried about you getting your due, is all. It isn't right that *she's* up there."

Collie took a deep breath and fingered the ribbon that hung around her neck. "I know." She looked over her shoulder, past the milling servants, to the family huddled together near the door, waiting.

She didn't look at Miranda Greer, couldn't without enduring a nearly suffocating rage, but she knew Miranda was there, waiting with the rest of them. All of them waiting—but none, she was sure, with more anxiety than herself—for *him*. For Lord Julian Northcliffe. Just saying the name to herself brought such a wave of joy and relief to her heart that she was hard-pressed to subdue a smile. He was *alive*, she reveled to herself once again. He hadn't perished. Her prayers had been answered.

She swallowed hard over the lump of joy in her throat. It blotted out everything, this tidal wave of relief, every time it struck her anew that Julian was alive and not gone from her life forever . . . not drifting pale and lifeless beneath the sea, his fine hands limp, his deep eyes sightless, as weeks of nightmares had tormented her. For those moments when she realized again that he lived and would return, all her fears and anger were displaced by exultation. Even the fact of Miranda Greer was overshadowed.

Now the moment of truth approached. Now he would return, he would step once again over the threshold of Northcliffe, to take back his life. And hers.

Because surely he would—he *must*—remember her, she thought, allowing a brief surge of hope. Surely God, after letting her suffer for weeks believing him dead, would not return Julian only to hand him over to Miranda Greer. No, this was providence. Fate. They were meant to be together.

With a brief smile at Pam, Collie turned and

edged through the row of people in front of her to stand apart from the assembled servants. After all, as governess to young Shelly she wasn't, technically, a servant, even if most of the family treated her that way. She was a lady, she reminded herself, and worthy of standing, if not with the family, at least near them.

Except for her inability to be with Shelly, Collie did not mind her current exile from their ranks, however, as they were not very friendly toward her. But Shelly was confused and afraid of Julian's return, and Collie wished she could be there to help her through the ordeal of being reintroduced to a brother who, apparently, would not recognize any of them.

Clasping her hands at her waist she tried to project an image of calm. In her mind's eye she'd seen him walk through that door a thousand times, each time striding right to her and sweeping her into his arms. Perhaps it would happen that way now.

"Yes," he always said in her dream, "I am back. Everything will be all right now. I love you. Only you, Collette."

Butterflies winged upward in her stomach at the thought. He promised he would come back to her and now he had. Somehow, he'd survived. Please, God, she prayed, please let him remember.

Near the door a commotion arose. A runner had come from the lane, no doubt informing the family the coach had been sighted. Lady Northcliffe and her son from a previous marriage, the odious Monroe Dorland, stood side by side. Behind them stood Mr. Horace Bafferty, the late earl's cousin. Shelly stood in front of them, and beside her, to Collie's ongoing mortification, stood Miranda Greer, supposed fiancée to the new Lord Northcliffe.

Miranda's deception had begun, pointlessly, after Julian's supposed death. As a beauty renowned as much for her physical perfection as for her money, Miranda had been expected to marry Julian for as long as anyone could remember. For a while, apparently, it had looked as though even Julian was resigned to the match. But that was before Collie had come to Northcliffe, she knew. Before Julian had pledged himself to *her*.

Unfortunately, no one else knew what had passed—virtually beneath their noses—between the heir to the title and the family governess. They were all too used to thinking of Miranda as the eventual countess. So when news of Julian's death reached the family, Miranda was treated as the grieving "widow" and Collie was forgotten.

But the worst part, the part that had so infuriated Collie, was that Miranda claimed Julian had proposed to her just before leaving for Italy.

It was a lie. It had to be. But Collie's outrage had paled in comparison to the enormous pain of Julian's loss. She'd been so devastated that she'd been unable even to contradict Miranda, though she knew without a doubt that the family would never have believed her claim. For Julian, just before leaving with his father, had proposed to Collie. He was to ask his father's blessing for the match—which he'd had every confidence of receiving—and upon his return he was to announce the betrothal to the rest of them.

But he had not returned. And now Miranda, the lying shrew, had convinced everyone it was *she* who was to be his bride.

Collie bit back her ever-present fury at the thought. Though it was torture to stand by and watch the woman manipulate the awful circumstances, she knew she could say nothing. Lady Northcliffe and her arrogant son Monroe would never believe that anyone of their standing, and most assuredly not the heir to the title, could fall for someone who was more servant than aristocrat.

So Lady Northcliffe had had no trouble believing Miranda was engaged to her son. Indeed, she'd campaigned for the match almost as long as Lady Greer had. Nobody questioned *when* it might have happened, Collie reflected sourly. Nobody even noticed that Julian had barely seen Miranda prior to his departure for Italy. No, it was enough that she was the daughter of a marquis, and a wealthy one at that.

Of course, the lie had scarcely mattered as long as Julian was dead; but now, Collie thought, *now* Miranda was to be presented to him as his fiancée. Collie wondered just how quickly he would remember it wasn't so, and hoped it would be instantaneous. She imagined his expression as the presumption would be presented to him, his initial confusion and then that ironic laugh. *No,* he would say, in his customarily blunt manner. *I'm afraid that's impossible, for I'm betrothed to Miss Travers.* Even the imagined words filled her with warmth.

Then again, she reminded herself, he might not remember at all. And if that were the case, would

he believe them? Would he believe and actually
marry Miranda Greer?

Fear clutched her heart.

Amnesia, they'd said. She had no experience with
the malady. It could be temporary, the doctor had
informed them, in the family meeting to which
she'd been invited as support for young Shelly. Or
it could be permanent. There was no telling. He
would have to let them know later, after interview-
ing the patient.

Collie wondered, if Julian truly remembered
nothing, was he not aware of his father's death?
The loss would be severe, she knew, for they had
been close, and her heart ached for him.

Hooves sounded on the drive outside and
abruptly all noise in the hall ceased. The servants
whisked into two long, disciplined lines and the
family stood stiffly by the door.

If it were me, Collie thought, *I'd be out that door
and down the steps the moment the carriage stopped.
But they just stand there, stupid as sheep, waiting for
the prodigal son to come to them.* She pressed her
lips together. *Don't be uncharitable,* she heard her
mother's voice chastise, and tried to feel contrite.

The hall was deathly quiet as footsteps sounded
on the outside steps. A moment later the door
swung open and there he stood on the threshold,
with Cuff beside him and a group of servants flanking them on the stoop.

Even dressed in peasant garb with the begin-
nings of a beard, he exuded all the pride and bearing of an earl as his eyes swept the entryway. He
looked remote, Collie thought, and he said nothing,

just let his hooded gray gaze scan the room.

As his slow, hard eyes traveled the line of servants, she remembered how much she used to fear him. When she first began working at Northcliffe he'd been stern and forbidding, a bit frightening. He'd eyed her with such intensity, such penetrating acuity, that she had always worried she would do or say something stupid and his patience with her would snap.

But somehow they'd discovered their mutual regard for Mozart and Greek philosophy, and when he found she could speak French he began to direct surprisingly funny, private comments to her in the language while in the company of his mother and brother, who could not understand it.

Collie's stomach fluttered as his eyes neared her and her knees threatened to buckle. Controlling the urge to run to him, she stood stock-still. But his cool gaze only touched her, and moved on.

A pent-up breath burst from her with a sound perilously close to a gasp. Her hands flew to her mouth and she bit her knuckle as several heads turned in her direction. His quick eyes returned to her, lingered, then turned to his family.

Collie sucked in a breath, light-headed, and grasped the arm of the butler, next to her.

Pulver looked at her with a surprised, disapproving frown, but she could not let go.

"Julian?" Lady Northcliffe's timid query could be heard throughout the hall. Her voice was high and tenuous, at odds with her sturdy, black-clad form. "Is it really you?"

Collie squeezed Pulver's arm and strained forward, her breath shallow and rapid.

The gaze Julian turned on his mother was blank, even cold. "You must be my mother," he replied.

Collie's skin shivered at the sound of his voice, quiet and deep, yet resonant in the silent hall. She closed her eyes. A knife twisted in her heart as his voice made it all real. He was home and he did not know her. He'd looked at her with a stranger's eyes.

Lady Northcliffe wrung her hands and gazed up into his face. "Oh, son," she said, tears choking her voice. "You know me, then? Can you not even give your mother a proper kiss? After all I've been through . . ." Her words trailed off and even Collie, little as she thought of the woman, felt pity at the sight of her, frightened and unsure.

Julian took a deep breath and strode the two steps required to reach her. Bending, he kissed her briefly on the cheek.

Lady Northcliffe's hands grasped his shoulders in a sudden, ferocious grip. Julian's face showed surprise.

"Oh, my boy, my boy," she cried, shaking him by the arms.

"I'm sorry," he murmured, but did not back out of her grasp. He shook his head, looking confused. "I'm sorry, madam."

At this Lady Northcliffe's wail spiraled upward. "I am your mother," she cried. "You are my son, Julian, my dearest, fondest son!"

Collie noticed that Monroe's head jerked at the words and his jaw clenched before Mr. Bafferty moved past him toward the wretched woman.

Lady Northcliffe's tears threatened to overcome her as Mr. Bafferty took her by the shoulders. "My lady. Should we not let the boy get reacquainted with the house? Perhaps his memory will return at that time."

She sniffled, wiping at her nose with a handkerchief. "Of course." She dabbed at her eyes and turned into the comfort of Mr. Bafferty's arms. "Of course. Julian?" She peered back at him. "Shall we—shall we show you around y-your house?"

Julian drew himself up and looked again around the hall. "No," he said finally. "First I should like some introductions." He turned to where Miranda stood with her hands on Shelly's shoulders.

"Introductions!" Lady Northcliffe wailed. "Oh, that it's come to this!"

Mr. Bafferty stepped forward, his bushy muttonchops writhing like a live animal as he smiled. "Julian," he said with a short bow, "if you would allow me, I would be happy to do the honors."

Julian's eyes scanned the man's portly form, then returned to his round, bespectacled face. "Perhaps you would be so good as to start with yourself."

Mr. Bafferty's face suffused with blood and he snapped his shoulders back to stand taller. "Of course." He bowed again. "Horace Bafferty, at your service. I am your late father's cousin."

"My late father's cousin," Julian murmured after him. "And you live here?"

"I, ah"—he cleared his throat—"yes. That is, since the tragedy."

"He came to help me," Lady Northcliffe said and

blew her nose into a handkerchief. "You have no idea how dreadful it's been for me."

Julian glanced at her and then returned his attention to Mr. Bafferty. "Then I thank you." No trace of warmth infused his voice.

Collie, witnessing the scene with the rest of the servants, felt hope spring up in her breast. He didn't like Bafferty, she thought with elation.

He'd never liked Bafferty.

"Well—ahem—well," Mr. Bafferty huffed in unaccustomed humility, "it was nothing, I assure you. Nothing at all. I'd have done the same for—for any relative, you know."

Julian's brows drew together, his eyes intent on Bafferty's face. "I'll have to take your word for that, won't I?"

His gaze shifted to Monroe.

"This," Mr. Bafferty said, attempting as cool a demeanor as Julian had, "is your brother, Monroe."

Monroe offered his hand and Julian took it. "Monroe," he said with a nod.

"Welcome home, Jules," Monroe said. "You look none the worse for wear."

One side of Julian's mouth kicked upward, causing Collie's heart to tumble with vivid, painful memories. "Good to know."

"Your sister, Shelly," Mr. Bafferty said, as Julian's attention shifted to her.

Shelly curtsied, her blond ringlets bobbing on her shoulders, and kept her eyes fixed on the floor. "Welcome home, brother."

Behind her, Miranda squeezed her shoulder and

patted her arm. "It's all right, dear," she said quietly.

Julian studied Shelly's blond head a moment before asking, "Was I always the type of brother to frighten you, Shelly?"

Shelly looked up at him, tears collecting on her lower lashes, and shook her head.

Julian's expression was sober. "But I frighten you now, don't I? Because I act like a stranger."

Shelly blinked rapidly, tears falling from her lashes to roll down her cheeks. Her lips parted on a tiny sob. "But you're not a stranger. You're my brother. Why don't you remember me?"

He looked at her intently for another moment before shaking his head. "I don't know."

Shelly sniffed and wiped her nose with the back of her hand.

"Shhh," Miranda murmured. "It's all right, dearest."

Julian glanced up at her, then returned his attention to Shelly. "How old are you, Shelly?"

"Eight," she said, then looked slyly up at Miranda. "Almost eight."

He smiled at the small fib and Collie, on the other side of the room, felt her heart constrict. He was always good with Shelly. He was the only one of the family who'd ever paid any attention to her. Even the kind old earl had considered her too young, and no doubt too female, to take much notice of.

"I'd have guessed ten," Julian said.

Shelly tried to stifle a smile, but shot Miranda a triumphant look. She started to say something further to her brother but stopped abruptly, as if remembering to be afraid.

"Lady Miranda Greer," Mr. Bafferty said, "your fiancée."

Julian turned his attention to Miranda, resplendent before him in yellow silk.

Miranda smiled tremulously as Julian's eyes met hers. He took her hand in his to bow over it. "Lady Greer."

Miranda covered their hands with her other one and raised a tragic expression to him. "Julian," she whispered, tears welling in her green eyes to roll down her cheeks. "Welcome home, darling."

Chapter Two

"It's been my experience," the doctor intoned, "that in cases such as this one a sudden resurgence of memory, an onslaught, shall we say, of things familiar and demands that he consider this thing or that for familiarity, does a great deal more harm than good."

Chewing thoughtfully on the end of his pipe, Basil Irwin, the doctor who specialized in ailments of the brain and whom Lady Northcliffe had summoned from London, circled the settee on which Shelly and Collie were perched before moving toward the fire. Collie watched a reflection of the flames dance across the surface of his monocle.

"But how shall he remember," Lady Northcliffe inquired, "if we do not remind him of things?"

Dr. Irwin pulled the pipe from his mouth and stroked his beard. "It is a natural process, Lady Northcliffe," he said. "The brain must be allowed to heal itself. In time, he could remember all, a little at a time. But were it all to strike him at once, well . . ." His thin, dark brows drew together. "It could prove too much for his mind to handle. There have been cases—and I don't wish to scare you, merely to impart to you the gravity of the situation—there have been cases where too much was demanded of the subject, resulting in, I'm afraid to say, insanity."

Collie gasped. "Insanity? Do you mean because of his inability to remember, or as a result of the return of his memory?"

"Really, Miss Travers, try to contain yourself," Miranda admonished, glancing fretfully at Lady Northcliffe.

Dr. Irwin turned to her gravely. "The swift return of it, in most cases, does the most damage. In fact, in the few cases I've known where the patient never regained his memory, the patient was much happier. Indeed, the release from former cares and worries seemed to do a great deal more good than harm."

Lady Northcliffe clapped her hands together in delight and turned bright eyes to Monroe. "And didn't we always say he was far too solemn and conservative for his own good? Don't you think this might be just the thing for him? Perhaps he might now be able to enjoy his life a bit more."

Collie stared at her, openmouthed. "Lady Northcliffe, you can't possibly mean you think he would be better off without knowledge of his life. That his insensibility is of greater use to him than his former intelligence."

"Miss Travers!" Miranda exclaimed, sitting forward. "Do you think it's your place to say such things? Think of Lady Northcliffe, please."

Collie felt her skin heat. It *was* her place—certainly more than it was Miranda's—but none of them knew it. From their point of view she was intruding where she had no business. She swallowed her pride and met Miranda's appalled gaze.

"I apologize if my tone offends you, Lady Greer," Collie stated with as much dignity as she could summon. "And I apologize to you too, Lady Northcliffe, for my outburst. However, these questions are important, don't you agree? Pray continue, Dr. Irwin; you were saying?"

Lady Northcliffe looked in bewilderment from one woman to the other, as Monroe regarded Collie beneath lowered lids.

Dr. Irwin cleared his throat. "Lord Northcliffe has lost none of his intelligence, I assure you. He has the same brain, the same capabilities. In fact, in most such cases, the subject can recall almost everything except personal details. He can read and write, calculate figures, ride a horse—mostly what he has forgotten is that which pertains to his personal, emotional life. Usually this is the case, we believe, because something unpleasant occurred that he does not wish to remember."

Collie's stomach sank at the thought. Emotions had run quite high at their last meeting. Perilously high.

"Not wish to remember!" Lady Northcliffe exclaimed. "Do you mean to say he doesn't *want* to remember his family? Oh, it can't be true. It would be too much for me to bear! It would be my undoing, I tell you, my undoing. In fact, I'm already undone by it! Positively undone, I tell you. Doctor, oh! My smelling salts."

Monroe produced the requisite salts from a box on the side table and waved them perfunctorily in his mother's face, bored with the routine.

The doctor smiled, a thin, pointed smile through his beard. "Pray, don't distress yourself, Lady Northcliffe. Lord Northcliffe *wants* to remember his family, I'm sure. But it is likely that something emotional happened to him just before the accident, perhaps a day, maybe a week, probably much closer to an hour, however, that upset him. Then, with the blow to the head, he simply erased it."

Lady Northcliffe fanned herself with great energy, but kept her eyes pinned to the doctor's face, not about to miss a single word.

"But he's erased his whole life," Collie said. "He doesn't even remember his home, or his own mother. How can that be, Doctor?"

Lady Northcliffe appeared mollified by this concern for herself and nodded. "Quite right. Why didn't he just erase whatever small portion it was he didn't like? Why must his whole family have gone too?"

"You must remember that he did not do this intentionally. The blow occurred, his brain was jarred, some memories were lost. But keep in mind how fortunate it is that he was not rendered completely insensible." With that he turned to Collie. "His state of being is quite rational, quite himself; he simply cannot remember. It is not so great a tragedy as it might have been."

"Of course not," Collie said, shaking her head. Did they all deliberately misunderstand her? Or did they truly believe a man's past was so expendable?

"I only meant that his memories are important, his—his knowledge, his feelings, his *relationships*." She turned a significant look on Miranda. "For us now to be cavalier—even happy—about their loss seems hideous."

Miranda stared hard at her in return, apparently trying to discover from whence the governess's hostility had come. "Miss Travers," she began slowly, her voice quiet, "I can't imagine that it makes such a difference to you. For you to become so emotional is unseemly. If *I* can stand it, as his fiancée who has promised to be with him for the rest of his life, surely you, as mere governess to his sister, can tolerate the circumstances as well."

Outrage clutched Collie's stomach and twisted it. "It seems to me, Lady Greer, that if you truly had his best interests at heart you would be as anxious as I that he regain his whole self."

Miranda's perfect features went slack with shock. "How can you doubt that I—I—But of *course* I have his best interests at heart. He's to be my *husband*." Two fat tears spilled down her pale cheeks and she turned her face away.

Beside her, Monroe pulled a handkerchief from his pocket and handed it over with a casual air. "Miss Travers," he said, his tone bland, "this will go much more quickly if you restrain your more inflammatory comments."

Miranda sniffed and patted the corner of one eye. "And the doctor has just finished telling us that people in Julian's condition are often much happier in their new state of mind. Did you not say so, Doctor?" She turned a bewildered expression upon the doctor. "I certainly did not mean to discredit Julian's life or accomplishments. I simply want him to be happy."

Dr. Irwin moved to Miranda's side and took her hand in his. "Of course not, Lady Greer. We all know you hope for his complete recovery. As we all do." He stroked the back of her hand with his thumb. "And I did say that those in a similar condition are frequently happier before regaining or if they never regain their memory, so we must bear the consequences of both possibilities in mind. Miss Travers, I understand your concern, but in framing your questions please try to consider the welfare of Lady Greer and the rest of the family, who suffer perhaps more than yourself."

Collie gripped the arm of the settee with a murderous hand. "But Doctor," she began slowly, "it is not Lady Greer's welfare that should be foremost in this conversation. Does not Lord Northcliffe suffer now, knowing he does not remember? Does he not wonder, even grieve for not knowing? Surely"— she swallowed hard and pressed on despite disapproving glares from all sides—"Doctor, with your vast understanding and experience, surely you know of something that can be done to ease *his* mind."

Dr. Irwin dropped Miranda's hand and moved back to the fire. "Yes, the patient does suffer some now," he admitted. "He blames himself for forgetting, which is, of course, absurd. But as I said, the danger of remembering too quickly should be of paramount concern. What he needs is to be cocooned by his family in an atmosphere of love and trust. In that way, he may learn to function again as the earl. Mr. Dorland, I understand you had taken over the running of the estate when Lord Northcliffe was feared dead?"

Monroe raised his chin and glanced at his mother before answering. "For the first month, yes. Then Mr. Bafferty arrived."

"Ah, yes, Mr. Bafferty. I'd forgotten him."

"He's showing Julian the grounds," Lady North-cliffe offered. "Should we summon him back? Should Julian not be burdened with memories of the grounds?"

Collie gripped her hands together in her lap until she thought the bones might snap. *Idiots*, she screamed mentally. *They're all idiots.*

As she gazed at her clasped fists, she felt a light touch on her arm. Then Shelly's small hand reached out and took her wrist. Releasing her grip, Collie took Shelly's hand in hers and looked into her face.

Shelly smiled, her gray eyes full of a wisdom beyond her years. "He'll remember someday," she whispered, leaning close. "He's sure to remember how much fun we used to have."

Collie closed her eyes against sudden tears, then opened them and forced a smile to her lips. "I know he will, honey," she whispered back. "You're right, everything will be fine."

But her heart bled with the words, because what if everything were not fine? What if Julian never remembered? Suppose he believed Miranda and married her? God, the agony was too much. She could not let it happen.

"Miss Travers?"

Collie's eyes snapped up and she took a short breath. "Yes, Lady Northcliffe?"

"Perhaps it would be best if you took Shelly upstairs to her studies now." She inclined her head toward the door. "I think she has heard quite enough to understand the situation."

"Yes, let's go, Miss Travers," Shelly said, scooting off the seat and tugging on Collie's hand.

Collie contained her disappointment with effort, wanting to know all she could of Julian's condition and chances of recovery. She rose with Shelly. "I should like to ask one more thing, with your permission, Lady Northcliffe."

"You may." Lady Northcliffe inclined her head again.

"I understand we are not to force Lord Northcliffe's memories, but if he should ask us questions, ought we to answer as completely and as truthfully as possible?"

Dr. Irwin tapped his pipe on the inside of the fireplace, letting the burned tobacco fall into the grate. "Why, yes, you must of course be honest, Miss Travers." He rose and looked at her through his monocle. "But you do not need to offer more in answer than the question demands."

"I understand," she said, with a brief curtsy. "Good afternoon." With a glance at each of them she headed for the door.

"I'm so glad to be gone from there," Shelly breathed the moment they were out the door and Collie had closed it behind them. "I don't like that doctor! Did you see how he kept touching Lady

Miranda?" She made an exaggerated face of disgust.

"I know," Collie said absently, turning toward the stairs. "He's a bit supercilious. But we must be patient."

Shelly danced across the marble floor toward the stairs, blond curls bouncing off her shoulders. "He's supercilious! Super, super silly. . . . *us!*"

Collie had to smile. She knew many would believe she should reprimand her charge, but Collie thought her dislike of the doctor an accurate assessment. And shouldn't one encourage an astute judge of character?

"Come back here, Shelly," she commanded, a smile in her voice. "Come here and turn around; your sash is undone."

"My sash!" Shelly sang, and danced back across the floor toward her. "I've come undone—I'm all undone!"

Collie recognized Lady Northcliffe's helpless words and bit her lip not to laugh. "Shelly Coletun," she admonished as the girl came closer, "you know it's not nice to mock people."

"So sorry, Miss Travers," she sang in the same lilting tone.

Collie laughed as she knelt to tie the sash. "You're quite the card today, aren't you?" She rose to her feet and bent to brush the dust off the bottom of her gown. "I expect you'll want to study drama now, won't you?"

"No, I want to read about Friday. You know, Mr. Carusoe's story." She skipped across the huge hall, her footsteps echoing up to the high ceiling.

"You mean *Robinson Crusoe*," Collie corrected. "But I think we've had quite enough adventure for today. We have not yet reviewed your French memorization." She turned, glancing around the marble floor. "Did I have my embroid—"

From the darkness of the back hall a tall, moving shadow caught her eye. She gasped, and raised a hand to her throat.

Julian emerged into the light of the marble hall, watching them. Collie'd forgotten how intimidating he could be, his face sculpted into wary stillness, and his eyes ice hard and direct. She was immediately thrust back a year to when she'd first arrived, when he'd frightened her with his swift, impatient intelligence and chilly scrutiny.

Of course, she'd known nothing then of his humor and kindness . . . of his passion and capacity to love. How strange that he should more resemble that distant vision now.

He was clean shaven, his hair freshly cut; but that same errant lock she knew so well still fell across his forehead. She wanted to brush it back and touch the new scar by his eye, ease the violence of it, dispel his torment. But of course, he did not know her now. . . .

He was dressed as if he'd just been outside. The bottom of his coat showed flecks of mud, and his high black boots gleamed as if wet.

"Tell me," he began. His heavy-lidded eyes, deceptively sleepy, watched her. "Have you always gasped at the sight of me, or is this something new?"

Collie had trouble finding her voice. To speak to

him as a stranger, to utter courteous, meaningless words after believing him dead for so long was too hard, too cruel. She could barely meet his eyes, so dear, so familiar, yet looking at her with little more than polite interest. So she looked at his throat, at the pulse point in his neck she remembered kissing that day in the field, that warm, sultry September day. . . .

"You are the young woman who gasped at me in the foyer yesterday, are you not? The governess?" His eyes did not leave hers. Penetrating, they snatched her breath, drew blood to her cheeks, made her head swim with an airless fear of loss.

"Y-yes," she forced from between frozen lips. "Ex-excuse me. Please. You startled me, is all."

He nodded. "And yesterday?" One side of his mouth rose ironically. "Surely you expected to see me then?"

Collie glanced over at Shelly, who stood motionless on the stairs, her earlier gaiety gone, her gray eyes fixed on her brother.

"You looked different than I expected." She raised a feeble hand toward her face. "Your beard . . ."

He raised a hand as well and rubbed it across his jaw. "Ah, yes. But now I look myself, is that it?"

Her throat constricted. *Oh, if only you knew,* her heart cried. Instead, she nodded. "Yes. You look yourself."

He didn't miss the emphasis on "look" she'd inadvertently uttered. She could tell by the barely discernible narrowing of his eyelids.

"Miss Travers?" Shelly's voice quavered.

Collie tore her gaze from Julian's face—at once a relief and a hardship. "Yes, Shelly?"

"I should like to study my French now."

She smiled at the child, hoping to reassure her but feeling no such calm herself. "Very well. *Va chercher ton livre tout de suite. J'irai à sa rencontre dans la chambre d'école.*"

"*Oui, m'amselle.*"

Shelly took off up the stairs, her slippered feet slapping the marble surface. The sound echoed away as she disappeared down the corridor and silence descended.

Collie turned back to Julian, who stood motionless, an inward-looking expression on his face. The hooded intensity of his eyes was gone. In its place she saw—fear?

His eyes whipped to hers, aware of her scrutiny, and the glimpse she'd had of—no, not fear, perhaps vulnerability—was gone.

"I speak French," he said in a guarded tone. "You told her to find her book, that you'd meet her in the schoolroom, is that right?"

Hope fluttered in Collie's breast, quickly followed by anxiety. The doctor had said not to prompt him, not to push him with memories of his life. But it had been accidental; surely that was not harmful?

"Yes, that's right," she said.

He looked at the ground, considering. "You're the governess," he said again, perhaps to himself, she was not sure.

"Yes. Miss Travers." She held her breath. Could he be remembering? How did this work? If his memory were to return, would it happen all at once? One memory at a time? And if he were to be driven mad by it—how would that happen? "I must go, my lord," she said quickly. "Shelly is waiting."

She took a step sideways, waiting for his release.

He looked up at her, his gray eyes clear and focused, but still unknowing. She breathed a sigh. Madness was a fate worse than death—certainly worse than amnesia.

"Libre à vous. Ne vous gênez pas," he said softly. *Go right ahead.*

"Merci," she breathed and had to force herself not to run up the stairs as Shelly had.

He watched her go. Miss Travers, the governess. The pretty woman with the lively face and quick brown eyes. She had wanted to say more. He'd thought it unusual that she didn't say more. Why?

And why would she hold herself back? He'd wanted to hear what she had to say.

The door to the drawing room opened and that bloody pompous doctor from London emerged, followed by Julian's mother, brother, and fiancée.

No wonder Bafferty had detained him outside for so long, though the weather was foul and the man obviously longed to be indoors—probably in a chair with some cake and a cup of tea, if his portly appearance could be trusted. Which Julian was sure it could be.

They looked guilty when they caught sight of him, he thought. Except for Lady Greer. She glided toward him across the marble floor, her gown of pale yellow and hair of honey gold making her look like an angel.

He searched himself and found nothing but objective admiration for her. No feelings, no love. She was beautiful, breathtaking, with green eyes and a voluptuous figure, yet he'd been more curious about the governess. Probably the influence of the Harrises, he decided. A result of his present unfamiliarity with having servants.

"Darling," Lady Greer said, her lips curved into a smile that was, perhaps unintentionally, quite seductive. "How are you feeling?" She took his arm in her hands and squeezed.

Julian felt a surge of pleasure at the contact. How long had it been since he'd been touched?

"I'm feeling fine," he said. "How are you feeling?"

She laughed up at him. "So much better, darling, upon seeing you. Have you been to see the grounds?"

He glanced at the assembled group. "Yes," he replied, "as you are all no doubt aware, I've been touring the shrubbery with Bafferty." He fixed his gaze on Lady Greer's face. "Did I miss anything?"

He was gratified by the flush that spread across her cheekbones. He'd angled for it instinctively. Why? It didn't matter why, he told himself. They'd been talking about him and she felt secretive about it. It was enough.

"Not a thing," she professed. "We've just had some tea. We tried to wait but you were gone for so long. Would you like some now?"

"Well, I'm off to town," Monroe said abruptly, starting across the hall.

"Oh, Monroe." His mother sighed. "Not again. It's so early."

51

Monroe shot his mother a hard, careless look. "Shall I pick you up something from Ford's? A bit of ribbon, perhaps, some ivory buttons? Would that make you feel better?"

"As if you'd even remember," his mother accused.

Monroe issued a curt laugh. "In that case, I'll just be off then. Good-bye."

Julian watched him go, Monroe's stride angry, aggressive. *To a pub*, Julian thought. *He's a drinker.* Did he know that, or was it just his mother's reaction that put the idea into his head?

The worst thing about this affliction was that he could not distinguish between memory and intuition. What did he know, and what did he simply surmise?

The house was unfamiliar to him. The landscape had evoked nothing but a cold chill, most likely due to the rain. His mother was flighty, his brother sullen and uncommunicative. The governess was nervous and tongue-tied. Shelly was afraid of him. To whom could he turn?

To the one person he must have trusted above all others, logic told him. His fiancée.

"Yes, Lady Greer, I would like some tea," he said. "Perhaps you and I could have some together. Alone."

She smiled and lowered her head, looking up at him through her lashes. "Of course, my lord."

She was beautiful, he had to admit. If nothing else, he'd had exquisite taste. Her skin was perfect, her eyes clear and intelligent, her lips perfectly formed into a naturally sensual pout.

He turned to his mother. "My lady, would you excuse us?"

His mother beamed and waved a hand at them. "You two go right ahead. I know you'll want some time together now, it's been so long. I know I can trust you, Julian, to be a perfect gentleman, but the sooner you two choose a date the better, I say. Nothing so bad as long engagements."

"But Lady Northcliffe, we have chosen a date," Lady Greer said, twining her arm through Julian's and shooting him an uncertain glance. "That is, it was fixed before he left for Italy, do you not remember?"

"Oh, well, of course I do," his mother said. Her eyes registered bewilderment. "Yes, yes, of course. When was it again, dear?"

"Don't fret, Lady Northcliffe," Lady Greer said, leaning forward to pat her arm, but not relinquishing Julian's. "No doubt Julian doesn't remember either." She smiled at him, teasing. "Your mother and I didn't speak much of the engagement after— after the accident. Too painful, you understand."

He tried to imagine what she must have felt, the sadness of losing the one she was to spend her life with, the uncertainty of her future without him. He thought he could understand such pain, though he was not sure how. "Lady Greer—"

"Miranda—*please* call me Miranda," she insisted. "It's too strange, your calling me 'Lady Greer' all the time. Especially since we grew up together!"

"We grew up together?" he asked, surprised.

"Yes, of course. And it was March the fifteenth," she continued, turning back to Lady Northcliffe.

"We'd chosen March the fifteenth as our wedding day." She squeezed Julian's arm against her breast. "Pray, don't worry if the date does not sound familiar, darling. Most men would not hold it firmly in their minds." She teased him again, yet he could tell by the way she clutched his arm and the worried look in her eyes that she was afraid of his response. He squelched the urge to comment that the date did sound familiar. *Beware the ides of March.*

"I'm afraid I don't recall," he said instead. The feel of her breast on his arm caused complex feelings inside him, a mixture of desire and trepidation, an impulse to take her in his arms and an equally strong resistance to the idea.

"Of course you don't," she said with a wry smile. "Do not even try to remember. I'm sorry if it seemed I was pressing you. Lady Northcliffe, would you mind sending Brenda with the tea? Julian, do let's sit down; you must be tired from your walking. Where's Pulver?" When the man arrived she whisked a hand in his direction. "Come quickly, please, and take Lord Northcliffe's coat. He's been standing here dripping for a quarter hour."

They removed themselves to the drawing room, where Julian noted there was no tea service, nor any used plates to indicate that the previous occupants of the room had been doing anything but talking. About him, he knew.

Miranda floated before him, her hips shapely beneath the clingy material of her gown. She carried herself like a queen, head high, shoulders back. When she turned, her breasts, high and firm above the tight bodice of her gown, were flushed and her hand lay over them in a breathless gesture.

Julian closed the door behind him.

"Darling," Miranda cooed as the door clicked shut, "it's so *good* to have you back. And alone." She all but ran toward him and he had no choice but to catch her in his arms. Laying her hands on his chest she looked up at him, her eyes filled with longing. "It's been so difficult, these last weeks. And now, to have you home, only to be unknown to you. Oh— it's too awful! But I don't care if you remember nothing about me, just tell me if I please you now. I beg you, tell me you're not unhappy to find such a betrothed waiting for you."

She gazed up at him with lips parted, her breathing shallow, her eyes glittering with unshed tears. He found himself torn between pity and indifference. It was like watching a play unfold, only the principal was himself and he had no idea what his next line should be.

At his silence she brought one hand again to her throat, a gesture at once protective and seductive, for his eyes could only be drawn to the creamy column and the bounty that lay beneath it. "It's so hard to believe you remember nothing about me," she whispered.

At the same moment a flash of memory hit him, an image of pale breasts and a back arched to receive him. The memory took him by surprise, and floored him with its vividness. She'd been naked, he thought. He could feel the softness of her skin on his tingling fingertips.

Almost as soon as the vision appeared it was

gone, and he was left shaken, a blast of desire skating through him.

Perhaps seeing the need in his eyes, or noting his suddenly flushed and clammy skin, Miranda seized the moment. She moved her hands up his chest and drew him near, gazing up at him with heat in those green cat eyes.

She wet her lips and his eyes followed the motion of her tongue. Physical sensation triggered a memory, he knew, and he wanted to feel the softness of her skin pressed against his, wanted to unpin her hair and let it fall through his fingers. He wanted to taste her lips and know that it was right, that she was home to him, all the home he needed.

She threaded her fingers through the hair at the nape of his neck and asked in a throaty voice, "Do you remember this, Julian? Do you remember the feel of my body against yours?"

His eyes scanned her face—her eyes at once afraid and on fire. "Did we do this, Miranda?" he asked. Just how far had he gone with his fiancée?

Her breasts pushed against his chest as his hands shifted to her back. His muscles gave in to desire and he pulled her to him.

"Yes," she said on a breath. "Yes, yes."

She raised her mouth and he took it. His lips covered hers; his tongue entered her mouth. She opened to him and grasped his coat in her hands, pushing herself against him. But as their breath mingled and his hands traced the curves of her body, the sensation was not the one of coming home that he'd anticipated. His body knew all the responses, but the comfort he sought was not there.

He did not know what he'd expected, but it was not this.

He raised his hands to her shoulders, seeking to extricate himself from her, to stand back and regroup. She would not be denied. The persistent pressure of her hips sent a roar of sensation to his gut. His hands descended down her back, along her the stays of her corset to the full swell of her buttocks.

Not this, his mind extolled. *Step back, take a breath.* But his body wanted more. It was as if physically he refused to believe this was not what he needed.

Behind him, the door burst open.

Miranda gasped as he pulled back and turned, one arm braced around her waist to keep her from stumbling.

In the doorway stood the governess, her face flaming and her hands spread open on her stomach. Her mouth dropped open and her fine brown eyes looked stunned.

"Excuse me," she said in a high, tight voice. "I'm so sorry. I'm so . . ."

With a short expulsion of air, she looked helplessly at the two of them. Then she took one weak step backward, her eyes rolled upward and she crumpled to the floor.

Chapter Three

Julian reached her in three strides. Kneeling, he lifted her head from the hard marble floor and brushed the hair from her forehead, noting her fevered brow with apprehension.

"Brandy," he barked at Miranda. "Get her some brandy."

Miranda hesitated only a moment before edging past him through the door to hurry across the hall.

The governess's face was as white as the marble beneath her, her brows dark arches against nearly translucent skin. Her thick, straight lashes cast a dusky shadow beneath her closed eyes, and he wondered if she'd been ill, so frail did she look.

There was something unnerving about the stillness of her face. Not even an hour ago she'd stood in the hall, scolding and smiling at Shelly with gentle irony, and he'd admired her expressiveness. Then he'd approached and those quick, intelligent eyes of hers had flashed with an unexpected astuteness.

"Come, Miss Travers," he whispered, patting her cheek. "Come now, wake up."

His heart pounded against his rib cage; he was strangely panicked by her lifelessness. He held her cheek and shook her head lightly. His pulse accelerated as the softness of her skin seemed to beg for a caress.

She looked as if she were sleeping, and for a second he imagined her head pillowed on a bed of cut grass and purple wildflowers, her high-necked gown open to the sun.

He flushed, shamed by the illicit thoughts as she lay helpless before him. Miranda had gotten him so stirred up he could not even look at the governess without erotic imaginings. He wondered if before the accident he'd been the sort to take his pleasures where he pleased, taking advantage of the prettier females in his employ without regard to their futures or feelings. Many men of consequence did, he knew. Had he been that kind of man? And who in the world could he ask?

"Wake up, Miss Travers," he repeated. He shook her head again, ignoring the way her hair felt and the vulnerability of her head in his hand. A maelstrom of questions hurtled through his mind. Was he simply not used to crises? Why, along with everything else, this sudden, bloodless panic?

He felt for her pulse, noting the contour of her lips, the delicate shape of her ear, how the sweep of chestnut hair away from her face carried an arc of shine even in the muted hall light.

"Come on, Miss Travers, come back to me," he whispered.

Her lashes fluttered; her lips twitched.

"That's the spirit," he murmured. "You can do it, come on, now."

Her head turned in his hand, and he felt the movement deep in his chest. A breathy sigh emerged from her lips.

He swallowed hard. "Miss Travers." Indulging the impulse, he brushed a knuckle fleetingly down the side of her face.

Her dark eyes fluttered open and took a moment to focus before her sigh became a swift, indrawn breath.

She sat up in a panic. "Julian—" She broke off and glanced wildly around herself. "What happened?"

But she'd sat up too quickly, he noted, for she swayed and clutched a hand to her head. He reached his arm around her to steady her. The crimson blush that colored her face relieved the pallor.

"You fainted," he said. The closeness of their bodies and quiet intimacy of their words sent an unmistakable current of pleasure through him.

Her effort not to look at him was obvious, but she curved into his body as he held her as if she sought refuge from the world. She closed her eyes a moment and took a deep, trembling breath.

"Lady Greer went to fetch some brandy," he said, thinking he should let her go, or take her into the parlor, or something.

Her eyes opened. "Lady Greer," she echoed. Then, "Oh! Lady Greer."

She tried to sit up straighter but he kept his arm around her shoulders. The way she was shaking he did not trust her at all not to swoon again. Her hands patted her pockets as if looking for something.

"I'd left my embroidery . . ." Her voice trailed off and she glanced at him, then forced her gaze to the floor.

He wanted her attention back, wanted her dark gaze upon him. There was something compelling about her face. She *knew* something. Her eyes spoke volumes, yet she said very little. Whatever the turbulent thoughts that graced her expressive face, she would keep them to herself, studiously, he felt. Why?

Was she lying about something? Hiding something? Could she possibly be behind the nameless dread that had followed him to Northcliffe from the relative safety of a simple cottage in Lyme?

He'd had such a strong reaction to her; stronger even than to his fiancée. As she'd lain unconscious his fear had returned tenfold; but how could she be the source of a danger perilous enough to penetrate the haze of his amnesia?

His thoughts took wild turns in an effort to conjure a plausible scenario. She was too intelligent for her position in the household, he thought. He'd known that the moment he saw her. Had he always thought so? Was that memory or intuition? Perhaps she'd been sent here for some devious purpose, perhaps to spy on the Earl of Northcliffe. But by whom? And for what?

He shook his head, struggling to analyze the array of emotions she provoked. Anxiety was definitely among them. Just kneeling here with her on the floor, he felt an apprehension aside from concern for her welfare. Had she threatened him in some way? Why did she look so secretive?

He was paranoid, he realized. Everyone could not possibly be hiding something, and yet he sensed deception at every turn. His family all looked at him with guarded expressions; everyone spoke carefully chosen words and placating sentences.

His fiancée simultaneously seduced and disturbed him. She had sought to appease him, yet she'd lied to him about the tea.

Monroe had cunning eyes and a deceitful curve to his mouth. He thought little of his family, it was obvious.

Bafferty glossed everything over, gave no particulars when Julian asked about estate affairs or even the state of his mother's mind after the death of his father.

Miss Travers was skittish as a cat whenever he was around, gasping when he entered a room, watching him with searching eyes. Was she afraid he would remember something?

Whom could he trust? And more particularly, which feelings within himself held the key to the truth?

A clatter arose from the direction of the dining room and both he and Miss Travers jumped at the intrusion on the reigning silence. A second later Miranda appeared, leading Pulver and three footmen.

"Here we are!" she called. Her voice echoed off the marble walls. "Help is coming! Is she all right?"

*   *   *

Collie shot Julian a glance, their faces still so close she could see the stitch marks on the vivid gash by his eye, could pinpoint the heart of the wound the ship's boom had inflicted, stealing his past—and her future.

His gaze shifted to hers, and for the moment their eyes locked—she in his embrace, he with his shoulder supporting her—his heavy-lidded gaze burned into hers, as if grappling with questions he could not voice.

Time stopped. They sat perfectly still for three thunderous heartbeats; then his attention left her for Miranda.

"Did you bring the brandy?" he demanded.

"Oh, the brandy!" Miranda's face showed instant remorse. "One of you, fetch some brandy immediately." She waved at the footman closest to the dining room. "Go quickly! I thought we would have to carry her to her room, so I merely grabbed all the men that I passed."

Collie dragged her eyes from Julian's face.

"I could have managed that alone, I should think," Julian stated, with a lift of one brow.

Looking from one to the other of them, Collie saw again in her mind's eye Miranda's hands in Julian's hair. With brutal clarity she remembered the curve of Julian's shoulder as he bent into Miranda's embrace, saw the flexing of muscle beneath his jacket as he pulled her close, saw the balanced splay of his legs as their bodies melded. . . .

Collie drew herself up straight. "I'm all right," she said, swiping a tendril of hair behind her ear.

He'd been kissing her when she'd opened the door, kissing Miranda passionately. The memory scalded away the pleasure of his touch.

"Please, let me rise." She pushed herself up from the floor.

His hand closed around her waist and she thought she might faint again at the contact of his fingers, hot through her gown. She gritted her teeth.

Resisting his help, she rose to her feet. "I'm fine. I'm sorry to have inconvenienced you." She stepped away from his encircling arm, away from the torturous familiarity of it. "I—I think it best I should go to my room."

"Yes, do go to your room, Miss Travers," Miranda said. "You must have overexerted yourself today. A more quiet afternoon is no doubt what is called for. I'm sure Lady Northcliffe will understand the intermission in your duties."

Collie shot her a cold glance. "Could someone . . ." She looked to Julian, but the sight of his disheveled cravat pained her so badly she turned her eyes to Pulver. "Could someone let Shelly know that I've been taken ill?"

"Of course, miss," Pulver said, with a short bow. "I shall go to her directly."

Collie swayed again, her head still swimming with shock and the effort to keep tears from choking her voice.

Julian reached for her. His hand closed on her forearm. "Will you be all right? Shall I help you?"

She glanced at his face, at his eyes, filled with concern. Or was it wariness? His expression was intense—could he be suspicious? Her heartbeat accelerated in her chest. Were they all suspicious? She grazed her eyes over the two remaining footmen. Both of them ogled Miranda in her filmy yellow gown. She glanced at Pulver, but he too watched Miranda as she spoke.

"I'm sure what Miss Travers needs is to be alone. Isn't that right, dear?"

Collie turned to her and could swear she saw genuine sympathy in her eyes. Could she know? As a woman, did she intuit the truth? Oh, why did the wretched woman have to be kind to her?

Collie swallowed hard and pulled her arm from Julian's grasp. "Yes. I'll be fine. If you would be so good as to let me go upstairs."

"Someone should help you to your room." Julian's hand remained outstretched. "You don't look very steady."

"No." The word was harsh. She could not for long keep from bursting into tears.

At the look on Julian's face, she instantly regretted her tone. "I apologize, Lord Northcliffe. I am—not well. But I do prefer to find my way alone, thank you."

He nodded and straightened away from her. His hand dropped to his side. "Indeed, you would have to lead me, I'm afraid."

She forced a brief smile and bowed her head. "If you would excuse me."

As she departed, a commanding nausea arose within her. She rushed to the back stair, nearly running once she was out of sight of the hall.

God, please let me make it to my room, she

prayed, grabbing the banister and pulling herself forward. She raced up the steps, head spinning and feet thumping on the wooden staircase. She fled down the wide, silent hallway to the end and burst into her room.

Slamming the door behind her she rushed to the chamber pot, sliding to her knees before throwing up into the bright, clean copper pail.

Dear God, she thought, dear God, dear God. But when she closed her eyes she saw only Miranda's perfectly manicured hands in the thick waves of Julian's hair and lost herself to the sickness again.

Her eyes teared and her throat closed. She clutched her hands to her stomach. The sick feeling had passed, almost as suddenly as it had come, but the fear that trembled through her limbs made a cold sweat break out on her brow.

It was true, it was happening, she thought for the hundredth time. How long did she have before it would show? Enough time for Julian to remember? Enough time so that no one would suspect?

But suppose before Julian regained his memory Miranda and Lady Northcliffe succeeded in getting him to the altar? Suppose she never had a chance to tell him?

"Oh, dear God," she whispered aloud, pushing loose strands of hair from her face with the back of one hand. "Oh, dear God."

"How long's it been happening?"

The voice behind her made her jump nearly out of her skin. She spun on her knees, hearing splinters from the floor catch on the fabric of her gown.

Pam sat on the bed, the door closed behind her, and regarded her with pity.

"W-what? How long has what been happening?" Collie attempted, her voice shaking. She brushed at the skirt of her gown, which twisted around her legs.

"How long has the sickness been happening?" Pam repeated gently.

Collie's shoulders drooped and she covered her face with her hands. Tears dripped through her fingers as she choked back a sob. "About a week," she said through her hands. "Usually in the morning, but every once in a while . . ."

Pam regarded her a moment, then rose and took her friend's arm. "Get up, now. Come sit on the bed. Pulver told me you fainted in the hall."

Panic swelled in Collie's breast at the thought of how many people had seen her. Everyone would know how she'd fainted in front of Lord Northcliffe and that wretched Miranda. Everyone would wonder.

"Oh, God, Pam, do they suspect? They mustn't suspect!" Her voice rose and the trembling in her limbs resumed. "But what else would it be? Why else should I faint? If they think for two minutes—"

"Shhh," Pam said, stroking her back. "They don't know a thing. It was just Pulver, and what does he know of women's bodies?" She continued to run her hand up and down Collie's back.

"But the footmen, the footmen were there too!" Collie continued, on the edge of panic. "Jones and Cleary. There might have even been another, I'm not sure. I was just—it was just so—oh, what am I going to do?"

"Nothing. You're going to continue on as if nothing happened. Nothing did happen, Coll. So you had a little fainting spell; what of it?"

Collie took a deep breath and placed her palms on the bed on either side of her, straightening her shoulders. "Of course. You're right. It's nothing, nothing."

Her gaze rose to the ceiling, as she imagined the suspicious looks she knew she'd get from the servants. Thank goodness she would no longer have to take her meals with them. Now that Julian had returned they could not relegate her to the kitchen without having to explain themselves. And perhaps she could request to eat in her room, at least tonight. The problem was that it was becoming difficult to disguise her revulsion to certain foods. The smell of turnips, for example, made her weak with nausea, whereas before she'd had no trouble with them. Likewise, butter beans and mutton. And then there was the third housemaid's body odor.

How she would continue to keep up appearances she did not know. She couldn't even begin to consider what her options would be farther down the line, when her condition wouldn't be so easy to keep secret. But even if she could somehow manage to keep the secret for two, or God willing even three months, by that time would it be too late? Would Julian be married to Miranda? Would Collie be cast out of service before he had a chance to recall what had been between them?

"It's his, of course, isn't it?" Pam said. "Lord Northcliffe's."

Collie shot her a wary look, then slumped with despair. "Of course it's his. Whose else would it be?" A mental image of the scene she'd just witnessed flashed into her head. "But, oh, Pam, he was kissing her. That Miranda. He was kissing her as if they'd been married a year. Her—her hands were in his hair—" She broke off, unable to continue speaking, and buried her face in her hands again. "God, he wants her now. He doesn't remember me, loving me, asking me to marry him. He wants her now."

"Shhh," Pam murmured. "He doesn't know what he wants. He's barely been back a day and he's being told what he wants by his family. A more self-serving bunch of people I have yet to meet."

But when Collie looked at her friend she saw more than just pity in her eyes; she saw resignation.

"I don't understand. How could this have happened?" she whispered. "It was only the one time, just that one first time, before he left for Italy."

Pam smiled, her eyes gentle. "It only takes one time."

"He said he loved me, Pam. Only me." She shook her head. "How do you forget something like that? How could he not remember all we shared? All we felt?" She sighed and added bitterly, "This is so pitiful."

Pam took a deep breath. "It's my experience," she said carefully, her hand still stroking Collie's back, "that men will say anything, at that moment."

The words took a second to register. Once they

did, Collie straightened and swung to face her friend. "What on earth do you mean? I told you, he asked me to marry him."

Pam shrugged. "As I said, they'll say anything."

Collie gaped at her in horror. "Pam," she said slowly, "he was to speak with his father on the trip. He may not remember, but he wouldn't lie. He would never lie to me."

Pam said nothing, so Collie continued despite the fact that the desperation of her words was obvious and pathetic even to herself.

"It was all arranged—we were to marry. It—it seemed so silly to refuse. And I did not want to refuse. I wanted to do it! It wasn't just him," she declared, as if that proved anything beyond her own profligacy. "Because I loved him. I trusted him. And I was so sure he'd come back. And then he died. When I thought he was dead . . . but he *didn't* die, and now he's lost to me still! Oh, Pam," she cried openly now, "it's all so dire. My mother—what in the world will I do—if I lose this position—if Lady Northcliffe finds out—but how will she not? Eventually they will all find out!"

Everything hit her at once, the terror and the uncertainty. She had to admit it now, now that someone else knew. She was without her monthly courses. At first she thought the grief had caused the delay. The shock to her system had been considerable. But then she'd begun to get sick. And then she missed her second, and now, oh God, now she was sure of it—she carried Julian Coletun's child and nobody would believe her. Even Pam, she could see, while she believed that it was Julian's, did not wholly believe that he'd intended to marry her, that he'd asked her—on bended knee, by God—to be his wife. And if Pam didn't believe her . . .

Panic enveloped her and she clutched her arms to her middle. "If I lose this position I'll have nowhere to go. I'll have to let Nurse Frederick go, and then what will become of my mother? We shall starve if I have no work."

"Collie," Pam said soberly.

Collie looked up.

"There is a way . . . it's still early." Pam eyed her friend cautiously, but with intent.

"What do you mean?" Collie wiped the tears from her face with impatience.

"The child, Collie," Pam said quietly, as if another set of ears in the room might overhear. "I know of a woman. Sometimes she can do it with herbs. Other times . . ." She bent her head sideways with a shrug. "Other times it takes more . . . direct means."

Collie's nausea returned as Pam's meaning became clear. "No," she said on a breath.

"Collie, I know you love him. But if it means the difference between you and your mother starving to death and—"

"I said no!" she nearly shouted, and slammed to her feet. "I would *never* do that to his child."

"Then what shall you do?" Pam asked, her voice harder now.

Collie's indignant gaze skittered to the floor, the wall, the window, then back to her friend. "I know him, Pam. At the very least he'll take responsibility for his actions."

71

Pam threw her hands up. "Listen to yourself. He can't take responsibility for actions he doesn't remember. And what will you do? Tell him about it? 'Excuse me, Lord Northcliffe, I know you don't know me from Eve, but you and I were lovers and now I carry your child. Please, would you make arrangements?' Is that what you plan? He's a nervous, wary man, Collie. And a noble at heart, no matter what he remembers. He'll recognize a scheme for money when he sees it."

"But it isn't a scheme! It *is* his child!"

"Not as far as he's concerned," Pam said. "Look at what they're all doing. His mother is dying to turn him into the social fop she always dreamed of; she speaks of it constantly. Miranda has convinced everyone, including him, she's his betrothed. Monroe—well, Lord knows what Monroe is up to, but you can bet it's something awful—and there you'll be, just one among the crowd, looking to get your own piece of him. Trust me on this, Collie. I'm speaking what must seem like terrible words for your own good. He's not a fool; he'll believe what will seem obvious. A poor, unmarried governess pops up with child and tries to pin it on him. Who would possibly take her word that the bastard belongs to the forgetful earl, for God's sake? It's just too convenient."

Collie stood trembling in the center of the room. Pam's words echoed with bitter truth in her head.

"Listen," Pam continued more gently. "If you won't consider taking care of the child, then consider taking care of yourself." She paused and took a breath. "Get married."

Collie jerked. "What?"

Pam smiled. "I said, get married. Give the child a name. Perhaps you could keep your position that way and continue to take care of your mother."

Collie's hands and feet, even her face, felt suddenly numb. "To whom?"

Pam shrugged. "Cleary's always been solicitous of you."

"Cleary? The second footman?" she asked, incredulous. "Has it somehow passed your notice that he's several hundred years old? What sort of life do you suppose that would be?"

"He's very kind," Pam offered.

Collie scoffed. "The man talks to bushes, Pam. No, no, actually he *argues* with bushes. Have you seen him in the rose garden? And he barely bathes!"

"Well . . ." Pam drew herself up. "We can't all set our sights on an earl, now, can we?"

Collie rubbed a hand across her brow. "Pam, I know you mean well, but listen to yourself. Cleary would not even be a good provider. How much could he possibly make? Besides"—she held a hand up as Pam started to interrupt—"I have no intention of marrying anyone without love."

"Very pretty words," Pam argued. "Shall we speak again in a month? Two months? I don't hear you coming up with any plan. What if Lord Northcliffe never remembers? What then, Collie? Catching a husband will be quite a bit tougher once you start growing round. While someone might have you now, when the secret will be between yourselves, who will have you when the whole village knows you carry a bastard?"

"Oh, stop it!" Collie cried, whirling away from her. "Don't call it a bastard!"

"Collie, listen to me," Pam said. "Now is no time for delicacy. You're going to have a child. And you're running out of time to deal with it."

Chapter Four

"Dr. Irwin." Lady Northcliffe's voice quavered; her low tone was tentative. "Tell me the truth."

Julian stopped in the hall outside the door. He had not meant to eavesdrop but the whisper had drawn him in as he passed, causing him to slow his step and strain to hear.

"If Julian has been found alive," his mother continued, "is there any chance, even a small one, that my husband might also be found—alive?"

A shower of chills rained down Julian's spine. His father, who had been on the ship with him . . . could he have survived as well?

A consuming, familiar fear awoke in his chest like a once-sleeping beast—a fear more threatening because it was undefined and had the power to paralyze him. With a roar of unleashed might, the beast reared up inside him and strangled his heartbeat, sucked away his breath.

His mind's eye was suddenly filled with the image of an unconscious man on the wet deck of a ship, head lolling with every lurch of the enormous waves. Though the vision was dim, Julian struggled to make out the man's face, to recall the core facts of this half-remembered dream.

Suddenly, the floor seemed to pitch beneath his feet like the deck of a ship and Julian grabbed for the marble column flanking the staircase. Good God, was he losing his mind? He squeezed his eyes shut, but the vision only became more vivid.

He saw his own hands grab hold of a broken plank. He felt the memory of his shoulders flexing as he hefted the heavy board over his head. Then, in mute horror, he recalled swinging the board downward to smash the unconscious man's skull beneath it.

He jerked now as if feeling again the solid contact and subtle give as the murderous blow met and crushed its mark. In his mind's eye he saw the blood pool and mix with the water washing over the deck.

Julian forced his eyes open, unsure if he remembered or imagined the way the man's hair floated in the muddy mixture, and the way the eyes, half-closed and lifeless, looked almost sleepy.

He turned and leaned his back against the cool marble column. His skin felt clammy; his breath was short. His stomach clutched uneasily.

After a moment he lifted his hands—shaking and damp—and pushed the hair back out of his face. Fear howled within his chest and he wanted to break something, to destroy the vision within. His muscles burned with the effort of control.

Merciful heavens, I have killed, he thought. And now, the rage within himself threatened to tear out of control. Lord help him, he was losing his mind.

Gripping the column behind him with both hands, he forced himself to take a breath and looked to the ceiling, afraid to close his eyes.

He had killed, he thought again. But could he not trust himself to have had justification?

The rage inside him scoffed. *Intellectualize if you will*, a dark conscience laughed. But it had been Julian and none other who had bludgeoned that skull and had watched the lifeblood drain from the man's head onto the deck. And if his flawed, incomplete memory could be trusted, he'd felt nothing of remorse. Only rage and more rage.

His father was dead. Julian knew it though he knew no other thing.

And Julian had murdered a man.

Had it been his own father?

Choking on dread, lashing himself with self-hatred for his inability to remember, he bent at the waist and propped his hands on his knees. He took one breath and then another, forcing himself to recall the face that had lain on the deck. But like a dream after its dreamer wakes, it was lost to conscious pursuit. Only shadows of feeling remained, shadows of frightening, uncontrollable emotion.

Slowly his heartbeat returned to normal. The sweat cooled on his face.

Is there any chance my husband might also be found alive?

Julian had not heard the answer the doctor gave his mother, though his vision had lasted but a moment. It mattered not, anyway. His father was dead; he was sure of it.

His mother queried on, with soft, indistinct

words, while Julian's soul burned within him.

Footsteps sounded on the stairs, light and quick. He straightened, unable to push himself off the column to stand alone, but at least able to stand upright. He could not show weakness. The dread governing him since his return dictated he always maintain control. That he was plagued with uncertainty, plagued now with the fear that he himself was a murderer, must never be shown.

"Lord Northcliffe!" A breathy sound—almost a gasp.

The governess.

Julian might have smiled but could not shake his disquiet. He shifted his eyes to her face, alight with surprise, and fear. Was she afraid of him? he now wondered.

"Are you all right, my lord?" She stopped several paces away.

Did she look upon a murderer? he asked himself. Did she know the vile character he possessed that he himself could not remember? If she knew—if any of them knew—they would all fear him, he realized. If they knew of the vision or the terrible rage simmering inside of him, they would be foolish not to be afraid.

"Do I not look all right?" His voice was cool but his eyes searched her face.

"No. You look pale. Can I get you something to drink?" Her hands were knotted at her waist, the knuckles white. Illogically, her nervousness disappointed him.

"Yes." He straightened from the column. "Yes, I'd like a brandy." He took one step away from the pillar, relieved that his legs held him steady. "Would you join me, Miss Travers?"

Her eyes shot to the door behind which his mother and the doctor dwelled. "Join you?" she repeated.

"Yes. In the library." He turned and walked away from the drawing room, his control returning. Steady now, he forced himself to breathe naturally.

He crossed the back hall and reached the door to the library, relieved to hear her footsteps on the marble behind him. Gesturing her inside with a brief movement of his hand, he said, "If you please, Miss Travers." His tone was uncompromising. He was, after all, the master.

She drew herself up and moved forward. Entering the room, she went straight for the liquor near the desk, uncorked the brandy and poured him a healthy dose. The amber liquid slid along the inside of the tilted glass, becoming an even pool in the hip of the snifter before she righted it and turned toward him. She held it out.

She'd done this before.

He closed the door, moved into the room and reached for the glass. As she came toward him with it, he felt a brilliant, momentary flash of emotion in his chest. Trust, he thought. Then, no, something else. Something he was not sure of.

He took the snifter, his fingers brushing hers. She pulled her hand back to her waist and clutched it with the other.

She feared him, he thought. Her eyes were direct, but she didn't appear to be breathing.

"Pour one for yourself," he said, swirling the liquid in his glass. "You look as if you could use it."

Her chin rose a fraction. "No. Thank you."

Suddenly he had no patience for the uncertainty in her face. What in God's name did she have to be afraid of? She couldn't know of his vision. She didn't confront dread at every corner, didn't wrestle nightly with unnameable fears and sourceless guilt. Why in the world should she look at him thus with those vulnerable eyes? What had he ever done to her?

At that, he laughed harshly. What had he ever done to her indeed? He knew not. Based on his scant evidence, she probably had every reason to fear him.

"My lord?"

With forced mildness he asked, "How long have you worked here, Miss Travers?" His hand clutched the glass.

"Just over a year, my lord." Her voice was strong, at odds with the look in her eyes.

"And did you know the family before you were employed here?"

"Barely. I am quite distantly related to the late Lord Northcliffe's friend, Lord Bretton."

Julian searched his memory. "Lord Bretton," he murmured. It struck a distant chord. He clung to it.

"Yes. You may recall—" At this she stopped, flushed, then continued. "His son, my second cousin, Lord Anthony Bretton, was—is a friend of yours."

"Is he?" Julian's heart leaped, until he saw in her face something like pity. It stung him.

She nodded. "Yes. Unfortunately, he's in India now."

He kept his gaze on her. "Why is that unfortunate, Miss Travers?"

Her brows drew together. "Because he's your friend."

Friend, his mind scoffed in rage. Friend. "Is he my only friend?" Julian demanded. "Is no one here a friend to me?"

She frowned and looked away. "I—I don't mean to say that people here—that you don't have friends among those here. Just—he is, perhaps, your closest friend. The one who might help you most."

He lifted a brow. "Help me what? Remember? What is it he might do that my entire family and Dr. Irwin cannot?"

"I only meant that he could be a comfort to you. Someone you could trust completely. Not that there aren't some you can trust here—but he . . . well, he—he knows you so well." Her thumbs worked over her clenched fingers.

Julian smiled slightly, his eyes narrowed. Her discomfort began to give him a much-needed sense of control.

"I would think no one would know me better than my family. How long have I known this Lord Bretton?"

"Your whole life," she exclaimed. "And—" She stopped abruptly. Noticing his smile, she frowned at him. "Are you baiting me, my lord?"

"That's an impertinent question," he said. He turned and circled the desk to stand behind it.

She bowed her head, lips pressed together. "I apologize."

He deposited his glass on the table and folded his arms over his chest. "Miss Travers, is there no one else here who might help me as Lord Bretton would?" he asked coolly. "Perhaps you could tell me who I appeared to trust most in my household."

Her eyes rose to his, her brows raised. "Oh . . . No, of course you would not know, would you? You cannot perceive their characters as yet."

Irritated, Julian sat down at the desk. With one hand he grasped the stem of the snifter and turned it on the burnished surface. "I am merely interested in your perceptions, Miss Travers. Just answer the question. It may be that it's *your* character I seek to perceive, so do not guess at my motives; you do it ill."

She was silent a moment. He watched her, expressionless.

"You were closest to your father." Her quick eyes flashed to him, her face transparent with pity. "I'm so sorry you've lost him."

Inclining his head briefly, he said in a hard voice, "Thank you. But as you know, your condolence can mean little to me now—as I cannot even remember the man."

The sadness on her face changed swiftly into shock. "Perhaps not now, no. But . . ."

The anxiety in her eyes intrigued him. "But what, Miss Travers?"

"But, perhaps—I was going to say, perhaps soon you will. We are—all of us—most hopeful that you will remember all, in time."

He scoffed and watched her face fall. "I do not think it would be wise to count on my ever remembering all, Miss Travers. My past appears to be gone. Perhaps for good." His eyes dropped to the glass in front of him.

She issued a strange sound, perhaps an unintended word, and he glared at her swiftly. "What was that?"

"Nothing. I . . ." Her fingers touched the tabletop beside her and she appeared to lean on them. "Nothing."

"There is no need to look so astounded, Miss Travers. Irwin assures me it's best not to remember," he said dryly.

Her eyes glittered with a brightness they had not had moments before. Was she relieved or upset? Was that excitement in her eyes?

He lifted the snifter to his lips, taking a long draw of the fiery liquid. "Tell me, did this Lord Bretton receive word of my death?" he asked, turning to stare toward the fire.

She cleared her throat. "Well, yes . . . I . . ."

Her skirts rustled as she moved around the armchair in front of the desk.

"Please sit down if you like," he offered.

Her hands were again knotted at her waist. She disentangled them to smooth her skirts before sitting. "I wrote to him when word reached us that— that you'd been lost."

He looked at her, at what sounded like a catch in her voice.

"Then I wrote him again when we heard you had survived. I do hope the second letter reaches him quickly. I hate to think of his pain, believing you dead."

"*You* wrote to him? Why you and not my mother? Or even my brother?"

"He is my cousin, and your mother was in no condition to write to anyone," she said, her voice breathy. "She was confined to her room after hearing the news. It was not until Mr. Bafferty arrived that she emerged and strove to participate once again in the household routine."

"And my brother?"

She frowned. "It would be quite unlike Monroe even to think of such a thing."

"Indeed," Julian said. "It was kind of you to think of informing Bretton." He kept his gaze on her face, on the blush that stained her cheeks.

"I thought," she began, her hands bunched in her lap, "that you would wish it."

"And would you ordinarily have knowledge of what I would wish?"

Her mouth opened but no sound emerged at first. "I—" She closed her mouth on the word. Her brow furrowed. She dropped her gaze to her lap. "Yes, I—"

"Come now, Miss Travers, if you did what you thought best there should be no confusion in it."

Her dark, expressive eyes flew to his face. "No—I mean, yes, I did do what I thought best. But I also did think you would wish it. I knew that you were close to him, closer to him than anyone, save your father. And truth to tell, I thought if he were here, if he could come quickly, that he might help—

help—everyone here, help us all adjust to your loss. Yours and Lord Northcliffe's."

"You thought he would help *you*," he said.

She looked at him with great energy. "Yes," she breathed, and sat forward on the chair, as if she might swiftly rise. "Yes, I did."

Julian downed the last of his brandy and set the glass on the desk with a thud. "I see," he said. "And no doubt Lord Bretton would have flown to your side. Therefore we can assume he received your second post, stopping him in his tracks."

"I—I don't know. Perhaps. I hadn't thought of it in that way."

He laid his hands flat on the desk, and then slid them back to grip the edge of it in his hands. Tension gripped his body. "You've heard nothing from him, then?"

"No. Nothing."

He studied her face. The eyes were sincere, but hid something nonetheless.

Isn't she to marry Bretton? He heard a voice he knew but did not know echo in his head as if the words had just been spoken. Hard on its heels came another vision. Rain-lashed decks and a churning sea. He could feel the stinging torrent on his face, on his hands, and felt a tough hemp rope pull at the flesh of his palms as he dragged himself forward through the gale across the planking.

He stood up behind the desk and barely heard the chair scrape across the floor behind him.

Instead, the memory of being struck by a massive wave consumed him. The breaker knocked him from his feet and dragged him toward the edge of

85

the deck, toward the surging lead gray sea. He looked down, and saw blood and sea foam stream around his knees on the deck. He looked up, and not far from where he knelt saw a limp body clutching a white piece of fabric slide helplessly out to sea . . . without resistance, with no effort to save himself.

"No," Julian said, clutching the desk as if it were the rope keeping him alive.

In his mind he saw the body ease softly off the side of the deck. Graceful, so slow as to be taunting. The white cloth in the man's left hand visible for the merest second before the body disappeared into the fury of the sea.

"No, no, no!" He squeezed his eyes shut, and shook his head in a vain attempt to free it from the vision, and to free himself from the pain in his chest the sight summoned.

As if he'd commanded it, the vision shifted. This time he saw the face and the blood-covered skull. This time he watched as the sea sucked the man's body into the yawning cavern of an iron gray wave.

"*No!*" he shouted again, clutching his hands into fists.

The beast in his chest awoke, swelling and clawing at his throat to escape. *Stop, stop, stop!*

He pulled at his cravat and spun to lean against the back of the chair, to battle the beast before him with both hands. Guilt and horror swept him with the violence of the ocean's waves. His fingers struggled against the knot at his neck. He had to breathe. *Stop, stop!*

Hands clutched at his sleeves and prevented his

fingers from reaching the knot. He opened his eyes and lunged at the intruder restraining him, grabbed at the flesh and fabric and crushed the warm limbs in his limitlessly strong hands.

"Stop!" her voice implored him. Her eyes were wide with terror, and he realized it had been her words—the governess's—he'd heard. The frightened, insistent pleading to stop.

He clutched her shoulders in a punishing grip. Yet even as he took in who she was, he could not make himself release her. Instead he sustained the grip with both hands, the beast inside him warming with the contact, retracting horror to breathe white-hot desire through his limbs instead.

Julian exhaled and focused on her face. Holding her at arm's length, his fingers pressed far too hard into her supple flesh. But she did not struggle against him. Indeed, her hands clutched his sleeves with the same intensity, the fabric balled into her fists. He could feel the muscles tensed beneath his fingers.

Her eyes were terrified, yet she had rushed *to* him, not away.

Slowly, with hitherto unknown control, he eased his fingers apart, gentling his grip in fractions, until his sight cleared and the raw force that possessed him released his muscles.

She breathed nearly as heavily as he. A lock of shiny brown hair had come loose from the knot at the back of her neck and drifted along one flushed cheek. She smelled soft, powdery. The scent stirred a longing deep inside of him.

"Are—are you all right?" she whispered. Her fingers loosened on his sleeves, but she still held them lightly. "Please—say something."

He took a deep breath; it coursed roughly into his lungs. He dropped his hands, and hers fell away too.

"Yes," he said, hating the gravelly sound. He cleared his throat. "Yes. I'm all right." His body trembled.

"What happened? What is it? Tell me."

His eyes narrowed. He concentrated on breathing. "Tell you?"

She glanced away, down at her hands now knotted again at her waist. "I thought you might have . . . did you remember something?"

She *was* afraid he would remember something.

He ran a hand along his forehead, felt the clammy, cool skin. "Yes. I did."

Her eyes flew upward.

He grasped the chair and turned it to him. He sat, abruptly, when his knees folded too suddenly.

"My father is dead," he said, just to hear the effect of the words said aloud.

She rounded the desk and sat again on the chair across from it. "Most likely he is," she said softly. "Though we also believed you dead."

He shook his head. "No, you don't understand. I saw him . . . washed overboard. I—I believe it was him."

She leaned forward, hands on her knees. "You're not sure?"

His eyes snapped to hers. "I *felt* sure."

She exhaled slowly. "Ju—Lord Northcliffe, pray do not mistake my intention, but I think it would be wise to keep this . . . this episode to ourselves."

He took slow, even breaths and looked at her steadily. "Why?"

Her eyes skittered from his face, to the floor, to the mantel. "Situations such as yours . . ." She paused.

Into the silence he interjected, "You're familiar with situations such as mine, are you?"

She looked embarrassed. "I only mean, you are in a very—what some would consider a—a dangerous position."

"Dangerous, Miss Travers? Do you mean with regard to my health?"

She fiddled with the fringe on a throw pillow next to her. "Of course. Yes, that too. But Northcliffe is a very wealthy earldom. There might be those who—" She glanced at him. "Please take my words for concern for your welfare only—but some people are not scrupulous. They may take advantage of the situation. It may be that some are deceiving you." Her gaze dropped and she brought her clasped hands to her chin. After a moment, she dropped her hands and looked at him again. "Then there could be those who might argue that you are not fit to make your own decisions. They could, perhaps, attempt to make you do something you might later regret."

He leaned back in the chair. "No one is going to make me do anything. I've lost my memory, Miss Travers, not my mind."

At his words she gave a sudden intake of breath. "No, of course you have not lost your mind," she said, looking distinctly unsettled. "But suppose you were convinced to do something? Suppose you were taken advantage of?"

"It would help me more if you could be specific, Miss Travers. Do you suspect someone of treachery? Who is it you are thinking of?"

That soft porcelain pink stole into her cheeks again. "No. No one. I—"

"No one?"

"I mean, I think of no one, specifically. I only warn you as a precaution. It is a fear, I believe, among some of the servants, that you might not be—well. If you were to be . . . if your command were to be overridden . . . They do not want someone to act in your stead."

"How commendable," he murmured, watching her.

"They are quite loyal, my lord," she said. Her fingers clutched the pillow in her lap. "You can trust them—most of them, I believe. But I would not trust everyone. Not even those you think you ought, by virtue of their relationship to yourself."

"What is it you know, Miss Travers?" he pressed. "You're obviously trying to get at something—"

Before he could finish the sentence she rose from her seat, the pillow dropping to the floor.

"I've said too much with too little evidence," she said, hands gripping her skirts, as if to lift them and run away. "Truly, I know very little—I only suspect. As you should suspect—but you don't—you can't know. Oh! This is too frustrating."

She stepped around the chair toward the door. Julian rose and crossed quickly to take her arm, turning her to look at him.

"Tell me, Miss Travers," he insisted. "Tell me what you know."

She was afraid again; he could see it in her face.

"I told you, I don't *know* anything—"

"You said you knew very little." He drilled her with his eyes. "Even very little is something." His fingers tightened on her arm.

She breathed heavily, and the fichu covering the neckline of her dress quivered with her heartbeat. An unexpected urge to run his hand down the bare skin of her arm assailed him.

She seemed to feel it too, for she gazed up at him with heat in her eyes. The current of comprehension that charged between them flared as if she'd acquiesced to something forbidden.

"You do not understand my position," she said, so quietly he would not have heard her were he not so close. "My place in your household is insecure at best."

"As is mine," he answered. "If you are correct."

She pressed her lips together and dropped her eyes from his. He loosened his grip on her arm, allowing her to pull away, but she did not.

After a moment she raised her face again. "Though I cannot voice my suspicions, my lord, I would advise you to be ever conscious of your own objectives. You would believe nothing I had to say now completely anyway, as you well know, not without proof for yourself. But I can tell you, you would be wise to be skeptical of everything you are told."

His pulse skipped a beat. "Skeptical even of you, Miss Travers?" he asked, not bothering to keep the irony from his voice. "Or are you the one person I should trust above all others?"

Her eyes flashed with anger. "Trust me not either, then, if that is what you feel," she replied. "It is not for me to say if I am worthy of your confidence." Her chin rose and the look she gave him was defiant. "But do not, in my stead, put your faith in Miranda Greer."

Chapter Five

Julian sat at the massive desk and stared across its surface. Wax candles glowed at either corner, and a silver tray holding a quill and cut-crystal inkpot lay between them. To the right a silver salver held a stack of opened letters, the envelopes torn haphazardly, the notes pushed back into them sideways.

The desk was situated at one end of a long gallery with three large windows along the left wall. The walls behind and to his right were lined with books, uniformly bound in leather with gold-leaf titles.

Appropriately, the room smelled of leather and the sweetly pungent residue of cigar smoke. He leaned back in the chair and studied it from his vantage point, thinking about his meeting with the governess the previous day, picturing her in the chair across from him.

She was not a great beauty like Miranda. She did not have his fiancée's delicate features, pale hair and air of fragility. But something about her was compelling. She had an expressiveness, an energy and grace to her movements that captured his attention, the way a flash of lightning draws the eye and holds it in anticipation.

And she was intelligent, of that he was certain. She knew something specific about his situation but for some reason would not voice it. Why? If she truly feared for his welfare she would confess it. Unless it implicated her in some way. But then why bring it up at all?

He sighed and ran his hands through his hair. It was too much to figure out. He had nothing on which to base his speculations. He could only wait to see what information came to light in the coming days.

The hour was early and little daylight came from the northern windows through which he gazed. He sank back in the chair, stretched his legs and crossed them at the ankle. Propping his elbows on the arm of the chair, he clasped his hands loosely over his stomach. He felt echoes of familiarity, had moments of awareness that floated past like seaweed on a calm blue sea. The room was not quite known, but it satisfied him as if everything were in its place.

A snippet of music passed through his mind and with it a vision of a dark-haired girl in a white dress spinning and laughing, dancing alone, toward him. The memory was brief, but he wondered if her similarity to Miss Travers was due to the fact that he'd just been thinking of her, or if she had been at one time so at ease with him as to dance and make fun when they were alone.

Perhaps it was no memory at all, but simple fantasy. Since he could not reconcile her apparent concern for him with her silence, he had not been able to stop thinking about her. She was, he decided, too watchful. Her caution was unnatural.

He did not try further to place the vision, did not push for more, for he was exhausted from his efforts of the last few days. Yesterday's cataclysmic remembrance had drained him, as had the fear that his uncontrollable rage might somehow tear him apart, or make him commit some other heinous crime. If he were to remember the past, the everyday patterns of his previous life, he would do best to let them come to him slowly. He could emulate what his life had been to see if the motions sparked something less traumatic.

Pushing himself upright, he pulled on the top drawer of the desk. It slid open on well-oiled rims to reveal neat stacks of writing paper and envelopes, along with extra pens and neat stores of ribbon, sealing wax and a gold press. This last he picked up and turned over in his palm. Gazing at the initialed crest—*JPC*, Julian Pembroke Coletun—he felt a stirring of uneasiness. He knew it to be the Coletun family crest, had seen the rearing lion and thorned rose on everything from the carriage to the butler's embroidered lapel. But it had never disturbed him until now, looking at the gold engraving of the sealing press. With a deep breath, he dropped the object back in the drawer and pushed it slowly shut.

He would confine himself to exploring pleasant memories today, he thought, unwilling to admit to any trepidation over the possibility of reliving yesterday's horror. He would concentrate on memories like the laughing girl in white. Perhaps it had been Shelly, he speculated, opening another drawer to find it virtually empty. A few pence rolled about inside, along with some string, a buttonhook, cigar clip, and a snippet of wrinkled newspaper tucked in a back corner, perhaps overlooked in the cleaning. He pulled this last out and smoothed it on the desktop. The article was from an issue of the *Times* months back, before he'd left on his ill-fated trip, and was a brief, uninspired description of the grand opening of some pavilion in India. Lord Anthony Bretton's name was mentioned.

Julian folded the piece of paper and pushed it into his breast pocket.

In opening each subsequent drawer he was struck by the fact that aside from the article on India he found nothing of any personal nature. The desk was well stocked as if ready for use, but showed no sign of having been employed by any one person on a regular basis. The further he looked, the more this disturbed him.

Where were his papers and his personal effects? Where were the household records, the accounts, registers, receipts? Bafferty told him this had been his study, the location from which he'd run the estate after his father had handed the operation over to him. And yet there was nothing here to indicate any work had ever been performed—personal or otherwise.

Slamming the last drawer, he glared at the items on the desk. The letters—surely here was something personal. He pulled the salver toward him and picked up the first note.

PRAY LOVE, REMEMBER

The Lord and Lady of Winchelsea request the honor of your presence at a ball, to be held on the evening of October the seventeenth, at Chatsworth Hall.

He tossed it aside and opened the next one, and the next. All were invitations of one sort or another. All were addressed to himself. All appeared to be unanswered and had either arrived or taken place during the first couple of weeks of his absence. Presumably, once the news had gotten out that the ship carrying him and his father had been lost, the invitations had stopped coming. But why were these saved? And why were they the only personal objects to be found?

At the far end of the room the door eased open. Julian raised his head and tensed until he saw his mother's capped head peer around the portal. Squinting across the distance at him, she lifted a hand and waved, her fingers twirling almost flirtatiously.

"Good morning, Julian," she sang. Her smile was tentative as she entered. "It is you, isn't it, Julian?" She squinted again and started across the Persian carpets toward him. Her bejeweled hands held her skirts aloft to ease her waddling gait. "My eyes aren't what they used to be."

He watched her approach, wondering what he'd called this woman before the accident. "Mother?" "My lady?" "Lady Northcliffe?" None seemed to fit.

"Good morning," he said as she neared.

"You see?" she said brightly. "Things haven't changed so very much. You and I are still the first

97

ones up and about, while the others laze in their beds."

She rounded a straight-backed chair across from him and settled herself upon it, for all the world like a hen settling upon her nest.

"Going through your things?" she asked with a timid smile.

He sighed and tossed the invitation he still held back onto the pile in front of him. "That was my intention," he answered, "but there don't seem to be any things here."

Her face puckered in condolence. "Oh, I know. And I'm sorry, Julian. It's just that after the—the accident—it was so painful to have all those personal effects lying about, staring us all in the face so horridly. So I had Horace clean it all out and Pulver burned it."

Julian started at her last words. "Burned it?" he repeated. "What on earth for? Stowing it in the attic didn't occur to you?" His instant irritation confounded him.

His mother looked unhappy, but not surprised at his tone. "Please don't be angry at me, Julian," she pleaded, a worried tremor in her voice. "I was all alone. And so upset! I'd just lost your father, you know, and I simply didn't know what to do. All those solicitors and farmers and tenants, even townspeople, wanting to know if we were going to settle this, or if we still wanted that. Who was going to take charge of this endeavor or that? I tell you it was awful, simply awful. And I don't know anything about settling accounts or collecting money— I'm just a woman, Julian, a helpless widowed

woman." Her voice broke and she plucked a handkerchief from her sleeve to dab at her eyes.

"I'm sorry," he said curtly, feeling nothing of the
kind. Perhaps he really was hard-hearted, he
mused solemnly, to be so unmoved by his own
mother's tears.

"And why should we stow all of that in the attic?"
she added, an obstinate note creeping into her
voice. "It wasn't as if we knew you'd be coming back
and needing it."

Julian smiled grimly at the words. "You seem put
out that I have."

"Julian! How can you say such a thing? I only
meant—"

"Yes, yes, I know what you meant. But surely,
madam, you recognized the need to save the household registers—the rents and the accounts?"

She drew herself up and gave him an injured
look. "I had Horace decide what needed saving. I
am not so much a fool as to think I would be able
to know what was what."

He fingered the invitation he'd dropped on the
top of the pile. "I imagine it was you who saw fit to
hold on to these, however." He pushed the salver
full of invitations halfway across the desk toward
her.

She brightened. "Yes, it was me! You see, I didn't
do everything wrong. At the time it seemed too sad
to do away with party invitations. Such merry
things, you know. I believe I felt as if . . . as if you
might return and want to attend one of them. . . ."
She sniffed and dabbed at her nose this time.
"Some of the parties have not yet occurred, Julian,"

she added, looking up at him through dewy lashes.

Julian stared at her. "So you burned all of my personal letters and files because I would never return to know the difference; yet you saved these invitations on the off chance that I might show up and want to attend a party?" He folded his hands together on the desk to keep from clenching them into fists of frustration.

"Don't be angry with me," she cried. "It's just that the invitations reminded me so much more strongly of you than those other things. You did always love a party so."

Guilt and annoyance stung him at once. It was nothing but sentimentality to save the worthless invitations. Yet to be angry with her was absurd. Unfair, even cruel to challenge her reasons for saving one thing and burning another. It wasn't, after all, as if she could have known he would be back. If he'd died and she had saved his personal effects they'd just be another box of moldering paraphernalia in the attic for future generations to pile things atop.

"All right," he said. "I've no right to question your actions in the wake of such a tragedy."

Her eyes popped back up to his.

"You did what you felt you must," he elaborated, irked by her surprise. "And if Bafferty saved the household accounts then I suppose nothing of consequence was lost." He tried not to think of all the clues to himself that were gone. Perhaps there'd been a journal, or a partially written letter . . . something that would have given a hint to his thoughts, his feelings, his actions when his life had been his own.

She beamed at him. "Oh, thank you, Julian. Thank you for not being angry. You know how I hate it when you're angry with me. Now"—she leaned forward and pulled the tray of invitations toward her—"would you like to go through these and choose which ones to attend? Oh, Winchelsea!" she exclaimed, picking up the top one. "Of course we must attend that one. Everyone will be there. And won't they be happy to see you!" She giggled like a girl.

"Pam, you should have seen him," Collie said, moving across the schoolroom's bare floor to close the door. "I thought I had done it. I thought I'd made him go insane. It was terrifying."

"What happened?" Pam perched herself on the edge of Shelly's little desk. "Did he remember you? No, of course he didn't or you wouldn't be here now. He'd have whisked you off to Gretna Green and woe betide anyone who'd stop him!"

Collie smiled wanly at her optimism. "No, he didn't remember me. But he remembered something. He recalled that his father was dead—"

Pam snorted. "That's hardly progress. Everyone's been telling him that since he returned."

Collie shook her head and moved to her desk. "He seemed to actually remember it this time, as well as something more, something quite shocking. He was positively mad with the memory, Pam, trembling and in a sweat. At first I thought he might be having some sort of attack."

Pam looked at her, enthralled. "Did he say anything strange? He didn't get violent, did he?"

Collie remembered the way he'd lunged at her, the fierce grip he'd laid upon her arms. She had not been frightened—not for herself—but she had been mortally afraid he might be losing his senses.

She shook her head. "He kept saying no. 'No, no, no.' As if the vision were too awful to be borne. Afterward he was as shaken as if he'd just awakened from a dreadful nightmare." She leaned back against her desk, half sitting. "I remember most clearly the terror in his eyes. No, not terror—horror. As if he finally realized something dreadful. His father's death, of course. I could see he wanted to talk about it, but he couldn't. Oh, Pam, he doesn't know whom to trust, and it's just awful to see. He does not even trust *me*."

Pam smiled gently. "And who is that most difficult for, you or him?"

Collie waved a hand dismissively. "Oh, I know it sounds self-pitying. But if you could see how lost, how frightened he is—"

Pam guffawed. "Frightened! Lord Northcliffe? I don't believe it." She shook her head and laughed again. Then, gazing at her friend, she sobered. "Dearest Collie, I know you care for him a great deal, but don't let your feelings color what his might be. He's not frightened. Out of sorts, maybe. Confused. But anger is what I see most. He's like an injured animal, Coll, and when they're wounded they're not at their most reasonable. Be careful. Don't assume too much."

"I'm assuming nothing," Collie said. "You forget, Pam. I know him."

"I know you've *known* him," Pam said, then laughed at the inadvertent lewdness of the statement. "I'm sorry. I didn't mean it that way."

Collie closed her eyes. "I wish I'd never told you."

Pam got up from Shelly's desk and came toward her. Taking Collie's hands, she said, "I truly am sorry, Collie. You know I would never make light of your situation. But the fact is, though you were close once, don't forget it was for a short time. Only two months, right?"

"Three," Collie corrected with some force. How it must sound to the objective observer, she thought. A mere three months of courtship—a term she could apply only loosely to the situation—and here she was pregnant. Most likely she appeared as gullible as the greenest village girl.

"Three, then. Long enough to be carrying his—"

"*Shhh*—" Collie stood so suddenly the desk scraped on the floor with the movement. A slight shuffling near the door had caught her attention. She'd heard something earlier and assumed it had been a mouse in the wall. But it was no mouse, she was suddenly sure.

Pam gaped up at her. "What . . . ?"

Collie listened, her heart thundering in her chest. "I thought I heard something," she whispered.

The two remained fixed for at least a full minute, until the distinct sound of heels on the bare hall floor sounded from the stairwell. The footsteps proceeded up the hall toward them and slowed near the schoolroom door. Staring at the doorway, they heard the low rustle of silk before the portal swung open and Miranda Greer appeared.

She appeared surprised at the sight of the two immobile women staring at the doorway. Then she recovered and inclined her head courteously.

"Good afternoon, Miss Travers," she said. Her eyes skimmed Pam in her maid's uniform.

A sudden trembling in Collie's body threatened to mar her ability to speak. How much had Miranda heard before entering? The door had been closed, but Collie had distinctly heard something much closer than the far end of the hall the footsteps had come from. Had the woman eavesdropped, then crept back down the hall to appear as if she'd heard nothing?

"Lady Greer," Collie forced through bloodless lips, then bowed her head with a curtsy.

Miranda gazed with pointed coolness at Pam. "Perhaps you have some work to do. I would speak to Miss Travers," she said, "alone. If that meets with your approval, Miss Travers?"

Pam shot Collie a worried look, then, at Collie's nod, curtsied and left the room.

As soon as Pam left, Collie turned away from Miranda and moved back to her desk. "Please come in, Lady Greer," she said, closing her eyes for a second before turning to face her foe.

Miranda strolled into the room, looking around as if entering some ancient, curious dwelling. Her white gown brushed the floor and made her look as if she floated as she neared Collie's desk. "What a charming little room Shelly has here. You must

enjoy tutoring her in such cheerful surroundings."
She smiled, perfectly at ease.

Collie's eyes flicked around the whitewashed
walls and bare floor, the two little desks, which she
knew to have been the same that Julian and Monroe had used, and the bookshelves crammed with
volumes of children's stories and tutorials. The
room was simple, sparse, but Collie did love it. She
only wondered at Miranda's ability to see its charm.

"I do enjoy my position," Collie answered. "Shelly
is a joy to be around no matter what the surroundings."

Miranda inclined her head. "A laudable conviction, Miss Travers. You do yourself credit."

"I do nothing of the sort," Collie replied, as if she
would say such things merely to impress Miranda.
She forced a smile to her lips. "The credit is all
Shelly's."

Miranda studied her. A moment before Collie
was going to ask her what the devil she wanted,
Miranda's gaze shifted to the two children's desks.

"Have these desks been here long?" she asked,
circling one and glancing at the other.

"Yes. I believe Lord Northcliffe and Mr. Dorland
studied here as children."

Miranda sighed and ran her fingers over one of
the desks. Collie's eyes rested despondently on the
woman's hands, graceful as birds. The same hands
that had cradled Julian's head as he'd kissed her.

"Which do you suppose was Julian's?" Miranda
asked. "I imagine he was a darling child, simply an
angel."

Collie knew exactly which desk had been his. Julian had told her once, pointing out the sanded places where he'd carved improper words into its surface.

"I've no idea," she said. "I imagine they switched off."

Miranda looked disappointed by the answer, then turned toward the window. "What a shame. It looks like the sun shall not triumph today. It is raining again."

"Is there something I can help you with?" Collie asked. "Or were you simply curious about the schoolroom? There's quite a collection of books in the corner. Perhaps you'll find something there that belonged to J—Lord Northcliffe."

Miranda turned from the window, her milk white skin silky in the light coming through the panes of the dormer. "I of course find all the artifacts of Julian's life interesting," she said. "However, I did not come here simply to explore."

Collie said nothing.

"I expect you've heard of the plans for my wedding," Miranda continued.

"Yes." Collie swallowed hard. "Yes, we were all quite stunned by the betrothal."

Miranda's brows raised. "Were you?"

Collie began to sit, then decided against it and picked up some of Shelly's papers from the desk. Setting them into neat piles, she added politely, "I know Lady Northcliffe was inordinately pleased. As were, I imagine, your parents."

Miranda's face was impassive. "Of course."

"Shocked and delighted, I daresay," Collie added, unable to resist.

"Delighted, yes," Miranda replied. "I would go so far as to say that everyone who's learned of the proposal has been delighted. Including Julian himself." Her slanted cat-eyes seemed to tip up with the smug smile she gave. "Speaking of which, Miss Travers, I did so want to apologize to you."

"Apologize?" Collie echoed.

"Yes." Miranda tilted her head. "About your swoon the other day—I do hope it wasn't, well . . . this is quite embarrassing." She laughed and gazed coyly through her lashes at Collie. "I hope you weren't shocked by the amorous display you accidentally caught sight of. You must understand it's only because Julian and I hadn't seen each other in so long. He apparently missed me exceedingly. I do apologize for upsetting you."

Collie's face turned to stone. She could not have returned Miranda's smile if her life had depended upon it.

"Julian has no idea who you are," she said, without thinking. "How on earth could he have missed you?"

With those words, Miranda the coquette disappeared. "He knows exactly who I am, Miss Travers. I am his fiancée. He was informed of that before he even arrived home."

"But, Lady Greer, was he informed of it before he *left* home?" Collie countered recklessly.

Miranda started as if she'd been slapped. "I beg your pardon? What are you saying, Miss Travers?"

Collie instantly regretted the words and gaped, speechless at her own audacity.

"Tell me I've misunderstood you," Miranda continued. "For I would hate, as the future mistress of Northcliffe, to have gotten off to such a bad start with the staff."

Collie's mouth closed with a snap and she pressed her lips together to prevent another unwise attack. No good would come of angering Miranda further. Indeed, as Miranda had Julian's ear so much more frequently than she herself did, it would be foolish to push her to the point of poisoning Julian against her. Once again it seemed Collie's capricious nature might have done her irreparable harm.

"I'm afraid," she began stiffly, "that now it is I who must apologize. I only meant the words as a jest on the sudden announcement of your betrothal. Pray, forgive me."

Miranda folded her arms across her chest. "A tasteless joke, Miss Travers. And beneath you to indulge in it."

Collie felt the sting of Miranda's reprimand all the more because Miranda was right. To make such a quip was beneath her. And no matter what her level of anger, voicing it only made her look ill-bred. Collie's shame turned her face scarlet.

"You're quite right," Collie admitted. But while she could voice her guilt, she was unable to bow her head or show any physical sign of apology.

Miranda looked upon her as she might a pickpocket brought to her for justice. "I shall, in this instance, pardon you, as I am well aware of your impulsive nature. But Miss Travers, I must confess I have often wondered why the family tolerates some of your more unseemly outbursts. Make certain that it never happens again, for if it does I shall be forced to bring it up to my husband. Governesses with unruly tongues should not be in charge of impressionable young girls. Do you understand me, Miss Travers?"

Collie bit the inside of her cheek to keep from pointing out that Julian was not yet her husband and that currently she had no say whatsoever in Shelly's upbringing. She'd been impulsive once today, and she could not risk whatever retribution Miranda might be able to engineer to satisfy her anger.

"I understand you perfectly," she said.

"Very good." Miranda nodded once. "Now, I came to you today for other reasons than to be abused by a cutting wit. Lady Northcliffe informs me that you are handy with a needle and embroidery thread. Is that so?"

Do you doubt Lady Northcliffe's words? Collie longed to reply. Instead she said, "I defer to Lady Northcliffe's opinion."

Miranda issued a cool smile. "Then I should like for you to sew my wedding veil. It must be perfect, and my own maid has a clumsy hand."

"I am sure you are aware that I am not a maid," Collie said, bristling. "However, I shall endeavor to do my best just the same."

Miranda nodded. "Good. I shall send for you, then, on Thursday. I have a fitting and you will be able to see exactly what I want. I shall give you the materials—which are quite costly, I warn you, so mistakes cannot be made. And it must be done by

Christmas, you know, as the wedding is to be soon after."

Collie's stomach jumped at the pronouncement, but she kept her face impassive. "Christmas?"

"Yes, it's imminent, I know. But Julian would have it so. He was so distressed at the uncertainty of my situation, the lamb, he insisted on putting my mind at rest with an early date."

Collie opened her mouth, then closed it immediately. Not one of the many unseemly things to say that sprang to mind could she utter.

"I imagine there are some who have questioned whether he would marry in his current state," Miranda continued, "but he is not so far gone as to renege on his obligations."

Collie's hands gripped each other. "How fortunate he has someone to tell him what those obligations are."

Miranda lifted a brow. "In this instance he has many to remind him of this obligation. It is important to both families. And I'm sure you are as anxious as I am that he maintain his reputation for honor and principle. Surely even you can see how imperative it is that he continue to act in as noble a manner as possible despite his affliction."

"It is not in his character to act otherwise," Collie said, "memory or no."

It was the one certainty that brought her comfort. Julian would act on what was right and he would condemn duplicity of any kind. All he had to do was remember.

Chapter Six

Julian trudged through the thick marsh grasses, trying to ignore the sounds of Cuff, Lord Greer and Mr. Bafferty thrashing along behind him. Who needed the spaniel with them along? he mused sullenly. No doubt they were flushing every bird for miles with their bluff conversation and heavy-footed tread through the underbrush.

To be fair, he thought, it wasn't Cuff so much as the other two. Lord Greer even insisted on puffing that infernal cigar along the way, while Bafferty simply stumbled along ineptly, no doubt hating every inch of the outdoors. Why the man persisted in accompanying him everywhere was beyond Julian. It was more than obvious he'd rather be home before the fire with a glass of port and a large plate of cheese.

"What say you, Julian?" Lord Greer boomed, setting flight to at least half a dozen thrushes in a bush up ahead. "How far out should we venture?"

"Yes," Bafferty said, wheezing. "Why don't we set up a—what do you call it?—a blind right here."

"A blind is for duck hunting," Julian answered,

wishing himself alone. "We could sit in a blind for a week and never see a pheasant."

"Right you are," Lord Greer agreed. "But we could stop for a spell and send the dog out, what? Let her flush something out for us. I tell you, hunting shouldn't be this much work, not with a good bitch in the lead."

Julian stopped and turned around. Lord Greer led the troop, cigar smoke billowing around his head as he slowed, followed by a red-faced, unhappy-looking Bafferty, and a resigned Cuff.

Despite the mist that had Bafferty's thinning locks plastered to his forehead, Lord Greer's thick mane of white hair waved back from his brow like the stripe down a skunk's back. His cheeks were pink but he did not look overexerted, and his black-caped overcoat looked to be ample protection from the clinging mist.

He grinned at Julian and came to a stop before him. "Look here, there's a log we can sit on while the bitch does her hunting. We'll see perfectly well if anything goes up from there."

Julian glanced at the drenched, rotting log, then back at Lord Greer. "You want to sit on that log and wait for a bird?"

"Criminy, but you're a tough one, Coletun. Yes, that's precisely what I want to do. Any objections?"

Julian shrugged. "Only that with the four of us on that log it'll be pulp in under a minute."

"Fine. I'm sure Cuff won't mind taking Horace a little farther along, then," Lord Greer said, ignoring Bafferty's pained expression. "They can ensure the spaniel doesn't stray too far."

"If you wish." Julian glanced at Cuff and nodded.

Cuff hefted his gun back onto his shoulder and said, "All right then, Mr. B. Follow me."

Bafferty turned, muttering a hopeless, "Perhaps there's another log," and plodded off after Cuff.

"What was it you wanted to talk to me about?" Julian asked, the moment the others were out of earshot.

Lord Greer shook his head and chuckled. He made his way to the log and lowered himself with a grunt. Then he fished in a pocket and pulled out a silver flask, grinning around the cigar. "Didn't have enough for everyone. Care for a snort?"

Julian let his gaze rest on the older man a long moment, then joined him on the log.

Lord Greer uncorked the flask, took a swig and held it out to him. Julian accepted it and took a swallow. Rich, mellow whiskey soothed the inside of his throat, banishing the chill air to a distance. He took another draft.

"Fine stuff," he said, handing it back to the older man.

"The best," Lord Greer answered, drawing long from the little flask.

Julian waited. He certainly had nothing to say to this man. In fact, he had not much to say to anyone. He only wished they'd all leave him alone to find his way around this stranger's life. But in the short days he'd been back, he'd had very little time to himself. His mother kept up a steady stream of visitors, such as Miranda and Lord Greer, and when that failed she simply exhausted him with chatter. Chatter that was all about what a gregarious and amiable man he used to be; how he would travel far and wide to attend parties; how he'd invite hordes of people to stay and hunt; or how he'd throw a ball for no reason whatsoever. Perhaps he'd like to do so again now?

Julian could only shake his head in wonder. He'd apparently been a much different man before his accident than he felt now. Now, the idleness of such a life threatened to drive him insane.

He'd wanted to help Bafferty with the accounts, but the doctor had unequivocally forbidden him to tax his bruised mind in such a way. Then he'd asked his mother how he could reach his supposed friend, Lord Bretton, but she'd warned him that Lord Bretton had recently gone through a difficult problem and should not be bothered with trivialities at this time. When Julian had asked what difficulty he'd just endured, she'd been unable to answer.

He decided he would wait and ask the governess how to reach the man. Because surely someone, somewhere, could tell him something about himself that would ring true.

After a quiet spell during which the thrashings of Cuff and Bafferty disappeared completely, Lord Greer said, "So you don't remember anything?"

Julian laughed. "I remember how to hunt, and this is not it."

"You know what I mean." Lord Greer's voice lost its jovial tone, revealing an uncompromising core. Clearly the man had an agenda.

Julian gave him a mild glance from the corners of his eyes. "I can get dressed in the morning, saddle a horse, do figures, read a book or write a letter.

I can"—he laughed—"speak French, which surprised me." He shook his head. "But I couldn't tell you my mother's maiden name. By God, I couldn't even have picked her out of a crowd before Monday last. And it struck me this morning that I don't even know what to call the woman, or what I called her before."

Lord Greer looked at him through narrowed eyes, considering him for a long moment. "Your mother's maiden name was Pembroke."

"Ah." Julian raised his brows and nodded. "Well, then."

Lord Greer cocked his head and watched him. "But Lady Northcliffe's not your mother."

Julian turned to Lord Greer and looked him straight in the eye. "Lady Northcliffe's not my mother," he repeated.

The older man shook his head, lips clamped firmly around the cigar.

Julian stared at him, nodding as the words sank in. At last, a revelation that did not jar him. He turned the idea over in his head, viewing it from all angles. It made perfect sense, fit logically into a place in his mind, though he could not have said he'd suspected anything of the sort before Lord Greer revealed it.

"She's your stepmother," Lord Greer continued. "Married your father when you were a boy. A right young one, as I recall. She had Monroe already, who was a year or two older than you, so she knew what she was doing. Main reason your father married her, everyone said, was because you needed a mother."

"So she," Julian said in a dry voice, "is my fault."

Lord Greer laughed, the sound loud in the close mist as it bounced off the damp trees. "By God, boy, you've not changed so much. No, you've not changed at all. You always were a wary bastard, even when you knew your own name!"

"I know my own name," Julian said, though he smiled at the man's mirth. "Unless there's something they haven't told me about that too."

Still laughing, Lord Greer punched out his cigar on the log between them. "No, you're Julian Coletun, all right. And a Pembroke to boot. Some of the finest bloodlines in Northern England."

"Good to know," Julian said. Whether his estimation of the man was improving because of his revelations or his character, Julian couldn't say. But he was beginning to like Lord Greer. Perhaps the appeal his daughter had once held would reveal itself eventually too.

"Yes, you and my Miranda will make fine, fine parents. She's got Lewiston blood, you know, on her mother's side. Then of course there's mine, but I also know a thing or two about making money, as you know. And my Miranda's got a head on her shoulders, that's for certain. She'll make you a bloody clever wife."

Julian studied the clouds on the horizon. Though the day was overcast, a darker, purplish hue darkened the skyline.

"I . . ." Julian began, then paused. "How long have I known Miranda?"

Lord Greer laughed again. "Funny conversation this is, I'll swear. You've known her all your life, boy. And she's been in love with you for most of hers. Glad you finally came to your senses and asked her to marry you." He pulled from his pocket a fresh cigar and rolled it appreciatively under his nose.

Julian nodded, pulled up a blade of marsh grass and began shredding it lengthwise with his fingers. "I wish I could remember it," he said almost to himself.

"Oh, she said it was quite romantic. Bended knee and all that rot women love. Can't say as I don't wish you'd spoken to me about it first, though, Julian. That's the right thing to do." He pulled a silver cigar clip from his pocket, snipped off the end of the cigar and tossed the stub to the side. "I would have thought your father'd taught you better than that. But then you always did believe in taking what you wanted, devil take the consequences." He pushed the clip back in his pocket.

Julian's brow furrowed as he tried to reconcile the man's words with something—anything—inside himself. "So, I didn't speak with you about it first. I simply—asked her?"

"Aye, that you did. Up and rode on over the day before you left. She said you spent most of the day with her, even though her mother and I'd gone to York, you sly dog." Lord Greer elbowed him in the shoulder and winked. "Good thing you proposed or I'd've had to call you out." He laughed heartily at the thought.

"Had we been courting long?"

"Bah! No need for that." Lord Greer waved his unlit cigar in front of him to banish the suggestion.

"You two'd known each other too long for that sort of silliness. Though I warrant you could do it now, couldn't you?"

Julian didn't smile. "Perhaps we should."

Lord Greer clapped a hand to his shoulder. "Now, now, don't worry yourself. You're just feeling strange because of this bloody brain ailment of yours. You and Miranda are an excellent match, everyone says so. Once you get your memory back, nothing'll bother you again. Don't give it another thought."

Julian looked away. Lord Greer fished around in first one pocket, then another, for a match.

After a few moments of thought Julian said, "I haven't mentioned this to Miranda yet, but perhaps after I do you could help her to understand. I want the wedding postponed until after I've regained my memory. I'm sure if she were to think about it she would see that it's best for her to know the man she's marrying is the same man she said yes to."

Lord Greer pulled a match from his vest pocket, struck it, and puffed the cigar thoughtfully before answering. "Hmm. Yes, I suppose I can see your thinking there. But what if you never remember? Irwin told us there's a chance of that, you know. Can't keep the girl hanging, Coletun."

"I don't expect that will be a problem," Julian said, recalling the horrific memory of the day before.

"But it could be." He tossed the dead match onto the ground and crushed it into the wet leaves with the heel of his boot. "No, I think it best we leave things the way they are. The wedding'll be after

Christmas. Besides, if you don't remember by then—by God, that's nearly two months away—chances are you won't ever remember."

Julian felt his insides curl with dread, but turned on his future father-in-law with studied calm. "I'm afraid I must insist, Lord Greer," he said. "I cannot marry a woman I don't remember. Surely you understand."

Lord Greer fixed him with a steely eye. The moment stretched long and taut. Julian's resolve was firm, yet he did not want to alienate the man.

Finally, Lord Greer said, "Give it at least a fortnight, son. If you remember in the meantime, no sense breaking the girl's heart now. If not, well, we'll cross that bridge when we come to it."

Julian expelled a breath. "I have no intention of breaking anyone's heart."

"No one ever does," Lord Greer said, blowing out a cloud of smoke. "But it happens all the time."

The words were just out of Lord Greer's mouth, the cigar smoke still hung in the air, when something ripped through the trees in front of them. The second after Julian registered the sound, a chunk of bark from the tree behind him leaped off the trunk, and a gun blast rocketed through the fog.

Birds erupted from the trees around them. Julian and Lord Greer were both on their feet before the last bit of bark had hit the ground. With unconscious fluidity, Julian raised his gun to his shoulder and cocked it. He spun in jerks, eyes probing the fog for any sort of movement.

A long moment of silence reigned.

"Bloody hell," Lord Greer said softly.

Julian exhaled as hard as if he'd been running. His heart thundered and his muscles bunched with the desire to act. Still, nothing moved.

A second later someone crashed through the underbrush toward them. Julian and Lord Greer whirled, rifles poised, ready to blast the intruder to kingdom come.

"My lord!" Cuff's voice, breathless and frantic. "My lord, are you there?"

Julian inhaled deeply and lowered the rifle a fraction. Cuff crashed through the last of the trees and into the small clearing. He came to a relieved, winded halt in front of them.

"Oh, thank God," he said, laying eyes on Julian. He closed his eyes and clutched his own rifle to his chest. "Are you all right, sir?"

Julian lowered his rifle completely. Lord Greer followed suit.

"Yes. Barely. Where's Bafferty?"

Cuff turned and waved halfheartedly toward the trees. "Out there, somewhere. He'd just gone off to relieve himself when I heard the shot."

"You didn't see him?" Julian questioned.

"No, I—" He shrugged. "I came straight here."

"Why?"

"To make sure you're all right, of course." The man's shaggy eyebrows descended in consternation as his chest rose and fell with exertion.

Julian placed his rifle butt on the ground and leaned on the muzzle. His nerves buzzed with adrenaline. "And what made you think I was in any danger? What made you think I or Lord Greer had not spotted a pheasant?"

Cuff's jaw tensed. Julian saw a muscle jump beneath his whiskers. "With all due respect, sir, I could tell the shot wasn't coming from this direction. But I could tell from the disturbance in the trees that this is where it went. The birds . . ." He gestured to the sky and breathed hard.

"Is that so?" Julian studied the man's ruddy face.

"Yes, sir. It is so." The gun he'd clutched to his chest he now dropped to his thighs, his shoulders slumping. He looked implacably back at his lord; then his eyes shifted a fraction to a spot behind Julian. "You see, sir," he said, lifting his hand and pointing.

Julian turned fractionally and saw the wounded tree bark.

Cuff traipsed past him, ignoring Lord Greer's cautious grip on his musket. "You can see where the ball hit. You can tell it came from back that way." He turned and pointed to a spot a degree or two north of where he'd come from.

Julian gazed at the mark. His limbs quaked slightly in the aftermath of shock but he stood silently surveying the evidence.

"You didn't see fit to pursue whoever fired that shot?" Lord Greer asked.

Cuff turned to the man. "No, sir. It seemed more prudent like to make sure his lordship was all right."

"Well, you can see the man's fine," Lord Greer said, obviously in the throes of recovery himself. "Go after the assailant now, why don't you? Jesus, the man's probably halfway to London by now."

"Exactly, sir," Cuff replied.

"Bloody Christ," Lord Greer spat again, turning on his heel to stride toward the area Cuff had indicated. "I'll go myself."

From a short distance away, a faint cry sounded. "Hallooo? Anyone? Help!" A brief bit of flailing crackled through the mist. Then closer, "Damnation! Anyone at all? I say! Where the devil is everyone?"

Lord Greer halted in his tracks and looked back at Julian.

Julian nearly smiled. "Bafferty," he said.

"I'll get him, sir." Cuff turned to return the way he'd come.

"No, I'll get him," Lord Greer said. "You stay here. I don't trust you out there in the fog."

Cuff drew himself up and glared at the man. "I've been serving the Northcliffes for forty-three years, sir, and nary once has any danger befallen them in my presence."

"Can't say that now," Lord Greer stated.

Julian laid a hand on Cuff's shoulder. "It's all right," he said. "Let Lord Greer go after Bafferty."

Cuff spun to face him. He stretched his gun out with one hand and threw his other hand down, palm up, toward it. "Christ's bones, look at my gun. Does it look like it's been fired to you? No, sir, it does not. He has no grounds to accuse me of this sort of treachery." He took a deep breath, face ruddy with indignation. "By all the saints, milord, you can't have a man as your steward if you can't trust him enough to be out of your sight."

"Are you resigning, Cuff?"

The man's florid face turned an even brighter

shade of red. "Resigning? Why should I, sir? I've done nothing wrong. No Cuff ever resigned from anything, 'cepting this earthly life when the time was nigh. I'm loyal as the day is long, milord, and if you were in your right mind you'd know as much."

Despite knowing the man had not intended the insult, Julian felt the sting of his words nonetheless. He wasn't in his right mind. Indeed, he was one short step away from insanity, according to Dr. Irwin.

"Then perhaps you can tell me, Cuff, why you really thought I was in danger?" he asked. "And don't give me that nonsense about knowing where the shot came from and where the bullet was going. A shot fired through the trees, in the fog, is not traceable by ear. And I may not remember much, but I know when a musket's fired any bird within range is going to take flight, not just those in the direction the bullet's headed."

Cuff gave him a guarded look. "It was what I thought, sir, and turns out I was right."

"You thought the shot was meant for me, I believe. But not because of the sound of the gun." Julian took a step toward him. "You're going to tell me it wasn't you, Cuff," he added. "But—"

"It wasn't me," Cuff interrupted, aghast.

Julian smiled. "If that's so," he continued, "I want to know who you thought it was."

Cuff dropped his gaze to the ground and shuffled one foot in the leaves.

"Bafferty?" Julian prodded.

Cuff scoffed and looked off to the side. "Bafferty,

ha! That's a good one, sir. He couldn't hit a barn door with a brick." He dropped his gaze to his feet again and hitched up his pants with one hand. "No, sir. I don't know who it was done the shooting."

"But you have ideas."

Cuff looked at him, brows raised. "About who done the shooting?"

"Of course."

Cuff shook his head. "Not exactly, I don't. No, sir. I guess after your accident I might just be a bit too worried about something else happening to you. My suspicious nature, I suppose, but a man's got a right to worry, don't he?"

Julian took an exasperated breath and pushed a hand through his hair. "It's a wonder you ever let me out of your sight."

"It ain't easy, sir," Cuff agreed.

Julian took another breath and felt his pulse returning to normal. "No doubt the culprit will have given up for the day."

"Yes, sir. I expect he will have."

Julian gave him an ironic look as Lord Greer and Bafferty burst back through the trees into the clearing.

"His gun wasn't fired," Lord Greer announced.

"Of course it wasn't, and I resent your implication that it might have been," Bafferty blustered. "I was merely answering nature's call when the racket ensued. I thought someone had spotted some—what do you call it?—prey, that's it."

"You didn't see anyone?" Lord Greer pressed. "Hear anything unusual—footsteps or the like?"

"Just Mr. Cuff's. And my own, of course."

"Of course," Julian repeated. "Cuff, why don't you go out and have a look around. Pick up anything that looks unusual, no matter how inconsequential. I'm going to dig this ball out of the tree and then we can head back."

"With all due respect, sir," Cuff said stiffly. "I believe it best if you go back now. Let me dig out the ball and have a look-see. The longer you're out here the more opportunities for disaster may arise."

"Nonsense," Julian said. "We're agreed that whoever did this is not likely to try again."

"You and I've agreed, sir. But that won't make much matter to a killer who may be of a different mind."

"I've got to agree with the man," Lord Greer said with obvious dismay at the prospect. "Best we get you home now."

Julian bristled at the words. "I've no intention of running at the first sign of trouble. For all we know this was some hunter's honest mistake and we're getting into an uproar for nothing."

"This is your land, sir," Cuff said. "Anyone else hunting on it has already broken the law, even without shooting at you. No, whoever it was wasn't making any 'honest mistake.'"

Julian glared at his steward in frustration. "Suppose it was Monroe? He has a right to hunt here, does he not?"

Cuff's answering glare became resigned. "Yes, sir, he does."

Julian threw out a hand. "Well then?"

Cuff sighed, not taking his eyes from his lord's. A moment passed. "If Mr. Dorland—or any hunter for that matter—made this 'honest mistake' you speak of, why wouldn't he show himself and apologize for it?"

"I don't know, maybe he was embarrassed," Julian said without thinking. A second after the words left his mouth his gaze shot back to Cuff, his eyes wide. "Monroe," he said quietly to the steward. "You—"

"Yes, sir, I'll go look around now," Cuff said quickly, his face closing up behind his whiskers. "Before any more time passes."

Julian's pulse raced again as the man turned and clumped through the leaves, out of the clearing. Cuff thought the culprit was Monroe. Sullen, drunken Monroe. But what reason would Monroe have to kill him? If what Lord Greer said was true, Monroe was only a stepbrother, and therefore not eligible to inherit the title or the money. Killing Julian would gain him nothing.

"It's best we go back now, son," Lord Greer said, moving forward to take his arm.

Somewhere along the way Lord Greer had lost his cigar, Julian noted irrelevantly.

"No sense tempting fate," Lord Greer added, an attempt at a grin on his no-longer-jolly face.

Julian turned numbly. The realization that he was completely alone hit him with renewed force. Someone had tried to kill him and he had no way of knowing who it might have been. Bafferty, Cuff, Monroe—hell, it could have been anyone but Lord Greer, who was as close to the bullet as he was.

"How do we know they weren't aiming at you?"

Julian asked Lord Greer as they traipsed from the clearing, Bafferty trailing behind.

Lord Greer glanced tellingly back toward Bafferty, then looked at Julian. "Did you know," he said quietly, his solid stride never missing a step, "there's an investigation into your shipwreck?"

Chapter Seven

Collie stood in the back doorway of the cellar, peering out the cobwebbed window. Three men emerged from the mist and her heart gave a panicked leap. Three men only, when four had gone out. With a surge of fright, she grasped the knob.

She hesitated.

Straining her eyes, she studied their movements as they neared. One was short and lagged behind. One stout and robust, and the third tall, with a long stride. Yes, she was certain the center figure was Julian. The athletic gait, the tilt of his shoulders with each step, the way his form seemed composed of balance and angles, rather than flesh and gravity.

He tipped his head toward the stocky man on his right and Collie quivered with relief. It was him. With a heavy exhalation, she closed her eyes.

She'd had such a feeling of dread all morning, as if something dire were about to happen to him, something over which she could have no control. With typical morbid inventiveness, her imagination had taken flight with countless events that might jeopardize Julian's safety. Though he'd gone hunting many times in the past and she'd never worried, since his miraculous return from the shipwreck she'd imagined tragedy at every turn.

The three men approached and she shrank back against the door frame, disregarding the dirt and bugs encrusted upon the wall. She let her eyes drink him in, reveling in the opportunity to stare without being seen.

Julian's hair was damp and curled with the mist, giving him a rakish air. With his gun swinging in one hand and his long coattails billowing out behind him, he appeared positively cavalier. Yet his face was grave, she could see as he and Lord Greer conversed.

Halfway across the lawn Bafferty gave up his effort to stay with them and sank into a plodding course that led him off toward the stables.

Collie laid her face against the door frame, her heart aching as she watched him through the glass. He was so beautiful—yet so remote. Even before she'd gotten to know him, when she'd just arrived at Northcliffe to take up her post as governess, as aloof and intimidating as Julian had been he'd never been so distant as he was now in his illness.

The mist had turned to a steady drizzle, making a sheer curtain between them, a screen through which she could behold her love but not touch him. She imagined the way his dark eyelashes would clump with the wetness, the way his gray eyes would appear clearer and deeper because of it. The drops raining down upon his head would slip down that roughened cheek and along the muscled neck to the sturdy slant of his collarbone.

Her breath caught with the memory of his skin, smooth and firm over dense muscle. She recalled the way her hands could cup his bare shoulders without coming close to encompassing them as she leaned over him for his kiss. He'd smiled at her, eyes crinkling against the sun so that a mere silver shard of their laughing depths was visible between the dark lashes.

One of her hands touched her breast where her arms were crossed, and she indulged in the memory of that day in the sun, the day before he'd left, when their love was enacted and her fate was ensured. She raised her other hand to her cheek, touching the skin there and remembering the gentleness of his fingers as he caressed her with his hands and his gaze.

He *did* love her. She would never have given herself to him otherwise, no matter how much she loved him. He loved her and Miranda was lying. She had to be.

Suddenly the voices sounded close and Collie was jolted back to awareness. They were heading this way—sweet Jesus, they were heading for the cellar door.

Collie jerked back and crashed into two chairs stacked seat to seat. The top one clattered to the ground.

Quickly, quickly, she thought frantically, turning to the darkness behind her. *No time to reach the stairs.* She pushed past low crates and unboxed furnishings, nearly falling behind a thickly cobwebbed marble nude on a high pedestal just as the door scraped open.

"Just a moment alone," Lord Greer was saying as the two entered the musty cellar. "I didn't want to insult the man openly, but there are a few things you need to consider. Not to mention that Pulver'll take kindly to us taking off our muddies down here as opposed to in his back hall."

"I don't believe Pulver takes anything kindly," Julian said. His voice sent shivers of aching pleasure down Collie's spine. "No doubt he'll believe we thought him not up to the job of cleaning up after us."

Lord Greer laughed. "Didn't take you long to peg the household, did it? Well, you always were a fair judge of character, I'll give you that."

Julian scoffed. "There's far too much unpegged for my satisfaction."

"Which brings me to my point," Lord Greer said, pulling off a boot with a grunt. Collie heard the footgear hit the floor with a wet thwack. "Here, son, here's a chair on the floor."

A noise ensued during which Collie pictured Julian righting the chair she'd overturned and sitting on it to doff his own boots.

"Whoever means you harm can do so with only one end in mind," Lord Greer said.

Harm? Collie thought. Who meant him harm? It was all she could do to keep herself from rising and demanding an answer.

"I assume you mean the title," Julian replied.

"That's right. Now, we know Bafferty inherits if you die without an heir—"

"Does he?" Julian asked, his tone surprised.

Lord Greer chuckled. "I know. Little hard to picture, isn't it? In any case, regardless of the fact that he was in a prime spot to have fired the shot, he's far too incompetent in my estimation to have come so close to accomplishing the deed."

"Could be a pretense," Julian murmured.

"His incompetence?"

Julian nodded.

"Then he's been pretending for years," Lord Greer countered. "Since birth, I'd wager. No, I'm wondering if it isn't a bit more than straight inheritance that drives this threat."

"What do you mean?"

"I'm not sure," Lord Greer mused. "But you've got to admit that Bafferty as the Earl of Northcliffe would be considerably easier to sway in matters of business than you would be. If someone were interested in manipulating the Northcliffe assets he'd be far better off with Bafferty in charge than yourself."

Julian said dryly, "Not if I'm insane."

Lord Greer laughed again. "Even then," he said.

"But I'm still not convinced the shot was not an accident," Julian said.

Lord Greer scoffed outright. "Don't be naive."

"Then who do you think it was? Who would be in a position to influence Bafferty?"

"Anyone, really. The man goes where the wind blows him," Lord Greer muttered.

Julian chuckled low, a sound that brought tears to Collie's eyes where she sat amidst the dust and spiders.

"All right, I'll grant you he'd be an easy mark. But

who would want to influence him? Who could profit?"

"There's the sad part of the matter, son. You're the most likely one to know that, but you don't know much of anything these days, do you?"

"Not one for delicacy on the subject, are you?" Julian said.

"But here's my real point," Lord Greer continued. "Rather than trying to figure out whatever motives the wretched bastards responsible for the plot have, your best bet is to ensure that their plan can never pay off even if they succeed. You see, that way, if they comprehend that their efforts would be for naught, they'd likely give up."

Silence reigned for a moment. "And how would I ensure their plan could never pay off?"

"Marriage, my boy!" Lord Greer crowed. "Marry Miranda and get the girl with child. Now, now," he added, "you're probably thinking I'm turning this quite neatly to my own ends. But listen to the logic of the thing. Whoever fired that shot today wants you dead. But if your heir were started, killing you would mean nothing."

Julian laughed lightly. "Thank you."

"You know what I'm saying. And it's so simple. You're going to marry the girl anyway—just do it a bit early and foil the cagey bastard's plans."

Collie held her breath, awaiting Julian's reply.

"Would that not then endanger your daughter?" Julian asked.

"What? No! Who'd kill a woman with child?"

"Who'd kill anyone?"

133

Collie slowly, silently let out a breath. He would not be coerced.

"The point is, once you've got an heir there's a whole lot more involved in the job. Killing one person is one thing; killing an entire family's another. Think on it, Julian. Just think on it for a day or two. I think the plan has merit."

Julian sighed. "I'll think about it. Though if you're right about the shipwreck, someone had no compunction about taking on both my father and myself."

"And see how difficult that proved." A chair scraped on the floor. "Come on, then, take your other boot off and I'll get us a nice warm brandy."

"You go on up. I'd like to take a minute alone."

A pause. Then, "All right then. Think about my idea, though, about Miranda, but don't be long. I'll have a fire made up in the library."

Lord Greer clumped sock-footed up the wooden staircase, and Collie heard Julian's other boot drop to the floor.

He sighed heavily; then a silence so complete descended that Collie reduced the depth of her breathing on the chance Julian might hear her.

Had someone made an attempt on his life? All of her earlier fears resurfaced with renewed credibility. Someone meant him harm, and Lord Greer's answer to the problem was to marry him off as soon as possible. The scheme made some sense, Collie thought. But what neither of them knew was that the very instrument that could save Julian's life already grew within her womb.

Should she stand up now and tell him? Surely

she owed it to him to say something. Suppose he greeted the news with relief? This child could save his life. But would the child then be in danger?

She kneaded her hands together. She longed to rise and speak to him alone, but something prevented her. The situation was too confusing. If only she could talk it over with him. She debated getting up, then imagined the look upon his face at the sight of her. He might think she had eavesdropped on purpose. In their last conversation he had treated her with barely concealed suspicion. To appear now as if she shadowed him seemed unwise.

Without the conversation to mask her movements, staying perfectly still was suddenly difficult. Collie was acutely aware of the piles of dirt upon which she sat. Her fingers were gritty with dust, and something crawled up her left forearm. Silently, she moved her right hand to brush whatever it was away, afraid to think what else might be crawling on her skirt or in her hair.

Just after ridding herself of the thing on her arm, something inched down her temple. Shuddering, she brushed at her hair, felt the thing cling to her fingers and, holding back a squeak of displeasure, she flung her hand out to the side to dislodge it.

Her fingers hit the side of a crate with a sharp pop.

The chair scraped as Julian instantly rose to his feet.

"Who's there?" he demanded. His voice carried through the darkness to wither her where she sat.

"Show yourself," he growled, "for I've no wish to destroy even this rubbish with a musket shot."

Cursing herself and the stupid, filthy insects, Collie rose from her cramped position. Her feet tingled from the awkward position she had held for so long.

"Get out here," he demanded, obviously hearing her shuffling.

She emerged from the shadows into the dim light from the doorway. Julian stood, musket at his hip, glaring into the darkness.

His face showed surprise upon her appearance and he lowered the point of the gun.

"Miss Travers."

She took a deep breath and stepped over the blasted crate she'd hit with her hand. She wavered a little on her prickling feet and he reached out to take her hand.

Feeling his fingers take hers, she could not restrain her own anxious grip. She held him tightly and let him lead her from the rubble, only letting go of his hand at the last possible moment.

"What are you doing here?" he asked.

She looked up into his eyes, her heart striking her rib cage like the clapper in a bell. His face was solemn, his eyes penetrating.

"I—I'm sorry," she began. "I'd come downstairs to retrieve . . . something, and when I heard you enter . . . I don't know, I thought it best not to reveal my presence."

She frowned and bowed her head, knowing the excuse was lamer than the truth.

"What was it you came to retrieve?"

Head down, she glanced furtively left and right in an effort to spot something that looked plausible.

Huge boxes and chairs, an old sofa and the marble statue were the things most immediately in sight. A long, rolled-up carpet just next to her was an equally impossible object.

"I, ah . . ." She swallowed and rubbed lightly at her nose where a spiderweb tickled.

The moment stretched as she searched for an answer, until it was too late. With a sigh she raised her head and looked at him.

"All right. The truth is I came down here for a moment alone. I was startled by your entrance, that's all. And in my muddled thinking I hid rather than attempt to explain."

Amusement lit his eyes, though his expression did not change. "Here?" he asked. "You came *here* for a moment alone, Miss Travers?" He looked around with exaggerated curiosity. "Tell me, what charms does this place have over your own chamber?"

It has a view of the forest, she thought, wishing she could voice it. *And the likely route upon which you would return to the house.*

"Expedience," she said instead. "At the moment I wished for solitude it was closer than my chamber."

Julian nodded, studying her.

But Collie could not contain her concern. "My lord," she began, crossing her arms at her waist and fingering the ribbon at her neck with one hand. "I know it's terribly rude to eavesdrop, but I could not help hearing portions of your conversation. Pray, tell me, has something happened to endanger you?"

He shook his head and looked annoyed. "Nothing

of consequence. A mere accident is all."

He would tell her no more, she realized, though they both knew the conversation she heard made his words, at the very least, an understatement.

She pressed her lips together. So many things she would like to say, but she was afraid all of them would only make him *more* wary and more reticent. She was not his confidant, she thought morosely. He would sooner tell Miranda.

She exhaled and dropped her hands to her sides. "I don't believe you," she said, "but I understand why you might keep your suspicions from me."

His lips quirked. "Miss Travers, I only seek to spare you any undue concern for me."

She laughed hopelessly and directed her eyes heavenward. "My lord, you cannot know. . . ." She stopped herself, then smiled sadly. "You cannot know. . . ." She shook her head.

The smile on Julian's lips remained, though it was more contemplative than amused. Collie could not keep her gaze from it.

They stood in silence for a long moment before Julian raised his hand toward her face. In surprise, Collie flinched and he stopped his hand in midair. Then his smile disappeared and he continued the movement, his fingers gently touching her hair.

Collie's lips parted on a shallow breath. Did he mean to kiss her? Did he remember . . . ?

She leaned almost imperceptibly toward him. But his hand pulled back after just the merest of touches, to show the wings of a tiny moth trailing strands of spiderweb caught in his fingers.

Collie looked at the insect and felt the ache in her

heart swell to her throat. She bit her lip and bowed her head as he tossed the bug to the floor.

"Upon my word, Miss Travers," Julian murmured, "you look at me with inviting eyes."

She forced her gaze back to his. His eyes were wary and intense, but beyond that inscrutable.

"I do," she agreed, her voice just above a whisper. Her chest rose and fell with her shallow breathing. Every nerve within her tingled. If he would just touch her, she thought, he would remember. If she could kiss him, he would come away knowing what they'd had together, she was suddenly sure.

She slid one foot toward him, closing the gap between them by half. She did not touch him, but as she neared his hands rose to grasp her arms—whether to draw her in or hold her off she was not sure.

His touch provoked a surge of pleasure along her skin and she closed her eyes with the sensation.

"Miss Travers," he said. His voice was brisk.

She met his gaze.

"What is it you want from me?" he asked.

Collie opened her mouth to speak. *I want you to love me, to make love to me, to remember me! I want to tell you what we had, of our love, our baby, our future.*

Her eyes searched his face, but the words jammed in her throat. She closed her mouth, wetting her dry lips with her tongue, and saw his gaze drop to her mouth.

With deliberate care, she moved closer, until her body touched his, her breasts against his coat. Her hands rose to his arms. Her fingers touched the damp wool of his sleeves. She moved one hand up to his shoulder, his neck, then allowed herself to touch a lock of hair that fell to his nape.

His lashes dropped so that he regarded her through slitted eyes. "Miss Travers, are you seducing me?"

A smile broke onto her face. It was the very thing he'd said the day he'd proposed, the day before he'd left on his trip. He'd gazed down at her in her flushed and disheveled state that he had brought about and uttered those very words with a wicked, taunting smile.

She opened her mouth to say the words she'd countered with then—*Make no mistake, my lord*—when the door at the top of the cellar steps rasped open with a hard yank.

Julian gripped her arms and he pushed her back into the shadows. She grabbed for his hands but they slipped away.

"Julian, wait—"

"Julian?"

Miranda's voice.

"Papa said you were down here. You've been sitting here a long while."

Her footfalls sounded hollow on the wooden stairs.

Julian aimed an intense look at Collie and she took two steps back into the darkness.

A moment later Miranda appeared at the opposite end of the room, stopping several steps away to smile at Julian. "Are you coming up? We've got tea waiting in the drawing room."

Julian moved toward her, pausing to pick up his

boots from the floor near the door. "I was to meet your father in the library," he said casually.

Miranda's smile deepened. "We've coerced him into the drawing room with us. While he had to leave his cigar behind, we did allow him his brandy."

He proceeded to the stairs and Miranda turned to lead him up.

"We have watercress sandwiches, which your mother said were your favorites," she continued.

Julian slowed as he reached the top of the staircase and turned his head to look at Collie.

Shame scalded her cheeks. The moment hung suspended between them. Then he turned and went up the steps.

Good lord, he'd nearly debauched the governess, Julian thought in amazement, slumped behind his desk at the end of the gallery. Of all the low and despicable things to want to do. What in God's name was happening to him? Had he had affairs with both Miranda *and* Miss Travers? During the last meeting he'd had with Miranda, she'd left no doubt that they'd indulged in much more than a chaste kiss or two upon their engagement.

But the governess . . . the governess. Of all the shabby tricks to pull. The next thing he knew they'd be talking of him the way they did Winfield Scarbrough, who bedded anything that moved and frequently had one or more maids carrying his bastards around the house. Oddly, his wife never seemed to mind.

He paused. Winfield Scarbrough was the second

son of Lord Pennybrook. Pennybrook resided in London, but his estate was in Surrey. Julian could picture Scarbrough's face, square and thick, with a large nose that was red from drinking too much. Julian's heart raced.

He *remembered* Scarbrough.

He searched his mind for further memories—even those as inconsequential as Scarbrough and Pennybrook—but could garner no more than the little that had returned in his distraction.

Winfield Scarbrough. Second son of Lord Pennybrook, he mused. But even of them further memories eluded him. He could not picture Lord Pennybrook's face, for example.

He sighed. Why couldn't he have recalled something that mattered? Why couldn't he have remembered whether or not he'd slept with Miss Travers? That would have been useful. For she had looked more than tempting in the cellar. More than seductive. She'd looked *expectant*. It made him more than a little suspicious that he'd partaken of her favors before.

If he had, her behavior toward him made sense. She'd been skittering around him for a week now. Perhaps she'd been wondering how to approach him, and had been afraid he would not want to continue the liaison. Well, her fears were justified, he thought roughly. He would indulge in no one until he figured out just what the devil he'd been up to before he left.

He knew, of course, that it was not atypical for a lord to wed one woman while bedding the servant of his choice. Like Scarbrough. But Miss Travers was not a servant, though she acted as willing as any tavern wench. Perhaps she was simply immoral. One didn't have to be a servant to like sex, he supposed. But *she* . . . she could have better prospects. She could marry a gentleman.

Julian leaned his elbows on the desk and held his head in his hands. Would that he could have stayed in Lyme rather than be dropped into this complicated existence. His relations with the people around him had been naturally complex, but now everyone expected him to complete whatever it was he'd started—without a thought to the fact that he knew nothing about any of it. He was to marry Miranda Greer, he was to sleep with Governess Travers, he was to attend a sea of parties and at the same time fend off a murderer possibly bent on inheriting his title.

Despite the multitude of confusing scenarios, however, Julian could not stop his mind from replaying the scene in the cellar. Miss Travers's parted lips, the pale expanse of cleavage revealed despite her lacy fichu, the transparent desire in her eyes . . . he felt again the onset of passion that had gripped him, the nearly overwhelming desire to kiss her and trail his mouth down the column of her throat to her bosom.

A knock at the door startled him and he straightened in the chair. Bloody hell, he thought, he was randy as a goat.

"Come in," he barked.

The door banged open and Cuff strode through. Debris from his mud-encrusted boots littered the floor with every step, and his rain-soaked coat spewed droplets of water on the furniture he passed. He held two muskets in his hands, and Julian had the brief thought that the man intended to shoot him right here in his own library.

"What the devil is going on?" Julian demanded, rising to his feet with an unwarranted surge of adrenaline.

"I found this, sir," Cuff said angrily. Water dripped from his thinning hair into his bushy eyebrows as he shoved one of the muskets toward Julian. "In the area near where I lost Bafferty this afternoon. It was partly hidden by leaves, like maybe he'd tried to bury it. Nearly tripped over it, I did, as I searched for clues."

"Near Bafferty?" Julian repeated. The man was a buffoon and not terribly bright, but Julian had not thought him so foolish as to attempt murder.

"Aye, sir. And it's obviously been discharged," he said. "Here's why he didn't try another shot." He held the gun out over the spotless desk, heedless of the rainwater he dripped, and pointed out the broken flint with stout fingers. "I also found another charge nearby, so he'd planned on attempting it again." One hand roamed around in his pocket, then came up with a muddy ball and shot.

Julian took the two from him and examined them. But Bafferty had come back with his gun, he thought, the same one he'd traveled out with. Where in the world would this one have come from? And why would whoever fired it drop it before fleeing?

"Shall I fetch the constable, sir?" Cuff asked,

straightening his shoulders and giving Julian a stalwart look.

Julian's lips curved as he fingered the extra shot. "No. Not yet." Despite the proximity of the discovery of the weapon, Julian was not convinced Bafferty was behind the shooting. The deduction had more to do with instinct than reasoning, but he trusted it nonetheless.

He gazed at his offended steward. "You know, Cuff, I did not suspect you this afternoon."

Cuff nodded once. "As you say, sir."

"But if I had," Julian continued, amused despite the situation, "this evidence would hardly clear you."

Cuff's intrepid expression faltered. "Wh—? I beg your pardon, sir?"

Julian shrugged. "If I'd suspected you of duplicity earlier today, what would keep me from suspecting it again now? I have only your word on where this musket came from."

"But—but, my lord!" Cuff protested. "It came from the woods, like I told you."

"I believe you," Julian said. "I'm only pointing out that as I believe you now, I believed you before. So you can dispense with your expression of martyrdom."

The man pulled his chin back and frowned. "I don't know what you mean, sir," he said indignantly. "But if you ask me this whole afternoon's been a bloody waste. We weren't going to shoot any grouse out there today, I'm convinced. And to come away with nothing but an attempt on your life, sir, well, it seems a very bad bargain to me. Whose idea was it, the wretched excursion, if I might ask?"

"A bad bargain, indeed," Julian agreed. Who *had* set it up? He could not remember. Good God, was his memory of even recent events going to disappear too? "I don't know whose idea it was to begin with. I believe Lord Greer and I discussed it at breakfast."

"Was Mr. Dorland with you then, sir?"

Julian looked up at him. "Yes. As was my mother, my sister and Miss Travers."

Cuff shook his head, his grizzled eyebrows drawing together. "I would never suspect the ladies, sir."

"Of course not," Julian conceded, thinking briefly of Miss Travers and her questionable actions. "But Monroe—?"

Cuff pressed his lips together and hung his head. "He's a gloomy one, that one. I'd not call him dishonest, but then there's something about his manner of late . . . well, he's just not been himself."

"How do you mean?"

"Drinking a lot," Cuff reported. "Don't a night go by where I don't see him down at the tavern, saucing himself till he can hardly walk."

"You see him every night at the tavern?" Julian repeated with the ghost of a smile.

"Aye, sir. And it's a sad, sad sight. He never was a happy one, as I said. Not even as a child, but now he looks downright pitiable."

Julian rolled the musket ball between his fingers. "But you say he wasn't a drinker until recently?"

"No, sir."

"How recently?"

"Oh . . ." Cuff puffed out his cheeks, thinking. "I'd

say since you and your father left for Italy."

Julian pondered this a moment. A man with a guilty conscience would have a lot of sorrows to drown. "Did he begin drinking before or after news of the wreck reached Northcliffe?"

Cuff cocked his head and looked to the ceiling. "Ah, now that's hard to say, sir. I believe it might have been before. Yes, I remember thinking it strange that he should miss the two of you so badly as to indulge himself so."

Julian sat down but kept his eyes on the steward. "Indeed, it would be strange of him to miss any two people who were destined to return in less than a month's time. Were we so close that he might have felt our absence so acutely?"

Cuff laughed. "Oh, no, sir. At least, not particularly close. But then you wasn't enemies, either. Just not the best of friends. And your father could be quite stern, as you well know." He coughed and glanced away. "Or I suppose you wouldn't know. Sorry about the expression, sir."

"It's all right," he said mildly. "I understand your difficulty. I'm not quite the man you knew before."

Cuff's pale blue eyes darted back to his master's face. "But you *are* the same, sir," he objected, then smiled ruefully. "Aye, I'll admit even your suspicion of me this afternoon was quite like your old self."

Julian's brows raised. "Was it?" he asked. "Did I never seem to trust you, then?"

Cuff's normally florid face went scarlet at what had just been said. "That's not what I meant, sir. No, not at all. I only meant to say as you were always a careful one. Always on your guard and test-

147

ing those around you. It warn't me in particular you didn't trust; you didn't trust no one. No one at all."

Julian exhaled slowly. "What a tiresome sort I must have been."

"Oh, no, sir. Just smarter than everyone else, and well you knew it." He laughed, then caught sight of Julian's face and looked mortified. "I'm so sorry, sir. Here I've gone and let myself run on at the mouth."

Julian forced himself out of his reverie and smiled at the man. "Don't apologize. I need to know your impressions. And your candor is helpful, if not exactly pleasing."

"Well, sir, let me add then that I had noticed the last couple months before you and your dear, departed father went off for Italy that you'd softened quite a bit. Aye, I believe—and I even told the missus—that with your father's trust and your new responsibilities, taking over the estate business and all, you were coming quite into your own. You seemed much happier, a good deal more relaxed, I vow."

"And what was my father to do, once I took over the estate?"

Cuff smiled. "Ah, he was ready to spend his days in this library here with a pipe, a good book and a strong fire, I believe I heard him say. He was a great reader, your father."

Julian glanced around the room at the books. He tried to picture the man whose face he'd seen in his horrible vision sitting in this room with a pipe and a book. He couldn't.

"Were we very close, my father and I?" Julian asked, perusing the steward's face.

"Oh, aye, sir. You were not just his right hand, he used to say, but his whole right side." Cuff grinned with the memory, showing a full set of tobacco-stained teeth.

So the governess had not been lying. Or mistaken. "And what about friends?"

"Friends, sir?"

"Yes. Did I have any? Was there anyone I was particularly close to, wary bastard that I was?"

Cuff shifted his weight from one foot to the other. "Well, you was close to your father, as I said. And then there was Lord Bretton, but he's gone now, in India."

Julian nodded. "Yes, I'd heard about him." He rested his elbows on the arms of the chair and steepled his fingers in front of him. "Anyone else?"

Cuff's face contracted in thought. "You had many acquaintances would come and go. Shooting parties and the like. And you always liked Lord Greer to go along on those. I suppose you could say Lord Greer was a friend too, though he was right close to your father, as well. Course, your father never liked to hunt."

"And Lord Greer's daughter, I presume I saw a good deal of her."

Cuff's gaze dropped to the floor and he shuffled his feet, shaking his head. "Not much, sir, no. In fact, I'd always believed you weren't especially partial to her, even though they all said as you'd end up marrying her in time."

"Who all?"

"Oh, everyone. Your folks, her folks, folks as came to visit. Aye, that betrothal's been expected since she was in the cradle and you just a boy in the schoolroom. She, I believe, expected it most of all."

"She got her way, then, didn't she?" Julian murmured rhetorically, staring at the desktop before him. "Did I get mine, I wonder?"

Cuff stared at his feet a moment more before looking up at him cautiously. "Aye, you might well ask it. I wouldn't say it but for your question, sir, but I remember one time you joked as how you'd sooner marry the governess than that there Miranda."

Chapter Eight

He hadn't remembered, Collie thought miserably as Shelly completed a French composition at the little desk in front of her.

Miss Travers, are you seducing me? His words echoed in her head. If she had looked into his eyes, really looked instead of convincing herself she could cure him, she'd have seen no spark of amusement, no teasing, nothing to indicate familiarity with her at all. She would have seen that he had asked the question because he really wanted to know if she was seducing him, because she had thrown herself at him like a harlot.

She held her head in her hands. Lord, what must he think of her? To him she was a stranger. Yet she'd come at him in the cellar like a dissolute parlor maid. As if, she thought in despair, her touch had the power to overcome the illness that a week in his own home, among all his family and belongings, had not done.

Her face burned and she slid her palms to her cheeks. How would she ever look at him again? She could not. She would take dinner in her room. She

151

would take every meal in her room. She would take to her bed and be sick until the memory of her humiliating behavior dimmed.

But no, she could not. After her fainting spell in the hall, people would talk. She could not give them any more reason to suspect something was amiss, for if they figured out what truly ailed her, nothing would save her. No, she must join the family for dinner and act as though nothing had happened.

She stifled a groan and covered her face with her hands, her elbows on the desk. What must he think?

He had just returned from hunting, where, if her perception of the conversation with Lord Greer was correct, a shot had been fired, ostensibly at him. Julian believed it an accident, or so he said. Lord Greer, whatever he thought of it, had taken the view that it was deliberate and used the threat to forward Miranda's claim.

Then, in the first moment Julian was alone Collie had thrown herself at him. The poor man had to be completely, dreadfully confused.

Collie closed her eyes and slid her hands from her face. There was only one thing to do, she thought. She must speak to Julian and tell him of her situation in as calm and rational a manner as she could. At this point she had no other choice. If she did not become emotional, if she presented the problem as a set of facts they should attempt to reconcile together instead of a plea for . . . for anything, then perhaps he would not suspect her of simply attempting to better herself with an extraordinary marriage.

She would contrive to do it this week, she determined. This evening was impossible because the Greers were staying for dinner and Lady Northcliffe had invited several of the more genteel neighbors for a small gathering afterward. Lady Northcliffe, Pam had told her, believed it would do Julian good to be in a social situation like those he was accustomed to growing up, so she had arranged the soiree and hired a quartet for dancing.

Pam had done all she could to dissuade her, she'd said, for she was still in mourning, but Lady Northcliffe would have none of it.

"Lord Northcliffe would have wanted it this way," she cried. "You know how he loved parties and gaiety. Everyone loves parties and gaiety, do they not?"

And so Pam had lost, in the face of Lady Northcliffe's habit of projecting her own sensibilities onto those around her.

Collie would not be expected to stay for the assembly, of course. As governess she would put Shelly to bed and keep to her own rooms. The only time she'd been to any of the Northcliffe assemblies had been the month before Julian had left, when their feelings for each other had grown so that he'd made a point of including her. Her presence at that time had not pleased his mother, she remembered, but no one had suspected anything more was between them than good nature on his part. Even Collie. Oh, she had known over the course of his attentions that *she* was falling in love with *him*; but she'd never flattered herself that he felt anything more than amusement with her.

Later, though . . . over the course of just a few days later, she had. When he'd confessed his feelings for her, her joy had held no restraints, no inhibitions. . . .

She shook herself out of the reverie. Speaking with him first thing on the morrow was out of the question because she was to go to Miranda's to consult about the veil. And despite her hope that the conversation with Julian would abolish any need for the veil, Collie knew she could not act on a mere *hope* for the future. No, she must take each step slowly and deliberately.

Though Collie knew her handiwork was good, she suspected Miranda had more pointed reasons for asking her to prepare it. Miranda could not possibly suspect her secret—unless she'd overheard her conversation with Pam in the schoolroom. But even then it was most likely she'd only gleaned enough to suspect Collie's feelings for Julian. Now she no doubt wished to make it gruesomely plain that Julian was to be married, and not to a mere governess.

That meant the earliest Collie could speak to Julian was tomorrow evening, if Lady Northcliffe had planned nothing else with which to divert her son from his predicament.

"Miss Travers?" Shelly's quiet voice broke into her thoughts.

Collie looked up. Shelly sat with perfect posture at the desk that had been Julian's, her favorite brother, she used to say, and regarded her with somber gray eyes very like her brother's.

"Yes, Shelly? Have you finished?"

"Yes, ma'am." She rose and circled the desk to bring the paper to Collie.

"That was quickly done, Shelly. I hope you haven't rushed at the expense of good work."

"Oh, no, ma'am," she said with an anxious smile. "I knew this lesson well. I always like the ones where Jeannette goes into town. This time she went to the milliner's. I had her buy a new hat."

Collie smiled. "A new hat. My goodness. Do you suppose Jeannette's family shall starve to death? Every time she goes into town she buys an article of clothing. Perhaps next time she should visit *la boucherie, que penses-tu?*"

Shelly giggled. *"Oui, m'amselle.* But I myself have never visited a butcher, so I wouldn't know what to have her do."

"Hm, perhaps we should remedy that as well. After all, your education would hardly be complete if you were someday to go to France only to starve to death." She scanned the paper.

"Miss Travers," Shelly chided. "You know I shall never starve. Mama said I am the richest girl in Yorkshire, and I shall marry the richest man."

Collie frowned. "You may well be the richest girl in Yorkshire, my dear, but it is most inappropriate and quite unladylike for you to say so. And you know you must be ladylike or no man shall consider you at all."

"You mean I should lie and tell everyone I am a pauper?"

Collie laughed. "Of course not. A lady simply does not talk about her wealth, whether of intellect, appearance or purse. If a gentleman is interested, you should leave that to your parents."

Shelly's eyes slid to the side. "You mean to Mama. Papa can make no match for me now. And what if Mama were to speak of my money? Perhaps no man will want me if she speaks inappropriately for me."

"Don't you fear," Collie said with perfect confidence. "You shall marry, and marry well, I vow. Your brother will see to that."

Shelly smiled. "Yes. Julian will look after me." She stopped, her face puckering. "Do you suppose he will still take care of me, even if he never remembers who I am?"

Collie took her hand across the desk. "Of course." She held the small fingers in one hand and smoothed them flat with her other. "He knows who you are now, dear, even if he doesn't exactly remember. As your brother he will take every care of you. But I don't think you should worry about even that, for he will most likely remember all before long."

Shelly's face lit up. "Do you think so really? Oh, I hope so."

Collie felt a stirring of guilt. Was it right to infuse the child with her own perhaps groundless conviction that all would be—no, that all *must* be—returned to rights before long? She lowered her eyes to their clasped hands.

"I believe he will remember in time," she said carefully. "Though of course we cannot know that for certain."

Shelly was silent.

With a final pat, Collie released her hand and

picked up the paper as if to be sure it was complete. *"Très bien, ma chérie. Ensuite, je crois que nous sommes finis pour aujourd'hui."*

Shelly smiled, her troubles forgotten with the promise of freedom. "Thank you, Miss Travers," she said, bounding for the door. "See you at dinner! *Au revoir!"*

"Au revoir," Collie called to the empty doorway, a wistful smile on her lips. To be so young and carefree . . .

She stayed an hour longer in the schoolroom to correct Shelly's paper—indeed a mess of mistakes, though she'd gotten every article right for the clothing—before heading for her room. She should wear something special, she thought. Something Julian might remember from before. The blue with the scooped neckline, perhaps. Or maybe the white . . .

She rounded the doorway into her rooms and stopped short, her hand flying to her heart.

Monroe stood in her sitting room near the writing desk, one hand hastily pushing a side drawer shut.

"What on earth are you doing?" she gasped.

He turned toward her, his face composed, unabashed. Monroe had no conscience to cause him shame, she knew. His heavy-lidded eyes drooped as he smiled in a devious way.

"Miss Travers," he said, sliding his hands into his pockets. "You're back."

"And unexpected, apparently," she replied, moving to her desk and casting an eye over its surface. Nothing seemed to have been disturbed and the drawers contained only paper and writing instruments, but what on earth could he have been looking for?

He slithered off toward the mantel. "No, not unexpected. In fact, I was waiting for you."

She looked at him doubtfully and he laughed.

"Mother sent me," he clarified. "You're to bring samples of your needlework to dinner tonight."

"All right." She nodded slowly. "What for?"

He chuckled again and shrugged. "How should I know? To show Lady Greer, perhaps." He meandered across the room, fingering a china figurine on the mantel, picking up a book from the table near the fire, putting it down and approaching the door.

"Since you were entrusted with the message," Collie said, bristling, "I naturally assumed you might know something about it."

"I don't."

"Then you are simply the messenger."

He bowed. "At your service."

His nonchalance infuriated her but she held her tongue. He was not here simply to deliver the message, she was sure of it.

Monroe paused by the door, regarding her with interest.

"Was there something more you wanted?" she inquired.

He shook his head, looking surprised. "Oh no. I thought you were formulating a reply. You looked so pensive."

"I have no reply. I will bring the samples. What more can be said?"

"I don't know. I waited to see."

She tossed out one hand. "And now you have seen. I have nothing more to say."

He shrugged again. "Very well."

She sighed and forced her tone to politeness. "Thank you, Mr. Dorland."

He bowed again and reached for the doorknob. "Oh, there is one other thing I've been meaning to ask you. . . ." He turned halfway back, his eyes narrowed, and watched her askance.

She raised her brows. "Yes, Mr. Dorland?"

"What do you think of Julian's progress?"

The question took her by surprise. "I? What do *I* think?"

He nodded. "You, Miss Travers. What do *you* think?"

"I—I don't know," she stammered.

He was such a cunning creature, he must have an ulterior motive, but she could not figure out what it might be. Perhaps he knew of Julian's violent attack of memory the other day. Perhaps he sought proof of something unbalanced about his brother, some way to prove him incompetent. The thoughts flashed through her head in an instant.

"I'm not sure what sort of progress you mean," she said.

"The obvious sort," he said. "Signs of his senses returning, his old life coming back to him. You haven't witnessed anything of that sort?"

Collie thought briefly of the wild, horrified expression on Julian's face when he'd been gripped by the memory.

"No," she said. "I have not."

He brought a hand up to his chin. "Haven't you?"

159

he speculated. "And yet you would be looking for it. . . ."

She feigned detachment, blood thundering in her ears. "Of course. Aren't we all looking for progress? I hope, just as you do I'm sure, that Lord North-cliffe will be his old self again as quickly as possible."

Monroe's lips twitched as the ghost of a sly smile crossed them. "Just as I do, Miss Travers?" he said, his voice ironic. "I recall," he continued then, in a conversational tone, "that you and Jules spent quite a bit of time together before his disappearance."

She fingered the quill she'd left out on her desk. "Do you? I suppose we did. Yes, he, ah, he wanted to help Shelly with her studies for a time," she said truthfully. "I don't think he realized how much he would enjoy her when he began."

"Shelly," Monroe said, nodding. "He was keen to be with Shelly."

She straightened her shoulders. "Of course."

"Do you think," he asked, laughter in his shifty eyes, "that being with Shelly was all he wanted?"

She opened her mouth to respond, but he held up a hand. "No, no, I'm being rude, aren't I? Sometimes I can't spot it myself, you know, until I see an appalled expression like the one on your face. Thank you, Miss Travers. I shall let my mother know of your acquiescence." He opened the door, turned within its frame and bowed.

Collie watched him close the door behind him, her heart tripping with several fears at once.

* * *

Julian had just turned the corner from the gallery when he saw Monroe back out of Miss Travers's room and close the door behind him. His air was so stealthy and he turned on such silent feet to creep toward the stairs, that suspicion tingled along Julian's skin.

Julian could tell the moment Monroe spotted him, for he started just enough to make his step falter, if not stop. Monroe said nothing, however, as they both approached the staircase from opposite sides.

"Was that Miss Travers's room you just came from?" Julian asked.

Monroe shot him a slanted smile as they started down the stairs together. "It was," he said and turned his head just far enough to wink at Julian.

Julian stopped, the implication startling him.

Monroe completed the staircase before looking back up at him. "Is something the matter?" he asked.

Julian opened his mouth to reply, wondering what to say. He would have liked to know, in words, just what Monroe meant by that insinuating wink. The obvious conclusion rankled him.

At his hesitation, Monroe gave a short bark of laughter, then continued around the newel post and disappeared down the back hall.

Julian gazed from the empty hall back up the stairs to the closed door of Miss Travers's bedroom. Perhaps she was not there. Perhaps Monroe had gone in there for some other purpose, something not altogether honest. Might he not then want to deflect suspicion by implying impropriety?

Suspicion of what, though? Julian wondered.

Exhaling slowly, he turned and started back up the steps. There was no point in puzzling over it, he decided. At the top of the stairs he turned toward her chamber and came to a halt as the door opened and she appeared.

Her eyes fell upon him and she flushed.

"My lord," she said, closing the door behind her before turning to curtsy.

He took the last two steps to the landing and inclined his head. "Miss Travers."

"Are you—that is, have you just . . ." She trailed off, obviously not knowing how to ask the question: *Did you see my lover just emerge from my room?*

He watched her, forcing her to figure out a way. If she was to engage in such behavior, she should be made to answer for it, he thought angrily. He didn't care if it was his brother; she had no right to make a mockery of respectability in this house.

"Were you looking for me, my lord?" she got out, finally.

"No," he said.

She colored further. "Oh. Well, then." She glanced around, then took an uncertain step toward him and the stairs.

He studied her, looking for signs of dishevelment. Lips swollen, perhaps, from Monroe's mouth; a trace of beard burn; the telltale splotches of lingering kisses on her neck. He could see none of this in the dim hallway, but still, anger built within him.

"I wonder if we might—"

"Have you seen my—"

They both spoke, then stopped, at once.

"Please go ahead," she murmured.

He did not resist; his desire to push her, to discover just what the devil was going on, was too strong. "Have you seen my brother?" he asked.

Her mouth opened and she looked alarmed, glancing down at her feet before answering.

"I—I believe he was looking for his mother."

Julian wanted to laugh, to shock her with his disbelief, his awareness of her behavior. "His mother, you say?"

She nodded.

"He looks for his mother," he repeated, allowing his lips to curl cynically. "He chooses odd places to look for her, does he not?"

Then he turned on his heel and descended the stairs.

Julian entered the drawing room, his mind seething with the significance of Monroe and the governess.

From across the room, Miranda rushed toward him. Her cheeks were rosy and her green eyes sparkled with her smile. She wore a white dress and he noted absently that the color made the fair skin of her shoulders sallow in contrast.

"There you are, darling," she said, her hands grasping his forearms. "Papa's just been telling me the news."

Julian's brows rose and he glanced at Lord Greer, seated in the armchair before the fire. "News?"

All he could think of was the surprising discovery that Miss Travers, for all her seeming intelligence, was carrying on an affair with one brother while attempting to seduce the other. For while he had not been blameless in that scene in the cellar, she had initiated it. Yes, she most certainly had.

"The news," Miranda repeated with an adoring smile. "And I could not agree more with your plan. You know I would do anything, anything at all to secure your safety."

This got his attention, and an uncomfortable misgiving awoke within him. "I'm afraid I don't understand." He moved her hands from his arms by taking her elbows in his and pulling back. She grasped his hands.

"About the wedding," she said, her eyes bright. "Papa told me what happened on your hunting expedition and, oh, Julian, it's just too awful, too frightening. You know I couldn't bear to lose you again now. I simply couldn't bear it."

He gazed down at her, saw what he thought was real concern on her face, and directed a hard glance in Lord Greer's direction.

"You've been needlessly worried, then," he said. He let go of her hands and moved farther into the room so he could look upon Lord Greer, who seemed intent on keeping his face behind a newspaper. "I wonder that your father thought it necessary to alarm you with such a tale. It was an accident, nothing more."

She pursed her lips and followed him. "He said you'd say that, didn't you, Papa?"

Lord Greer grunted and did not look up.

"But I'm a strong woman, Julian. If you remembered anything you would surely remember that.

And besides, Papa could never keep a secret from me." She laughed.

Julian saw Lord Greer's ears color.

"Darling . . ." She took his hand again and held it between hers at her breast. "I'll do whatever is in my power to keep you safe. And I think Papa's plan that we marry as soon as possible a sound one. After all, who would take on two such powerful families as the Greers and the Coletuns? Nobody. We shall be united against their treachery."

Julian gazed at her fierce expression. Whatever else might be said of her, he thought, she was not timid. He felt a stirring of admiration for her. Was this the quality that had led him to propose?

"You are quite the bold one, then, aren't you," he said with a smile. "But I'm afraid I cannot allow you to be the more chivalrous of the two of us. I will not consent to putting you in such danger."

Her face simultaneously glowed and crumpled with the juxtaposition of his compliment and his decision. Lush, amber lashes lowered over her eyes. "Oh, Julian," she said breathily. "Danger means nothing to me." She looked back up at him, her head still lowered, and added, "You know I would do anything."

She was beautiful, he thought, in the same way a work of art was beautiful. Lovely to look at, mayhap to touch. He could study her with pleasure in an effort to find the artist's secret brushstrokes, the slash of white that made her eyes appear to glitter like a gem, the hint of carmine whisked across her cheek, the ocher that warmed her golden hair.

Her skin was soft beneath his fingers where she

held his hand to her breast, her heartbeat fast above the low neckline of her gown. She was his, they all said. He could have her at any time.

With a quick inward breath, he extricated his hand from hers and turned to the divan.

Why then, in the face of all Miranda's beauty, and his own—he must admit it—his own desire for the warmth and physical comfort of a woman, why could he not get the image of Miss Travers and Monroe from his mind? Had they just had a tête-à-tête? he wondered. He frowned at his own perverse imagination. As if they could simply hop into bed together in the middle of the afternoon.

On the heels of that thought he had a mental image of purple flowers strewn haphazardly in the grass. Tall, cut stems, tangled with matted grass . . .

He shook the vision from his head. Silliness, he berated himself. Stupid to be so concerned about the woman's actions.

But what other reason would Monroe have for creeping so quietly from her bedroom? The two must be lovers.

He clenched his teeth and sat.

Miranda sat beside him. "Papa agreed there is no real danger," she said, arranging her gown around her. "So you would not be putting me in any undue peril. But all the same, he thought it better to be safe than sorry, did you not, Papa?"

Lord Greer lowered his newspaper and looked from Miranda to Julian. Meeting Julian's eyes he said, "Now don't be angry, son. She forced it out of me. She's got a will, that one." He chuckled uncomfortably.

"I can see there's no point in trying to talk sense to either one of you," Julian said, holding his anger in check. "But you must respect my determination. I cannot subject an innocent to possible danger, no matter how slight the chance." Monroe and Miss Travers. He would never have guessed it. He pictured the governess's face, her head laid back on a pillow, her satiny hair loose and spread about her, her lips parted. No brushstrokes there, just flesh and blood. Hot flesh and racing blood.

"Yes, well." Lord Greer harrumphed, rising. "Think I'll just step outside a moment." He reached into his pocket and pulled out a cigar. "Don't want to . . . you know . . ." He waved the cigar in Miranda's direction and made for the door.

Julian watched him depart and regulated his own breathing. He should not be this angry. If the governess was acting irresponsibly, the solution was simple. Sack her.

The thought brought a new surge of irritation.

"Julian?" Miranda laid a hand upon his sleeve. He felt the pressure of her fingers through his jacket. "Is something the matter?"

He turned to her, fixed his eyes upon her face. Here before him was a woman of uncommon beauty and refinement. She was his equal in rank, she was meant for him since childhood, and she was in love with him, from what he could tell. Yet he dwelled on the unseemly conduct of his brother, now a well-known lush, and the governess, who had shown herself just yesterday to be of questionable morality.

"No," he said. "No. Nothing is the matter." He

took a breath. "Miranda, I would like to speak with you about the wedding."

She leaned toward him, grasping his arm with her hand. "Yes?" She looked up at him through her lashes, wetting her lips with her tongue.

His gaze dropped to her lips and the perfectly sensual pout they formed. The governess had a sculpted mouth that in repose gave her a knowing look, a near smile, with firm lips that would be soft to his questing tongue.

"Miranda," he said, refocusing on her. Miranda, he told himself.

She leaned forward; the side of her breast touched his sleeve. He shifted his gaze to her chest, to the high, firm cleavage displayed for his perusal.

She slid her hand down to his and pulled it toward her, skimming his fingers, clasped in hers, along the skin above her bodice.

His body answered the touch immediately, his gut tightening and his heartbeat accelerating. He closed his eyes and imagined the white gown dropping from her shoulders to reveal creamy breasts with tawny peaks. He pictured them, saw himself dipping his head to taste them, felt her back arch up to meet his lips.

He opened his eyes as she flattened his hand over her breast and placed her lips on his. He froze, neither responding nor pulling away. His body told him one thing—take what was offered—while his mind rejected the idea.

She pulled back and looked at him with hot, determined eyes. "I love you, Julian," she said. "I always have."

He imagined seeing her naked and on her back. He envisioned tasting those high, firm breasts he could see so clearly in his mind's eye. He had taken her before, he felt sure. He thought he could remember the forbidden thrill of it, the moment of pushing into her, feeling her maidenhead give way and her body close over him.

He could remember thinking he would stay there forever.

"Miranda," he started. How to ask such a question? And yet it seemed so vitally important to know. If he had taken her before, their marriage was fixed. He could not discount it now; the decision had been made in that other, previous life.

"Take me, Julian," she whispered, her eyes alive with excitement. "Take me, I don't care what anyone thinks." She brought her hands up slowly to her shoulders, pushing the gauzy sleeves of her gown lower. "We shall be married before anything could come of it, before anyone would know. Take me, my love, right now. I am yours."

She pushed her sleeves even lower and her chemise and bodice fell forward, exposing pale, aroused breasts.

Julian's chest tightened.

Her face was bright red, her eyes fevered. She lowered her lashes in an attempt to look demure. But with her clothing at her waist the effect was lost.

Her words, her embarrassment, all seemed to indicate they had not done this before, he thought. But her boldness said something else, and he had to know for certain.

169

"Miranda," he said in a throaty voice, shaking his head. "I cannot. I don't—I don't remember—"

"No," she said severely, her eyes flashing up to his. "Do not protest, my love. Do not stop me. I *want* to do it, Julian. I've wanted to almost as long as I've known you."

He lowered his eyes, unable to hold her yearning stare and at the same time disguise his hope that they had not done the forbidden, that he had not been so stupid, that his future was not inexorably sealed. He glanced at her white, youthful breasts, high above her corset. Their pink tips stood erect with anticipation and the cool air of the room. Pink, he thought, not tawny.

"Have we," he began again, then directed his eyes straight into hers. He had to know the truth from her own lips. "Have we done this before?"

She lowered her eyes and drew a deep, trembling breath. For a long moment she stared at her hands, clasped white-knuckled in her lap. "Yes," she said finally, and dipped her head lower. "Yes. So you see it does not matter if we do it again now." She did not raise her eyes to his.

He felt the weight of obligation descend upon his heart. Did she lie? he thought, knowing the hope naive. This was an intelligent, respectable woman, from a family whose rank and lineage were above reproach. Surely she could not be of a character to invent such an enormous lie.

Besides, hadn't Lord Greer said he always took what he wanted, and devil take the consequences? Well, the devil was giving him back the consequences now, it seemed. But the anxiety it brought him had nothing at all to do with Miranda.

Chapter Nine

He had not done it. God help him, he couldn't have taken her then if his life had depended upon it. He'd pulled himself away from the whole situation and Miranda had fled, furious. Clearly, he thought, it was obvious to them both he did not feel about her now as he had when he'd proposed. Now she would not speak to him.

Well, he amended, she spoke to him. But only in polite sentences while others were present. Dinner had been excruciating, with Miranda's icy silence and the governess's shamed reticence both working on his nerves. Disgust with himself—that previous self who had compromised Miranda—and a lingering disappointment in Miss Travers's possible profligacy, combined with pity and irritation for Miranda to make him into a truly unpleasant dinner companion.

He'd thanked God when the meal had ended and the neighbors had appeared for the dancing.

At that point Miss Travers withdrew to take Shelly to bed, and the rest of them moved to the large back parlor where the furniture had been removed and the musicians were set up. He'd not had to look at the two of them then—the two women of anger and shame. Or rather, he'd not had to struggle with his own past in their presence.

Julian escaped the hot confines of the drawing room for the terrace and stood looking out over the lawn. Inside, the musicians played a minuet and the notes drifted out the French doors to mingle and disappear with the breeze. The light from behind him revealed little more than dark shapes on the lawn, representing shrubbery and trees, but the pleasure he felt from the wind on his cheek and the scent of earth and fading leaves told him he must have loved this place once.

He raised his eyes to the stars above and relaxed with the perspective they gave him. He knew them—Polaris and Orion, the Dog Star and the Pleiades. Their permanence, and the fact that he could name them, gave him hope that he had not lost himself completely. It was just his life that was forfeited to the curse and confusion of this thing called amnesia.

He relished the deep-root scent of the earth and the fixed pattern of the sky. They seemed promises that the universe provided constants, foundations one could guide one's life by. Like people one could trust. He paused in his thoughts. People one could trust. There was the missing element, the one lack he felt the keenest. He had to determine who stayed true to him, even in his current state, and who was changing with the circumstances. He could do that with the common sense left to him, he thought.

One did not need memory to spot a liar or a charlatan.

The frustration, however, arose because he was governed now by the actions of a man he no longer knew, or no longer was. Whoever he'd been when he'd deflowered Miranda, whoever he'd been when he'd murdered on board that ship, that man truly was dead, he thought, for Julian neither condoned nor understood those actions.

Could he possibly be so different now than he was before? Surely his innate sense of right and wrong had guided him in the past, the way it did now. There had to be some mistake, or some piece of information withheld that would make clear why he would have killed a man and made love to a woman for whom he had no feelings.

He closed his eyes, willing himself not to think about the murder he saw constantly in his mind's eye. It might have been a dream, he told himself. He had no reason to believe himself capable of killing, not when the thought filled him with such revulsion.

He opened his eyes and considered walking down to the lawn, letting the night air clear his head. He imagined the frosted grass, the crunch of it as he walked, and relished the idea of the darkness enveloping him the farther he got from the house.

But they would come looking for him, he knew. Lord Greer, he thought, and that Miranda woman. The words burst into his mind in an unmistakable tone. It was almost as if he hadn't thought the phrase so much as heard it from someone else. *That*

Miranda woman. Disgusted, disparaging. Someone had not liked her very much.

He spent a moment searching his mind, reaching for the source of the elusive voice, then gave up. The more he tried to recall something, the hazier it became, he'd found. He was better off letting things come to him, in fragments or one piece. For when he forced memories they grew distorted and confusing.

He let his thoughts turn to Lord Greer, with his broad, friendly face and ever-present cigar. The smell of that cigar had sparked a memory in Julian when he'd first smelled it, or rather, it had sparked a feeling of comfort that seemed familiar. Lord Greer would certainly seek him out if he were to go walking. Miranda's father seemed to be taking it upon himself to keep a close eye on his intended son-in-law.

A motion to his left, near a large rhododendron, caught Julian's eye. He shifted his gaze and searched the darkness. There, again. The merest shadow, flitting. He strained his eyes and saw it once more, on the other side of the bush. Someone was walking.

Miss Travers, he knew immediately. He could tell by the way she moved, quick and self-contained. She rounded the hedge and continued across the lawn toward the maze, pausing to look up at the house.

When she saw him up high on the terrace, she started. For a moment, across the distance, Julian felt their eyes meet and hold. An aggressive thrumming started up in his heart, and agitation skittered through his veins.

After a long pause, she turned to continue her walk, slower now, contemplative. He watched her, defying an impulse to follow, until she was directly across from him. He could walk down the stone steps and be with her, just the two of them cloistered by the dark.

"Miss Travers," he called. The night was quiet; his voice traveled easily.

She paused, and drew her shawl closely around her before turning.

He moved to the stairs and descended unhurriedly. With every step he wondered what he'd say, why she waited, what he expected. But he did not let the questions faze him.

"It's cold," he said as he approached her. "Why are you not inside dancing with the others?"

She gazed at him, curtsying with habitual politeness. Her face was pale in the night. "I am not invited to join them."

"Are you not?" he asked.

"No, my lord. I am the governess. Not a houseguest. I don't expect to be included in the social events of the household." She said it without bitterness, but there was something in her tone that made him pause.

He studied her. She looked away, readjusting the shawl again. "I imagine the servants do not include you in their gatherings either. What do you do for amusement, Miss Travers?"

A smile flitted across her features, small and wistful. "I enjoy walking. And reading. There are many diversions other than social ones." She glanced back at him. "As I'm sure you would agree," she added, in what sounded like a sudden afterthought.

What he would agree with was something they could all speculate on at length, he thought cynically. Chances were she knew better than he did what his attitudes had been. "So, you do not enjoy dancing?"

"Oh, no. On the contrary, I love to dance. But I have other activities to occupy me here."

The way she said *here* gave him a sudden curiosity. What had her life been like before she'd come here? What drove her now to associate with Monroe, to offer what she had offered to himself? "Where are you from, Miss Travers?"

She studied the fringe on her shawl, her expression softening with whatever memory the question evoked. "Derbyshire."

"And your family is still there?"

She pulled at the fringe. "No. My father passed away two years ago. My mother and I had to move after that." She dropped the fringe and met his eyes.

"Entailed?" he inquired. It seemed the most likely reason for them to have lost their home. The house was probably required to be left to some male relative, who in this case obviously felt no compunction to care for them.

She nodded. "My mother now lives in London."

"And you have gone to work."

"Yes."

Her father had died and her whole life had changed, he surmised. No doubt she was supporting the mother with the wages she earned here.

He inhaled and shifted his gaze out across the lawn. The tiny strains of a minuet traveled the cold air to tinkle like a music box around them.

"We had frequent dances in Merrifield, where I grew up," she added lightly. "It seemed everyone in the county would come. I can remember returning home exhausted from all the dancing, with my feet hurting and my hair coming loose from so much spinning. It was lovely there."

So lovely she'd left it, he thought. Had someone seen an unsuitable beau leaving her bedroom in the middle of the day? he wondered irritably. "So why did you leave such a bastion of happiness? Surely there was something you could have done there."

She glanced up at him, obviously noticing the bite in his tone. "After my father died, we were in such—reduced circumstances," she said carefully, "we did not want our neighbors to feel obliged to charity. There was no work for me there that would have covered our expenses, and to stay as a sudden burden on that kind society . . . well, I could not do it. I felt it best to leave the area completely, lest someone should feel obligated to assist us beyond their own means."

"How commendable," he murmured, meaning it.

She scoffed and looked away. "How proud," she corrected.

He stood uncertainly for a long moment, feeling admiration for this composed, confusing woman and distrusting it. "Come with me and I'll take you inside," he said finally. "That should qualify as an invitation. How long has it been since you've danced?"

Her small smile flashed again, like a wraith in the night, and she said, "It has not been overlong, my lord."

"Come along anyway." He extended his hand, knowing she could not refuse him. "I find myself with a desire to make your feet hurt."

A second passed before she moved forward, a ghost in her white gown and shawl. Indeed, he felt a chill shimmer along his nerves as she came toward him, as if he sought and somehow managed to capture a spirit.

She placed her hand in his. As his fingers closed over her cool skin and fine bones, he felt her return the pressure, very strong and decidedly alive. Here was no ethereal angel, but a woman whose presence took up the entire scope of his attention.

He felt suddenly bouyant, as if her sadness and his confusion canceled each other out. The lightening of his mood made him realize just how dark was the cloud of apprehension under which he'd been dwelling. Imagining Miss Travers dancing at her country ball made him yearn for something good, something pure and reliable, and something else he could not name. He savored the feel of their clasped hands, and lost himself in the magnetism of her gaze.

"You're quite sure your mother will not mind?" she asked as they walked toward the house and mounted the flagstone steps to the terrace.

"I don't particularly care if she does." But that was not completely true. He actually enjoyed the idea of his mother's agitation. He enjoyed the idea of challenging the whole stuffy crowd inside with a presence they did not expect. Let Miranda protest, let Lord Greer disapprove. They could do nothing about it. He was the earl.

But as they approached the doors to the parlor, Miss Travers's apprehension won out. She drew back. Her hand, now warm, left his. "I'm sorry—I cannot. My lord, it would be awkward," she explained. "I would feel awkward."

"Awkward?" he repeated. "Do these people frighten you, Miss Travers? And here I thought you were made of stronger stuff." He tempered the words with a smile.

"They don't invite me to the dances," she explained. "They don't want me there."

He crossed his arms over his chest. Her timidity irked him. It wasn't right, somehow. "Have you never been to a dance here, then?"

She glanced downward. "I've attended one or two. Not many."

"Then we shall add this one to the list."

She shook her head and her eyes caught on something near the door. She took a step backward.

He turned to look at what she saw. Miranda strolled past the door with Dr. Irwin, gazing at him as if he told her a riveting tale.

"Lord Northcliffe," the governess said. "Since we find ourselves with this moment alone, I would like to speak with you, just briefly, if you wouldn't mind."

He looked at her. "Ah," he said knowingly. "Might

179

this have something to do with the incident in the cellar?"

She nodded, biting her lower lip. Then, as if noticing the childish gesture, she stopped and collected herself.

"Perhaps," he continued, taunting, "you wish to make an excuse for your behavior? Or do you mean to repeat it?"

The words brought an instant flush to her face and she turned quickly away from him, moving out of the light from the parlor to the wall that surrounded the terrace. When she reached it she turned again, gathering her shawl around her in the chill air.

She took a deep breath. "I don't blame you for saying that. But I wanted to apologize for it."

He took several steps toward her and stopped, watching the light glitter in her eyes.

"It was . . . a misunderstanding," she said. "You see, I thought you . . . that is, you seemed to be saying . . ."

A couple, laughing, emerged onto the terrace and sat on one of the iron benches near the doors. The governess clamped her mouth shut.

Julian remembered the feeling he'd had as she'd looked up at him in the cellar. He'd wanted to touch her, to run his fingers along her skin. He'd reached up to take a cobweb from her hair, and the desire to cup her face with his hand had nearly overpowered him.

He lowered his head for a long moment. "I believe I confuse a lot of people these days. We needn't dwell on the incident."

"I cannot forget it," she said. "What a trollop you must think me. If you only knew why I did it, if only I could tell you."

He recalled the evidence pointing to a tryst with his brother, and didn't believe that this quiet, embarrassed woman could be carrying on illicitly with Monroe. Her embarrassment over the episode—which had, after all, amounted to nothing and did not even come close to what he'd just experienced with Miranda—spoke of more modesty than one could expect from a woman whose lover had visited her room that very afternoon.

"Why can't you tell me?"

"I—it's wrong. It's not my place—"

"Miss Travers, you and I always seem to be talking at cross purposes—saying one thing and meaning another—never quite getting to the point," he said. "Tell me now, Miss Travers, and let's clear the air once and for all. Why did you do it?"

She opened her mouth and her eyes met his, a clear mix of anxiety and anticipation in them.

His blood raced. For some reason he had the curious expectation that she might reveal his life to him. He had to force himself not to take her arms in his hands and shake the truth from her.

"Northcliffe!" Lord Greer's voice boomed from the doorway. "Come inside and dance. The ladies are tireless, I tell you, tireless, and my old knees are threatening to give out."

The governess looked away.

Julian expelled a breath.

The moment was gone. He'd lost her. He took a moment to regulate the beat of his heart, then extended his hand to her again. "Come inside and dance, Miss Travers." He gave a courtly bow. "And then I shall release you."

She let go of the shawl with one hand, but did not reach out to his. She bit her bottom lip again, undecided.

Lord Greer stood blocking the light from the doorway. "Are you coming? Who is that with you?"

"No one will question your presence since I've invited you," he added. "They're just starting the next set. I promise I won't let anyone bite you."

She laughed slightly and his mood lightened. She took his hand.

He turned and they approached the door. "I've convinced the governess to join us," Julian said to Lord Greer. "She was reluctant but I've pointed out that as a member of this household she is welcome at its festivities."

Lord Greer, frowning, held the door for them. "Yes, quite," he said gruffly.

"She was afraid," Julian added with a pointed look at the older man, "that people might treat her as if she didn't belong here."

Lord Greer harrumphed and muttered, "Heavens, no. More than welcome. Quite an unnecessary fear."

They were the first couple in the new set, so when the music began he took her in his arms directly and swept her between the lines of men and women. As his arm circled her waist, the sensation of her body beneath his hand gave him a surge of adrenaline.

"You move like the wind across a field of wildflowers," he teased in French with a grin, just to see how she would react. He felt as if it were the most natural thing in the world for him to compliment her so lavishly, and in a foreign language.

Her dark eyes snapped to his and a becoming glow swept her cheeks. "How poetically you speak, my lord. You are too kind," she murmured in the same language.

"I am never kind," he said. "Honest to the point of rudeness."

They circled each other and stood back while the other couples performed their steps.

"You seem to recall yourself, at least, very well," she said after a moment.

"Do you think so?" he asked. "I have no way of knowing."

Would she know? he wondered. The idea of her telling him what he'd been like intrigued him.

"I'm afraid everyone in this room has the advantage over me," he continued. "You have no idea how disturbing it is to think they know me better than I know myself."

"I imagine it would be," she said, circling him as the other ladies in the dance circled their partners. "Though I don't believe even they knew you all that well."

He took her in his arms and spun her, reluctantly letting go as they resumed their positions.

"I wonder," he said, still in French, as a couple swirled past. "Miss Travers, would you tell me something about myself?"

She looked at him. "What would you like to know?"

"Anything," he said.

She smiled and seemed to think a moment.

"Tell me what you thought of me the first time you met me," he prompted, taking her into his arms again to sweep through the middle of the dancers.

Her lips curved and her eyes shifted, unfocused, with the memory. "You frightened me," she said.

"Ah," he said. "It would appear not much has changed. I imagine you gasped every time you saw me then too."

"Oh, no," she protested, her eyes meeting his. "There was a time, between then and now, when you did not frighten me at all. Indeed, you were nothing but kindness. It's just something you project that intimidates people, something you do when you are not—comfortable," she finished, and glanced downward. "If you'll forgive my impertinence."

He studied her. "I asked you, Miss Travers. And I always get what I ask for."

They finished the dance and bowed to one another.

"Thank you," she said in English. "That was lovely."

"I must know what you two have been talking about," Lady Northcliffe demanded, charging across the room toward them. "I could hear snatches of that infernal language from where I stood with Mrs. Gilbert. I'm sure I told you both months ago how rude that is. It's like whispering. I cannot stand it."

Julian looked at her in surprise. "I can't imagine

what business it is of yours," he said, letting his indignation show plainly.

His mother shrank from the rebuke, the wind taken out of her considerable sails. She fumbled for her handkerchief and made great work of unfolding it and pressing it at her temples, as if she were overheated.

"Well, I just don't see why you couldn't conduct your conversation in English, for pity's sake. We are in England, you know."

One side of Julian's mouth lifted. "Do you mean to say you thought we engaged in inappropriate conversation?"

"I didn't know. That's just the point," she exclaimed. "You should speak intelligibly so that we might know if you are speaking inappropriately."

The governess fought to hide her smile, he could tell. He felt an answering amusement rise up inside himself and let his go in a laugh. She joined him, briefly, but averted her face when Lady Northcliffe's wrathful gaze fell upon her.

"The next inappropriate conversation I have," Julian said to his mother, "shall be in English and loud enough for you to hear it. Would that please you?"

Lady Northcliffe glowered at him. "Certainly not. I do not seek to hear inappropriate conversation, only to quell it."

"Had we been speaking inappropriately, you would certainly have done that." He caught Miss Travers's eye and conveyed a subtle smile.

"Oh! You tease me. You always were such a disrespectful boy." Lady Northcliffe turned on the governess. "And *you*."

"I should go," Miss Travers said quickly. "Thank you for inviting me in, Lord Northcliffe." She curtsied and turned for the door.

"Where are you going?" Lady Northcliffe asked. "Your room is that way." She raised a plump arm and waved her handkerchief in the direction of an interior door.

Miss Travers stopped on her way to the terrace. "I was walking outside—"

"I'll escort you back out," Julian said. "My mother apparently doesn't understand about those 'other diversions' we spoke of earlier."

"I'm sure I understand perfectly whatever you were talking about," Lady Northcliffe said. "I know all about diversions."

Julian turned on her. "Yes, I'm sure you do. But I would like to speak," he said firmly, "with the governess. So if you will excuse me, I'm going to escort Miss Travers outside." He settled a final glare on her, knowing that while she might grouse and complain till she was blue in the face, she would never argue with him.

"Fine, then, fine. I will not stop you."

"Good." He moved toward the doors and took Miss Travers's arm, leading her onto the empty terrace.

"You see?" she said. "Now I have caused a scene."

"No, you haven't," he said mildly. "My mother did."

She looked over her shoulder as they walked.

"Stop looking so guilty," he told her. "You've done nothing wrong."

He thought briefly of that afternoon's episode with Monroe, then pushed it from his mind.

"You were saying, Miss Travers," he said as they gained the terrace, "in answer to my question, that I frightened you, and then I was the very soul of kindness. What brought about this transformation?" He studied the way the candlelight shone on her hair.

She looked thoughtful. "I don't know. I believe getting to know you better dispelled most of my intimidation. You began spending time with Shelly, and so you and I became better acquainted. I remember it started when you showed Shelly your old hiding place in the cellar. She was so impressed with your bravery in descending to the cellar, even when you were a boy."

"The cellar is a scary place?" He thought of the day he'd found Miss Travers hiding amongst that ridiculous assortment of junk.

"If you're a child it is," she said. "And your hiding place was quite remote. A room no one ever noticed. I believe it used to be a wine cave or something, but now it's just dark and damp and empty."

He nodded, and thought for a moment. "Just now, my mother said something about having reprimanded us before for speaking French in company."

They neared the edge of the terrace and he saw the curve of her cheek as she smiled. He slowed so that she would turn toward him.

"Yes, we used to do it rather often," she admitted.

"I'm afraid we were quite rude about it at times. You see, none of the others speak French. It started as a joke; you would mention some obvious point or other that everyone else had missed and then I would notice something else. Unpardonable, really."

He enjoyed her relaxed expression. "I'm sure I started it," he said. "Drawing you unconscionably into my web of impropriety."

She laughed. "You certainly did start it. I would never have presumed to impose such irreverent wit upon the heir to the title."

He found himself smiling in response. This was more like it; he goaded and she answered with a tease of her own.

He reached out impulsively and touched her cheek. Soft as satin, he thought, as he'd suspected it would be.

Her smile faded at the contact and she stared up at him, a fire igniting behind her eyes just the way it had yesterday in the cellar.

Their breath fogged in the cool air. The night felt colder, he noted irrelevantly, to distract himself from what he was about to do. He cupped his palm to her cheek, just as he'd wanted to in the cellar, and his fingers touched her hairline. The strands were soft on his fingertips.

The passion he could not feel for Miranda washed over him now as the governess's lips parted. Her eyelids blinked rapidly, then closed as she inhaled and turned her cheek into his palm.

Desire slammed into his gut. He stepped toward

her, taking her waist in one hand and the nape of her neck in the other.

He could not deny himself. He would not. He was in the grip of something much larger than his conscience, and much more powerful than reason.

He dipped his head and captured her lips, those full, sculpted lips that he'd known would be soft upon his. His left hand pulled her into him. Her willowy body bent to his, her breasts, her hips, her legs, met his body and made it explode with exquisite sensations.

Her mouth opened beneath his. Her hands grasped his arms, squeezing with unexpected strength, and he deepened the kiss, drinking her in, his tongue dipping and tasting, exploring her mouth while his heart threatened to burst from his chest.

His hand swept from her neck to her side, grazing her breast as it went. Their lips broke apart and she inhaled with the contact.

He looked down at her, amazed that he'd gone so far, and she raised her arms to his neck, pressing herself against him. One by one his reasons for restraint fell away.

"Oh, Julian," she whispered, burying her face in his shoulder. Her body quivered beneath his hands. "Julian," she pleaded, and he answered her by bending his head to her neck. He kissed the soft skin and she tilted her head to accommodate him. He moved his lips to the spot below her earlobe. She sighed and her hips moved into his slowly, instinctively, with a rich, melting heat that fused them together.

He tightened his arm around her waist, wanting his skin against hers, his body around her, *inside* her. She seemed to liquefy against him, her body fitting into every curve of his form. Her arms were a web, a net, a magnet.

Never had he known such a powerful force as the one he submitted to now. His body demanded and her body answered. He felt as if he were possessed by some demon of desire, and yet he did not care. He wanted only her, the feel of her supple limbs and the taste of her skin. . . .

The knob on one of the doors behind them rattled and Julian pulled back. The governess clung to him, her breath coming unevenly. "No," she said on a breath.

"Someone is coming," he said.

She moved her head to glance behind him. A long strand of hair had come loose and curved along her neck to her breast. He closed his eyes, gripping her arms tightly before finally letting go.

She inhaled sharply and he looked down into her face.

"I must go," she said, grabbing the ends of her shawl and pulling it around her. She glanced up at him and a smile flitted across her lips. Eyes bright, she took his hand. "Good night," she whispered, bringing his fingers up to graze a kiss across them. Then she turned, swept down the steps to the lawn and disappeared into the shadows.

Julian could tell the door had opened by the increased volume of noise that emerged.

"Mother insisted I come find you," Monroe said.

Julian ran a hand over his hair, hoped he did not

look as disheveled as Miss Travers had looked, and turned to his brother.

"What have you done with the governess?" Monroe asked. "I was sure I saw her leave with you."

"Yes," Julian said, his voice husky. He cleared his throat. "She . . . left." He gestured down the stairs. "She did not feel welcome, I believe."

Monroe snorted. "Well, I don't doubt it. Mother can be a bit dotty but she doesn't miss *everything* that goes on right under her nose."

Dread crept into Julian's stomach as the significance of Monroe's wink that afternoon came tumbling back to him. "What do you mean?"

Monroe studied him, as if to be sure he could be trusted, Julian thought.

"I mean," he said slowly, "that if the governess was becoming a little too, how shall I say it, *involved* with a member of the family, Mother would not take kindly to it, I don't think. What do you think?"

Julian's muscles iced over with the chilling comprehension of Monroe's words. "No, I don't expect she would," he answered.

"She'd want to sack her, no doubt," Monroe continued, coming closer, moving the drink in his hand in a circular motion. "Which would be unfortunate, wouldn't it?"

Julian forced himself to move and sat rigidly on the stone wall behind him. "Would it?"

"*I* think so," Monroe said. "She's a nice sort of girl. I like to think of her as being rather a permanent part of the family, don't you?"

Julian's fingers contracted into fists, his nerves

still shaken from the onslaught of desire. "Do you intend to make her one, then?" he asked. "A permanent part of the family, that is."

Monroe raised a brow and regarded him for a moment. "Me? Are you implying I should marry the governess?"

Julian lifted a brow, not trusting himself to further expression. "It seemed to me you were saying as much."

Monroe laughed, then polished off his drink. "I'm sure if she's not right for you, she's not right for me."

Of course not, Julian thought. Though he'd never inherit the title, his brother could still marry well; his indiscretions would matter not at all to legions of wealthy mothers anxious to wed their daughters into an alliance with Northcliffe. Monroe didn't have to settle for a penniless governess. Not unless he loved her.

"What have I to do with it?" Julian asked, the whole inside cavity of his chest growing cold.

Monroe looked into the empty depths of his glass. "I had the thought that you might want her, that's all. Do you?" He lifted his gaze.

The question burned in Julian's brain. Monroe's question could not be innocent. Monroe did nothing innocently. He wanted the governess, he thought. At the same moment another thought of much greater magnitude struck him.

Monroe wanted this girl, and this girl appeared to want to trade one brother for the other. The motive for an attempt on his life by Monroe was at hand. Monroe was jealous. How many acts of violence were perpetrated out of just such passion?

I had the thought that you might want her, he'd said. *Do you?*

Julian crossed his arms over his chest. "No. Do you?"

Monroe laughed and ignored his brother's question. "You sure about that?"

"I'm engaged to Miranda," Julian said, forcibly reminding himself of her with the statement, as he'd forgotten her. Standing with Miss Travers, touching her, kissing her, he'd forgotten completely that he was betrothed, and had apparently partaken of all the sins of the flesh he was allowed before marriage. But while his feelings had been dead for Miranda, they were not dead within him.

His passions had apparently been altered by his accident. For he no longer desired his fiancée.

Monroe laughed again, but he did not look amused. "Yes, you have Miranda."

Chapter Ten

Collie heard the footfalls on the steps and rose quickly from her bed. She strained her eyes in the darkened bedroom, made out the furniture standing like sentries along the walls, and felt her nerves tingle. It was well past midnight. She crept to the doorway and opened it a crack. The light of a single candle disappeared down the back hall.

It was him, she knew. Julian. She felt almost as if she'd been waiting for him, she'd woken so quickly at the sound of his steps.

Her heart thrummed in her chest. Anticipation quivered in the air around her. They'd come so close that evening, as they'd danced and then afterward, when he'd kissed her. He'd almost remembered, she was sure of it. If nothing else, his body had remembered. And the taste of him had nearly made her weep.

She moved back to her bed and sat down, unsure what to do. She wanted to follow him, to try to coax more memory from him. But something else told her it might be best to let him think about the events of the evening on his own, and perhaps the past would come back to him naturally. The doctor had said he should not be forced to remember things, that it was dangerous for him to be pushed too hard. But she felt so *close*. He was on the very precipice of remembering her.

She lay back on the covers, telling herself she would only gratify her own anxious desires by following him. She should follow the doctor's advice and let Julian alone. He had enough to think about without being confronted again. She ought to try to sleep again.

But something inside her refused to lie tranquil while Julian roamed in tortured seclusion somewhere below. He searched for answers, she knew, more ardently even than she ached to give them to him. She could not simply tell him what she knew—that would come as too great a shock. But suppose she were to lead him to his old behavior, suppose she simply made it possible for him to act on his impulses; perhaps that would help him more than anything.

She sat up again and eased her legs over the side of the bed, each move another decision. Her feet found the chilly floor and she stood, telling herself again that she would not prompt him, would not tell him anything. She would simply look at him, let him see how it felt to be alone with her again after sharing what they'd shared that evening.

She donned her robe, moved to the door and stopped. She placed her hand on the cool wood, her ear attuned to the silence, ready to catch any chance sound from the hallway. Nothing.

What if it was not Julian? she asked herself. It

didn't matter, she answered. She would go to the kitchen and get something to eat. It was not unheard of. Besides, she knew it was him.

She placed her hand on her abdomen and inhaled. They were connected, she and Julian, by the life that grew inside of her. That life, and the love that had created it, would prevail, she told herself. That life was the answer to all her uncertainty. She had to go to him. They belonged together.

She opened the bedroom door and stepped out. A floorboard creaked under her weight as she passed. Down the hall to the stairs she crept, eyes wide in the dark, picking out only the largest shapes and broadest paths through the furniture. Her descent was quiet, and at the bottom of the stairs she turned right toward the drawing room. No one stirred.

She passed through the double doors to the dining room, from there through the short hall to the pantry. There she heard a noise. From beneath the pantry door she spied a dim light, as if a single candle burned. Then she heard a thud and a whoosh, like the sound a sail makes when it catches the wind, as a log when thrown onto the hearth fire.

On silent feet, she moved to the door and opened it a crack. In the dim, low-ceilinged kitchen she saw Julian peering into a cabinet, a snifter on the counter next to him. The amber liquid inside the glass glowed like another flame. He was dressed in the clothes he'd worn to the dance, minus the jacket. His cravat was loosened at the throat, his hair slightly mussed, with a lock falling onto his forehead.

His shoulders moved easily under the loose cotton shirt as he pulled a loaf of bread from the cabinet. With the brandy in one hand, bread in the other, he turned toward the rough table in the center of the room. The light from a fire in the hearth made dark hollows under his high cheekbones, made his eyes a mere glitter in the dark, mysterious and strangely alive with the firelight.

He palmed the brandy snifter and drew off its amber contents. Ripping a piece of crust from the loaf, he stared hard into the fire.

"You're hungry. You should have eaten more at supper," she said quietly, stepping from the shadows of the pantry.

He did not jump or appear startled; he merely turned to face her, his eyes hidden amidst the dancing play of shadows.

"Perhaps," he said as quietly.

Collie breathed inward at the silken sound of his voice; it was so long since she'd heard it so low and intimate. Here, in the cavernous reaches of the kitchen, it seemed a dream to see him alone. After the weeks of believing him dead, he sometimes still struck her as a phantom. A demon angel come to taunt her—here and not here. Hers and not hers.

She stood motionless by the door and felt awkward. His face was inscrutable. Perhaps he deplored her for her wanton ways. Perhaps he deplored himself. It was impossible to judge what he was thinking.

"Thank you for asking me to dance," she half whispered, drowning in the sight of him.

He raised the snifter to his lips and drank, his

eyes not leaving her face. Then he lowered the glass slowly. "You're welcome."

The fire snapped and popped, then fluttered like a flag in a distant wind. A clock ticked dimly.

She moved farther into the room and stood opposite him across the table, her back to the fire. His face was lit now and she could see the wary alertness in his eyes. Did he regret what had happened?

"I'm sorry I ran off earlier," she said. "Monroe . . . makes me uncomfortable."

He studied her a moment. "Does he?"

"Yes." She took a breath, as if she might expound upon this, then found she had nothing more to say about it. She reached for the loaf upon which his hand still rested.

He pulled it from her reach, then took a knife from the block. "Are you very hungry? Or just looking for something to do?" he asked, holding the knife over the bread.

She felt a blush warm her cheeks and was glad for the darkness. "I'm hungry."

He cut her a slice, then turned to retrieve a wheel of cheese from the counter behind him. "Large piece? Small piece?" he asked, brandishing the knife in the air over the wheel.

When she didn't answer he scored the skin of the cheese with the tip of the knife. His raised eyebrows inquired of her. She nodded. With the quickness of a cat he raised the knife and slammed it into the cheese, precisely along the line he'd drawn. It hit with a dull thud. He pushed the cheese toward her with the flat of the blade.

She did not reach for it but held his gaze, knowing her face was in shadow, her expression of desire hidden. He stood still for a long moment. She could see the rise and fall of his chest beneath the open collar of his shirt and longed to lay her hand along his neck.

Finally, when she didn't move he turned back to the counter. There, next to each other, were the candle and the bottle of brandy, both of which he brought back to the table with him. It was a tall table for cutting, no chairs, and they stood across from each other silently, Collie's face lit now by the candle, Julian's by the fire.

"I don't understand what it is," he began in a quiet, unhurried voice, "but you provoke me, Miss Travers. You're either doing something I consider wrong, or you're saying something that sounds incomplete. Right now, seeing you here in candlelight, with your hair down, in your white robe, I wonder at your motive. There's something about you I don't trust, but at the same time I . . . I find myself fighting the feeling." He stood looking at her enigmatically, a wary expression in his eyes despite the gentle tone of voice. "You're trying to tempt me. Why is that, Miss Travers?" He drew a ragged breath, the look in his eyes growing angry. "What is it you want from me?"

"I—I just want to be near you." Collie's throat constricted, but she kept her eyes riveted to his face.

"Why?" His gaze shimmered into her, shooting sparks into every nerve and muscle.

Because I love you, her heart cried. Would that

be too much to say? Would it damage him to know that?

Collie stopped breathing, believing she'd never wanted anything or anyone as much as she wanted Julian right now. Steeling herself against fear, she moved around the table toward him, softly, so softly, with a stealth she didn't know she possessed.

She would not push him with words. No, she would let his own actions speak for her. For while he didn't remember their past, he remembered their passion.

His face was all angles and shadow in the fire-light. "We can't continue whatever we might have had before," he stated.

Collie stopped, startled. But he didn't remember. She could see it in his eyes—confusion, conjecture. He assumed.

"Can't we?" she asked.

Julian's eyes glittered as they followed her movement toward him. His lips parted; his jaw clenched. "Are you saying we had an affair?"

"I'm saying nothing," she said, closing in. She reached up and laid her hand along his neck, just where she'd wished to a moment ago, running her fingers beneath his shirt, along warm skin, rough hair.

He caught her wrist in his hand. A hot, hard, painless grip. But he did not pull her hand away. He simply held it tight a fraction of an inch from his skin.

"Stop it," he whispered harshly. "Why do you do this? Why do you degrade yourself this way?"

The words stung, but she didn't move.

"You know that I am betrothed to Miranda," he said, watching her. "You'll get nothing from this— endeavor. No future, no settlement. Nothing."

She pressed her wrist against his hand and he allowed it to move. She brushed her thumb over his lips, her breath coming quickly. "Don't talk." Then she raised her other hand to his head, buried it in the thick curls of his hair, and pulled his face toward hers. His fingers dug into the soft skin of her forearm.

Her mouth found his, and they came together with a shattering desire. He released her wrist to grab her roughly around the waist. Her breath left her as his mouth opened and his lips claimed hers.

She wrapped her arms around his neck, pulling him as close as she could. Their tongues mingled. Their breath hungered. His hands pulled her hips nearer, squeezing her against him then descended to her thighs, where he spread them, adjusting her nightrail and pulling her legs up and around his hips.

She clung to his neck as he pulled her hard against his body, stepping forward so that she sat upon the table and his body lengthened against hers.

He kissed her savagely, his stubble scratching her cheek, his lips moving down her neck. She lay back against the table as his mouth descended along her body. His lips trailed a wet path to her collarbone, from there to the top of her nightgown. One hand reached to untie her robe and he pushed the material away. He ran his lips down the front of the thin nightgown, capturing a nipple through the cotton material and sucking, then pulling lightly with his teeth until a moan escaped her lips.

"Is this what you wanted, Miss Travers?" he asked in a low voice. "Is it?"

"Yes," she whispered.

His ran his hands up her ribs to her breasts, the heat of his palms searing her through the nightgown.

"Are you sure?" he demanded, lowering his hands to her thighs and pulling her along the table toward himself.

Her nightgown rode up as he pulled, exposing her most private part to his hardened sex. He clasped her legs around his waist as he stood at the end of the table. Slowly he pushed his hips against her, his stiff member fitting closely to her through his pants, and Collie felt a pulsing sweep through her.

She looked up at his flushed cheeks and diamond eyes. "I'm sure, Julian," she said, raising herself up, her eyes not leaving his. Her hands reached down to the source of his heat; her steady fingers unbuttoned his pants.

He grasped her nightgown and pulled it over her head, his erection pressing against her, hot and demanding. She opened her thighs, and with his hands on her hips he pushed himself inside of her.

Collie closed her eyes in relief and could not restrain a soft, throaty sound of completion. Her legs tightened around his waist, pulling him closer. He thrust deeper, his mouth buried in the nape of her neck. She pulled his shoulders toward her, crushing his chest against her breasts, and felt his arms hold her with the same desperate intensity. She threw her head back.

Deeper and harder he thrust, the fire casting eerie, gyrating shadows along the stone walls and ceiling. Collie's breathing became more rapid as her fingers kneaded his back.

He drew back to gaze into her face, his skin bronzed in the candle's glow. Slowly, he lowered his mouth to the peak of one breast.

Collie arched her back, holding his head to her breast and pulling his hips closer, deeper, nearly writhing under the waves of pleasure spiraling outward from her breasts, her loins, everywhere his hands touched.

"Please, oh—" she pleaded, for what, she did not know.

"God. My God." His voice was a growl of satisfaction against her hair as, finally, with a deep, low groan, he released himself inside her. His body quivered with energy and completion. His hands ascended along her back, squeezing the breath from her lungs and the last low moan from her lips.

A moment passed with the trembling of their bodies suspended in the crackling firelight.

"Tell me, Julian," she whispered finally, her face buried in his shoulder. "Tell me you remember what we had."

Julian pulled back. Something he could only call shame burned through his mind, even as his body still thrummed with the aftermath of desire. She was beautiful, perfect, and she inflamed him beyond anything he'd ever felt—but he could not place the emotions warring inside himself. Guilt, longing, fear, trust.

Memories batted against his consciousness, stupid as birds at a glass window. He could almost grasp them but something held them back.

That Miranda woman.

The words echoed in his head in that disparaging voice as she blossomed in his mind. With the onus of obligation, he remembered her, the woman he was promised to marry.

"You expect a lot from a simple act," he said. How easy it was to put the blame on this complex, artful woman. She'd come to him. *She* had seduced *him.*

He pulled away from her and straightened his clothes, keeping his eyes on the task. He hated himself, he decided. Hated himself for the desire he could not control. For the act he had decided he would not commit and which he'd succumbed to anyway. And for the anger he felt now at having to deal with the whole sordid scene.

He couldn't look at her, couldn't face the pain he knew he had inflicted. It would show plain as day on her face. Something in his chest twisted viciously.

Peripherally he saw her sit up. She collected her nightgown and donned it, pushing the hem down with a trembling hand.

She was no virgin, he made himself note. He supposed she would tell him he was responsible for that, at one time or another. And even if he wasn't, he might as well be now.

"Don't be this way. Please." Her voice was tenuous, as he'd known it would be.

"What way? I told you at the start you'd get nothing from this. I told you before we did this there was no future. No settlement," he repeated through his teeth. Jesus, why was he being so cruel? It wasn't her fault. He knew, he *knew*, dammit, how he'd feel after giving in to his lust.

"You don't remember," she said simply. There was such sadness in her tone he felt it sting to his very soul.

He jerked around and grabbed her by the upper arm. "What did you expect? Hm? Some miracle cure? Some blast of memory that would enable me to resume some contemptible affair under the very nose of my family? My fiancée?"

She shrank back from his grip, her eyes welling with tears. Her fine, lively, wounded eyes . . .

He closed his eyes. "I can't do this." He shook his head. "I can't live this way. I lay with you. I lay with Miranda—"

"*No!*" she burst out. The fierce look on her face was at odds with the tears that dripped down her cheeks. "You *never* lay with Miranda."

He laughed harshly. "That's what you think."

She looked at him in horror, her mouth opening, then closing abruptly.

"That's right, my love. You *and* Miranda. I'm quite the prince, aren't I? Perhaps you'd do better with Monroe."

He swiped his hand through his hair and turned away from her. Jesus help him, what he wouldn't give to be back at the cottage in Lyme. Perhaps God had given him a second chance there, a chance to redeem himself and lead a simple, sinless life.

But no. He'd had to return here, to this place with its endless complications and temptations. All the peculiar thoughts and disjointed memories, each one at odds with the other.

"When?" she asked.

He turned a quarter of the way back to her, not looking at her, his head thrown back in fatigue and despair. "When what?" he snarled.

"When did you sleep with Miranda? Did—recently?" she asked.

He turned a hard look on her. "Unseemly curiosity, my love," he said.

He saw a muscle twitch in her jaw and knew she clenched her teeth together.

"Do you remember doing it, or did she *tell* you you did?" she insisted.

He shook his head, thinking of the arched back, the purple spray of flowers, the tawny breasts. "I remember." Then he thought of Miranda's pale, pink-tipped breasts. "I don't know. I don't know—what to think." She'd looked so *sure*, Miranda had, that afternoon when she'd exposed herself to him. So perfectly confident that he would take her. He shook his head again.

The governess pressed a hand to her mouth, but he heard the sob anyway and hated himself for it.

The fire had dwindled and crackled dimly behind them. The shadows were deeper. The room was growing cold. He picked up the bottle of brandy, sloshed some into the snifter, and handed it back to her.

"No," she said, a mere breath of sound.

He downed the contents himself, then filled it up again. "I'll give you—some money," he said finally.

Her intake of air was high-pitched and shaking. "No," she said again.

"No," he said, not looking at her. "Let me. I owe you something."

He thought she said, "You have no idea." But when he looked at her she did not continue. She sat staring at her hands in her lap, her fingers limp and graceful.

"I assume," he began, then stopped. "You realize this cannot happen again."

She pressed her lips together, her throat working against her tears, then slid from the table to stand next to it. She looked very slight in her white cotton nightgown, her hair loose on her shoulders, her feet bare. He felt a nearly overwhelming urge to take her in his arms, to lay her head on his shoulder and cover it with his hand. Her pain was like a knife to his chest; her dignity twisted it into a gut-wrenching torment.

"You should get out of here," he said. "God knows what further indignities you might suffer at my hands if you stay."

She lifted her head. "Julian," she said quietly. Her voice was composed now; her little frame seemed suddenly sturdy and full of more strength than he possessed. "Don't do this to yourself. Don't blame yourself."

He looked at her, incredulous. In one way she saw through him. But she could never know the self-loathing that came with his actions. It would be one thing if he hadn't known better, but he had. He'd watched himself make every single wrong move and he'd done nothing to stop himself.

"You don't know anything about it," he said. "You don't know the first thing about it." The rage he'd kept in abeyance for so long threatened again to burst free. He felt it burning in his chest, along his limbs, behind his eyes. He blinked rapidly—the stinging in his eyes from the smoke, the dry air, the musty room.

"I want to remember," he said, the words emerging in a growl low in his throat. A log shifted, sparks sprayed upward with a sound like a sudden shower. "I want to remember you. But I don't. I can't. The more I struggle the farther away it gets. And it's going to drive me crazy, this not knowing, this feeling my way in the dark." Panic welled up and threatened to choke him. "I don't think I can stand it. I honestly don't think I can stand it."

She came to him and laid her hand on his sleeve. But her kindness only shamed him more. He pulled away and drained the brandy glass, striding across the room to look out the high, narrow window. He saw nothing but blackness.

"I'm sorry," he said, meaning it so much more than she could ever know.

He heard her shift slightly behind him and guessed that she donned her robe. He pictured her as she'd looked standing in the doorway when she first arrived. He'd conjured her from his thoughts. His terrible, tormenting angel.

"I've made it worse, then," she said.

He couldn't contain the ironic laugh that burst

forth. He turned back to her, letting her see the cruelty and anguish in his face. "Yes. Yes, you have. I was fine until you came in." He moved toward the table to lean against the counter. "You should leave now, Miss Travers. There's nothing more that can be said."

She lowered her head, pulling on the ties of her robe. One hand lingered on her stomach as the other pushed the hair from her face.

"There is one thing that must be said." She lifted her head. Her dark eyes penetrated deep into his. "I love you. I just want you to know that."

With great dignity, she turned back to the pantry and disappeared through the door.

Chapter Eleven

Collie awoke the next morning—the morning she was to go to Miranda's—feeling mentally drained and physically sicker than she'd felt in days. Her muscles resisted movement as if they were made of lead, and when she glanced at the clock she was shocked to see that it was half past eight—far later than she ever arose. Miranda's coach was to arrive at nine.

Where was Pam? she wondered, forcing her legs over the side of the bed and pushing herself up. Every morning for the past week her friend had brought her cold milk to start the day and help her feel better after the morning sickness. Perhaps Pam was getting a late start too.

Collie sat on the side of the bed, her head bent and pounding, and her eyelids heavy with the desire for more sleep. After a moment the familiar nausea assailed her, rising up from her soul like a tidal wave, it seemed, to propel her across the room.

As swiftly as her listless legs would carry her, she rushed to the gleaming chamber pot and sank to her knees.

A minute later she heard the door open behind her and, relishing the relief that Pam had not forgotten her, she rocked back onto her heels.

"Oh, Pam, I tell you I don't know how much longer I can take this. How can a babe scarcely visible cause me to feel so very wretched?" She wiped her face with a hand towel and turned to smile wanly at her friend.

But it was Lady Northcliffe's stunned countenance she encountered behind her. Lady Northcliffe, who in treating Collie like a servant was the only person other than Pam who never knocked before entering her bedroom. Now the woman's considerable bulk, rigid with shock, blocked the doorway.

"Miss Travers!" The countess gasped. "What is this all about?"

All the blood left Collie's head as she stumbled to her feet. "Lady Northcliffe, I—I beg your pardon." She swayed and grabbed the footboard of the bed to steady herself.

"Miss Travers, I demand instantly to know what you are about. Were you just ill? What is the meaning of this?" Lady Northcliffe's voice was reedy with outrage.

Collie glanced involuntarily back at the chamber pot. "I—yes, I—I think I ate something that did not agree with me. I'm better now." She forced her eyes to Lady Northcliffe's, her limbs trembling violently. It would, she believed, be a miracle if she did not drop into a dead faint before the woman's imposing wrath.

"That is not what you just said," the countess insisted. "I distinctly heard you say something about a baby. Tell me what you meant about a baby."

Collie's face ignited in a blush hot enough to singe her hair, and she noticed one of the housemaids tiptoing past the door with a curious look inside the room.

"I—" She swallowed and had trouble catching her breath. "I don't recall what I said just then, ma'am. I thought you were someone else."

"That's right. You thought I was my maid, Pamela. I heard you," Lady Northcliffe said. "I heard what you said. Now I demand you tell me the meaning of it."

More people collected at the door. The first housemaid Sadie, the parlormaid Marianne . . . She closed her eyes and swayed.

"Miss Travers!" Lady Northcliffe commanded. "Don't you dare attempt a swoon. I won't have it. Do you understand? I know you did so the other morning, in the hall, and at the time we thought nothing of it. But now . . . now I begin to comprehend."

Collie opened her eyes and willed herself to remain upright. Lady Northcliffe glared down her long nose at her.

"You will dress this instant and present yourself to me in my sitting room in a quarter hour." She spun on her heel to leave, scattering housemaids with the swirl of her skirts. But before taking a step she turned back abruptly, holding one finger aloft. "One quarter of an hour, Miss Travers, do not go anywhere else first, do you hear me? One quarter of an hour."

The countess swept out the door and down the hall, shooing away inquisitive servants who dared step in her path. But Collie did not move from the center of the room. She should close the door, she thought, before the peeping housemaids returned, close the door and crawl into bed, never to rouse herself again.

She swayed again, light-headed, and stumbled to the bed, sitting down hard on the edge, her weight propped upright on one straight arm.

This was it, she thought blankly. She was to be sacked. Just when it seemed things might finally be resolved, Lady Northcliffe had discovered the truth and now she would dismiss her.

She had to find Julian, she thought with sudden resolve. Now was the time to tell him, whether he seemed ready to hear it or not. After last night, he would probably not be surprised, not about most of it. It was the part about Miranda that gave her the most pause, and about his proposal to herself. She just prayed to God that despite everything he would at least believe her, even if he didn't remember.

She pulled off her nightrail and yanked a gown from her armoire. Gray wool, serviceable. Her best governess dress. If she could not feel steady and virtuous, she could at least look the part.

After a moment of frenzied energy she sank down onto the bed, her gown in place but unfastened, and took a deep, exhausted breath. How in the world could she face Lady Northcliffe when the simple act of getting dressed fatigued her so? She had to be strong. She had to be calm.

She bent her head to pull up her stockings.

Julian's actions last night proved one thing, she thought. Even if he didn't remember her he was attracted to her, as he had been in the beginning. He did not recall what they'd been to each other, but if she explained the circumstances to him now, would their shared passion be enough to convince him she told the truth?

If it wasn't—if he, God forbid, agreed with his mother that she should be sacked—Collie would have to leave. And she'd have no place to go but her mother's, she thought with a shudder. That depressing little house in east London that was the only lodging she could afford on her salary and still have enough to pay for Nurse Frederick.

She did not realize she was crying until a tear hit her hands as she buckled her shoe. She straightened and looked down at the wet trail on her hand, her eyelids forcing more tears over her bottom lashes. She watched the droplets roll off the backs of her hands.

He wouldn't remember. He would look at her as he had last night, as if she were a harlot, a liar, a fraud.

No, she argued. He would give her a chance to speak. He would listen with an open mind. He was a fair man. She knew he was a fair man. . . .

The door slammed. Collie blinked and looked up.

"Is it true, what the servants are whispering?" Pam asked, rushing to kneel by her side. She took Collie's hands in hers and wiped them dry with her apron. "Did she discharge you?"

"Pam," Collie said. "Pam. I thought she was you.

I thought . . ." More tears cascaded down her face. She wiped them furiously away. "I've done it now, Pam."

"Oh, Collie." Pam squeezed her hands and lowered her head. "So it is true."

Collie sniffed and shook her head. "She hasn't done it yet."

"She hasn't dismissed you yet?"

"No. Not yet." Collie disengaged one of her hands from Pam's to brush again at her cheeks. "I'm to meet her in her sitting room in a few minutes. She plans to do it there, I'm sure."

Pam rose and sat next to her on the bed. "Perhaps not. If she meant to sack you it seems she'd have done it here, in the heat of the moment."

Collie shook her head again, working away the lump in her throat so that she could speak intelligibly. "No, if there's one thing the nobility work to maintain it's their dignity. And you can trust me when I tell you there was none in this room this morning."

Pam sighed and patted her hand. "What can I do? How can I help you?"

"I need to know where Julian is. Have you seen him this morning?" Collie asked, rising.

"Julian?" Pam repeated.

"Yes. I'm going to tell him first, and he can do what he will. But I won't let Lady Northcliffe send me from this house before I speak with him. If *he* decides I must go, then I will. But not before." She ran a brush quickly through her hair and pulled the dark tresses back into a simple, severe bun.

"But Julian isn't here," Pam said. "He's gone off

somewhere with Cuff. I heard Pulver telling Brenda not to bother with his tea."

Collie's arms dropped and she turned toward Pam, feeling tears spring again to her eyes. "He's not here? When did he leave? When will he return?"

"I don't think they were to be gone long. But to be sure it will be longer than a few minutes." Pam chewed her lower lip. "Shall I try to stall Lady Northcliffe?"

"Pam!"

The voice from the doorway startled them both. Pam jumped to her feet.

"What is it, Sadie?" she snapped, irritated.

"It's my lady. She's screamin' and carryin' on, callin' for you. She's in a state, she is." The corners of Sadie's mouth quivered and drew downward. "She nearly smacked me when I told her I didn't know where you'd gone."

Pam and Collie exchanged a horrified glance.

"Tell her I'll be right there," Pam said.

But Sadie shook her head and stepped backward. "I'm not goin' back there, neither for love nor money. I've found you and told you and that's all I'm bound to do. You'd best hurry, though. Waitin' aren't likely to sweeten her temper any."

Pam frowned and pushed some loose curls up under her cap. "Fine, then, be off with you. I'll go straightaway."

Sadie disappeared and Collie rose to her feet. "I'll come with you."

"What in the world could the old bat want with *me?*" Pam questioned, brushing at her skirts to smooth them, her brows drawn together.

Collie felt the wretched tears sting her eyes again and bit her lip to stop the swell of emotion. She had to control herself. It was all up to her now.

"She heard me mention your name when she came in. I thought it was you coming with the milk. But now she must suspect you know something." She moved to Pam's side and grasped her arm. "Pam, I'm so sorry. You've only tried to help me and now I've gotten you into trouble."

Pam sniffed and raised a cavalier smile to Collie. "Well, it'd be different if you weren't in the right, Coll. Since you are, I guess it's all worth it." She sniffed again and rubbed the back of her hand across her nose.

Collie put an arm around her shoulders and pulled her tight. "I'll make it up to you," she said, her voice hushed, as they were so close. "I promise, Pam. I'll make it up to you."

Lady Northcliffe awaited them in the sitting room adjacent to her bedchamber. Despite the early hour the room was dim. Funereal, Collie thought as she and Pam entered, their hands clasped behind their backs. The curtains were drawn and the deep red walls glowed in the light of the fire and a single table lamp. Her ladyship sat erect and intimidating in a plush chair by the fire.

Collie and Pam stood together, several paces away from the formidable woman. Collie forced herself to breathe, to hold her chin steady and to meet the countess's eyes.

Lady Northcliffe gazed upon them with the practiced superiority of years of nobility. "I have informed Lady Greer that you won't be joining her this morning, Miss Travers. We shall send to London for the veil."

"I understand," Collie said.

"Not that it shall matter to you," Lady Northcliffe continued as if she had not spoken, "for you shall no doubt never see it. You will confess to me now what manner of illness I was unfortunate enough to witness this sorry morn."

Collie took a deep breath and opened her mouth to speak.

Lady Northcliffe held up one bejeweled hand. "And you will tell me no lies."

Collie straightened her shoulders. "I shan't lie, Lady Northcliffe, for I do not believe it to be any of your concern."

Lady Northcliffe's mouth thinned and she glared at the young woman before her. "Do you mean to say that you'll tell me nothing?"

"That's correct." Collie clenched her teeth against a growing panic. Obstinence could ensure her dismissal, she thought, but the truth would get thrown out faster than anything. "I do not owe you an explanation."

"What—not *owe* me an explanation," Lady Northcliffe repeated, flabbergasted. "Have you forgotten who it was plucked you from obscurity to wait upon a countess? Have you forgotten the honor bestowed upon you by this titled family when you were hired to educate my daughter? Miss Travers, you owe me everything."

"My lady," Pam interjected, "there is a story behind the circumstance—"

Lady Northcliffe waved a plump hand in front of her as if to discourage a fly. "I have no wish to hear *stories*, Pamela, though I believe that is all I'm likely to get from either of you. Let me instead tell both of you something. I know that you are with child, Miss Travers. And I know that you, Pamela, were party to this information. Therefore I have no other recourse than to require you both to leave this household immediately. I will give you no severance. I will give you no letter to recommend you to another employer. You have, both of you, betrayed my deepest trust. You, Miss Travers, by corrupting the innocent mind of my daughter. And you, Pamela, by keeping from your mistress the details of this vile situation."

Pam's breath shook audibly as she inhaled. "So we are both sacked?"

Collie could hear the panic in her voice. Pam had no family, had nowhere to go, no one to look out for her or take her in while she looked for another post—without references.

Bracing herself for the first lashings of Lady Northcliffe's storm, Collie said, "My lady, you are right to reprimand me, as I am the one who has erred. But Pam's done nothing—"

"Do you admit, then, that you are with child?" Lady Northcliffe demanded, snatching the opportunity to make her confess the way a cat swipes at and downs a moth.

Collie swallowed. "I do. But my circumstances have nothing whatsoever to do with—"

"You are? You, a single woman with no husband?" Lady Northcliffe exclaimed with such repugnance that Collie wondered if the countess had not truly believed it before. "Gracious heavens! To think that you were the person most responsible for the education and refinement of my impressionable daughter. And now you are pregnant!"

Collie had time only to open her mouth with the intention of drawing her back to the point—that Pam had nothing to do with it—before the woman took off again.

"How on earth did this happen? Who in the world is the father? Does he intend to marry you? Well, it matters not, for I cannot possibly have someone of such low behavior and lack of virtue in my employ—in charge of my child, no less. Lord only knows what failings you have already instilled in her, what depravations of mind, what degeneration of morals. Your very proximity to her has no doubt warped her innocence—I shall have to send her to a convent school to cleanse her now. Heaven help her, she will have to be purged of such turpitude somehow."

Collie stared at her, unsure how to proceed. She could feel Pam's presence beside her, both of them suspended in the eye of Lady Northcliffe's storm.

"Well?" Lady Northcliffe demanded. "Are you going to explain yourself?"

"I—I don't believe I have anything more to say," Collie said, so stunned she could not formulate even one thought that might turn the tide swirling around them.

She lowered her eyes, shaking her head. Lord, did pregnancy make one stupid as well as tired and ill?

"Lady Northcliffe," Pam said, "the circumstances are most unusual. Collie should never have been in this situation otherwise. I must tell you, even if she won't, who the father of her child is, for surely he bears the responsibility for her predicament."

"Pam, no!" Collie burst out on an exhalation of air.

"But I must implore you to listen to my whole story," Pam continued quickly, "as otherwise it might come as quite a shock to you."

Lady Northcliffe snorted. "No more of a shock than discovering my trusted governess is a tart!"

Collie bit her tongue. "I am no tart, my lady."

"Your ladyship, Collie was set to marry when her intended became the victim of a most unfortunate accident," Pam explained.

Collie felt faint.

"An accident? Surely he is not dead?"

"No—"

"Pam, please don't do this," Collie implored, taking a step toward her.

But Pam would not look at her. When Collie had moved, Pam had taken one step forward, her hands clasped together at her chin, practically begging Lady Northcliffe to listen. "He's alive and would do right by her if he were able—"

"It still doesn't signify," Lady Northcliffe pronounced, running over Pam's words with the vehemence of her own, "because the fact of her loose morals remains. This would never have happened had she waited for the sanctity of the marriage bed before indulging her sordid, lowly nature."

"I agree," Collie said, "but—"

"But however the case might have been, I would tell you how it happened," Pam insisted. "For weeks after her intended's accident we all believed him dead—"

"But you just said that he is not."

"No, he is not—"

"Then why is she not married?"

"Because he doesn't remember anything!" Pam burst out.

Collie closed her eyes. She thought she might collapse; her knees trembled beneath her. She took a deep breath, and her head spun with the sudden influx of air.

Lady Northcliffe stared at her maid without comprehension for several long moments; then she shifted her gaze to Collie.

The moment the truth dawned the countess's great bosom heaved with her outraged gasp and her face went crimson. She rose from her chair, the fringe of her shawl quivering with her rage.

"Do you stand there, insolent, abhorrent girl, and accuse my son of lying with you, of intending to marry you, a servant?"

"I am not a servant," Collie said miserably, struggling to keep her head high. "I am a governess and the daughter of a gentleman."

"And what would that gentleman think of you now?" Lady Northcliffe said, her voice ominous. "It's disgusting. Get out! Get out of my sight this instant, before I have Pulver throw you out. Pam— fetch the doctor, I fear I am going to faint."

Indeed, the moment after the color had flooded her face, it had just as quickly drained. She looked ready to collapse and sank back into her chair.

Collie took a step toward her. "Lady North-cliffe—"

"Do not even speak my name, impudent chit!" Lady Northcliffe recoiled as if she were to be struck.

Pam stood rooted to the spot, unable to take her eyes from the spectacle before her.

Collie stopped, astonished. Then, slowly, heat and mortification flooded her. "I see. Yes, you think me little better than a leper now. And you may feel you have every right to denigrate me, but you do not. I carry within me your grandchild, the Earl of Northcliffe's rightful heir, and he should know it."

"Liar!" Lady Northcliffe shrieked.

Shaken, Collie plowed onward. "We were in love, Julian and I, and planned to marry as soon as he returned from Italy. He was to speak with his father on the trip." Lady Northcliffe was shaking her head vehemently, her eyes closed. "My lady, this is the truth, I swear it—"

"The truth!" the countess burst out, her eyes flying open. "You wouldn't know the truth if it were emblazoned upon your forehead. No, you are not worthy of my forbearance any longer, Miss Travers. I will not have a soiled woman in my household!"

Collie glared at her. "Very well, I will not explain further. I shall speak to Julian and then I shall be gone."

Lady Northcliffe shot to her feet. "Speak to Julian! Good lord in heaven, child, do you wish to drive him mad? He is ill, extremely ill. Reckless falsehoods of this sort could be the very thing to put him beyond saving. Have you such an unholy wish for his destruction? Imagine the nerve," she exclaimed to the ceiling, circling her chair to stand behind it, gripping it with gnarled claws of fury. "A penniless harlot seeking to pin such a claim upon the Earl of Northcliffe. He would die of apoplexy before insanity even had a chance at him."

"Your ladyship, despite your treatment of me I understand your skepticism. But I am not a liar and I am not a woman of loose morals. You've known me nigh on a year now; surely you know me to be of good character—"

"Good character! No, I have known you to be impulsive and headstrong. I have frequently tolerated your unreserved speech, as you were recommended so highly by Lord Bretton, whom you obviously deceived; but Miss Travers, by this indiscretion you have shown yourself to be of no character whatsoever. In truth, I should have seen it before but I was blinded by your prettiness and Lord Bretton's regard. Indeed, I have learned my lesson now—a pleasing appearance does not a virtue guarantee."

"I may have made a mistake," Collie said, willing herself not to cry and yet fatigued beyond measure. "But your son loved me and he intended to marry me. I believe with all my heart that when his memory returns he will feel the same, and fulfill that promise. But in the meantime, I carry his child and I tell you I shall not leave this house without speaking to him."

Lady Northcliffe stomped to the corner and yanked hard on the bellpull. "Don't move an inch," she ordered, one accusing finger outstretched.

"I will remain as long as it takes Julian to arrive."

"Julian!" she repeated. "She calls him Julian, Lord in heaven help me."

The door opened and the maid Sadie poked her head in, her face awash in curiosity. "Yes, my lady?"

"Fetch the doctor. And quickly!" the countess ordered.

"And Lord Northcliffe," Collie added with a hard look at the maid.

"No!" Lady Northcliffe screeched. "Get Monroe—Mr. Dorland, and be quick about it! Do not under any circumstances fetch the earl."

"Yes, my lady," the maid said with a rapid curtsy and disappeared.

Pam edged toward the door.

Collie swung back to Lady Northcliffe. "Do not fear that I won't leave your house," she said, all pretense of patience gone. "I shall go to London, to my mother, but I *will* speak to Julian."

"Julian is in no condition to speak to anyone, particularly not someone who slanders his very name and besmirches his character with vile accusations."

Footsteps thundered down the hall, and a moment later Pulver and the doctor burst through the door.

"My lady, what is it? The maid told me you had an emergency," the doctor said, dropping his bag on the table and pulling a vial from its depths.

"Oh, Dr. Irwin, thank God you've come! Pulver,

expel this woman from my house immediately," Lady Northcliffe commanded.

The doctor put an arm around Lady Northcliffe's shoulders and waved the vial beneath her nose. She closed her eyes and inhaled deeply.

Pulver turned to Collie, his flat brown eyes unreadable but clearly unsurprised.

"I must speak to Lord Northcliffe," Collie maintained, not moving. But her hands gripped each other hard in front of her.

Lady Northcliffe's eyes flew open. "Take her bodily from this dwelling if you must, Pulver. I want her gone before another moment passes."

Pulver took a step in her direction, his face set. Collie had just enough time to wonder if he would drag her kicking and screaming from the room when Monroe appeared silently in the doorway.

"Oh! Monroe!" Lady Northcliffe exclaimed in relief, breaking free of the doctor's grasp and rushing toward him. "Help us! Help us oust this Jezebel from our midst."

Monroe's sleepy eyes surveyed the scene as he leaned against the door frame. "I heard there was a commotion."

"She is telling the most vile lies, Monroe." Lady Northcliffe took one of his hands and held it between hers at her heart. "She must be banished at once."

Collie stood as if balancing on a wire, unsure which way she should fall. Pulver eyed her with malevolence, yet stayed his approach in view of Mr. Dorland's presence.

Monroe studied her with a laziness she was sure

was deceptive, for something behind his narrow countenance seemed alert, and aware of more than what simply met the eye. His perusal made her palms sweat, his keen gaze somehow more threatening than his mother's overt hostility.

"What sort of lies is she telling?" he asked.

Lady Northcliffe glanced uneasily at Pulver. "I'd rather not say before the servants."

Monroe laughed, the sound strange in the charged room. His lips drew back over his teeth, but it was not precisely a smile that resulted.

"Doubtless the servants could tell us a thing or two *we* don't know about what's gone on here today," he said. The words were indolent, yet Collie could not tell if he was drunk.

Lady Northcliffe grabbed up her skirts and turned away from her son. "Pulver, wait outside," she directed with a wave of one hand.

With a parting glance at Collie, Pulver sidled around Monroe and left the room. Pam was nowhere to be seen, Collie noted, and prayed that she was searching for and would find Julian.

Monroe pushed off the door frame and entered, swinging the door shut behind him with a flip of his wrist.

For the first time, Collie studied his face, hoping to glean from his expression something of his intentions. But his features were enigmatic. Dark brows slashed over long, slanted eyes. His nose was thin and his mouth hard, with no hint of warmth. Tall and gaunt, he nonetheless moved elegantly, with a stealth that Collie now realized had always unnerved her. He had the shifty look of a criminal, she noted, and wondered why that had never occurred to her before.

"What is the lie that you have told, Miss Travers?" he asked mildly.

Collie held herself so rigid she had difficulty turning her head toward him, where he lounged against the chair his mother once again occupied. The doctor stood by the fire, his medical bag at the ready.

"I tell no lies," she said.

"Blasphemy," Lady Northcliffe hissed. "Monroe, the trollop is with child."

His brows raised fractionally. "And she lies to deny it?" he asked, keeping his gaze on Collie.

"No! She admits it." Lady Northcliffe shook her head with an incredulous look at her son. "But she claims the child is Julian's. Can you think of anything so vile?"

The doctor started and uttered a low "Good lord."

Monroe gave his mother a long look, then turned back to Collie, his head tilted, considering. "So you're claiming the child is Julian's," he said finally.

"I claim only what is true, and ask only to speak with your brother before I leave this house."

"How can she speak with him, Monroe?" his mother demanded. "Dr. Irwin, she cannot, can she? Not while he is so ill. He is"—she turned back to Monroe—"the good doctor has informed me, on the very verge of catastrophe. If she were to accost him now, Julian would surely suffer greatly."

Monroe lowered his eyes to the doctor. "How would he suffer, Doctor?"

"You know very well," Lady Northcliffe exclaimed. "He could go insane. And then lord only knows what manner of harm could befall him. Insane people injure themselves all the time. His very life could be imperiled."

"It's true," the doctor said carefully. "Something of this nature, so personal and so shocking, could easily wound him beyond all power of saving. He is at a critical point, one where the situation could be reversed by the slightest surprise. An accusation of this sort . . . well, it doesn't bear contemplation."

Monroe's face darkened and he looked back up at Collie. "I don't believe we can risk your talking with my brother," he said.

Collie's heart had risen to her throat at the doctor's pronouncement. That Julian could be so close to such tragedy took all the energy from her conviction.

"But you and I both know you needn't really speak with him, don't we, Miss Travers?" Monroe continued.

The words were so silky and companionable Collie wondered if she had missed something obvious in the conversation.

"I don't understand. If you mean—"

"I mean," Monroe said over her, "that you and I both know quite well whose child it is you carry."

Collie looked in confusion from him to the doctor to his mother, all of whom stared up at Monroe with equally perplexed attention.

"Do you know with whom she has lain?" Lady Northcliffe inquired in a breathless voice, her eyes rapt. "I knew it wasn't Julian! Do you know who really fathered the brat?"

Monroe laughed shortly. "I do indeed." The

slanted eyes turned a languorous look from her to Collie. "The child she carries is my own, Mother."

Collie's breath left her in a whoosh and the room whirled around her. She grabbed at the back of a nearby chair.

Lady Northcliffe's mouth dropped open and she uttered, "Yours?"

"That's untrue!" Collie burst out. "The child is Julian's."

Monroe issued a thin smile. "Apparently my sweet Miss Travers thinks she might do better than to secure the untitled son's affections," he said with unfeigned bitterness. "But your game shall not succeed, my dear. Because, you see, I am here to disprove your claims."

"Is this true, Mr. Dorland?" the doctor inquired.

"Of course."

Collie searched Monroe's face. "Mr. Dorland, what are you doing? Why do you say these things? You know perfectly well you and I have never shared a conversation of any duration, let alone any intimacy."

"Ah, I see you are quite determined," he said, taking several steps toward her.

Collie recoiled. "I am determined the truth be known—"

"Then stop this folly, Miss Travers," he commanded, his voice suddenly hard. He came within a foot of her and grabbed her by the forearms.

Collie was so astonished she could not move. She could not even speak. Staring into his eyes, the full import of his lie struck her with horrific clarity. With his obvious willingness to perpetuate this falsehood to his family, her assertions had no chance. No one would believe the proud and aloof earl would betrothe himself to a mere governess; but not a soul would doubt his ignoble brother capable of trifling with a woman so sinful as to find herself with child out of wedlock.

At the moment she grasped the hideous truth, Monroe raised a brow and inclined his head so slightly she thought she might have imagined it.

"On second thought, Mother," he concluded, turning to face the countess and the doctor, and slipping one hot arm around Collie's waist, "perhaps we should set Miss Travers upon him in order to prove beyond a doubt she speaks false."

"What on earth do you mean?" Lady Northcliffe gasped.

"I mean," he said, "let us take her to Julian."

Chapter Twelve

"Take her to Julian!" the doctor exploded. "Are you mad?"

"It's what she said she wanted." Monroe turned, releasing her waist, and raised his brows. His hands slid along her forearms, as if to hold them, but she wrenched free. "Isn't that right, Miss Travers? You would speak to Julian, you said. You would not leave before speaking to Julian."

"That's right," she said breathlessly, backing away from him.

"You're willing, then, to risk his sanity to tell him your tale?"

Collie felt the world shifting beneath her. Words jammed in her throat. She must speak to Julian, she thought, she *must*. "He—he has a right to know." But her voice was weak and lacked her previous conviction.

"So," Monroe said, nodding, "that is the level of your affection for him."

She took a shallow breath. "What do you mean?"

"Think about it, Miss Travers," he said. "Your intention is secure your own future without regard to his. You wish to announce your version of the truth, without thought to the truth of this situation." He paused to take a breath. "Do you think you're so much better than we are?" He swept a hand out, encompassing them all—Lady Northcliffe, the doctor, himself. "Do you believe your story has more merit than the wishes of his family for his recovery? It's funny. I never imagined you to be quite so self-serving."

She noticed something odd as he clenched his teeth around the final words, something that snapped her out of her daze. Monroe was furious. The realization was sudden and shocking. Sly, laconic, drunken Monroe did not toy with her for his amusement. He was apparently involved in some dreadful game with stakes high enough to make him savage and desperate.

She swallowed, her palms slick against each other, and looked from Monroe to his mother. Lady Northcliffe stood stolid as a bulldog, her face set in hard, uncompromising lines.

Collie looked to the doctor, and his face unnerved her the most. The monocle and the glare from the lamp obscured one eye, giving it the blank, unreadable stare of a button-eyed doll. But the other was narrowed, and his arched brows descended over both like winged birds of prey.

His mouth thinned to a line, but his words were incongruously gentle. "Whose child is it, Miss Travers?" he asked. "Tell us the truth."

Monroe's hand gripped her forearm, and he twisted viciously. She cried out, but had no choice but to turn to him.

"Tell them," he said, drilling her with an intensity she'd never seen in his face. "Tell them it is my child," he commanded, "or by God live forever in hell for your perfidy."

"*My* perfidy!" she exclaimed, shaken. She glanced again at the faces around her. Panic colored her thoughts, made her confused, but the expressions that surrounded her bore a single message—she was defeated. The more she asserted her story, the more enraged they would become. They'd never help her reach Julian. The only one who could help her was Julian himself. But was the doctor right? Was Monroe? Could her cares be the death of him? "My perfidy," she repeated, and looked back into Monroe's eyes.

"My dear, what else would you call it?"

"Why are you doing this?" she asked, her voice breaking. "Why do you wish to destroy me?"

He breathed deeply through his nose, his nostrils flaring. "Why do you wish to destroy my brother?"

His gaze did not relinquish hers. Tears pricked her eyes, but she would not blink and let them fall. "I don't," she whispered. "I just . . ." . . . *wish to save myself,* she thought weakly, then shook her head with disgust. She did it all for herself, without thought for Julian, without thought for the awful future that could befall him.

"Then tell them," Monroe continued in a calm voice, with a grip on her forearm that belied the tone, "tell them it is not Julian's child."

She yanked free of his grip. "How can I?" she said savagely, rubbing the place on his arm that he had held. "I cannot! I will not." She could keep it to herself, she thought, but she would not lie about it.

"We should send her away," Lady Northcliffe said, breaking her infuriated silence. "We shall send her to her mother, in London. She shall not be allowed back on the premises."

Monroe spun on his mother. "Oh, very clever, Mother. Send her to London where she can spread her blasphemy from Cheapside to Mayfair. All of London is already talking of the muddled Earl of Northcliffe, whose life was spared, but for what? To bring misery and insanity to his poor, bereaved family. Add a story like this to the mix and we'll find Julian barred from the House of Lords, our good name questioned at the exchange and creditors beating down our door for their money. Just until," he added snidely, "this 'unfortunate incident' is behind us." His lips twisted with the words.

"Don't be absurd," his mother said in horror. "They would never do such a thing . . . not to the titled!"

Monroe scoffed. "It is the very title that ensures it, Mother. If Julian were a simple, unfortunate businessman, anyone might take over for him, and society at large would care naught. But he is an earl, and as such he represents all the aristocracy. I daresay the Lords would be the first to toss him out. His very existence besmirches their superiority: his questionable reason sullies them all."

"Then he should pass the title!" Lady Northcliffe declared. "He should pass the title on! Or he should be *made* to do it if he is not competent."

"He cannot," Monroe growled, frustration with his mother's naivete obvious. "He is the heir. It is written into Lord Northcliffe's will in the same way it was written into the wills of his grandfathers, generations back. Nothing short of death can—" He stopped abruptly, his mouth snapping closed and his face suddenly looking as if he'd said far too much. "His title cannot be passed on," he said with more control. "Competent or not."

Silence descended for a long moment after this speech. Collie found herself holding her breath. So much more was at stake here than she'd realized. Julian's sanity, his credibility, his very position in life was called into question by his affliction. To add her scandal to the commotion would only hurt him further, in ways more far-reaching than she'd ever imagined. Creditors, peers, competency . . .

She exhaled slowly. Monroe shifted his eyes to her.

"Do you begin to see my point, Miss Travers?" he asked.

She jerked her head up and down once.

"I have a sister," the doctor said into the stifling hush that enthralled the room, "who lives in Lincoln, not so very far from here. Miss Travers can go there and wait out her confinement. You could visit her there, Mr. Dorland, if you wished. Or not, as you pleased. I'm sure for the most reasonable sum good care and lodging could be provided for her. My sister is quite . . . capable."

Monroe looked at her, the fierceness gone from his eyes. Collie had trouble catching her breath.

"Shall I write to her, Mr. Dorland?" the doctor inquired.

"Yes," Monroe said instantly. "Yes, do. We

needn't make the decision whether or not to send her until we receive an answer. Up to that time Miss Travers should stay here, where we can keep an eye on her."

"Here!" Lady Northcliffe exploded.

"Yes," he said. "She should continue to tutor Shelly, of course, so that none will suspect. We cannot have the servants talking. But I believe we've convinced her not to go to Julian, have we not, Miss Travers? You know now that going to Julian will get you nothing."

Collie hesitated, hating Monroe for his horrid, slanderous lie, but knowing she must do all within her power to stay in the house and near Julian. Her only hope was for Julian to remember, completely and on his own. If he were to lose his wits, or be judged incompetent, everything would be lost. He might remain the earl, but he would be powerless, perhaps even incarcerated. His life would be meaningless.

"I will say nothing," she said, adding to herself *at present*. But she would pray with every shred of her soul that Julian's memory be restored. And if it was—*when* it was—she would be there to dispel the lies that swarmed around him.

Lady Northcliffe clapped her hands together. "There," she said briskly. "That's settled then."

Monroe turned to her, his expression skeptical. Even Collie found the countess's tone of satisfaction and confidence odd a split second after her outrage.

"Miss Travers will stay here until the good doctor's sister can be petitioned to take her in." Lady

Northcliffe fixed a stern eye on Collie. "And you should count your blessings, child, that Monroe Dorland is of the character he is. Any other man would have disowned you completely after such a heinous attempt to secure such a match. The gall, Miss Travers, the utter gall of thinking to attach yourself to an earl! Well!" She gave a giddy laugh. "It's simply laughable. Laughable, I say. Is it not, Doctor?" She turned her smile to Dr. Irwin.

His face did not lighten. "I find nothing amusing in the situation."

"No," Lady Northcliffe immediately concurred. "There is nothing amusing in the manipulations of unscrupulous women."

Monroe's hand tightened on Collie's arm. She gritted her teeth.

"To be given a living at all after such a scene as this is far more than you deserve," Lady Northcliffe continued to Collie. "Since you have proven yourself so unworthy, I shall not address you further on this or any other topic. You are henceforth beneath my notice, Miss Travers."

The doctor shot Lady Northcliffe a hard look. "Pray, do not forget, my lady, that Miss Travers was not alone in her promiscuity. You and I, as purveyors of morality, must lay blame where blame is due. But not without some compassion, I think. It is our duty to help those less morally gifted."

"Yes, I see what you are saying," Lady Northcliffe agreed, fixing a beady eye on Monroe. "You have greatly disappointed me, Monroe. I would have thought you bright enough to choose a doxy from amongst the servant class. To have chosen the governess, when you see what aspirations she has—well, I only hope you've learned something today. But from now on, you must stay away from her. I won't have that disgusting behavior going on beneath my roof. I run a moral house here, a moral house. And I really don't think she should continue to tutor Shelly, for pity's sake. Should we not lock her in her room or something, Doctor?" She turned worried eyes to Dr. Irwin.

"Heavens, no," the doctor said, and Collie closed her eyes in relief. Thank God he was here, she thought as he took a moment to consider the situation. Thank God he was here.

Monroe kept his grip firm. Collie focused on the feel of it, hot and bruising, telling herself that once she was free of this room she would formulate her own plan. Somehow, some way, Julian must remember. But it must be done gently, in such a way as to preserve his reason. She bit her lower lip.

"First of all, we must keep this matter as private as possible," the doctor said, as if collecting his thoughts verbally. "I'm sure Miss Travers wishes that as well. After all, she is not without a reputation to preserve."

He looked up at her and she nodded slowly.

"At the very least," he continued to Lady Northcliffe, "to lock her away would cause unnecessary gossip among the servants, as Mr. Dorland pointed out. And that could get back to his lordship. No, I believe we can trust Miss Travers to say nothing. She seems to have learned her lesson here today. She has admitted the child is not His Lordship's, have you not, Miss Travers?"

Monroe's hand tightened again.

A queasy sensation slid through her stomach. If she insisted the child was Julian's they would not let her stay. They did not believe her anyway, and it would not matter how strenuously she insisted. Her only hope was for Julian to remember. She must only ensure that she stayed in the house. The doctor, for all his siding with Lady Northcliffe, was at least being kind. And it was due to him that she was not to be locked away, unable to reach Julian.

"Miss Travers," the doctor repeated gently, his one visible eye trained on her. "Must you think on it so hard?"

Collie raised her chin, knowing she should recant the truth and assert the lie, but unable to get the words out. It was almost as if renouncing the truth aloud might relinquish her claim to it.

"The child is mine only," she said.

"Not Lord Northcliffe's?" the doctor pressed.

She felt him focus on her with a queer, quiet insistence. The doctor didn't mean her harm; Monroe did. Did the doctor somehow sense that? For some reason, Monroe hated her enough to debase her publicly. But Monroe's words were the ones giving her the chance to stay in the house. Lady Northcliffe would never allow her to stay if she believed Collie's story, so with Monroe she must side—temporarily.

"No." She nearly choked on the answer, wished it back the moment she spoke it, and felt unexpected tears dash down her cheeks.

"Hah!" Lady Northcliffe burst out. Her jowly face quivered with delight. "I knew it."

"I take it, Mr. Dorland," Dr. Irwin continued, "you do not intend to marry Miss Travers?"

Collie opened her mouth to protest, but Lady Northcliffe beat her to it.

"Marry!" Lady Northcliffe gasped. "Surely not! Monroe, marry a governess? No, absolutely not! Doctor, what an absurd question."

"Indeed, marriage was not part of our bargain," Monroe said smoothly. "But I intend to take responsibility for my actions. I won't turn her out without support."

"Commendable, in its way," Irwin murmured, studying Collie.

Shame burned her cheeks and she battled the urge to scream out her frustration, to pummel them with the truth and damn anyone who did not believe it.

But she could not damn Julian. She could not condemn him to a life of derangement. He would sooner die, she knew. And so would she.

Collie didn't notice his appearance until she saw Shelly shrink in her seat in the schoolroom and give the door a sidelong glance. Collie turned her head.

Monroe leaned against the door frame, his hands in his pockets.

"Good afternoon," he said.

Shelly glanced uneasily at Collie, who nodded her head.

"Good afternoon, Monroe," Shelly said sullenly. "What are you doing here?"

He pushed a shoulder off the door frame and sauntered into the room. "I've come to see how you're doing, and to speak with Miss Travers for a moment. What's that you're working on?"

Shelly shrugged and concentrated on her paper. "Latin." Then, realizing the distraction at hand, she added, "I hate it," and looked up at her brother with eyes that guilelessly invited conversation.

"I hated it too," Monroe said, propping one thigh on the opposite desk and half sitting down. "When I was your age I told my teacher I wouldn't do it anymore."

Shelly looked at him in awe. "You did? What did she say?"

"*He* rapped my knuckles with a book and told me to do it anyway."

Shelly unconsciously closed her hand as she gaped up at her brother. "Did you do it?"

Monroe laughed and shot Collie an irreverent look. "No."

"Nevertheless," Collie said sternly, "you, Shelly, will complete it. Your brother can talk to you later, after your lesson is finished. If you still want him to."

Monroe's mouth curled. "What a severe teacher you are," he said. "Making your students perform such unpleasant tasks." He pushed himself off the desk and strolled toward the windows. "I suppose you'll be ramming all those Renaissance fellows down her throat next . . . Chaucer, Milton, Shakespeare. . . ."

"Chaucer wrote in the Middle Ages," Collie said stiffly, "therefore his works are not considered Renaissance literature. And Milton—"

"Fine, yes, whatever," Monroe said, leaning one

arm on the dormer windowsill so that his hand drooped casually. "I didn't come here for a lesson."

Collie stood ramrod stiff by her desk. "What did you come here for?" she asked sharply.

Shelly's head rose and her gaze rested with interest on her teacher.

Collie took in a slow breath. Monroe raised his brows at her, his expression amused.

"Yes, well," he said, laughter in his tone. "Speaking of Shakespeare—"

"She's a few years away from Shakespeare yet," Collie said. "We're very busy here. Why don't you get to the point, Mr. Dorland?"

"Yes, but *you're* familiar with him, are you not?" Monroe asked, ignoring her impatience. "Shakespeare, that is."

"Of course." She picked up a book, turned it in her hands, then put it down again. What did he want? She longed for the ability to speak freely, to demand he explain why he'd lied about her that morning. But she could not in front of Shelly, and she knew that if he wanted to talk to her without revealing his motives that was why he'd come to her here.

"One of my favorite lines from Shakespeare, as I recall from my imperfect education, was 'Frailty, thy name is woman!'" He smiled at her broadly.

"How intriguing," she snapped, "that *Hamlet* should be a favorite of yours. 'Something is rotten in the state of Denmark,' has ever been my favorite line."

Monroe straightened from his leaning pose, his eyes unexpectedly intent. "Exactly."

Collie looked up at him, her brows drawing together. What in the world was he getting at?

He took several steps toward her, speaking quietly as he came. " 'I could a tale unfold whose lightest word would harrow up thy soul.' "

The low, threatening timbre of his voice startled her, sending an uncomfortable chill down her spine. He did not relinquish her gaze.

"Your—you seem to remember his plays quite well," she said. She glanced at Shelly, who studied her paper, apparently uninterested in their verbal sparring.

Monroe lifted one brow, his lips forming a small, cool smile. "Aye. And how well do you remember it, Miss Travers?"

He stood close to where she leaned against her desk and looked down at her with an unsettling concentration. Did he think to threaten her? she wondered, her heart hammering in her chest. He'd already managed to silence her; what more did he seek?

"I remember it all," she said, making her voice hard. She rose and moved around him toward the window. "I remember it all, in all its vile treachery." She turned back to face him, forcing fear to the back of her mind.

He studied her, that smile still on his lips. "Treachery, indeed."

She laughed without humor. " 'Smiling damned villian,' " she quoted with an arch look. " 'That one may smile, and smile, and be a villain.' "

Monroe followed her to the window. She felt herself trembling as he neared.

"I am no villain," he said quietly.

She shivered and crossed her arms in front of her. "You merely behave like one for no reason, I suppose."

"Surely in studying that play, as you obviously have," he continued, "you learned that things are not always what they seem, that people are not always as they seem."

She raised her chin. "Not always, but mostly." He stood before her, too close, and she felt her back against the wall as she tried to retreat.

He scoffed. " 'You speak like a green girl, unsifted in such perilous circumstance.' "

She was out of her depth, she realized. Danger surrounded him like a cloak and she was ill-prepared to deal with it. Color rose to her face and her heart took up a panicked flutter.

"What do you mean?" she demanded, her voice too low to disturb Shelly, but agitated enough to wipe the smile from his face. "Speak plainly, Mr. Dorland, for I have lost the thread of our conversation. Do you threaten me?"

"Do I need to?" he asked. He too spoke in a low tone so Shelly couldn't hear, and his sober expression unnerved her more than anything.

"Are you telling me I am in perilous circumstances?" Her voice quavered. She forced herself to hold his hard gaze to belie it.

"You are." His eyelids drooped lazily, but his eyes were still cold. "As is my brother. And I have no wish to see either of you . . . hurt, in any way."

She inhaled swiftly. Terror pounded around her eyes. "You wouldn't harm him."

His head cocked a fraction. "No sooner than you would. Would you?"

"Of course not!"

"Your silence, then, is . . . secured?"

Sweat prickled in the palms of her hands and along her scalp. "I have already said—"

His face was rigid and his insistence easily stopped her equivocation. "Your word, Miss Travers. I would have your word that you will say nothing to Julian of your earlier claim."

Shelly looked up from her paper again and Collie ducked out from behind Monroe. "Are you finished already, Shelly?" she asked brightly.

"Not yet," Shelly mumbled, resting her head in one hand.

"Miss Travers," Monroe insisted.

She turned back to him, her hands fluttering to her sides, then back up to grip themselves in front of her.

"I would have your word." His voice was like ice, smooth, hard, distorting all that lay beneath it.

Shelly looked nervously between the two of them.

Collie forced an amiable smile onto her face. "I don't recall that line. Are we still in *Hamlet*?"

"No." His eyes, dead cold and determined, skewered her where she stood. He took a step toward her.

Shelly cocked her head at him, a gesture so similar to the one Monroe had just made it calmed Collie's rippling nerves. He would not hurt her. Not here, in front of his sister. He might make oblique threats, but all he sought was her word that she would not go to Julian.

"I will say nothing to harm him," she said.

"Harm who?" Shelly asked. Her expression was alert and interested now.

Collie managed to smile at her. "Nothing, dear. We're discussing characters. From the play. Finish your translation, please."

"But I hate this," she complained.

"That doesn't matter," Collie said, more sharply than she'd intended. She softened her voice. "You must sometimes do things you do not like in order to learn. And this one should be easy. It's the same as the one in the book we read yesterday."

Shelly pursed her mouth and went back to the paper in front of her.

Monroe walked to the door, his pace unhurried, his movements relaxed. But when he turned to face Collie she saw again the rigid lines of his face and the uncompromising look in his eyes.

"Do we understand each other, Miss Travers?" he asked. "I think I've made myself clear."

That she was in danger. That she must keep silent or he would ensure it, somehow. Yes, he'd made himself clear. On that issue, at any rate. But she still did not know why he'd lied, why he claimed her child as his own. And she could not ask him, not with Shelly listening so attentively. She would have to find him later and demand the truth.

Yes, she would find him when they could be alone, and she would discover just what he was doing.

"I understand you," she said.

He let his gaze stay upon her until she was sure the depth of her discomfort showed on her face.

"And I," he said quietly, his lips curling again into that cynical smile, "understand you, Miss Travers."

Chapter Thirteen

The knock on the door was so light that Julian barely heard it. He looked up from the ledger before him, and then glanced at the clock on the mantel. He'd told Pulver not to disturb him until noon. He was far too busy mulling over his disgusting behavior with Miss Travers to tolerate any company.

"Come in," he barked, irritated. He marked his place in the ledger with the ruler and leaned back in the chair.

The door opened on well-oiled hinges and the doctor eased into the room. He bore a tray with a cup, a teapot and a plate of biscuits on it. Julian could see the steam rising from the cup.

"Good morning, my lord," the doctor said, his smooth Oxford accent grating on Julian's nerves as it always did for some reason.

"Good morning." Julian watched him approach down the length of the room.

"I've brought you something." He neared the desk and inclined his upper body toward Julian a mere degree, his version of a bow.

Julian dropped his pen across the page and

leaned back in the chair. "Apparently."

"It's a tonic, my lord, that I believe may do you some good. Taken on a regular basis—every morning about this time, perhaps—it could help to restore your memory."

He took the cup and placed it in front of Julian on the other side of the ledger. Julian looked at it.

The doctor continued, placing the teapot and biscuits at the corner of the desk, "It has soothing properties that pacify the nerves and enhance the synchronous processes of the brain, allowing the memory and the conscious mind to merge despite the contused state of the cortex."

Julian shifted his gaze from the steaming cup to the doctor, studying the pointed face, the thin mustache, the gold-rimmed monocle.

"And what's in it?" he asked, leaning forward to pick up the warm glass and smell it.

"Just a few herbs and plant extracts. Nothing complex, though the combination is known to have quite restorative effects. It's a special tincture—that is, a solution of medicines in an alcoholic menstruum—that I manufacture myself." Irwin turned his head and the light from the window obscured his left eye. His chin rose and he managed to exude an air of injured pride at being questioned. "It has proven very effective in other, similar cases, my lord."

"I see." Julian lifted a brow, then added dryly, "And I know what a tincture is."

The doctor inclined his head.

Julian sniffed the concoction again. "It smells like tea."

"Quite right, my lord. It is mixed with tea, and as this is only the beginning dosage it is quite small. The amount is naturally increased if the patient does not respond, so do not despair if results are slow in coming." Irwin gave the thin-lipped smile that made Julian's flesh crawl. "You must have patience, my lord. But I shall go so far as to say that if your condition is not significantly altered through use of this tea within a fortnight I shall forfeit my right to attempt any further ministrations."

"A fortnight," Julian repeated. "You believe I could improve within a fortnight?"

"I believe," Irwin said firmly, "your situation will resolve itself to the perfect satisfaction of your family within that time, yes. I would stake my reputation on it."

Julian narrowed his eyes, wary of the hope he felt. "A fortnight."

"Unequivocally." The doctor raised his chin again and pursed his lips. "It is, however, imperative that you let me know if you remember anything—anything at all—no matter how inconsequential it may seem to you. You see, what might appear trivial in your estimation could open broad doors to my understanding of your condition."

"Hm," Julian said, setting the cup down on the desk and glancing at the ledger in front of him, as if anxious to get back to it. "Fine," he said distractedly, "I'll drink it. You may go now."

Irwin's knuckles went white on the tray and he sniffed. "With all due respect, my lord, I make it a policy to stay with the patient to whom I am administering medicine."

Julian looked at the doctor. "You don't believe I will drink the stuff, is that it?"

"Certainly not, my lord. I trust you implicitly. But as a physician it is my responsibility ensure that no ill effects overcome you upon drinking the mixture. Though I take every precaution, one can never tell with medicines exactly how a body will react."

Julian regarded him silently.

The doctor tucked the tray under one arm and looked pointedly at the register of rents open in front of Julian. "Considering that you've chosen to disregard my other medical advice, I would think at the very least—as a courtesy to your mother and your entire family who suffer under your affliction—that you would try to better yourself with the means at your disposal. At the risk of censuring myself, I should like to point out that my services do not come cheaply. Your mother is going to great effort and expense to ensure your recovery."

"My *step*mother," Julian said, "is expending nothing. The money is mine, Dr. Irwin. You stay at *my* leisure."

The doctor pursed his lips again and his eyelids drooped in an infuriating expression of wronged dignity. "Yes, of course, you are correct. However, I feel it my duty to inform you that in other cases that I have had the sad misfortune to witness, the patient who does not recover has been subjected to such things as inquests and competency hearings to judge whether he is fit to resume his business. In the case of the titled, there is even more reason to protect the family resources and honor." He glanced again at the register. "And after all, my lord, you must admit it is not quite sane to forget one's entire life." He looked at Julian. "Is it?"

Julian glared at him and rose slowly to his feet. "Are you threatening me, Irwin?"

The doctor watched him rise, coughed and took a step backward. "Of course not," he said. "No. I merely wished to point out the difficulties in your situation—"

Julian forced a laugh, closing his hands into fists to stop their involuntary infuriated trembling. "You think I don't understand the difficulties of my situation?"

"Well, of course, you understand some—"

"You have no idea what I'm going through, Dr. Irwin," Julian interrupted. His muscles quivered with the desire to hurl the man physically from the room. "Your medical presence may be desired by my mother, but I for one do not think so highly of your powers. Condescending to me, in that case, is not your wisest course. You stay, Doctor, because for the moment I think it best to placate Lady Northcliffe. In the meantime I suggest you tread carefully."

Irwin drew himself up and stared at the earl. "I have only your recovery in mind, my lord, if you would but listen to my—"

"You may go now," Julian said, driving his fist down onto the table and leaning forward onto it. His voice dropped ominously. "And don't come back until I summon you."

The doctor closed his mouth and took another

step backward, his eyes slitted resentfully. "Yes, well . . ." He motioned toward the cup and teapot. "I'll have the maid come collect the cup . . . later."

"Much."

Irwin coughed again. "Yes, well . . ."

Julian nodded. "Yes, well." He laid a hand out, palm up, toward the door. "Good day, Doctor."

"Good day," the doctor replied, then turned on his heel and stalked from the room.

Julian sank back into his seat, staring at the closed door. *Idiot*, he thought. *Pompous imbecile.* He clenched his right hand into a fist over the arm of the chair. That he should entrust such an arrogant, patronizing blockhead with his life, his future, his—his sanity . . .

After all . . . it's not quite sane *to forget one's entire life. Not quite sane. Not quite sane.* He looked at the cup on his desk; the steam had diminished to a trickle. He glanced at the register, at the columns of numbers, the headings, the notes in the margins, all in his own distinct, slashing hand. Notes he barely understood now. *To forget one's entire life . . . one's entire life . . .*

He wanted it back, he thought with such longing his throat closed. He was sick with wanting it back . . . his entire life.

Without further thought he lifted the teacup and downed the vile mixture in three swallows. Wincing at the flavor, he slammed the empty cup back down on the desk and glared at it.

There, he thought. *There.*

* * *

Julian leaned back in the chair, letting his eyes drift shut. He'd been working so long he couldn't decipher the numbers in the ledger anymore. Though he found what he'd thought were several large sums of money extracted for no apparent reason, he could not concentrate long enough to figure out where they might have gone. Even his eyelids felt swollen, closing over hot, gritty orbs that no longer focused properly.

The moment they were closed, however, the vision came to him, flickering with the dim oil lanterns along the rough-hewn walls. The room rocked around him as if he were in the belly of a ship, but he could not open his eyes. He turned his head—and saw his father.

He knew it was his father—his kind face and faded gray eyes filled with concern as he looked back at his son.

"You'll make it back, son," Julian heard his father's voice say, gravelly and deep. "You'll make it back, son."

Sitting at the desk, Julian felt his limbs tremble with the force of some vile energy. He raised his hands to his temples and clutched his head. His lungs felt thick, his throat too narrow. He forced his eyes open and stared, unseeing, at the desk in front of him, inhaling slowly, deeply.

"Something for the missus," another voice said, and the vision in his mind's eye coalesced.

Thin and pale, with a slender mustache, the man who'd spoken in his mind had a pointed smile and a shimmering, curved blade. His voice was familiar, the Cockney accent a fake.

With the impossible slowness of a dream, Julian looked down to see his father's hand spread awkwardly onto a solid block of wood. His third finger was extended, the others bent painfully under his palm while a big, beefy hand held it steady. His father's ring gleamed gold in the lamplight, shooting starlike reflections off the metal to hurt Julian's eyes, blinding him.

A burly, unkempt man held his father's hand to the block, one meaty fist curled in his father's collar at the back of his neck. His companion, similarly large and dense, held a pistol pointed at Julian's heart.

"Something for the missus," Julian heard again, and his pulse accelerated, his heart threatening to burst with the exertion.

Then the blade swung downward, cutting through the air so swiftly it seemed to whistle. It hit the wood with a *chunk*. The finger on his father's left hand rolled sideways, separated from the muscles and brain that ruled it. An inhuman cry arose from his father and Julian surged to his feet.

"Restrain him!" the thin-faced man shrieked, his Cockney accent gone.

Large arms circled Julian's chest from behind.

The man with the pistol bound his father's hand with a dirty white rag, then let him drop back against the wall, his eyes glazed, nearing unconsciousness.

"You will die for this." Julian's own words, but his voice was unrecognizable. Rage billowed through his chest.

The thin-faced man plucked a handkerchief from

his pocket, picked up the finger that still wore the ring and wrapped it tightly. "No," he said calmly. "*You* shall die, my friend," he said with that sly, pointed smile. "And I shall become very rich."

"No!" Julian howled, fury burgeoning within him. He broke free of the arms that bound him and stumbled forward. Something crashed into his thighs and he opened his eyes.

The library reeled around him and he clutched the desk to keep from toppling onto the floor. He gasped over the gauzy thickness in his chest. In his mind he saw the flickering lamps against the mildewed plank walls. He saw the block of charred wood upon which his father's hand had lain, upon which his fingers, all but the one that wore the ring—the gold, glittering ring—had jerked outward with the impact of the blade.

Around him the library lay unnaturally quiet. Julian returned to the scene of home sluggishly, the crash of the waves against the hull and the wail of pain receding in his mind with infinite torpor. His eyes took in the lamps on the desk, which did not flicker. They were in fact unlit. Light streaming in the windows made his eyes jerk away, but the couches and chairs around the hearth on which he focused instead loomed real in its illumination.

But this scene was not real, he thought illogically. The scene that was real existed in his head, playing out horrid scene after horrid scene again and again. He closed his eyes to catch a glimpse of the ring, now surreal in its brightness, gleaming like a star fallen from the heavens. The ring . . .

He opened his eyes and yanked open the drawer

in front of him. The press. He pushed through the contents of the drawer recklessly until his fingers knocked into the heavy metal object. The gold sealing-wax press.

He pulled it from the drawer and turned it upward, his breath frozen in his chest. Engraved deeply in the gold were the letters *JPC*. Julian Pembroke Coletun. Just like the ring. The same pattern, the same curling letters in heavy polished gold. Only the initials on that ring stood for Jonathan Pellham Coletun. His father. His father's ring. No wonder the gold press had caused him unease that first day he'd picked it up. Someone had murdered his father. And it had not been himself.

He slumped back in the chair and raised quaking hands to untie the cravat at his throat. The damn thing was too tight. He couldn't breathe. He tore the material away, buttons popping off in all directions, then dropped his head in his hands, inhaling deeply. He wanted to cry out with the pain throbbing through his temples, with the memory that surged in his mind like the turbulent sea, but he dared not.

Someone had murdered his father.

He remembered the bark ricocheting off the tree behind him as he and Lord Greer had sat talking, and the memory took him by surprise.

And someone had tried to murder *him*.

He closed his eyes, felt tears sting behind his lashes. He clenched his teeth to quell the unbearable rage mushrooming within him and inhaled again as deeply as he could.

"Thank God, son," he heard clearly, unexpectedly, and knew his father's voice. "Thank God, son." The words echoed in his head, mocking the tragedy he had just relived.

Julian sucked in another breath, drawing his brows together as hard as he could and pressing his lips closed to keep the howl of violence and fear from escaping. But there was something more now . . . there was sadness. Intense, vulnerable, and irrevocable sadness. For he remembered not just his father, not just the face and the eyes and the hand of the man who'd raised him; but the respect, the love and the loss. The hideous, unbearable loss.

Light exploded behind his eyelids with a sharp, shooting pain. He squeezed his head between his hands and laid his elbows on the desk in front of him. Pain screeched through his brain, streaking from his eyes to the base of his skull and back again.

His muscles twitched and trembled, in the grip of something outside of his body, not under the control of his mind. His elbows knocked against the desk with the violent shivering that encompassed him.

Tea, he thought. The tea . . .

He opened his eyes and stared straight at the door. His hands lay flat on the desk before him, writhing and quaking with the tremors that shook his body.

Dr. Irwin had given him that wretched tea. What had he said? Something about its soothing properties . . . about pacifying his nerves . . . it was supposed to help him remember, he thought.

He stood and lurched around the desk. His knees

quivered. Dizziness assailed him. He pulled in another breath. He had to find someone, tell them that his father was murdered.

He had to find the doctor, collar him and demand to know what the devil was in that tea. He stumbled across the room, grabbed the doorknob and staggered into the hall.

Pulver spun from the railing where he polished the newel post. He took a step toward Julian and stopped. "My lord," he said, "can I help you?"

"The doctor," Julian said. His voice grated across his throbbing, tortured mind. Dimly he recognized the need to appear normal. If he were judged ill, or out of his wits, he would be dispatched and his opportunity to discover what the doctor had done to him would be lost. Indeed, he might be put under the doctor's care and *all* would be lost. With great effort he tried again. "Where can I find the doctor?"

"Upstairs," Pulver said. "He was conferring with your mother not half an hour ago."

Julian strode toward the stairs, grasping the newel post and feeling the polish slip between his fingers. The hallway seemed to pitch slightly under his feet. He held tightly to the railing, not knowing if he staggered up the stairs or if he managed to ascend normally. All he knew was that he felt Pulver's eyes upon him until he reached the top and moved out of view.

Somehow Julian made it to his mother's room. At the thick, carved door he stopped and leaned his head on its surface. He needed control. He needed to find out what the doctor had done to him and make him stop this wretched, evil distortion that gripped his brain.

Julian knocked upon the door, and heard nothing from inside. He closed his eyes and pictured the governess, her eyes determined and her jaw set.

He needed to find the doctor, he told himself. Something was terribly wrong with him. He turned the knob and pushed open the door to his mother's bedroom, the hinges creaking softly in the dead silent air. He found himself in her sitting room. The curtains were drawn and the bloodred walls seemed to undulate in the light of a dying fire.

He looked around himself; everything looked so very far away. He took two steps, then three, into the room. She was not there, he noted slowly, and neither was the doctor. He drew in a deep breath and held on to the mantelpiece for balance. Good God, he thought in sudden panic, how would he ever make it out of this room? And where would he go?

Miss Travers, he thought again. He should find Miss Travers. But what could she do? No, he must get to Lord Greer. Lord Greer knew about the investigation into the shipwreck. Lord Greer had been there when someone had fired at him. Lord Greer would believe the possibility of foul play.

He pushed himself off the mantel and the room spun around him. He stumbled drunkenly, lunging for one of the chairs and missing, scattering what seemed to be dozens of figurines from a low table beside it. They crashed to the ground, the pieces jumping as they hit, glimmering in his bruised and unfocused sight like a million tiny diamonds, like the shooting sparks of light off the ring on his father's severed finger.

He rolled away from the fragments and tried to push himself upward. The ground rocked beneath him. He was on the ship. He heard the crash of the waves. He had to get to his father before the storm washed them both out to sea.

He forced his eyes open and focused on the door. The door through which he'd just come. He was *not* on the ship. No, it was his mother's sitting room. The fact that he'd confused them terrified him.

Something for the missus, the voice cackled, and the lamps flickered against the dark, sooty walls. He thought the face belonging to the voice was the doctor's. He could even see the monocle gleaming in the flickering lamplight of the ship's hold.

The room rocked and he rolled with it, knowing it was the breakers from the coming storm that threw them about. The bastards couldn't hold them if the storm proved fierce, he thought. They'd need every man on deck, lowering the sails and battening the hatches to withstand the approaching squall.

The flickering lanterns dimmed further as Julian felt the energy leave his limbs, vaporizing like a spirit exposed to sudden daylight.

Thank God, son. He heard his father chuckle, and Julian relaxed. His arms let his body go and his head hit the glass-strewn carpet.

Thank God, son, his father said, and Julian felt relief wash over him. *I thought you were going to marry that Miranda woman.*

The world went black.

Chapter Fourteen

Julian awoke to the creak of hinges. He raised his head slowly, the effort as strenuous as if he lifted a bell from the church tower, and looked toward the door. He had to blink several times before Miss Travers's face came into focus, peering cautiously into the room but not catching sight of him on the floor near the hearth.

He pushed himself up. Glass crackled beneath his palms but he felt no pain and wondered how long he'd lain there. He was in his mother's sitting room—what had he been doing? He sat up straight, brushing the bits of glass from his hands, and recalled a sense of urgency. But his mind did not seem to connect and he could not remember his purpose.

The governess gave a cry and rushed toward him. He turned his head and looked at her through narrowed, unfocused eyes.

"What's happened?" she asked, kneeling beside him. She took his arm to help him up. "I heard a crash. Are you all right?"

She smelled of flowers, he thought. Her touch

was light yet firm. He tried to rise, but had to lean heavily on her arm to do so. He could tell she struggled under the weight.

"Miss Travers," he said, shaking his head to clear it. But the fog would not disperse; it swirled in his head, lightening for brief moments, then returning, circling his thoughts like a flock of birds.

"I'm here. Come, sit here. Let me get you a blanket, you're trembling."

She tried to lead him toward a chair but he stopped. The confusion mocked him, made him powerless; he felt foolish.

"No," he said. The word emerged as a growl and reverberated painfully in his head.

He must not sit down, he thought. Something had to be done. He had to get somewhere, to someone. Something dreadful was happening. He rubbed his forehead with one hand. If he could just pull the gauze from his brain and think clearly . . .

The governess still clutched his arm and he shifted his weight from her. He could at least stand on his own. *Show no weakness,* he thought. *Show no weakness. No one must know.*

He tried to move away from her, but his step was jerky. He gritted his teeth and searched his mind for the source of this bewilderment, flexing his hand into a fist and releasing it several times in a row. The motion inexplicably gave him back a small feeling of control.

Her hands gripped the tense, corded muscle of his arm beneath the fabric of his jacket. "Is it your head?" she asked. "Did someone hit you?" She looked about the glass-strewn floor.

Had someone hit him? he wondered vaguely.

"What time is it?" he asked.

"I beg your pardon?"

"The time, Miss Travers." It was important, though he was not sure why. He laid his hand over his eyes and bit back a groan.

She glanced at the mantel clock. "It's not yet noon."

He lowered his hand and bent his head back, face directed to the ceiling though he did not open his eyes. "Exactly, please."

"Ten minutes before," she said.

He felt her anxious gaze on his face. "Ten minutes before noon," he repeated. "Ten minutes before noon."

"Let me call the doctor," she said quietly. "You're not well."

He winced. The doctor. No, not the doctor. Yes, he countered, shaking his head. He'd been looking for the doctor. But he did not want to see the doctor. God in heaven, he was losing his mind.

Noon, twelve o'clock, Cuff was due. They were to go over the tenant roster and the—the yield. Yes, the harvest . . . what—what—how much. He struggled for the exact task, then gave up.

He said, "Cuff'll be here soon." Had he been anxious to see Cuff?

"Perhaps he should help you to your room. Julian, do you feel ill?"

He shook his head.

She squeezed his arm again. "Please tell me, Julian. Please tell me what has happened." Her voice shook.

Perhaps it was some manifestation of his condition, he thought. Perhaps he was going crazy not remembering anything. But he knew there was something urgent he needed to do. Could his brain have had some sort of seizure? Perhaps she should call the doctor, pompous fool that he was.

But he had seen the doctor. . . .

"The tea," he said vaguely, rubbing his forehead again and squinting his eyes open.

"Tea?" she repeated. "Shall I ring for some tea? It's early yet but I'm sure—"

He laughed then, hard and harsh, battling his disorientation. He didn't *want* tea; he'd just *had* tea. Yes, he'd just had tea. . . .

"Irwin," he said suddenly, remembering, "gave me some tea. Made me sick, I think. Irwin did." He lowered his eyes to the floor, to the broken fragments of the figurines. Half a face stared up at him, a china blue eye on a face fractured from forehead to neck. He closed his eyes and saw Miss Travers's face in place of the piece of china. Her head on the floor, her hair spread loose around her. A spray of purple flowers lay next to her. And she smiled, a lovely, tranquil smile.

"Did you fall?"

Her voice brought him back. He turned to look at her, seeing the concern in her eyes, feeling her hands knead his arm though he no longer needed the support. "Please, come sit," she said.

The fog cleared for an instant. "I was thinking . . ." he began. "I had something to do. Something urgent."

This time he let her lead him to the chair. She sat

beside him on the arm and did not relinquish her hold upon him.

"Miss Travers," he said, picturing her again with her hair spread loose around her face and the spray of purple flowers by her head.

"Yes?"

"I believe I was coming to find you."

Her eyes lit and color flooded her cheeks. "Me?" The word was barely a whisper.

She was beautiful, he thought suddenly. How had he not noticed that before? Or had he?

He stood abruptly, swayed on his feet, then turned and pulled her up beside him.

She gripped his forearms and he leaned into her, his head swimming, the fog whirlpooling, the spinning room dodging his best effort to control it.

Her hands on his arms were stable and warm. She was an anchor, the only sure thing in the absurdly revolving room. He took hold of her upper arms and they stood there, locked on to each other, while the world circled them.

"It's all right," she murmured, and he desperately wanted to believe her. "Everything will be all right, Julian. Do not distress yourself. Please don't push yourself any more."

He closed his eyes and lowered his head to hers until their foreheads touched. Her breath brushed his chin.

"There's something . . ." he began.

"Yes," she whispered.

They stood quietly a moment longer. The room slowed, then righted itself.

"Miss Travers," he said, reaffirming her presence.

He lifted his head and gazed down at her.

Deep, dark-lashed eyes stared back up at him. He had the sudden urge to take her head in his hands and kiss her, kiss her until passion ruled his blood and this dizzy, disoriented, world-crashing fog was banished from his system.

He thought of the night before. No, two nights ago. She'd given herself to him. Sought him out and brought him into her. He had a sudden, clear memory of the moment he'd entered her.

"Tell me the truth," he said.

She nodded, slowly, as if mesmerized.

"You and Monroe—"

She expelled a quick breath and looked away.

He stopped, watching color mottle her neck and cheeks.

"No," she said emphatically.

He drew back a fraction. "No, what?"

She glared up at him and her grip tightened on his arms. "You were going to ask if Monroe and I— had relations. We have not. We do not. No."

He loosened his grip on her arms and let go. She did not release his.

His head swam. He took a deep breath. "How did you know what I was going to ask?"

She pressed her lips together. "Because they've all asked it. They're all asking it still. It isn't true. You, Julian, must know the truth. After what— what we've shared. You must know, somewhere inside of you, that I wouldn't lie—I would never lie to you."

A sardonic smile crept onto his lips. "It's my belief . . ." he began; then the words followed one after the other as if memorized, "the one who claims never to lie, breaks his word at the moment he expresses the conviction."

She shot him a startled look, then, unexpectedly, smiled. "Yes," she said weakly. "It was your father's belief as well."

He drew back. She let go of his arms and he walked slowly to the mantel. His head was clearing. The throbbing eased. He rubbed a hand at his temple.

She denied a relationship with Monroe, he deliberated, struggling to order his thoughts and return to the plan he'd had when he came to this room. Yet she acknowledged that everyone thought they had one. And she'd already demonstrated she was willing to give herself away.

"Why does everyone ask you about Monroe?" he asked, turning.

"I don't know."

He scoffed; it resounded in his head. "Come, now. There has to be a reason. Tell me, Miss Travers. You promised you would tell the truth."

She seethed at him a moment, then said in a rush, "Because he wishes it." She threw a hand out with the statement and averted her eyes.

"He wishes it," Julian repeated. "He wishes to have a liaison with you. And you don't?"

"No," she said fervently, looking back at him. "How can you think such a thing? After . . . after what happened," she finished in a whisper.

She took a step toward him and he stiffened.

Monroe wanted this girl, he remembered slowly. But she wanted one brother and not the other. She wanted Julian. Attempts at murder circled through his mind; the shot in the woods, Cuff's silent indictment of Monroe.

He took an involuntary step backward. This girl, this pretty, passionate, meaningless girl could be behind the whole episode.

He rubbed a hand over his face and turned back to the mantel.

"What is it?" Miss Travers asked, her voice holding a frantic note. "Tell me! Why did you look at me so?"

"You," he said, "and Monroe."

"No!" She charged up behind him and grabbed his arm, spinning him to face her.

His fingers caught on a vase as he turned, toppling it. He reached for it, catching it by its base as it rolled off the edge of the mantel, but something dropped from its depths.

A ping, loud in the room, sounded on the brick hearth. A flash of gold caught his eye, then bounced underneath the chair. He closed his eyes—saw the dark, sooty walls of the ship's hold—and opened them immediately. The red walls and thick, drawn drapes of the sitting room greeted his sight. He expelled a long breath.

Miss Travers bent and picked up the thing, turning it in her fingers with a strange expression on her face. Julian glanced away from her to the object in her hands and felt his stomach plummet to his feet.

Thick, gold, shining—

"What is it?" he demanded.

She opened her mouth, then snapped it shut as he grabbed the thing from her fingers.

Clumsily, he righted it in his hand and stared at the engraving on the heavy gold ring. *JPC* Swirling, interconnected initials etched deeply in the solid, heavy metal under the family crest.

The image seemed to echo in his head, growing larger as he stared. "What is it?" he repeated, stupidly.

"It—it looks like—it's a signet ring."

He looked up at her. She was white, paper thin and fragile.

"*Whose* is it?" He kept his gaze pinned to her face, as if the expressions there held the key to all the turmoil in his soul. His heart thundered and adrenaline flooded his veins.

"It must be your father's."

The answer rang in his chest like a gong. "My father's," he said derisively. He was breathing hard, as if he'd just run up the stairs. His mind no longer felt fogged but he trembled with the truth of what he held. "But he wore this, did he not? Did you ever know him to take it off?"

"No." Her voice was but a whisper. Her fingers toyed with a ribbon at her throat.

"Did no one else have a ring like this? Could this belong to anyone else?"

She didn't answer at once and he glared at her. "Answer me!"

She jerked her head toward him. "You had one."

He inhaled swiftly and turned the ring over in his hand. The thought that he should try it on burned in his brain, but he didn't. He could not force his hands to perform the task.

"Do you think," he asked her then, his voice radiating pent-up agitation, "that this ring could be mine?" He flicked his eyes up to hers, squeezing the ring into his palm and releasing, squeezing and releasing.

She shook her head, her eyes on his, afraid. Of what? What did she have to be afraid of?

"Why not?" he demanded. "What is it, Miss Travers? Why do you look so afraid?"

"I'm not afraid," she answered. "That is, I am afraid for you."

He clutched the ring hard in his hand, felt the edges bore into his skin. "Afraid for me? Why? What do you know, Miss Travers? For weeks now every time we've talked you've acted strangely, alluded to things, approached me and backed off. Even the other night, in the kitchen, you would not talk. What is it, Miss Travers? What is it you won't tell me?"

Her eyes grew large and she backed away from him a step. "Nothing!" she cried. He could see from where he stood that she trembled.

He lurched away from the mantel and grabbed her by the wrist, pulling her toward him, their faces inches apart. "Tell me," he demanded. He knew he must look like a madman, but he had to discover the truth. "You know something, dammit, I can see it in your eyes. Now tell me."

They stood close together for a long moment, their breathing rapid and evenly matched. Julian's blood thundered in his ears and his eyes probed her face, from the downy soft hair at her hairline to her trembling lower lip.

"I can't," she whispered, lowering her eyes, but not attempting to get away. "It would not—help you."

He stared at her lower lip, at its full, expressive shape. She was hiding something; she was too agitated for him to believe she was not.

"Why wouldn't it help me?" he asked. Her body close to his radiated warmth. He could feel her tremors as if they were his own and watched her lips part with the intention to tell a lie. He knew it, because he saw her so clearly. . . . because he knew her so well.

Without thinking, he covered her lips with his own, a hard kiss, demanding. He felt her breath in his mouth and the twitch of her hand in reaction where he still held her wrist.

He pulled his face back, but did not move away. Their breath mingled and she held perfectly still.

"You have something to say to me," he said, his voice a low, quelling caress. She trembled beneath his grip and he pulled her tighter. He turned his head and kissed the side of her face, close to her ear. "Something to tell me." He kissed her lightly just below the lobe and felt her shiver.

He'd loosened his grip on her arm to the point that she could easily pull away. But she did not.

She breathed shallow and fast, rippling the hair at his temple as she leaned her head back. He opened his mouth and sucked lightly at the skin below her ear. She sighed. Her hand rose and grasped his coat beneath his elbow, pulling ever so slightly.

"You'll give me this," he murmured. He moved his hand to her waist, then took another light bite at her neck. "And yet . . ."

She quivered all over. He pulled her closer, running the hand holding the ring up her back, squeezing their other clasped hands between their bodies, his grip caressing now rather than holding her captive.

"Julian," she whispered.

He shifted and his mouth covered hers. She opened to him instantly and they dove together into a kiss that moved with passion, a kiss that was practiced and sure.

She leaned into him, her mouth opened, her tongue searched, her hand rose from between their bodies to circle his neck, pulling him closer, deeper, further into her.

His body awoke to the memory of the night in the kitchen. His hand at her back clutched the ring and used two fingers to grab the base of her neck. He broke free of the kiss, trailing his lips down her neck, telling himself with each taste of her skin that he needed to stop, with each arch of her body that he should pull himself away, with each gasp of her pleasure that he had to get from her the information she withheld.

He let his left hand caress her breast, his fingers gripping her rib cage and his thumb teasing the crest of her breast through her gown.

"Why will you give me this," he began, "give me yourself, again and again . . ."

She inhaled sharply as his fingers lightly pinched the hardened nipple.

"And yet hold back what I ask for," he insisted.

She tried to draw back but he held her close. His hand at the base of her neck pushed her into his shoulder and his lips found her neck once again.

He tasted her skin, this time slightly harder, and she gasped. "Tell me," he said, covering her breast fully with his other hand. It was heavy and full in his palm. Desire pushed upward through his loins.

"Tell me," he growled into her neck. "Miss Travers, you have something to tell me."

She froze in his arms. He kissed her again, where her collarbone met her shoulder.

The action seemed to jerk her to life.

"I don't," she said, breaking away from him. She looked shaken and guilty and passionate all at once.

His body throbbed with need of her. He could have taken her, he thought. She'd have let him take her again, he was sure of it. And he wanted to, Lord God, how he wanted to. But she wouldn't help him.

"Please," she said, her eyes beseeching.

"You beg me," he said, hunger shifting insensibly to ire. "You beg me, Miss Travers, and yet it is I who need something from you. Why won't you help me?"

She seemed to struggle with the question. Her hesitation infuriated him. What in God's name did she want?

"Tell me!" he shouted, flinging his hand out to sweep the unlit lamp from the table. It tumbled to the carpeted floor, spraying oil as it went, but not shattering.

Her eyes widened in panic. "Julian, I implore you," she cried, hands clasped under her chin. Her hair was dislodged from its bun and trailed down her cheek to her neck. "Calm yourself. I don't—I won't—there is *nothing* I can tell you. You have to keep calm."

He stared at her where she stopped several paces away. "Please," she said, her voice breaking and her eyes brimming with tears, "do not do this. Do not search further. The answers will come to you in time. They must. But you cannot force them. Please, do not force them."

"Look at you," he said, his voice quaking with wrath. "Giving yourself to me. You'd have surrendered everything, again. Anything I wanted." He prowled close, relishing in his anger her stunned and frightened expression. "But you won't tell me what you know. You'll sleep with me. But you won't help me. What does that make you, Miss Travers?"

Her lips parted and she went white. "Don't do this," she said mindlessly, her eyes glazed. "Please don't do this."

"Why not? What don't you want me to remember?"

She laughed, a breathy, hopeless sound, and looked away from him, her shoulders drooping.

"You're protecting someone," he said slowly, an idea forming in his head.

Her eyes whipped back to his. "Yes, you! I'm protecting you!"

He laughed cynically. "If you wanted to protect

me, you would help me. But instead you keep your silence."

The hinges creaked and the door swung open. Miss Travers spun toward it. Julian turned his head to see his mother standing in the doorway.

"What are you doing here? What's going on?" Her beady eyes focused on Miss Travers, then bounced from her to Julian. She looked startled.

Julian slipped his hand into his pocket and dropped the ring. It fell heavily to the bottom.

"Ah—n-nothing," the governess stammered. Every inch of her testified to what they'd been doing. Even the shoulder of her gown was askew, showing the thin strand of ribbon she wore around her neck.

"What have you told him?" Lady Northcliffe asked, her face going crimson with indignation. "What have you said to him?"

Julian stared at the woman, then shifted his eyes from one to the other of them, his stomach clenching convulsively. They *were* keeping something from him. Both of them together.

Miss Travers gawked at his mother with guilty terror. "I've said nothing. We—we were simply talking."

Lady Northcliffe looked from her to Julian and studied his face. Her tone changed instantly, placating him. She smiled a gruesome smile. "What did she tell you, Julian? You know of course that she's a liar. We've only just discovered it this morning, but you mustn't pay her any mind. Monroe can tell you." She began to look slightly anxious. "Yes, we shall call Monroe and he will tell you the truth of the matter—"

"I have told him nothing," Miss Travers insisted, drilling the older woman with her glare. "Lady Northcliffe, I have told him nothing. You must believe me. I would not spread that—that lie that you accused me of earlier. I gave you my word and I would not do it."

"Your *word*," Lady Northcliffe scoffed, stepping further into the room, inspecting the premises like a suspicious constable. "As if that meant anything at all. Which is exactly my point, Julian. She'll say anything to get her way. Scheming, manipulative little baggage." She came to the broken figurines and stopped, raising her head to Julian. "What on earth's happened here?"

"What are you talking about?" Julian said.

"Right here, this broken glass," she said shrilly. "My nymph! My dancing nymph!"

Julian grabbed her by the wrist. "No, what are you talking about? What are you afraid she would have told me?"

He could tell by the look on her face that he'd blundered, a stupid, overanxious misstep. She knew now that the governess had in fact told him nothing. She knew now to hold her tongue.

Cursing himself, he dropped her arm.

"Where's the doctor?" he demanded. His limbs felt heavy with fatigue.

"Irwin? Why, he's gone to town," she replied, looking relieved. "I just ordered the carriage for him. He needed medical supplies, he said. He should be back by supper."

"Send him to me the moment he returns," Julian said. Without another look at either of them he strode from the room.

Chapter Fifteen

Julian descended the stairs in a rage, blackness encroaching on the edges of his sight. His head throbbed and his limbs shook. He felt as if he stood upon the precipice of a great black void determined to swallow him up.

Miss Travers's duplicity fanned the embers of his wrath into a raging fire. It was now more than obvious she kept something from him—she and his silly, overbearing stepmother. Between them they knew something about him, something important, or they would not be so anxious to keep it to themselves. Why?

Why? Why? Why? He was so sick of the question he could hardly see.

He reached the bottom of the steps and swiped at a marble bust of Caesar tucked into a wall alcove. The head went flying, bouncing heavily on the marble floor. A portion of the laurel headdress shot off and skittered across the hall. But the chip wasn't enough—Julian wanted more, he wanted to shatter something, take something whole and ruin it.

He looked around at the elaborate embellishments adorning the hall, thinking they all belonged to him, each and every one. Ancient swords, shields and helmets had probably hung on the wall since kingdom come, busts of men long dead stood like sentinels on pedestals, ornately carved chairs waited for suitably awed visitors, and the long, filigreed oak railing edged one side of the stairs.

He wanted to tear it all down, tear the whole house apart. It was his, after all, he thought hatefully. He owned it, every last twig and dust mote. If they were so determined to keep his life from him he would destroy it. Then they could see what it was like to lose something, though they could never understand what it was like to lose everything.

Everything, he thought, everything that mattered. These things didn't matter, and yet they thought he should be contented with this. This and no more.

His hands shook as he grabbed one of the bobbin-turned chairs. He hurled it to the floor and felt his muscles jump with adrenaline. Two of its legs cracked to a drunken angle as it slid to a corner.

The brief sight of his own hands swinging a plank of wood flickered in his mind. He'd killed that man. He closed his eyes, saw his hands take up the board . . . his hands, he thought, his hands that bore no signet ring.

He opened his eyes and pressed his teeth together so tightly the throbbing in his head extended to his jaw. He strode past the chair and picked up a metal globe. Turning, he sent it crashing toward one of the great leaded windows near the front door. It glanced off the sill and rolled jauntily back to him, ready for more.

He retrieved it, ready to throw it back through the window, when Pulver rushed into the hall.

"My lord! What has happened?" he asked, panic and worry in his fastidious face. He surveyed the article-strewn hall in horror.

Julian turned to him slowly, the globe still raised in his hand, and eyed him with unconcealed malevolence.

"Someone has broken in and wrecked the place," he stated, tossing the globe a little in his hand.

Pulver looked at him in surprise. "Good lord," he breathed. "Which way did he go? Who was it? Did you know him, my lord?"

Julian's lips curled and he laughed. "Did I know him?" he repeated. Rage once again darkened the corners of his sight and he turned, throwing his body into the act of heaving the globe across the room to the window.

This time it struck dead center. Glass shattered around the lead paning and showered to the ground in a symphony of sound. The globe itself bent with the impact, and one protruding band of brass caught on the lead windowpane. The globe settled there, bouncing in the cold breeze that blew through the hall.

"No," Julian said, icy calm. "I didn't know him." He turned back to the butler and drilled him with a challenging eye. "Perhaps you can find someone else who might identify the madman."

Pulver looked confused, and not a little afraid. After a moment of consternation, he bowed. "Very good, sir," he muttered and backed out of the hall.

Julian laughed, relishing the crazy sound as it bounced off the marble walls and surrounded him with lunacy. It was, indeed, the sound a madman would make. He turned around and around the room, his eyes scanning the festival of objects.

Very good, sir. Pulver's words echoed in his head, and Julian's blood boiled in his veins. They'd been that way since he'd returned, all of them, agreeably going along with his confusion, humoring the mad lord who did not even know himself, yet telling him nothing. They were happy in their ignorance of him, safe and secure, never knowing the torment Julian fought, the danger he spared them daily, hourly. . . .

For if they knew what his few memories gave to him—visions of murder and bloodshed, spurring feelings of insensible rage—they would not be so sanguine. He was capable of violence they could not imagine.

He pulled a ceremonial sword from the wall. The muscles in his back sang with the familiar weight of it. So, he thought, I fence. Another thing they'd never told him. He swung the sword with both arms toward the newel post. The blade whistled through the air. With the weight of his body behind it, the weapon thudded deeply into the thick, carved wood. The impact resonated up his arms and into his shoulders. He had to pull hard to extract it.

He himself had been the worst of them, he thought viciously. Spending his time watching and waiting—for what? For memory to descend like some guardian angel? For the blackness to recede and the rage to be vanquished like a fog by the burning sun?

Yes, he thought, swinging. The sword plunged into the seat of another chair, mate to the first. The wood split down the center and the chair collapsed in on itself. The blade rang against the marble floor. He lifted it again, swung at the pedestal next to the splintered chair. The base split in two. The bust upon it seemed to hover in shock a split second before it dropped to the floor, hitting just the right spot and shattering. He turned, and turned again, swinging the sword at whatever item stood before him. Heads rolled, wood split, fabric rent, glass shattered—nothing was spared. The blade knew no foe too great.

Finally, he stood still in the center of the hall, fractured artifacts strewn about him like leaves from an autumn tree. He breathed heavily from the exertion, closed his eyes and listened to the silence of the house. They cowered, he thought, hiding from his insanity as if they hadn't wished for it . . . as if they hadn't caused it.

He opened his eyes. His jaw clenched and un-clenched rhythmically. He hefted the sword to his shoulder and strolled along the wall. Another bust caught his eye—Brutus, he hoped—and he swung the heavy blade at its throat. The head rocked off its base, broken cleanly away at the neck.

Satisfaction swept him and he turned triumphantly as the front door opened.

"What the devil is going on?" Lord Greer's voice boomed through the carnage.

At the same time quick, light footsteps descended the staircase, slowing as the bearer took in the broken remnants of the hall.

Julian directed the point of the blade to the floor and leaned upon it.

"Good morning," he said. His muscles ached pleasantly and his head no longer throbbed.

He glanced up the staircase and saw the governess flanked by Pulver halfway down the steps.

Here was something interesting, he thought. Pulver, in his panic had retrieved the governess. Not his stepmother. Not Monroe. Not any of the burly field hands capable of restraining him. Simply the governess.

He cocked his head at them. "Have you something to add to our earlier conversation, Miss Travers?"

She stared down at him. His midnight hair was wild, his eyes brilliant as icicles in a noonday sun.

"Well?" he asked, mocking.

His gaze darted back up the stairs behind her and she turned her head swiftly. Lady Northcliffe peered out from behind the curtain to the gallery. Collie must choose her words carefully.

"Stay away, Lady Northcliffe," Julian called derisively. "He's on the rampage. Run, call your precious doctor." His lips curled into a sneer with the words.

Lady Northcliffe skittered off, most likely to do his bidding. Or perhaps simply to choose another, less obvious location from which to listen.

"Why did you do this?" Collie asked, hoping ridiculously for some sane, reasonable answer. Surely, despite its appearance, this scene wasn't one of madness, but frustration. "What do you want? How can I help you?"

"What do I want?" He laughed.

Collie shuddered with the sound. Lady Northcliffe could return with the doctor and they might constrain him—perhaps take him off to an asylum.

"You ask how you can help me, Miss Travers, and yet you do all in your power to confound me," he said. "You're more than anxious to offer diversions, but when I ask you simple questions you stammer and shake and tell me exactly nothing." He took several steps toward her. "Information, Miss Travers. I want to know what it is you won't tell me. What everyone won't tell me. But it seems I am to be given everything"—he lifted an insinuating brow—"but information."

"*I've* got some information for you, boy," Lord Greer said impatiently from the door. "If you're sane enough to absorb it." He glanced around the floor. "Which I doubt."

"Lord Greer—" Collie began.

Julian spun and pointed the sword at Lord Greer. "You," he said imperiously, "speak."

Lord Greer harrumphed. Julian was nowhere near enough to be a threat, but his facetiousness appeared to irritate the man. "I have here the ship's manifest."

"The ship's manifest," Julian repeated.

"The *Persephone,* the ship you were taking to Italy, that somehow ended up on a course for France."

Julian lowered the sword. Collie thought she saw his body shudder as he did so. Sweat dampened the back of his white shirt from his exertions, and the hair at his collar curled with it.

"What did we carry?" he asked. His cuffs were undone and the full sleeves fell back as he lifted the blade to his shoulder again, showing sinewy forearms.

"Nothing. The ship was empty."

She watched his chest rise and fall with his breathing. "We sought to fill it," he said. "Brandy . . ."

Lord Greer's mouth curved. "No doubt. Someone did, anyway. But there are a couple of other items that will be of interest to you here."

"And you wish to inform me of these things?" Julian asked suspiciously.

Lord Greer's bushy brows drew together. "Of course."

"Lord Greer," Collie said quickly. "Did your daughter not tell you? In speaking with the doctor . . . that is, I'm not sure . . ." She trailed off as Julian turned toward her, his eyes frigid.

"Not sure of what, Miss Travers?" he demanded. "That I should be told anything? Why do you strive to torture me this way?"

She clasped her hands together. Oh God, she thought, shaking her head. Something was wrong, she thought for the hundredth time since finding him in Lady Northcliffe's room. Something was terribly wrong. "I do not seek to torture you."

"No? I can think of no other reason for you to withhold vital facts that could help me. That is unless," he added, "you have something to fear from my memory. But let me tell you, Miss Travers, you have a great deal to fear as it is, because I know now what I only suspected before."

Collie felt desperation flood her heart. The more she tried to save him, the farther away from her he got. And the only means she had of reaching him were those that could damage him forever.

But now there was something worse, a suspicion far more dangerous than even the threat of madness. The person who sought to kill him was in this house. The person who'd attempted to take his life had left that ring in Lady Northcliffe's sitting room.

She stood on the stairs awash in indecision. What was right? She had no idea. Should she go to him and enlist his help, risking madness; or keep her silence while his brain healed by itself, risking death?

But as her eyes slid from Julian's and took in the wreckage on the marble floor, she found her decision had already been made. His actions proved he was far closer to madness than he might be to peril, for at this point her suspicions were just that: speculation. Her misgivings were so extraordinary and distressing she should not even speak them aloud, let alone risk Julian's health by telling him. Yet, if they were correct . . .

"Well?" Julian asked. "Have you nothing to say?"

She pressed her lips together and shook her head.

"Nothing to deny?" he asked, mocking her with his smile.

She swallowed, the look on his face tearing the

already weak foundation of hope from beneath her. "You hate me now," she whispered.

"Hate you?" He laughed, shaking his head. "What does it matter whether I hate you, Miss Travers? What does any of it matter?" He laughed again without a trace of humor. "That's what you don't understand," he added, his face bitter. "You and my mother and Irwin and Monroe . . . you don't understand that none of it matters. Not really. Not if it can be taken and kept from you as easily as this."

Silence gripped the hall for a long moment. Julian's gaze rested on her coldly, with an inward-looking aspect. "How much worse can it get?" he asked, with a slow curl of his lips. "I am tormented by old women and governesses."

Lord Greer, apparently growing weary of the theatrics, cleared his throat and stepped through the doorway. Plucking the globe from the window frame, he approached through the rubbish, trying not to step on anything but managing to kick part of Caesar's head across the floor toward Collie. She looked down at it. His ear, she noted blankly.

He stopped in front of Julian and dropped the globe at his feet. "Do you want to hear what I've got?"

Julian looked curiously unconcerned, Collie noticed, then thought, He's given up.

"Of course," he replied, his voice cool.

"My lord," she called, as the two men turned toward the library.

Julian stopped and turned around. Lord Greer took several more steps, then turned as well.

"Yes?" Julian asked.

"Might I—do you mind if I come with you?" Perhaps, she thought, if Lord Greer could be trusted . . . if she could hear what Lord Greer had discovered, if she could see the effect it had on Julian, she could more readily assess whether he could handle what she had to say. Lord Greer might even be able to help. "I'll be silent, I promise. I'll sit off to the side. Just—please."

Julian eyed her speculatively. "I can't imagine why I should grant this request."

She shook her head. "And I don't know what to tell you. Except—that you can trust me, my lord." She gripped her hands together and brought them to her heart. "You can trust me."

Julian stared at her a long time. "Miss Travers," he said finally. "At the risk of being impertinent to a lady, I must confess that I don't trust you."

She exhaled and dropped her hands.

He shrugged a shoulder and added, "I don't trust anyone." Then he turned to Lord Greer and inclined his head toward the library, making a sweeping motion toward the door with the sword. "Shall we?"

Lord Greer shook his head, his expression weary, and entered the library.

Julian tossed an ironic look over his shoulder at Collie. "Don't worry," he said, one side of his mouth lifting. "I don't trust him either."

He entered the room and closed the door firmly behind him.

Collie waited in the front hall for what seemed like forever. Long after the servants finished cleaning up the wreckage, Collie sat on the step and waited, going over and over in her head the benefits of confiding in Julian, against the danger of jarring his fragile memory.

The servants' voices echoed dimly from points beyond, the clock ticked loudly, and yet she heard nothing from behind the library doors. With each swing of the pendulum she wavered—tell Julian? No, the risk was too great. But if she were correct? It was too awful, too outlandish, to be true.

She tried to reason it out again. Lord North-cliffe's ring had been hidden in Lady Northcliffe's room, but Collie remembered so clearly the day Julian and Lord Northcliffe had left. In taking leave of his wife, Lord Northcliffe had patted her on the shoulder and in doing so had somehow caught the ring in the fringe of her shawl. It was a tiny moment, one she was sure no one else would have noticed, yet she remembered at the time she'd wished it had been more entangled, for freeing it had taken only moments at the end of which Julian had been obliged to depart with him, leaving her behind with a swift, private smile that made her heart swell and her legs weak.

Collie clasped her hands under her chin, resting her elbows on her knees. She closed her eyes.

For Lord Northcliffe's ring to now be here, in this house, when Lord Northcliffe's body had never been recovered, something ungodly must have occurred. She did not even know what to think, except that someone had to have seen Lord Northcliffe between the time he left and the time he died. And that someone had to have procured the ring and sent it back to Northcliffe Manor.

She thought of Monroe, of his shifty, independent ways. She knew unequivocally he lied about one thing, so he was capable of lying about others. But what reason would he have for retreiving the ring? And how would he have done it?

She shifted one hand to finger the length of ribbon at her neck. Beneath her dress, at the other end of the ribbon between her breasts, hung the proof that the ring Julian had found was Lord Northcliffe's.

The front door opened and Dr. Irwin appeared. Collie stood as Pulver floated out of the sitting room to take the man's hat, gloves and cane. As the doctor plucked at the fingers of his gloves, Collie pensively handled the ribbon at her collarbone.

She did not want to tell him of Julian's discovery of the ring. Nor did she intend to tell him of the scene Julian had made after he'd been with her upstairs. But perhaps she could ask him what harm it might do to restore something to Julian that had belonged to him. After all, he'd already heard her confession of the truth, though she'd had to recant it immediately.

Discovering that she possessed Julian's signet would tell him nothing more than he already knew. . . .

"The first thing I've got to tell you is that there's a witness," Lord Greer said promptly, as he seated himself near the fire.

"A witness?" Julian repeated.

"Yes. Another survivor of the wreck. Mostly likely

the only other survivor, from his description."

"Another survivor and they've only just found him now?" Julian lifted a brow and leaned against the mantel. "Don't tell me he's got amnesia as well."

Lord Greer laughed. "No, thank God, though I imagine he wishes he did. They found him several weeks ago and have been holding him in London. The tale he had to tell was something fantastic and no one was quite sure whether to believe him or not, especially in view of the fact that you have said nothing of the matter. But portions of his story seem to jibe with what the authorities already knew about the journey."

"That they were heading for France for contraband brandy," Julian said. "I imagine that implicates me, and my father, somehow."

"Of course not. Don't be ridiculous. Everyone knew you weren't going to France, but to Italy. That the ship was found on a course for France was the first clue that something was amiss, prompting the investigation." Lord Greer produced a pair of reading glasses and perched them on his face, peering through them at a letter he unfolded. "This letter, from the man heading the investigation . . . one Lord Crandall, a baronet . . . hm, let's see. Ah, here it is. He says, 'Lavolet'—that's the witness—'Lavolet swears that the man in question was holding two prisoners destined for the gallows at Versailles. They were agents, he swears again, who had double-crossed the emperor and were neither seen nor heard from beyond the moment they boarded the ship.'" He peeked over his glasses at Julian, who stood frozen at the mantel.

"But here's the strangest part," he resumed. " 'Lavolet's been most cooperative through most of the questioning, hoping, I am sure, to secure himself an easier sentence after being discovered in the act of smuggling, by providing the necessary information to the investigation. He even admits their mission. However, he solemnly avows, and this with an expression most sincere, that he never knew the vessel to be carrying any Lord Northcliffe or his son, nor did he see anyone who fit the description of having noble blood.' "

Lord Greer removed the glasses and looked at Julian as if he might be able to shed some light on the subject.

Prisoners, Julian thought, picturing the dark, scarred walls and the flickering light. Remembering the burly arms that held him as his father's hand was mutilated.

He dropped his hand in his pocket and fingered the heavy gold ring that lay at the bottom. It warmed quickly to his touch. *Prisoners.*

"Who was 'the man in question'?" he asked.

"Eh?" Lord Greer said. "What man in question?"

"At the beginning of the excerpt, he said something about 'regarding the man in question,' or some such thing."

"Oh, yes." Lord Greer put his glasses back on and scanned the previous pages. "Oh, yes, I'd forgotten. The man who held the prisoners was an Englishman . . . name of . . . Gilpin. He was in question because they knew who he was. He was wanted on other charges, I believe, but they weren't sure what he was doing mixed up in an apparent smuggling operation. In any case, he got what was coming to him because they found his body washed up not far from Lyme as well and his head'd been smashed in. Seems someone gave him a bit of his own medicine."

Julian stared at Lord Greer. *His head'd been smashed in.* Did Lord Greer suspect he was guilty of murder? No, his expression was unconcerned with the man's fate.

"Gilpin." Julian rolled the name around in his mind. He pictured the face of the man who wrapped his father's finger in a handkerchief. Narrow, pointed, with a little, affected mustache. *Something for the missus.*

He pictured the face of the man on the deck, the face of the man who'd lain unconscious as Julian had hammered the life from his body, crushing his hateful face with every last ounce of his strength. That man had killed his father, as surely as if he'd shot him. Weary from loss of blood, his hand continuing to bleed long after the handkerchief had grown soaked, his father had not been able to withstand the punishing wind and waves that had pummeled the deck. His father had not been able to hold on, Julian remembered, and Julian had not been able to get to him.

Clenching his teeth together until he thought they might crack, he regulated his breathing to concentrate on Lord Greer.

"Yes, ah, Irving Gilpin, I think. Spent years in petty criminal endeavors, apparently. Always being brought up on charges of one thing or another, but was bailed out by relatives most of the time. Seems he was from a respectable family."

Something for the missus, Julian thought again, the voice striking a familiar note in his fragmented memory, but the essence of the familiarity hung just out of reach, an elusive shadow of remembrance. His accent had not been real, Julian knew, for he could recall the man slipping more than once. He'd been masking a diction far more cultured than the dockside Cockney he'd affected.

Lord Greer ran his finger down a page of the letter. "Not Irving, Irwin. Sorry."

Julian's head jerked fractionally. "*Irwin* Gilpin?"

"Hm . . . yes. Irwin," Lord Greer confirmed, then looked up. "Something the matter?"

Julian shook his head slowly. "No. Nothing."

Chapter Sixteen

"Dr. Irwin," Collie said, descending the last few stairs. "Might I speak with you a moment?"

The doctor eyed her through his monocle. "Ah, Miss Travers. I've just posted the letter to my sister. I've no doubt we'll hear from her within the week and then your immediate future shall be assured."

Collie stumbled in her determination. A week, she thought. They would receive the reply from his sister and she would be sent off, away from Julian, away from any chance of knowing how he was, of ensuring that he remembered her. And if he regained his memory without her, would they tell him where she was? Or were they all too anxious for him to marry Miranda?

"Th-thank you," she said. She swallowed. "But there is something else I wished to ask you."

He stopped before her in the hall and looked down from what suddenly seemed to her an imposing height. "Yes, what is it? Are you feeling ill again?"

"No. Thank you, no, that's not it." She glanced behind her. "If you wouldn't mind, sir. A little privacy . . ." She gestured toward the back parlor.

"My dear," he said, not unkindly, "it is a truth most people overlook, that in trying to hide something, oftentimes the least obvious place is out in the open."

Collie thought immediately of the ring she and Julian had found. In a vase, on the mantelpiece.

"If you and I were to closet ourselves away, more people would wonder what we were about than if you and I were to chat quietly here in the hall," he continued. He swung his hand, palm up, out beside him. "There is no one nearby. You may speak quite freely. What is it, Miss Travers?"

She closed her arms over her waist and raised one hand to feel the ribbon at her neck. "It—it's a question about Lord Northcliffe's condition. You see, I—have something of his, something he asked about, and I just wondered what harm it might do to, um, give it back to him."

Irwin's brows descended, their fluted ends curving upward and making him look somewhat demonic, though of course that was ridiculous. He was the only one who'd been kind to her since her condition had been discovered. The only one who had treated her as if she still merited some respect.

"You have something of his? I'm afraid I don't understand, Miss Travers. Everything here belongs to him. If you have something in your possession I suggest you put it back where it belongs, unobtrusively, where he might run across it in the natural course of things."

Collie lowered her head and stared at the swirls of darkness in the marble floor. Like clouds in the sky, or constellations, she thought. "This item is more—personal."

"Personal? What sort of personal item? Where did you get this thing?"

She hesitated.

The doctor reached out to pat her arm, his hand soft and plump. "My dear, the more personal the item, the more likely it is to startle him, to tax his memory in a sudden, unsatisfactory way. I really must know the nature of the item before I can answer your question."

He smelled of cologne, she noticed. Just faintly. Smelling the scent made her feel as if their conversation were unsuitably intimate. She took a step back and his hand dropped.

Her eyes flashed up to his face. Once again, his brows drew together, descending over his eyes in that ominous way, though his expression was otherwise impassive. "I—I just . . . It's something he gave to me, so it really isn't anything he's missing. I just thought it might answer a question he had, something that disturbed him in his mind. Perhaps it would quiet him, in a way." *And make him trust me*, she wanted to add, but she knew how she must present this to the doctor. She didn't want to deceive Dr. Irwin, for then she would not get an accurate answer to her question. But at the same time, she did not want to inflame him overmuch. He seemed a bit . . . excitable when it came to Julian's condition.

"I'm afraid I must know what it is," he persisted.

Again, she paused. But, she asked herself, if the doctor was being cautious, should not she be too?

Why should the doctor be more careful than is warranted? She imagined giving Julian the ring and knowing that it was she who'd driven him past the point of saving. She had a bleak, horrible vision of him swinging that enormous sword again, shattering everything in his path. She imagined guards bursting through the door to subdue him, trussing him up and carrying him off to the asylum.

Her mother had been in the asylum once, before Collie got this job and hired Nurse Frederick. Julian would never recover there, she knew with a dreadful certainty. He would only make himself crazier with anger and frustration, though the attendants would conquer even that, with time.

Slowly, with great trepidation, she pulled the ribbon from her neck. She could feel the warm metal rise up, past her breasts to the edge of her gown. She looked up at the doctor. His eyes were intent on the length of ribbon in her hand. Finally, the ring came free and she laid it in her other palm.

"What is that?" he asked.

"His signet ring," she said quietly, in almost a whisper. "He—he gave it to me before he left. He asked about it this morning."

The doctor's face became immobile and he lifted his eyes from the solid gold piece to her anxious gaze. "Am I to understand that Lord Northcliffe *gave* you this ring? This valuable, significant heirloom?"

She looked at him warily, suddenly unable to read his face. "Well, he was not Lord Northcliffe at the time. But yes. He gave it to me."

"Why?" he demanded.

She started at the tone. "I—I believe I made that reason clear in Lady Northcliffe's room."

"What you made clear, Miss Travers," the doctor said, enunciating each word carefully, "is that Lord Northcliffe was *not* responsible for your current condition. I believe I asked you that specifically."

She closed her fingers around the ring and moved to put it back inside her gown. But he stopped her.

"Wait. Let me see it again."

She opened her fingers.

"No. Take it from around your neck. I wish to examine it."

Instinctively, her hand closed around the object again. "I'd rather not."

For a moment she thought he might grab her hand and yank the ring from her. But the doctor sighed and pulled a handkerchief from his pocket. He took the monocle from his eye and began to rub it with the cloth. Collie saw the indentations of flesh around his eye where the lens had been and noted he looked much younger without it. He also looked much less intimidating.

"I don't mean to be difficult," she said. "But I suppose I'm rather—superstitious about taking it off. You see, I've had it here, close to my heart, since he left. It's been something of a talisman, I believe, because he came back. He came back when all hope was lost."

She stopped as the doctor replaced the monocle, unsure why she'd rambled on so. She felt the need to explain herself to someone, to make someone understand her situation, and the doctor was the most likely one to do that. He, of all of them, had nothing to lose by believing her. And he, as a member of her class, might not feel such abhorrence for the good fortune that had made Julian Coletun, Earl of Northcliffe, fall in love with her.

"Am I to understand," the doctor began again, "that you now reassert your claim that Lord Northcliffe is the father of your child?"

Collie glanced behind him at the statement. She resisted the urge to turn and search the hall behind her to make sure no one was listening.

"I thought perhaps you understood," Collie said. "Upstairs I was . . . pressured. Mr. Dorland . . . I don't know why, I suppose he wished his mother to believe something other than that Julian is responsible."

"But you agreed. When I asked you, you said the child was not Lord Northcliffe's."

She lowered her eyes. Why did he not understand? She thought he'd seen through her in that encounter, that he understood she'd do all in her power to stay in the house. But now he seemed obtuse. Perhaps he shared Lady Northcliffe's horror of the circumstance. Perhaps he believed she was unscrupulously trying to better herself.

She clutched the ring in both hands. "I went along with Mr. Dorland to prevent further argument. I felt it useless to belabor the point when she would obviously never believe me, nor help me to ensure that Julian knows the truth . . . *before* he makes further commitment to Miranda." She could not help the bitter way the other woman's name came from her lips.

The doctor examined her slowly. "Lady Greer," he started, then stopped, thinking. "Lady Greer has said that Lord Northcliffe asked her to marry him. And indeed, he has gone along with that since his return, not fighting it as he has . . . other things. Do you call Lady Greer a liar, Miss Travers?"

She glanced up at him through her lashes, then lowered her eyes again, reluctant for him to see the insubordination she knew blossomed there. He was as determined as the rest of them, it seemed, that Julian marry Miranda. "No, of course not. She's mistaken. Perhaps."

"Perhaps *you're* mistaken," the doctor said gently. "A betrothal to a beautiful woman of his own station makes far more sense than marriage to a governess of no consequence. And Lord Northcliffe strikes me, even in his injured state, as a man of politic good sense. A man with the consciousness of nobility."

Collie felt her face flame with indignation. "Nevertheless, he promised marriage to me. Otherwise I would never—never have—" She broke off. The doctor did not need to know the details. It was obvious he was not going to help her, was not, it seemed, even going to answer her question. She should leave before the interview went any further and she said something in anger she might regret.

"You would never have given yourself to him?" The doctor smiled. "How many men have made similar promises for just such a reason, I cannot even begin to count. I've seen hundreds of girls in your predicament, Miss Travers. Hundreds. All with the same story. 'He promised marriage.' 'I'd never have done this if he hadn't promised to make an honest woman of me.' 'He was only waiting until he got his parents' approval.' I don't need to tell you what became of those women. It's a tale older than time, Miss Travers."

Collie swallowed over the outrage lodged in her throat and met his eyes. "It wasn't like that," she said heatedly. "He didn't lie. Surely you can see, he is not the type to lie." She pulled her fisted hand out to the end of the length of ribbon. "And I have this. He gave it to secure the promise. How else would I have gotten this?" she demanded.

He looked at her obliquely, the light winking off the lens at his eye. "I don't know," he said quietly. Too quietly. "Why don't you tell me?"

Her eyes widened and she took a step backward. "What are you insinuating? Are you saying you think I *stole* his ring?"

"You said he asked about it. Did he wonder where it had gone?"

She looked at him incredulously. "He doesn't remember!"

"What made him think of it?"

Her breath caught in her throat. She couldn't possibly tell the doctor about the other ring. She did not yet know what it meant to have found it in Lady Northcliffe's room but she could never betray the family to an outsider. Especially one who proved to be so quixotic. No, Julian must know. Julian must figure out the implications. But he could not do that without proof that it wasn't his ring in his mother's room, and without proof that he could trust her to help him.

She pressed the ring between her palms. "I don't know what made him think of it—"

"Why did he ask *you* about it?"

She shrugged and averted her eyes. "I don't know. We happened to be together when it occurred to him—"

"Do you mean he *remembered* the ring? He noticed its absence?"

"Not precisely."

"Miss Travers, this could be important. What, precisely, did he say?"

She shook her head, wishing she'd never spoken to him. He would not help her, and even if he would she could never tell him the whole truth.

"I . . . I don't recall, precisely. He—he saw . . . something that prompted him to ask. But he was not reminded so much as curious. It was a logical question at the time, if he had a signet. Just please tell me, Doctor. Would it harm him to see it, do you think? Could it precipitate . . . something untoward, just to be told it was his?"

The doctor took a deep breath. "I don't know. It's too personal—"

"But it's really just another article of clothing," Collie reasoned. "And he was given all of those without a second thought. His box of cuff links and shirt studs; this could have been with those."

She wasn't sure why she tried to convince him. It just seemed so logical, she thought, to give him the ring. She wanted someone else to see the rationality of it so that she could be sure she wasn't wrong. But the doctor wouldn't see it; he was too wedded to his course of denying Julian every scrap of information available. A course Collie was becoming more and more convinced was wrong.

"I don't think it's a good idea. Not at this time," he said pensively. "But if you were to give the ring to me, just for a while, I could present it to him at what I think is an appropriate moment." He nodded, convinced. "Yes, give it to me and when he appears strong enough I will present it to him and gauge his reaction." He held out his hand expectantly.

Collie gripped the ring and stepped back. "No. You—you can call me when you think the time is right. I'll bring it."

"You'll bring it," he repeated. "And will you then be tempted to tell him your disgraceful lie?" He advanced toward her.

"It's *not* a lie—"

"This morning it was," he said. "How am I to believe you now when just hours ago you claimed the child was Mr. Dorland's?"

"But I was—surely you saw that—I was persuaded to lie, for Lady Northcliffe's sake. I was under duress—"

"Why would Mr. Dorland try to claim a child that was not his own?"

"I don't know! I don't understand him. But I'm telling the truth."

"Come, now, Miss Travers. Don't do this to yourself. Mr. Dorland is ready to give you a living, to care for you through your confinement, to help you after the child is born. Not many men would do that for their mistresses. Count yourself lucky. You will not have to find your own way in the world with a bastard child."

The doctor stepped close, made a quick grab for her and snagged his fingers in the ribbon as she jerked away.

"No!" She gasped as the ribbon broke and slid through her fingers.

The ring jerked from her hands and flew outward. She heard it hit the marble floor with a tiny chime of sound. It hit again and Collie's eyes darted toward the sound, but she could not see where it had gone. She thought she heard it skitter on the floor toward the library door. She stepped quickly after it, the doctor behind her. She started to sink to her knees, to run her fingers along the floor, when the library door opened and Julian stepped out.

Julian's eyes flicked from the doctor to Collie, off to his side on the floor. She straightened and stood sedately, her heart hammering.

"What's going on out here?" he asked.

"Julian," she started, out of breath, "there's something I wish—"

"Nothing, my lord," Dr. Irwin stated. His stentorian tone overwhelmed Collie's words. He shot her a hard, meaningful look. "We were having a mild disagreement. I'm terribly sorry for disturbing you."

"A disagreement?" Julian asked, with a lift of his brow. His gaze shifted to Collie. "What about?"

He looked tired, she thought, and was still disheveled from his earlier rampage. She thought she ought to tell him of the ring, now before she lost her chance, but she hesitated. She did not have the ring, for one thing, and the doctor would dispute her ever having it. But most important, Julian looked too weary. She was too afraid of what might become of him.

"Nothing," she said finally, her eyes darting to the floor in search of the ring. "I—nothing."

Julian's eyes followed hers.

Lord Greer appeared in the doorway behind him. "What's all the ruckus out here?"

Julian turned. "It seems the doctor and Miss Travers were arguing. About nothing."

The woman looked torn, Julian thought. Not secretive, or calculating, but afraid. His gaze flicked back to the doctor, who stood just a little too close to Miss Travers.

Irwin smiled, a chilling smile. "We shan't disturb you further," he said, taking Miss Travers's arm. "Please, go on with your meeting." He nodded to the man behind Julian. "Lord Greer."

The doctor started to turn, propelling Miss Travers with him. But the governess resisted. "No—I, I think it's important that we speak, Lord Northcliffe," she said, her eyes imploring.

"She is overwrought, my lord," the doctor said, turning back. "She hasn't been feeling well for a week now and has not gotten over her fainting spells. They tend to make her agitated and unwise in her actions. Isn't that right, Miss Travers?" He gave the governess a starched look that she stiffened under.

Julian's eyes fell to the doctor's grip on her arm.

"Perhaps if you were to let her speak freely, Irwin, we would get to the point that much quicker."

Miss Travers's eyes met his and she seemed to be barely breathing.

Irwin dropped her arm. "I merely meant to support her. She was unsteady moments ago."

Julian looked away from him. "Now, what is it, Miss Travers?"

Her glance shot from him to Lord Greer; then she lowered her eyes. "It—it can wait. Until you've finished your business."

"Are you sure?" Her expression unsettled him, as did the doctor's. "Lord Greer and I were almost finished, were we not?" He turned his head to Lord Greer, who shrugged.

"Almost," the older man said. "I was just going to add that the witness will be coming here, along with several emmissaries of the inquiry from London. They should arrive within the next couple of days."

"Here?" Julian asked. "What for?"

"Witness, my lord?" the doctor asked. "Witness to what, might I ask?"

Julian turned to the doctor. "No, Irwin, you may not."

Lord Greer chuckled behind him. "You might want to tell him, Northcliffe. Make sure the shock won't send you into some sort of destructive rage." He stepped out of the doorway and looked around the hall. Not a trace of the earlier chaos remained. "Hm. Fast work. Believe the place even looks better without all those heads around. Damn me if I didn't feel I was being watched every time I walked through the place. Pardon me, Miss Travers." At her questioning look he added, "For the language."

She expelled a breath on a slight laugh. "Oh. Quite all right." Her gaze descended again to the floor.

"I shall just take Miss Travers back to her room now," the doctor said, taking her arm again. "You both obviously have further business to discuss. You can call her when you're ready to speak with her, Lord Northcliffe."

"Fine," Julian said, keeping his eyes on Miss Travers. "I'll send for you when I'm finished."

She looked up and her gaze sparked a tender heat in his chest. "Thank you," she said.

The doctor turned her and they headed for the back hall. Julian watched them go, studying the back of the doctor's head. There was something in the way he walked, as if he were on the balls of his feet, that aroused Julian's hostility toward him.

The two disappeared down the back hall. Lord Greer turned behind him to head back into the room. Julian turned as well when his foot struck something and sent it shooting across the marble floor. A tiny metallic sound accompanied it across the bare floor. Julian's eyes caught on the gold as it came to rest, spinning like a top in the center of the hall.

Lord Greer turned back. "Drop your ring?" he asked.

Julian's neck stiffened, the sensation spreading from there down the muscles in his back. He walked slowly across the floor to the ring and looked down. His hand went to his pocket. He could feel the outline of the ring he'd found earlier through the fabric.

He closed his eyes. He pictured himself taking the ring from his finger. Memory? Or imagination? Over and over he watched himself take the ring from his finger. He had to work to get it over the knuckle. Then, the ring still warm from his wearing, he pressed it into a white palm, a feminine palm. He saw his own hand close the other's slim fingers over the ring, then rest atop their clasped hands.

He felt Lord Greer's eyes on his back. He bent and picked up the ring. It was cold. He turned it over in his hand, saw the crest, the swirled initials—*JPC*. Something churned in his gut.

Slowly, he reached into his pocket and pulled the other ring from it. Holding the two next to each other, he felt an overwhelming emotion swell in his chest. His eyes blurred. He found himself struggling for breath.

The ring in his right hand, the one he'd found in his mother's sitting room, was duller, the metal no longer quite round, as if it had been banged up through many years' wearing.

The ring in his left hand had a slightly newer cast to the engraving. The polished surface of the gold shimmered with a luster the other did not have.

He slid the left-hand ring onto his finger. It settled into place and warmed to his body immediately. The smooth weight of it felt right—more comfortable than his finger had been without it.

He looked at it on his hand. *I'll be back soon,* he imagined himself saying. *Don't worry.*

He looked at the other ring. *Something for the missus.*

Lord Greer was suddenly beside him. Julian hadn't even heard him approach.

"Is that your father's ring?" he asked.

Julian heard him as if from a great distance. A roaring in his head obliterated the finer points of sound and he found himself breathing hard.

"My boy," Lord Greer continued, his voice still remote. "Come sit down. Come back here and sit down."

Julian inhaled and felt his head swim. He closed his eyes and saw the blade descend, saw his father's finger roll simply to the side, disconnected. *Something for the missus.*

"Was my father ransomed?" he asked, his own voice disconnected, far off.

Lord Greer's hand touched his back; his other took Julian's arm. "Come sit down, Julian. For God's sake."

"Was he ransomed?" Julian demanded, turning fierce eyes on the older man.

"No, of course not."

"Would you even know? Would you have been consulted if he had been?" Julian pressed.

"Yes. I'm sure I would have been," Lord Greer said, his florid face concerned. "Son, your father died. In the wreck."

Julian shook his head. "No." He shook his head again, vehemently. His hand clenched around the ring. "No. My father was killed. His hand was mutilated, and his ring was sent back here. Here. What for? How would it have ended up here if he were not ransomed? If it was not offered as some sort of proof that they had him?"

Something for the missus. He ran a hand through his hair, felt the blood rushing through his veins. A sudden nausea rose in his stomach and he swallowed hard. "Jesus," he muttered. His head throbbed.

"How do you know this?" Lord Greer asked.

"I remember." The ship's cabin came back to him. The dark, scarred walls, the flickering light, the block of wood, his father's hand. "I remember," he said again, the memory familiar now. "*We* were the prisoners, my father and I." He felt the rope on his wrists. "We were held by Gilpin." The name spun off his lips and with it a crystal-clear memory of the man. Sharp, pointed features. A small, chilling smile. A thin mustache. The man dressed well, but he spoke with a falsely uneducated accent. "Gilpin," he repeated, "had every intention of killing us both, before the storm came. He was trying to get away . . . they lowered a boat . . . several men got in, but not Gilpin." He shook his head and laughed harshly. "No, I got to Gilpin before he got to the boat."

Lord Greer's hand tightened on Julian's arm. "Come into the library, son," he said gently.

Julian turned and focused on his face. The man's eyes were sad. "Do you believe me?" Julian asked.

Greer nodded slowly. "Yes." He took a deep breath. "Yes, I do. Come back to the library."

They turned and walked slowly across the empty hallway.

Chapter Seventeen

"Where did you find this?" Lord Greer held his father's signet, turning it in his thick fingers, studying the lettering, the shape, the scratches.

"My mother's sitting room. It was in a vase, on the mantle. I found it by accident when she was not in the room."

"Was anyone else with you?"

Light winked off the gold, hurting Julian's eyes. He turned away. "Miss Travers."

Julian felt rather than saw Lord Greer's eyes shift from the ring to him.

"Miss Travers," Lord Greer repeated. "Did she have anything to say about this ring's appearance?"

Julian tried to think back. He remembered kissing her, and his miserable idea of using seduction to gain information. How quickly those tables had turned. For though she'd trembled under his touch, it was he who had found himself struggling to keep his purpose in mind.

He ran a hand through his hair. "She said it was not mine."

Greer scoffed. "That would have been obvious,

with yours on your finger. What else did she say? Why was she there with you?"

"Mine *wasn't* on my finger," Julian said, more to himself than to Lord Greer. "I didn't have mine, and I didn't have it on the ship." He looked down at his hand. It looked right now, normal. Before, when he'd first been told who he was, even his hands had looked foreign to him. Now they looked familiar. The ring had been missing.

Lord Greer was silent a moment. "If you didn't have it on the ship, and you didn't have it when you came back, where on earth did it just come from?"

Julian turned to him. "I don't know. Irwin and Miss Travers were arguing. I suspect one of them had the ring and dropped it." Hadn't Miss Travers been staring at the ground when he'd emerged from the library? Hadn't her gaze returned again and again to the floor as he'd questioned them?

He pictured the slim white fingers closing over the ring. His own hand holding it there, in her hand. *I'll be back soon. Don't worry.*

The obvious burst upon him with blinding significance.

He'd given her the ring.

His eyes flew to Lord Greer's, and a thundering broke free in his chest. Why would he have given it to her? There was only one reason he could think of.

"Irwin and Miss Travers arguing over your ring?" Lord Greer puzzled. "What on earth for? And how would either of them have gotten it?"

"What do you know about Miss Travers?" Julian asked suddenly.

"Me? Know about Miss Travers?" Lord Greer scratched his ear. "I don't know. She came recommended by Bretton. Your father didn't need any more than that. Trusted Bretton implicitly. I'm not sure any other scrutiny was given her." He eyed Julian.

"But what do you know of her character?"

He shrugged. "Good character, as I recall. Didn't pay her much attention, really. She did a good job with Shelly, kept to herself a lot, kept out of the way of the household, for the most part. A good governess." He nodded. "Your father liked her quite well, I believe."

Thank God, son. Julian's father's words.

"What did *I* think of her?" Julian asked, knowing Lord Greer would not be able to give him the answer he sought but needing to ask anyway. He had no one else to turn to. "Did I seem to like her?"

Lord Greer's eyes narrowed. "Sure," he said carefully. "Everyone did, as far as that went. I think Monroe was the one smitten with her, though. At first anyway. Think she might have given him the mitten early on, however. He's been surly about things for a while now."

Monroe. Julian shook his head. The thought made him agitated, but it didn't ring with any truth. Not on that deep, awakening level where he recalled giving away his signet. The thought of Monroe and Miss Travers bothered him because of what he'd seen since he returned—the wink in the hallway, the conversation on the terrace. But deep down, it wasn't important.

"But this is absurd, Julian. Miss Travers is inconsequential. Most likely Irwin had your ring. You know how anxious he's been to keep things from you." Greer laughed. "Or maybe you don't. Miranda said he's sworn everyone to secrecy. Not supposed to upset you, you know." He lifted a shoulder. "I figured since I was never here when he gave his instructions I didn't have to pay attention. Never did believe in keeping things from people anyway. Does no damn good, in my opinion."

Julian felt something click into place. "Irwin swore everyone to secrecy?"

"God, yes. He and your mother've been militant about it. Scared Miranda out of her wits. She begged me not to tell you anything. I finally told her I wouldn't discuss it with her anymore. She thought you'd be heading for Bedlam or something, if you were told anything you couldn't figure out for yourself. Though I have to say, when I arrived here today I thought she might be right."

No wonder Miss Travers wouldn't tell him anything, he thought. It made perfect sense now. And the more insistent he was, the more determined she became. She thought he was losing his mind.

Julian said, "Miranda didn't seem to mind my being reminded of our engagement."

Greer's face flushed. "Well, no, of course not. She'd waited far too long for that to risk losing you over something ridiculous like amnesia, or whatever the devil it is. Not to mention that she was devastated when we'd thought you were dead. I suppose the relief overcame her cautious disposition, at the time."

317

Someone knocked on the door. Julian and Lord Greer looked at each other.

"Come in," Julian ordered.

The door opened and Cuff appeared. "My lord, I'm sorry to be so late in coming, but the most extraordinary thing has happened. We've found Mr. Bafferty, sir. He's dead."

"I do not need your help in getting to my room," Collie said testily. "The main staircase would have been quicker. And besides, we need to find the ring." She tried to pull her arm free of the doctor's grasp but he only tightened his hold.

"No, first we're going to continue our talk, Miss Travers," he said. "You don't seem convinced that my proscribed course of action is the best, when it comes to Lord Northcliffe's affliction. And I've determined that we do indeed need to find someplace more private."

"I should like very much to hear your justification for what you've done, but as the ring is now lost I would prefer to find it before it's swept away. If you like, I'll go retrieve it and meet you afterward. The back parlor is generally neglected this time of day." She pulled harder at her arm, and his grip tightened more blatantly.

He jerked her forward. "No, I have another location in mind."

Collie stumbled in surprise. "If you please, sir," she snapped, yanking her arm loose at last. "You forget yourself. What in the world has gotten into you?"

He inclined his head slightly in apology, then gestured for her to continue. "I'm sorry. I'm afraid I'm just . . . anxious."

She eyed him. "Anxious about what?"

"I would like to tell you something, Miss Travers," the doctor said, evidently coming to some decision. "Something I've been contemplating for a while now, but we need absolute privacy. I think I know just the place. Will you come?"

"Does this have to do with Lord Northcliffe?" she asked.

He nodded wearily. "And Mr. Dorland's claim that your child is his."

Collie's chin lifted, but she was too aware of their public location to allow any conversation about her pregnancy here.

They moved through the back hall to the cellar door, where the doctor stopped. With a swift glance behind him, he opened the door.

She shot him a wary look. "The cellar? Surely there are places less . . . obvious. As you said, the more secretive we appear . . ."

He took hold of her arm again and urged her forward. "Doorways can be listened through, keyholes used as spyholes. Trust me, please. This will be safer." He pushed her toward the stairs. But something in his face made her stop.

"No," she protested, stepping back. "I won't go. You can say what you have to say right here."

Footsteps sounded on the hardwood floor of the dining room. "Quickly," he said in a hushed voice. He grabbed her wrist and preceded her down the stairs.

She followed, closing the door behind her. "What

is it? What do you have to say?" she hissed as they reached the dirt floor of the cellar. He was right about the secrecy, she thought. The stone walls seemed to absorb her voice into a bottomless well of silence.

He shook his head and pressed a finger to his lips. "They could still hear." He turned and passed through the open room of furnishings in which Collie had hidden the day Julian had gone hunting.

Nerves quivering with apprehension, she stood where she was at the bottom of the stairs, uncertain.

He turned back to her. "Miss Travers," he said, beckoning her forward. "Come."

"Where are you going? We can speak right here. I don't understand what you're doing."

He shook his head in frustration and came back toward her. He looked at her intently, taking her shoulders in his hands in a grip that was not tight so much as imperative. "I have some . . . suspicions," he said finally. "I've been reluctant to confide them to anyone since I haven't known whom to trust. But the object of my disquiet is such a one who might be lurking anywhere. Please follow me, Miss Travers."

She stared at him. "Monroe," she said quietly. "You suspect Monroe of something."

The doctor frowned and looked down at his feet, dropping his hands from her shoulders. "I'm afraid so. And he's so cunning, I do not trust him not to be watching me, watching all of us, for some sign that we've caught on to him. You know, of course, about his attempt on Lord Northcliffe's life."

Collie's eyes widened. "Are you speaking of . . ." Her glance flicked to the cellar door, through which Julian and Lord Greer had come from hunting. They'd been speaking of an attempt on Julian's life.

He nodded. "The shooting. He tried to kill Lord Northcliffe that day in the fog, but Mr. Bafferty foiled him. Quite unintentionally, of course."

"But how do you know it was Monroe?" she asked, leaning toward him.

He looked behind him, toward the door with the window in it. "Miss Travers, I'd really prefer to be less visible when we speak of this. You know as well as I do how clever Mr. Dorland is. Even now he could be listening to us. Come with me."

He turned and negotiated his way through the collection of objects. Against her better judgment, but unable to forgo hearing his suspicions, Collie followed him to the door to the canning room. He opened it and they went inside. The room was small, well swept, but musty.

Fresh jars of preserves lined one wall, with bags of potatoes, turnips, beets and other vegetables stacked along another. The third wall held jars and bottles covered with dust—foodstuffs unused from the year before—while the fourth had a low plank door, boarded tightly shut.

Collie knew the room beyond that door. It was the old wine cave dug into the side of the cellar wall. Julian had showed it to Shelly one day. Then he'd boarded it up because when they'd visited they'd seen that one side of the earthen wall had collapsed. The room was dangerous, Julian had said, and ready to collapse. Certainly not fit for little children's hiding places any longer.

The doctor closed the door to the canning room carefully behind them.

Collie turned to him. "How do you know this about Monroe? If you have proof you should go to Lord Northcliffe immediately."

He didn't answer her at once. He just studied her through his monocle and came slowly toward her.

Collie's pulse accelerated. "Doctor, Lord Northcliffe's life is in danger. You must do what you can to protect him. If you do not tell him of Monroe's treachery, I will."

"I have no proof," the doctor said, still looking at her with that curious intensity.

"Then how do you know it was Monroe?"

"I don't," he said. "I think it was you."

His words were so abrupt it took a moment for them to sink in. When they did, she laughed incredulously. "What?"

He reached into his pocket and pulled out a small silver pistol. She stared at it, the disbelieving smile frozen on her face.

"I think it was you, Miss Travers, and I have been charged with securing you down here until the authorities arrive from London." The doctor's hand was perfectly steady holding the gun.

"What?" This time it was an expulsion of breath more than a question.

"There is evidence that links you to the location. The fact that you had Lord Northcliffe's ring was the last piece in the puzzle."

She backed up, away from the gun and the malevolence in the doctor's face. "I told you, Julian gave me the ring. And I don't see how having it proves I tried to kill him." She laughed, a note of hysteria in the sound. "Of all the people in the world, I would be the last to want him dead."

The doctor kept the gun on her as he approached the low, boarded-up door. Reaching out, he pulled at one of the boards. Without much effort it came away in his hand. He leaned down, pulled at another that came off just as easily. They'd been loosened previously, she saw. The nails were bent and twisted as if wrenched with some sort of tool.

When he'd piled all the boards next to the door, the doctor kicked open the door.

Collie jumped at the sound and saw the door bounce inward. The doctor motioned with the gun. "Go on."

She stared at him stupidly. "You want me to go in there?"

He laughed. "Very good, Miss Travers. Yes, I want you to go in there."

"What are you going to do?" She imagined herself lying on the floor in the little room, a bullet hole in her head. She shuddered.

"I'm going to put you in there, reseal the door and hold you until the proper people come to take you away. You'll be arrested for attempted murder, Miss Travers."

She backed up without thinking. "You must be joking. You haven't any proof. You couldn't have. It's Monroe, of course. Just as you said before."

"Yes, of course." The doctor smiled. "We know it was Monroe. But he was not alone. He was working with his mistress. The woman who would claim to carry the heir to Northcliffe in her womb. Then the two of you would control the earldom until your bastard grew old enough to rule for you."

"You're not making any sense." Collie shook her head, though she dreaded that to some he might make a good deal of sense. With Monroe's lie, the story had a bizarre element of plausibility.

"Get inside, Miss Travers," the doctor said. "Tell it to the authorities when they arrive."

"You can't hold me here," she said, desperation making her voice shake. "I'm not under arrest. I've done nothing wrong. Why are you the one doing this? Why have you got a gun?"

"Lady Northcliffe has entrusted me with the welfare of her son. I am merely extending that charge beyond my medical abilities."

"But Julian isn't even her son! You're accusing *her* son, Monroe, of attempted murder. I can't believe she would be party to that."

The doctor smiled thinly. "Get inside," he said again.

"I'll scream. Lord Northcliffe is just upstairs. The servants . . . someone is bound to hear me."

"Scream to your heart's content, my dear," he said smoothly. "No one will hear you. Look around you; you're surrounded by stone. Now get inside. I'll make sure the police know whether or not you've cooperated." He gestured with the pistol toward the door.

Collie knew she had no choice. The man had a gun, and she was not going to be able to talk him out of his miscalculation of the truth.

She moved to the doorway and peered through. It was dark in the little room, and something told her Dr. Irwin would not be leaving the candle. She remembered the room had been empty but for the old wine shelves and that one wall that had collapsed in a heap of dank soil. She wondered about mice, then decided that if there were any, most likely they'd be in the room where the food was.

She ducked her head under the low door frame and clutched her arms together. Cold, clammy air touched her skin like skeletal fingers. The doctor followed her in with the candle. She glanced around herself. The walls were still lined by the old shelves with half-moon shapes cut into them, and the one wall was still crumbled. She thought perhaps it had disintegrated beyond what she had seen several months ago but she wasn't sure.

It was when she turned to the far corner that shock hit her. Coiled on the floor was a length of chain. One end was securely fastened to one of the beams holding what was left of the sagging ceiling, and the other end sported a manacle.

Collie felt her blood stop. She spun on the doctor. He smiled and inclined his head toward the chain.

"If you please, Miss Travers."

She didn't move.

"I assure you," the doctor said quietly, with calm self-assurance, "this gun is loaded. It would probably be months before anyone got around to looking in here for your body."

That his mind had run in the same direction as hers was chilling. But why would he kill her if he really held her for the authorities?

Because he wasn't holding her for the authorities, she realized with a rising, lucid dread. He had plans for her himself. He knew she wasn't conspiring with Monroe. *He* was probably conspiring with Monroe.

Her teeth began to chatter. She clenched them together. "What are you going to do with me?" she asked in a low voice.

"I've told you," he said and gestured again with the gun. "Go on. Lock that manacle on your right ankle."

She backed toward the corner slowly. If he was going to kill her, he wouldn't very well need to chain her, she thought. "How long before the police arrive?"

Dr. Irwin shrugged. "A day. A week. I'm not sure." He rubbed one hand along the arm holding the gun. "It's quite chilly down here, isn't it? I'll bring you some tea. Yes, that should warm you sufficiently. Some of my special, herbal tea."

Collie sat on the cold dirt floor and raised the hem of her dress. She picked up the manacle and fitted it around her ankle, closing it so that the ends met but did not connect. She dropped her dress back over the chain.

"Oh, Miss Travers," he said sadly. "I thought we had an understanding. I respected the trick you tried to play to win yourself a marriage. And I thought you respected my ingenuity in getting you down here. Now I see you think I am not quite as clever as you are." He pursed his lips and shook his head. "I *am* disappointed."

He strode toward her, flicked up her hem and

clicked the manacle together. Then, pocketing the pistol, he extracted a key from his waistcoat to lock it.

Sensing her only chance for escape, Collie kicked out with her foot and sent the doctor sprawling. But despite the fact that the manacle was unlocked, she could not get it unfastened. Before she could figure it out, the doctor was on his feet again.

He lunged for her, grabbing her arms. "You think that gun was the only thing keeping you down here?" he said with a growl. He shoved her back against the wall. Her breath left her in a whoosh. "You think you can outsmart me, Miss Travers? You think because you are a woman and can lure men into your bed that you can win against me?"

Collie pushed off the wall and struck him with both hands in the chest. He stumbled back a step. She kicked outward with her left foot, but missed her mark and struck him in the thigh.

Before she could regain her own balance, Irwin's fist connected with her cheek. She dropped to the floor. Blackness edged her vision. Her cheek immediately felt larger than the rest of her head. Her fingers dug into the dirt.

"I could break your neck right now," Irwin said. His voice was low, controlled and menacing. "I could fracture every bone in your body, naming them as I went. Your clavicle, your sternum . . ." With each part he took a step closer to her. ". . . your ribs, your femur, your tibia, your fibula . . . shall I go on, or have you got the idea?"

Collie raised her head and probed her cheek with shaking fingers.

The doctor knelt beside her. She flinched at his closeness, averting her face, and felt him lift the hem of her gown. Then she heard the metallic click of the lock being fastened on her leg. The iron was cold through her stocking.

"Where is Monroe?" Julian demanded, kneeling beside the couch where Bafferty's body lay. He'd been found in the woods behind the stables and moved to Cuff's cottage nearby.

"I don't know, sir," Cuff answered, wiping his brow with a handkerchief. "I haven't seen him since the morning."

"What about Lady Northcliffe?"

"Pulver said she's napping," Lord Greer said. "Do you want me to go tell her?"

Julian frowned. "Someone has to, but we don't need to do it immediately. She'll be upset; we should find the doctor first." The damned doctor who had more than a few questions to answer, Julian thought. Well, let him be of service first.

"What a god-awful mess," Lord Greer muttered. "I suppose it was natural causes. There's not a mark on the man."

"But look here," Cuff said, "where his neckcloth and shirt are all loosened. We found him that way. Didn't nobody touch him except to move him. Why do you suppose he'd be all askew like that?"

Julian fingered the edge of Bafferty's cotton shirt. The buttons were missing, as if he'd ripped them off in an effort to open his shirt. As if he couldn't breathe, Julian thought.

"Who saw Bafferty last?" he asked.

Cuff and Lord Greer looked at each other.

"Have someone ask around. Check with Cook first; see if he ate or drank anything—peculiar."

"I'll do it, sir," Cuff said, picking up his damp overcoat from the chair on which he'd thrown it.

"And find that damned doctor," Julian said, rising. "I want to see him first."

"Yes, sir." Cuff slid into his coat and left hurriedly out the door.

"What are you thinking?" Lord Greer asked, eyeing him.

Julian turned to him. "Irwin gave me some tea this morning. . . . God, was it only this morning?" He ran a hand through his hair. "I didn't drink it all—one small cup out of a whole pot—but about fifteen minutes after taking what I did of it I couldn't breathe. I started clawing at my own throat. I ripped at my clothing just like this—"

He broke off. Jesus, he thought. The doctor had taken Miss Travers off. To her room, supposedly. But now that he thought about it, Julian remembered seeing the doctor, his hand securely around Miss Travers's upper arm, leading her down the back hallway. *The back hallway.* When they'd been right next to the main staircase.

Julian swore. They'd been arguing over the ring and Irwin had taken Miss Travers off somewhere. Not to her room.

"What is it?" Greer demanded.

"Miss Travers," Julian said, grabbing up his own coat.

329

"She was with the doctor."

"That's right. But the doctor didn't take her to her room. The doctor," Julian ground out, "is going to kill her."

Chapter Eighteen

"What are you talking about?" Lord Greer demanded, lumbering after him as they charged from Cuff's cottage toward the main house. "Why would the doctor want to kill Miss Travers?"

Julian's long gait easily cleared an icy puddle. "I'm not sure. And I hope to God I'm wrong." He rubbed his temple, where vestiges of the tea-induced headache still lingered. "But I believe it has something to do with the fact that I gave Miss Travers my signet."

"Gave her your signet?" Lord Greer burst out, incredulous. "What the devil for?"

Julian stopped abruptly. Lord Greer came to a sudden stop behind him.

"Lord Greer," he said steadily, "I don't wish to offend you, but I think it's possible your daughter was not completely honest about our engagement."

Greer's face suffused with red and he puffed his chest outward in indignation. "What? You think Miranda lied? What a ghastly thing to say about a woman, any woman, let alone my daughter. What on earth are you about?"

The rain began, first splattering around them in fat, occasional drops, then growing smaller and more rapid.

"I'm not about anything," Julian snapped. "I've been trying to make sense of it all, the conflicting stories—my conflicting feelings—and my betrothal to her has never rung true. I've searched myself for some reason, some inkling that she and I—hell, I don't know. And now this."

"Now what? By Christ, boy, you've known her since she was born. She's not capable of a lie like that."

Julian shook his head. "That's just it, Lord Greer. I *haven't* known her since she was born. Not now. And I think I can see pretty clearly what she's trying to do. Think about it. No one knew about the betrothal until after I was believed dead. She mentioned it to no one, despite the fact that there was time after I left before the wreck."

"It was probably a secret—"

Julian held up a hand. "You yourself told me I didn't ask your permission first. And you admitted that it surprised you. You're also the one who told me Miranda and I had never courted." Julian turned toward the house and started walking again. Lord Greer took up beside him. "Why would we keep it a secret if it was what everyone wanted all along?"

"First of all, there wasn't a need for any courtship. Our families have been close since—"

"My mother was lost when asked what the date of the wedding was supposed to be, even though she'd supposedly been in on the planning. Monroe found the whole idea of the engagement amusing, which is never a good thing. Even Cuff told me I'd never shown the slightest interest in marrying Miranda before I left. Now Miss Travers pops up with my ring. Tell me, Lord Greer, if you can set aside your subjectivity, what do you make of all that?"

Greer panted beside him to keep up, his face drawn into a frown, his eyes looking inward. "I did say you hadn't courted, but like I said, there wasn't any need for that. And you were always such a cagey bastard; nobody ever knew what you were thinking. It made some sense, your asking her without giving a clue to it beforehand."

"So I never, at any time, gave you any indication that I might ask for Miranda's hand?"

Lord Greer's head shot up. "No. Nor did you ever give me any indication you meant to marry a damned governess." His mouth worked in anger, searching for words. "And now you're trying to tell me that you'd engage yourself to a penniless, unconnected woman and spurn my Miranda, a woman of blood, of lineage, of *beauty*, for chrissake. She's a *lady*, and a better match could hardly be found!"

"I don't dispute Miranda's claims to nobility, nor her charms, which I admit are considerable. I only dispute my proposal, which in light of what I've discovered today seems highly unlikely."

"The governess could have stolen that ring from you, did you ever think of that?"

They neared the house. The back door opened as they approached and Monroe stood in its frame.

Julian slowed for a second and drilled Lord Greer

with an unyielding eye. "I don't believe she stole it," he said quietly. "Because I remember giving it to her. And I can think of but one reason I would have done that."

Greer stopped and put his hand on Julian's arm. "But you don't remember the reason, do you?" he asked fiercely. "You're assuming the reason you gave it to her but you don't remember. You don't remember, for example, deciding that she deserved to become—or could even handle becoming—your countess."

Julian looked down at the hand on his arm and briefly closed his eyes. "You're right," he said carefully. "I don't remember deciding to marry her. I don't remember falling in love with her or promising her anything." He let the words hang in the chill air for several heartbeats before coming to a decision. Then he smiled slightly, sadly, at the man in front of him. "But I know how I feel now, Lord Greer." His voice was quiet and firm. "And I'm going to marry her."

Lord Greer's jaw clenched; Julian could see the muscles jump in his cheek. "Then you're a fool, boy. You're a damn fool."

"I'm sorry you feel that way." Julian turned and moved toward the door.

"Is he dead?" Monroe asked, his brows drawn together until a crease formed between them.

"Bafferty?" Julian asked.

Monroe nodded once.

"Yes."

"How?" Monroe's face was shuttered, a mask of impersonal curiosity.

Julian watched him closely. "We're not sure. Poison, maybe."

"Could have been natural causes," Lord Greer injected.

Monroe scoffed. "It wasn't natural causes."

Julian's eyes shot to Monroe's. "Why do you say that? And where is Miss Travers?"

For a second, Julian could have sworn Monroe looked startled. Then he raised a noncommittal brow and asked, "Why? Is she missing?"

"She went off with the doctor and I have reason to believe he might be dangerous."

"Christ," Monroe said on a breath. A long moment stretched between them in which Monroe did not elaborate. Julian watched calculations flit through his brother's eyes and resisted the urge to shake the truth from him.

"Well?" Julian asked.

Monroe looked down and shook his head.

Julian swore and shouldered past him through the door. "We've got to find her. You can help if you want."

Monroe turned as Lord Greer entered the hall and stopped Julian with his words. "I don't—I don't have any proof."

Julian turned. "Proof of what?"

Monroe pressed both hands back through his hair, looking more disconcerted than Julian had ever seen him. "I think Mother's in on it. I suspect . . . Jesus. But I didn't, I still don't know for sure."

Julian took a step toward him. "What are you talking about? Don't know what? Speak plainly, dammit."

ELAINE FOX

Monroe looked up at him, his eyes, usually so cunning, now filled with apprehension. "All right. I do know this: the doctor, who Mother brought here to 'help' you, is no doctor at all. Or at least, not under the name he's been using. No one in London has heard of a Dr. Irwin, and he was supposed to be a 'renowned specialist,' " he quoted sarcastically. "At least according to Mother. And himself."

"How do you know this?" Julian demanded.

"Because I had him checked out. I hired a man, an agent in London—"

"Why?" Julian pressed.

"Because I don't trust Mother!" he exploded, his face tortured. He scoffed and shook his head. "It started before you left for Italy. She was . . . strange. And she was corresponding with Bafferty often, more often than Father knew. As soon as you both left, though, her spirits rose dramatically. Bafferty showed up not two days later and they were inseparable. Even," he said slowly, "at night." His narrow gaze shifted to Lord Greer and lingered a moment before returning to Julian. "Then, just before we got word of your death, a man came. He was"—he shook his head and looked at the ground—"swarthy-looking. Not anyone who should have had business with the Countess of Northcliffe. Yet he did. And she saw him. And she was quite satisfied afterward."

"What did he want?"

"I don't know." He looked at Julian, his gaze hooded again.

"What do you *think* he wanted?"

"I really don't know," Monroe said heatedly. "But

336

when news of the wreck reached us, Mother was not surprised. I was with her. *I* was shocked. Bafferty was even shocked. But Mother was quiet. And she had the strangest look on her face. . . ."

Julian felt in his pocket for the ring and pulled it out. "Do you recognize this ring?"

Monroe's face went white. He held out a hand and Julian dropped the signet into it. Monroe turned it in his hands thoughtfully. "It's Father's," he said finally. He met Julian's gaze. "Where did you get it?"

"You don't know?" Julian asked.

Monroe's expression clouded. "What do you mean?" Then, as realization dawned, his face went slack.

"I think you know what I mean," Julian said quietly.

Monroe stared at him a long, long moment. Then, eyelids descending in that now familiar, enigmatic way, he laughed. "Oh, it's all very simple for you now, isn't it, Julian?" he said with such vehemence that Julian's muscles braced for an attack. "You come back here without memory, without knowledge of having ever done anything wrong yourself, and it all looks quite neat and simple to you. Well, I've got news for you, *brother*. Nothing is as simple as it appears."

"Then why don't you clear it up for me," Julian said, his low voice shaking with the effort of control.

Monroe's lips twisted into a grimace. "You've got me pegged, haven't you, Julian? You show up here to find us all virtual strangers, and yet you've figured out just what sort of degenerate I am. I've got to hand it to you, Jules, you really nailed this one. I'm no better than a drunkard, desperately jealous of you and your title, capable of any sort of despicable behavior." He lifted his hand in salute. "Irresponsible. Corrupt. Deadly." He took a long look at his stepbrother. "That's why I investigated the doctor. That's why I've been protecting your mistress, for pity's sake, at great personal risk to my own reputation." His sarcasm was bitter and unmistakable.

"What mistress?" Lord Greer demanded before Julian could get the words out.

Monroe's brow lifted and he glanced from Lord Greer to Julian. "Should I say? Well, what the hell. Miss Travers, of course. I'd have thought you'd have figured it out by now. While you were supposedly courting Lady Greer." He shot a look at Lord Greer and smirked. "According to legend, anyway. You were really satisfying yourself with the governess. And, oh, Julian," he said direly, "that can lead to the most unwanted sort of consequences. Particularly when the lady of the keep has other plans than your inheriting the castle."

Julian stared at him, stunned.

"That's right," Monroe said. "You and Miss Collette."

"Collette," Julian repeated. The name chimed in his head. Images flashed behind his eyes, a sun-dappled field, Miss Travers's laughing face, the spray of purple flowers by her head. They'd made love, that day in the field, before he left.

"But you've been so busy being the good son, the

heir, the master of the manor," Monroe continued bitterly, "and denying your attraction to her to whomever may have asked—and you'll remember I asked, brother—you've let her fall right into their hands."

Memories rocketed through Julian's head like shooting stars, spawning whole constellations of pictures, voices, events—blessed remembrance.

Collette, dancing toward him in the library in her white gown, her smile radiating joy and love. Collette, correcting Shelly's French, glancing slyly up at him with that seductive curve to her mouth. Collette, teasing him in French in the presence of his family that he really ought to listen to his mother and attend more parties so that he could meet women more suitable than the governess with whom to spend time.

But he hadn't wanted to spend his time anywhere else. It was she whom he wanted. Collette whom he looked upon with throbbing heart and fiery anticipation. She made him laugh, she made him think, she struck him dumb with desire.

He raised his hands to his head and pressed the heels of them to his temples. "Collette," he said again, his heart bursting with combined memories of the then and the now. What she'd gone through. What he'd put her through since he'd returned. He hadn't trusted her—hadn't remembered enough to take her back. How terrified she must have been.

How terrified she must be now.

He jerked his head up. "Where is she now? Jesus, the doctor—"

"I told you, I don't know," Monroe said coldly.

"Damn it," Julian exploded, grabbing Monroe by the coat and pushing him through the door and against the wall. "Where's your mother? Where's the doctor?"

Monroe glared back at him, anger oozing from every pore. "Where did you find this ring?"

"In Mother's room," Julian answered promptly. "In a vase. On the mantel. She had Father killed. Is that right?"

Monroe inhaled sharply through his nose, his nostrils flaring and his eyes narrowing. "Yes. I think so. But I have no proof."

"This ring." He grabbed Monroe's hand and yanked the ring from his fingers. "This ring was brought to her. As proof."

Something for the missus. Julian closed his eyes and stepped back, gripping his head again in his palms. *Something for the missus.* And the finger was wrapped and dropped into Gilpin's pocket. *Something for the missus.*

He remembered now, the whole dreadful plot. Gilpin had told them, just before he'd hacked off his father's finger. His stepmother didn't want either of them around anymore. If they were gone, her lover, Horace Bafferty, would inherit all. And he, Irwin Gilpin, was being paid an exorbitant amount of money to ensure they never returned.

Julian suddenly remembered the huge sum missing from the accounts. He'd tried to figure it out this morning, where it had gone, but his brain had been too fogged by the tea.

The tea.

"Who is in the most danger of her now, Monroe?

Me? You? Miss Travers? Who is she after now? Is the doctor doing her bidding?"

"The doctor's gone. He hasn't been seen since this morning. Mother is in her room taking a nap. I suggest we take the liberty of locking her in there now. Until we can—"

"There you are, Lord Northcliffe." Cuff, winded, came swiftly down the back hall toward them. "I've been looking for you everywhere. I've spoken with Cook, who said the only thing Mr. Bafferty had today was the tea you didn't drink this morning. Drank the whole pot, he did, and ate all the biscuits you didn't touch. She said he missed breakfast, as did Lady Northcliffe, and came through the kitchen a couple hours ago."

"Where is Miss Travers?" Julian asked, brushing by Monroe to meet the steward.

"I don't know, sir. Pamela just asked me the same thing."

"Pamela," Julian repeated, memories popping up like rabbits out of well-hidden holes. "My mother's maid."

"Yes, sir. She said your mother'd been looking for the governess and couldn't find her. Then she sent for the doctor, who couldn't be found either."

"Did anyone leave the house? Have any of the carriages been used?"

"No, sir. I checked. After Cook told me the doctor prepared your tea I went to ask him what was in it. But he weren't around so I talked with Jem. Nobody's left by horse or carriage."

Julian ran a hand through his hair and looked back out the door behind him. The rain was steady now, slapping the already wet ground anew.

"We'll search the house," Julian said. "Get the servants together." He turned to Lord Greer. "If you wouldn't mind helping . . . ?"

Lord Greer straightened his shoulders. "I've known your family too many years to desert you now."

Relief coursed through Julian. "Thank you. If you would detain my mother until the authorities can be summoned, I would appreciate it. And find Shelly. Make sure she's someplace safe."

Lord Greer nodded and moved past them down the hall.

"Cuff, get moving. Monroe, are you going to help?"

Julian turned and the two faced each other.

"What makes you think I would be of any help?" Monroe asked, his face shuttered, his lips pressed together hard. "For all you know I'm lying right now. Perhaps I have been behind the whole thing. Perhaps I hid the ring in Mother's room. Did you happen to think of that?"

Julian's lips curved upward. "Yes." He took a step toward his brother. "But then I remembered something. You gave me a warning before I left for Italy."

Monroe's brow lifted but the look in his eyes was not nearly as self-assured as the gesture suggested. "You remembered," he said skeptically.

Julian nodded. "You said, 'Watch your back, Jules.'"

Collie wrapped her arms around her knees and rested her chin upon them to keep her teeth from chattering. The first few hours she wasn't so cold, but the longer she sat the more deeply the chill penetrated. She had tried to get up and move around to keep herself warm, but the manacle on her ankle had rubbed her skin nearly raw.

The only good thing about the situation was that Dr. Irwin had not been back since he'd left her there this morning. She gently probed her cheek with her fingers, feeling the hot, swollen skin and the ache of the bruise. He would come back, she knew, and then what would happen?

She closed her eyes and imagined Julian coming to her rescue. He would not be able to find her, she imagined, would come looking for her, and—in some way she could not logically account for in her fantasy—he would remember talking with her about this little room. He would search for her, come to the canning room, see the unboarded door and break through to find her.

He would take her in his arms and she would tell him of the doctor's insanity. Then she'd tell him about the ring, and the baby, and the life they'd planned together.

Tears stung her eyes and a lump grew in her throat. She opened her mouth to breath over it and a sob escaped.

But he wouldn't find her. He didn't even remember her. And he was ashamed of what had happened between them in the kitchen. She had seen it in his eyes that night. If his memory never returned, she had driven him away from her forever by throwing herself at him.

He'd tried to offer her money. The memory of it bathed her in shame.

She blinked quickly to dispel the tears. If she gave in to them now she'd never stop.

No, she had to think of what to do when the doctor returned. She'd already searched the barren room for something to use as a weapon, and come up with nothing. The shelves could be used as a cudgel but they were too sturdy to be pulled from the wall. Other than that the only things left were the chain around her leg and the mound of crumbling earth.

She stood and shuffled to the beam around which the chain was secured. Squatting, she pulled at the chain as hard as she could. The beam shifted a hairbreadth in the hard-packed mud of the floor, just enough to make a tiny ridge in the dirt. She stopped and looked up. Thick and rough-hewn, the beam would make a formidable club. But aside from the fact that she probably couldn't lift it alone, it supported what was left of the roof of the room.

She pulled again on the chain. The beam shifted slightly farther. An idea crept into her mind.

She stood and walked over to the shelves along the wall. The bottom one rose about a foot and a half off the ground, and extended about a foot out from the wall.

She looked up at the ceiling, at the crossbeam supported by the pillar to which she was chained. If she were to lie under the shelves and pull the pillar out, she could possibly slip the chain off and be protected from any falling debris. The danger was if the whole roof collapsed instantly. Then she'd be trapped, the chain buried even if the shelves protected her, and she would be unable to reach the door.

Just as she had the thought the door burst open. She whirled, the chain clinking, and clutched her arms around her middle.

Dr. Irwin entered, the pistol in his hand and a frenzied, almost euphoric expression upon his face. "They're coming," he said breathlessly. He came to her, stepped behind her and pressed the point of the gun into her side. "Make a move that I don't sanction and you will quickly find yourself in need of medical attention."

Collie twisted her neck to look at him and he laughed down into her face.

"Who's coming?" she asked.

He smiled. "Everyone who is supposed to."

She heard the hollow footsteps on the wooden stairs, fast, clattering, coming to her. Muted voices—"which way?" "Over here," "The door's open." They entered the canning room and stopped.

"Irwin?"

Julian's voice. Collie expelled the breath she'd been holding and felt tears sting her eyes. She longed to cry out to him to be careful, but she knew the doctor would retaliate.

"In here, gentlemen." Dr. Irwin's voice sounded almost pleased.

Collie felt the point of the gun pinch her skin just as Julian ducked his head under the low lintel of the door. Behind him ducked Monroe.

Collie's breath froze in her throat. Had Monroe

ELAINE FOX

brought him down here at the doctor's orders? Were Monroe and the doctor conspiring, as she'd suspected? Her eyes flew to Julian, and she found his gaze on her—angry and worried. She found herself with the illogical thought that at least now he knew he could trust her.

"What do you want, Irwin?" he asked in a low, controlled voice. "Or should I say Gilpin?"

Collie felt the gun jerk with the doctor's surprise.

"So, you've remembered something. I guess my tea did the trick, eh?"

Julian's eyes narrowed and Collie felt some of the panic inexplicably leave her body.

"Your tea all but killed me, which I believe was your intent."

"It would have been a bonus, but it was not my direct intent at the time. If you were to be sick for a while first, that would have been best." His breath brushed Collie's ear, ruffling the hair at her temple.

Monroe stood warily by the door. Neither of them was armed, Collie noted, but they both still managed to look dangerous. She wondered at the doctor's calm.

"As it happened, though," Julian continued, crossing his legs and leaning against the wall, "I remember meeting you on a dock in London, where I and my father were handed over to your son as prisoners. I also remember your son killing my father. Is there anything I've left out?"

Collie's heart leaped in her chest. If Julian remembered all of that, did he remember everything? Her body shook with a sudden blast of adrenaline and she swung her gaze from him to Monroe and

346

back again. But they both had their eyes pinned on Irwin.

"You left out, Lord Northcliffe, the part where you killed my son. Where you bludgeoned him to death with a piece of wood. Isn't that right? Or don't you remember that part?"

Julian crossed his arms over his chest and cocked his head. "Actually, in the beginning that was the only thing I remembered. I just didn't know who it was or what he'd done."

"So you admit that you killed him," the doctor said.

Julian shrugged. "I try to do one good deed a year."

Collie felt the doctor's hand grab the back of her arm, and the gun pressed harder into her side.

"How cavalier," the doctor said with a sneer. The trembling in his body spread from his hands into her. "I don't suppose you care to reflect on the fact that I have the power to kill your paramour—well, my goodness, paramour to *both* of you, isn't that right, Mr. Dorland?" His voice rang with a smile. "Right here, right now, before your very eyes, I can take her life and stand by with all of my medical knowledge, watching her die. It isn't nearly an equal trade, but she's all I had to work with. How advantageous that it will inconvenience both of you."

Julian dropped his head back a fraction and looked through lowered eyelids at the doctor. "And then Monroe and I will kill you. Which I would not consider an equal trade, but it's all I have to work with."

Silence reigned for a long moment. Collie wished she could see the doctor's face, but he was behind her, still clutching her arm and pressing the barrel of the gun painfully into her side.

Just when she'd determined that he must have decided not to answer at all, he laughed. "You think my life matters to me?" he asked wearily. "You think I have one thing to live for, now that my son is gone? I don't care, gentlemen. You can kill me, but not before I damage you. Not before I get some kind of satisfaction. Because my son was a good boy, a clever boy, who did not deserve to die."

"Your son was a pig," Julian spat.

Collie jumped at the suddenly harsh tone and felt Irwin's fingers dig into the flesh of her arm.

What was he doing? she thought. Why was he deliberately angering the man? She saw Monroe's glance flick to his brother. Monroe's face, as usual, was unreadable.

"He and his cronies all deserved to die," Julian said. "I'm only sorry one of them survived long enough to come claim his bounty."

The doctor's breath came fiercely now, close to Collie's ear, hot and vaporous. He squeezed her arm and pulled her roughly forward. She stumbled, tried to catch herself and felt her leg hit the end of the chain with a solid clank. The beam shifted as the manacle bit into her tender skin. She gasped. A handful of dirt rained down from the ceiling.

Julian's eyes flew to her, then descended to the floor where the chain was plainly visible, drawn taut between her ankle and the wooden support. He looked back up into her face and their eyes met.

She felt as if he spoke directly into her mind with the look, as if the deep, intimate touch of his gaze infused them both with the same thought.

She nodded her head, slowly.

"What?" the doctor demanded, a shrill note creeping into his tone. "What are you doing?" He grabbed her hair and stabbed the gun into her side at the same second Collie pulled her leg forward as hard as she could.

She felt the beam shift but it did not fall. More dirt splattered from the ceiling. She couldn't turn to look, couldn't see how far she was from success. Would one more tug do it? Or would he simply shoot her as she tried?

"What are you doing?" the doctor said. "I could kill you right now!"

She clenched her teeth, her breathing heavy. The low, inhuman groan of bending wood came from the corner. She felt the doctor twist to look behind them.

"Oh, my God," she heard him say, just before a sharp crack rent the air, followed by the rumble of falling earth.

The doctor was thrown forward. Collie heard the gun go off as she tumbled with him to the floor. Searing heat flashed across her back, sharp as a lash from a whip.

"Julian!" she yelled, as dirt buried her legs, feeling at first just like a pile of blankets being thrown upon her, until the weight became unbearable. She clawed at the ground in front of her.

Rocks and thick, musty-smelling soil rolled up her legs to her back. Then someone was holding on to her arms. Someone was pulling her toward them. She tried to help, tried to bend her legs to at least push herself forward, but she couldn't move them. They were powerless, pinned under the rubble.

Another crack rocked through the room. She closed her eyes and bent her head into her arms as something heavy fell over her. Voices yelled. Wood cracked and split. She thought she heard the doctor scream. The air became thick with dirt and dust, choking her, choking them all.

Then, abruptly, the rumbling stopped.

Collie gasped for air and tried to lift her head but could not. She was caught in some sort of pocket. Then the weight upon her shifted, and she felt it move up and away. She raised her head, gulping in the dusty air, and tried to open her eyes. But they were full of dust and she blinked fitfully.

Someone turned her slowly onto her back, as other hands worked to free her pinned legs. Tender fingers brushed at her face. She laid her head back on a pile of dirt.

"Look at me," Julian said, his tone low and distressed. "Collette, look at me, please."

She heard the anxiety in his voice and felt her heart twist at the familiar use of her name. Collette—he'd called her Collette.

Her eyelids fluttered and she forced them open, not sure if they teared from the dust or sheer joy at the sight of his dear, agonized face. He remembered her, she realized. It was there in his eyes, all the love, all the depth—the defensive wall of mistrust was gone.

"Julian," she choked out.

He took her head in his hands and kissed her. She reached up to hold his palms against her cheeks and kissed him back with all the strength she could muster.

He pulled back. "Oh, Collette," he said, running his hand over her forehead and smoothing her hair back. "I'm so sorry. Sweetheart, I'm so sorry. Are you all right?"

She felt suddenly sleepy, as if the events of the day had drained her suddenly of every ounce of energy, but her happiness knew no bounds. "Julian," she said again, a smile on her lips. But as much as she had to say to him she could not get more out.

"Julian." Monroe's voice. "Look here. I think Irwin's bullet hit her."

Julian swore under his breath.

Collie didn't understand. They must be mistaken, she thought; she felt fine. She was not in pain. In fact, she had never been happier. She was just so sleepy. So very sleepy.

"We need to get her out of here. Help me." She wondered at the urgent tone of Julian's voice.

I'm all right, she wanted to say, but night was falling too rapidly.

She felt her head rise. Then she heard Monroe's voice again.

"Careful, Jules. She's pregnant."

Chapter Nineteen

Julian felt his head spin with Monroe's words. *Pregnant*. The sun-dappled field rose immediately to his mind. He saw the curve of her neck, her parted lips, half smiling, as she arched with pleasure.

Pregnant.

His hands felt suddenly large and too clumsy. He held her half in his lap, her head cradled in the crook of his arm, and yet she was too fragile to bear. He was afraid if he moved he would lose her again—afraid she would disappear back into that blank, black void of forgetting. The torment of the last weeks whirled with the sweet agony of remembering, of realizing that *here* was what he'd been searching for, *here* was that home he'd hoped to find, *here* was everything he had missed, all in this one woman.

He glanced over to where the doctor lay buried in the dirt. One of the crossbeams from the ceiling had fallen and knocked him in the head. Monroe leaned over and felt the pulse point in his neck.

"He's dead," Monroe said flatly. "We'd best get out of here before the whole place goes."

Julian jerked his head up. What was left of the ceiling was cracked and crumbling. He slid his legs out from under Collie's head and took her gently in his arms. Lifting her as carefully as he could, he followed Monroe through the door.

As he walked, he could feel the hot stickiness of blood dampen his shirt and wanted to squeeze her to him, to take the injury into himself and banish her pain.

They made their way up the stairs, Monroe preceding him through the doors and holding them open, the three of them forming a silent procession of fear and exhaustion. When they reached the first floor Julian spoke.

"Find Cuff," he said. "Send him to York for Mr. Sperry."

Monroe turned. "I'll go. No sense wasting time searching for Cuff."

Julian nodded. "Thank you."

"Be sure to tell Greer. I'll bring back the constable as well. Tell him not to let Mother out of his sight."

The two stood motionless for a split second. Then Monroe turned swiftly and headed out the back door toward the stables.

Julian strode through the empty front hall, his footsteps echoing on the marble floor. The odd sensation of remembering his days of not remembering assailed him, suffusing him with the unreal sense of being two people at once. He felt the strain of two minds in different times struggling to become one.

But when he looked down at Collie, he felt his whole being unite in a flame of love for her. He'd

ELAINE FOX

loved her before. And he'd loved her again when he'd returned. With a past or without, he knew he was hers, and she was his.

Pamela, his mother's maid, came racing out of the back hall as Julian ascended the stairs.

"Collie!" she cried.

"She's unconscious. She's been shot," he said. Pam gasped but he didn't give her time to think. "Get some bandages and some hot water. Mr. Dorland's gone for the apothecary. I'll take her to my room. Meet me there as soon as you can."

She stopped in midflight. "Y-yes, sir. Is she all right? Will she be all right?"

He turned when he reached the top of the stairs. "Yes," he said, as if the word had the power to make it true. "Yes. She will." He started to turn.

"Lord Northcliffe." Pamela's face was tight with worry. "Did you know—I feel I should tell you—she—she's—"

"I know," he said quietly. "I know. And if there's a God in heaven, this child will live."

When he reached his bedroom he laid her down on the bed, unfastening her gown and pulling the torn, muddy fabric from the ruptured skin at her back. The swath the shot had cut across her lower back was deep and bled heavily, but the bullet had not entered her body.

He expelled a deep breath of relief. She would be fine, he told himself, barely able to believe it. She would heal. He closed his eyes and held her fingers to his lips.

She would be fine.

Pamela raced into the bedroom bearing towels,

followed by two housemaids with a cauldron of steaming water and another with a jar of salve and a bowl of leaves. Behind them strode Cook, issuing orders with the command of a drill sergeant.

"Strip back those covers. Mary, pour some water over those herbs and stir in the ointment. Sadie, help Pamela get the miss's dress off." She turned her graying head and steely eyes to Julian. "Lord Northcliffe, I'm afraid I'm going to have to ask you to leave. This is no place for a man."

"No, I want to stay," he said firmly.

"Lord Northcliffe," Pamela said, her eyes meeting his timidly. "I know you care, and if she wakes I'll call you to her. But you know it's improper for you to stay. You don't want anything to look improper, do you?"

An objection about the relevance of propriety at a time like this died on his lips as he looked into Pam's intimidated, yet determined face. She strove to protect her friend's reputation. And she was right. It didn't matter that he planned to marry her. As it was they'd have an "early" child. To preserve Collie's dignity he should leave her to their care. It was the least he could do for her now.

He would have Collette Travers for his wife and he would have her with the approval and good feelings of everyone who knew them. No shame would mar this marriage.

He rose slowly to his feet. "You'll call me the moment she awakens."

"I will, sir," Pamela said, a tentative smile on her lips.

"I'll be just outside the door." He motioned with

his hand, but still had trouble making his feet turn for the portal.

Her smiled broadened. "I know."

"The *moment* she awakens," he insisted, donning an expression as stern as he could make it.

"Please," she said.

Julian nodded and turned for the door. He was instantly forgotten in the frenzy of female activity. He lingered at the exit, watching them minister to her, feeling his heart thunder at the paleness of her skin and his brow prickle with dread at the limpness of her arms. It was all he could do not to throw them all out and fold her into his arms. He wanted never to let her go, never to let her out of his sight again. But that would not help her, he knew. She needed tending and there was little he could do in that area. He had to leave her to them.

He turned and grasped the doorknob.

"Lord Northcliffe," Pam called.

He spun toward her voice and saw only Collie's face. Her eyes flickered and her lips opened on a sigh.

"Julian," he heard.

He was across the room, scattering housemaids as he went, and by her side before she'd opened her eyes. He took her hand in his.

"Collette," he said, his voice low, his hands huge and warm over her cold one.

Her mouth curved slowly and her eyes opened. She looked up at him, her gaze sleepy and unfocused.

"Am I dreaming?" she murmured. "Are you really here? Do you know me?"

"Yes," he said, stroking her face with one hand, smoothing the hair back from her temples. "I'm here. Everything will be all right now. I love you. Only you, Collette."

Epilogue

Fat clouds scudded across a cool blue sky, but the breeze that blew through the fresh green leaves was touched by early summer's warmth. Collie and Julian walked toward the stone chapel at Northcliffe, their footsteps crunching through last fall's untended leaves to the green grass below.

All around them early morning birds chirped and sang riotously, fluttering between tree branches, then diving one after another through the open spaces to a new perch. The soft air smelled verdantly of earth and new growth.

.Theirs was a slow, contemplative walk. Collie's hand looped through Julian's elbow to lie across his forearm; his own hand rested atop hers.

The wrought-iron gate to the graveyard stood open and they moved through it by tacit agreement, strolling among the ancient headstones and huge, gnarled trees to a spot in the far corner where a bench sat under a weeping willow tree.

"Sit down and rest," Julian said when they reached it, taking her hand and turning her to face him.

"I don't need to rest." Collie smiled. "You have to stop treating me as if I'm breakable, you know. I'm actually feeling quite good."

"*I* need you to rest," Julian said, placing his hands on her shoulders and pressing her into the seat. "I get exhausted just looking at you."

Collie laughed and sat down. She was lucky, she thought; she still didn't feel too ungainly, though the babe was due to be born any day.

Julian remained standing and propped a foot up on the seat next to her, looking up into the branches of the tree above them. "We should have painted the baby's room pale green," he said, gazing at the soft hue of the new growth on the tree. He let his eyes drop to Collie. "If she has your coloring it would suit her perfectly."

Collie felt herself grow warm under the heat of his eyes, and marveled again that he was hers. That he'd come back, *twice*—first from the wreck, and then from that place he'd been when he could remember nothing. He'd told her about it, how disoriented and afraid he'd felt, and it sounded like a terror Collie could not have withstood. For though she'd suffered many moments of fear and anxiety herself in the weeks he'd been gone, and then in the time he was back and did not remember her, she had never lost her *self*.

And then she'd always had the baby, too; their baby, to comfort and reassure her that a piece of him lived within her, a piece of *them*. She lifted a hand to her belly and felt the life flourishing there.

"We can't possibly paint that room again," she said, laughing. "As it is, it's probably several inches smaller due to the number of times we've changed our minds. I think it's a lovely shade now. The very color of the sky, in fact."

He frowned and looked at the sky. "It's not a very feminine color."

"He might be a boy," she pointed out.

His gaze slid to hers and he looked at her from the corners of his eyes, a shrewd smile on his lips. "Your cousin, Bretton, said he was sure of it in the last letter, but I think she'll be a girl," he said. "Mark my words."

"What makes you so sure? You've been saying that for months and I want to know why."

"I just know," he said. "And she'll bedevil me the same way you do."

"I don't bedevil you."

He laughed and rolled his eyes heavenward. "That's the worst part of it. You don't even know."

She curved her hand around his calf, propped next to her on the bench, and felt the muscle through his breeches. She massaged it gently. "Julian," she said, studying the stitching on his boot, "do you have any regrets?"

He leaned forward and captured her hand in his, resting his elbows on his knee. "Regrets, love?" he asked softly.

She looked up at him and caught the gentle smile in his eyes. "Yes. You know, about us, about how things have happened. Perhaps you would have liked—oh, I don't know—a wedding more suited to your station. . . ."

"Like Miranda's?" He chuckled. And they both laughed at the memory of Miranda's stunningly elaborate, if hasty, wedding to one of the men who'd pined after her for years. Julian had seen no reason to expose her deception, mainly due to his respect and gratitude to Lord Greer, but the simple fact of his marrying Collie, the governess, instead of Lady Miranda Greer had been enough of an embarrassment to propel her into the arms of the obese yet wealthy Earl of Bolling.

Collie's laughter dwindled and she continued pensively, "But really, Julian, perhaps you might have liked a wife whose first act was not to give birth to an 'early' child. I just wonder if you would have liked a situation with more—dignity."

Julian let her finish and studied her, rubbing her fingers in his hand with his thumb. "Collette, if I regret those things it is for your sake only. The only regret I can claim for myself is the one of missing the time I might have been with you, helping you, comforting you. When I think of how you must have felt during my . . ." He laughed dryly. "*Absence*, I guess we can call it, in all its forms. It makes me sick to think of you struggling with no one to help you."

She gripped his hand with her fingers. "Oh, but that's not so, Julian. I had a great deal of help, much more than I even knew. Who would have thought, for instance, that Monroe would prove to be so noble?"

"Monroe always had a noble streak," Julian said thoughtfully. "Most often it was overshadowed by a brooding disposition, but still, he came through for me more often than not as a child, I remember."

Collie's lips curved pensively. "You remember," she said on a sigh.

"And he's even coming through for Shelly."

"I know," she agreed, wonder in her tone. "He made sure it was possible for her to visit her mother at the asylum—and found a location away from the other patients so it would not be so strange for her. I believe it's good for both of them to go. And good for them to go together."

Julian continued to rub her hand, gazing down at it as he did. "Yes. She's the lynchpin of the family now."

"Shelly was a big help to me too," Collie said. "Always so cheerful and caring for me so. I don't know what I would have done without her. Or Pam. Even Lord Greer, indirectly. All that time I was so wretched about Miranda, I was in a way glad he was there, so you had someone you could talk to."

"He pulled through for me at the end too," Julian said. "Most men in his position would have defended their daughter's position come hell or high water. He only sought the truth. And getting the truth out of Miranda was no small feat, I can tell you."

Collie sat forward to lean her head against his knee, and Julian's hand rested on her hair.

"You sought the truth too, Julian," she said. "You never stopped seeking the truth."

"For much more selfish reasons."

Collie's eye caught on a headstone much newer than the rest just past the willow tree near the stone wall. She lifted her head.

"What is that one?" she asked, pointing.

Julian turned, lowering his foot from the bench. He reached a hand back for her and she took it, rising.

"That," he said with some satisfaction, "is one reason I wanted to come here. I wanted to show you this."

They walked forward and stopped before the tall stone. Around the edges was carved a vine that when studied closely revealed among its leaves tiny books and pens and parchments, even a tiny ship off to one side. Inscribed on the face was the name *Jonathan Pellham Coletun*.

"Oh, Julian. It's beautiful," she said, leaning to run her fingers along the engraving.

"I never told you," he said slowly, "that I asked my father's permission to marry you. Before we arrived in London."

Collie turned, feeling trepidation twist in her stomach. "No, you never told me that. Was he surprised?"

Julian laughed and ran a hand back through his hair. "You could say that." He laughed again. "Yes, you could definitely say that. I believe he was struck dumb for a full three minutes after my little speech."

Despite her worry, Collie found herself smiling with him. "And what was your little speech?"

Julian shrugged. "Oh, you know, the usual— fallen in love, can't live without her, extraordinary girl, sure you'll agree, and so on." He wound a hand out in front of him with the words.

"How eloquent," she said, smirking.

He shot her a wry look. "Yes, well, there's something about professing one's love for a woman to one's father that makes one . . . how shall I say . . . prosaic."

"And what did Lord Northcliffe have to say in return to such eloquence?"

"He said, once he'd gotten over his shock . . ." Julian turned and narrowed his eyes at her, a smile playing at his lips. "And I quote, 'Thank God, son. I thought you were going to marry that Miranda woman.' And for the longest time once I'd returned, and before I remembered, all I could remember about Miranda was that voice, in that tone, saying *that Miranda woman*. I suppose in a way it kept me from truly believing in the betrothal."

" 'Thank God, son.' " she repeated, feeling her heart lighten with the tale. *Thank God*. He'd actually been happy about the marriage! Inexplicably, she felt tears prick her eyes. "Oh, Julian."

He took one look at her and moved to take her in his arms. "Collette, he was happy for us."

"I know," she said tearfully. "And it's so wonderful."

He chuckled and kissed her hair, holding her tightly to his chest. "So you see, the situation could not have had more dignity. It was timing we lacked."

Collie laughed in spite of her tears. Then she gasped sharply as a pain shot through her abdomen.

He pulled back. "What is it?"

She swiped one hand beneath her eye and dropped her other hand to her stomach. "Oh, Julian," she said, then inhaled sharply as another pain began. Her eyes flew to his. "I think we'd better get going."

His eyes widened and he stood stock-still. For several long heartbeats, the two of them stood looking at each other in a sort of shock. Then laughter burst from both and they started for home.

Cuff gingerly placed his teacup on the corner of his desk and pulled out the straight-backed chair. Seating himself and arranging his paper and pen precisely before him, he bent his gray head to the task before him.

He'd taken to writing in a journal ever since the master had returned from the dead. He'd decided that it wasn't every household that experienced the sort of curiosities this one did, and he had a notion that the record of its goings-on might make for some pretty entertaining reading in years to come.

Yes, sir. With His Lordship's permission—and that of his lovely wife, of course—he might even be of a mind to try to publish the journal someday. Taking out all of the more personal details, of course, and making sure the principals weren't recognizable as Lord and Lady Northcliffe. He could use a nom de plume, he thought. Something like *Master X* or *Lord Anonymous*. And he figured if he bound it up right and sent it off to London, some discerning publisher would snap it up and set it on the public, where it would cause quite a stir, Cuff was very sure. Yes, quite a stir.

He trimmed the end of his pen to the precise angle he liked, then dipped it with great ceremony into the inkwell. He glanced down at the paper before him and stopped. Dropping the pen back in the ink, he repositioned his paper to the proper slant.

Once again he took up his pen and ran the tip along the edge of the inkwell.

Where to begin, where to begin? he pondered, rubbing the tip of the quill under his chin. The day's events were so extraordinary, he thought for the dozenth time. He needed to get the wording just right. This chapter would be one of the most interesting, he reflected with delighted anticipation. Audiences worldwide would be hanging on his every word at this point in the story.

With a deep breath, he brought the pen to the paper and wrote:

Lady Collette Northcliffe gave birth today more than a month early. So unexpected was the birth that it occurred in the churchyard, with nary a one to help but His Lordship, who had no special knowledge of the procedure beforehand, but who claimed to have had no difficulty in figuring out the gist of it.

It's a girl, just as His Lordship said it would be, and they named her Juliana.

Lady Northcliffe said she chose the name so that His Lordship would have no trouble remembering it.